D1231702

*The Shorter Novels
of Stendhal*

---

*VOLUME I*
# ARMANCE

12.50

# MARIE-HENRI BEYLE
## (DE STENDHAL)

# THE SHORTER NOVELS
## OF
# STENDHAL

ARMANCE
THE ABBESS OF CASTRO
VITTORIA ACCORAMBONI
THE CENCI
THE DUCHESS OF PALLIANO
VANINA VANINI

*Translated from the French by*
### C. K. SCOTT-MONCRIEFF

# LIVERIGHT PUBLISHING
## CORPORATION
### NEW YORK

1946
BLACK AND GOLD EDITION
LIVERIGHT PUBLISHING
CORPORATION

COPYRIGHT 1946 BY
LIVERIGHT PUBLISHING CORPORATION

THE ABBESS OF CASTRO AND OTHER TALES
COPYRIGHT, 1926, BY BONI & LIVERIGHT, INC.
LIVERIGHT PUBLISHING CORPORATION

ARMANCE
COPYRIGHT, 1928, BY BONI & LIVERIGHT, INC.
LIVERIGHT PUBLISHING CORPORATION

\* \* \*

*All rights reserved—no part of this book may be reproduced in
any form without permission in writing from the publisher, except
by a reviewer who wishes to quote brief passages in connection
with a review written for inclusion in a magazine or newspaper.*

*Manufactured
in the United States of America*

# PUBLISHER'S PREFACE
## TO THE
### BLACK AND GOLD LIBRARY EDITION

Marie-Henri Beyle, better known by his *nom de plume* of Stendhal, was born at Grenoble on January 23, 1783. With his father, who was a lawyer in the parliament of Grenoble, he was never on good terms, but his intractable disposition sufficiently explains his unhappy childhood and youth. Until he was twelve years old he was educated by a priest and later on sent to the Central School in Grenoble, and in 1799 to Paris. Shortly after that he followed Napoleon to Italy. Most of his time in Italy was spent in Milan, a city for which he conceived a lasting attachment.

He was a spectator of the battle of Marengo and afterwards enlisted in a dragoon regiment. With rapid promotion he became adjutant to General Michaud, and in 1802 returned to study in Paris. After many amorous escapades his father cut off his supplies and he was reduced to serving as clerk to a grocer. Through influence he obtained a position in the commissariat, and on the fall of Napoleon refused to accept a place under the new regime, and retired to Milan, where he met Silvio Pellico, Manzoni, Lord Byron and other men of note. In 1814 his publications began with biographies of Rossini, Hayden, Napoleon, many series of Promenades, essays, novels, and an amazingly interesting correspondence down to 1839, when his LA CHARTREUSE DE PARME, the last and most successful of his publications, was issued. It was enthusiastically praised by Balzac. Stendhal remained at Civita Vecchia, discharging his duties as consul perfunctorily and with frequent intervals of absence until his death, which took place in Paris in 1842. He was buried in Montmartre Cemetery, followed there by Mérimée, and many others.

Stendhal's real reputation began in 1880 and since then in France and England his cult has been growing. He is one of the enduring figures of French literature and one whose influence has spread far beyond the frontiers of French letters. It is difficult to come under the spell of Stendhal without becoming a permanent enthusiast for all of his work. In this country he has affected men like James Huneker and others to a point where they could only discuss him in terms of ecstasy, and this can be readily understood by anyone who has read any three or four of Stendhal's works in French. His critical work has begotten a chain of critics beginning with Goethe in 1818, and afterwards including Taine, Sainte-Beuve, Mérimée and Victor Cousin.

The eminent critic, M. André Gide, when asked lately to name the novel which stands, in his opinion, first among the novels of France, declared that since, without a doubt, the place belongs to one or other of the novels of Stendhal, his only difficulty was in making his choice among these; and he finally decided upon LA CHARTREUSE DE PARME. According to this high authority, Henri Beyle was indisputably the creator of the greatest work of fiction in the French language.

Georg Brandes writes of him; "Beyle stands to Victor Hugo in much the same position as Leonardo da Vinci to Michael Angelo. Hugo's plastic imagination creates a supernaturally colossal and muscular humanity, fixed in an eternal attitude of struggle and suffering; Beyle's mysterious, complicated, refined intellect produces a small series of male and female portraits which exercise an almost magic fascination on us with their far-away, enigmatic expressions and their sweet, seductive, wicked smiles.

"Henri Beyle is, without doubt, one of the most complex minds of the rich period to which he belongs. What chiefly distinguishes him from his brethren of the Romantic School is his direct intellectual descent from the severely rational sensationalistic philosophers of the eighteenth century. Not even in any short youthful or transition period is there a trace to be found in his soul of the Romantic reverence for religious tradition so prevalent in his day.

"No other novelist approaches Beyle in the gift of unveiling the secret struggles of ideas and of the emotions which the ideas produce. He shows us, as if through a microscope, or in an anatomical preparation, where the minutest veins are made visible by the injection of colouring matter, the fluctuations of the feelings of happiness and unhappiness in acting, suffering human beings, and also their relative strength."

In recent years his popularity has increased immensely and he has been acclaimed by the foremost modern critics. His writings contain everything complete: masterly novels, intelligent criticism that only can come from a distinct personality; correspondence, most of which was among the most interesting in the nineteenth century, conversations, observations and love—all of his life Stendhal was in love. Huneker said it was his master passion; Stendhal wrote a fascinating book on the subject (De L'Amour).

No better assurance of the quality of the translation need be offered than the mention that Mr. Scott-Moncrieff, the famous translator of Marcel Proust into English, has translated Stendhal.

# VOLUME I

---

*The Works of Stendhal*

# ARMANCE

To
RICHARD ALDINGTON

C. K. S. M.

# PREFACE

A woman of character, who has only a vague idea of what constitutes literary merit, has asked my unworthy self to correct the style of this novel. I am far from sharing certain political sentiments which seem to be blended with the narrative; so much I am obliged to explain to the reader. The talented author and I hold opposite views upon many subjects; but we have an equal horror of what are called *applications*. In London we find highly sensational novels: *Vivian Grey, Almack's, High Life, Matilda* and the like, which require a *key*. They are very good-natured caricatures of persons whom the accidents of birth or fortune have placed in an enviable position.

This is a kind of literary merit for which we have no desire. The author has not since 1814 climbed the stair of the Tuileries; such is her pride that she does not know even the names of the persons who have doubtless made themselves conspicuous in a certain class of society.

But she has brought on the scene industrial magnates and privileged persons, she is therefore a satirist. If we were to ask for a description of the garden of the Tuileries from the doves that moan on the topmost branches of the trees, they would say: "It is a vast plain of verdure where one basks in the brightest sunshine." We, who stroll beneath, would reply: "It is a delicious shady walk where one is sheltered from the heat, and above all from the glare of the sun, so trying in summer."

So it is that each of us judges everything from his own angle; equally incompatible are the expressions used of the present state of society by persons of equal respectability who intend to lead us by different paths to prosperity. But each party makes the other appear absurd.

Would you impute to an evil turn in the mind of the author the malicious and false descriptions that each party gives of the other's drawing-rooms? Would you insist that passionate people ought to be sage philosophers, that is to say, devoid of passion? In 1760, one required charm, wit, not overmuch humour, nor overmuch honour, as the Regent said, in order to win the favour of master and mistress.

It requires economy, stubborn toil, solidity, a brain free from any illusion to make anything out of the steam engine. This is the difference between the age that ended in 1789 and the age that began about 1815.

Napoleon, on his way to Russia, used constantly to hum the words he had heard so well rendered by Porto (in *La Molinara*):

*Si batte nel mio cuore*
*L'inchiostro e la farina.*[1]

[1] Shall I become a miller or a lawyer? . . .

# PREFACE

They are words that many young men might repeat who are endowed at once with good birth and with intelligence.

In speaking of our age, we find that we have sketched in outline two of the principal characters in the following story. There are perhaps not a score of pages in it that run the risk of appearing satirical; but the author follows another path; the age is gloomy, out of temper; and one has to handle it with caution, even when publishing a pamphlet which, as I have already told the author, will be forgotten in six months at the latest, like the best works of its kind.

In the meantime, we beg for a little of the indulgence that has been shown to the authors of the comedy, *Les Trois Quartiers*. They have held up a mirror to the public; is it their fault if ugly people have passed in front of that mirror? Does a mirror take sides?

The reader will find in the style of this novel artless forms of speech, which I have not had the courage to alter. Nothing is more tedious to my mind than Teutonic and romantic emphasis. The author said: "Too zealous a search for noble turns of speech ends by producing an admirable dryness; they make one read a single page with pleasure; but this *precious charm* makes one shut the book at the end of the chapter: and we wish our readers to read any number of chapters. Spare me, therefore, my rustic or *bourgeois* simplicity."

Remark that the author would be in despair if she

thought that I considered her style *bourgeois*. There is an unbounded pride in her heart. It is the heart of a woman who would feel ten years older were her name made public. Besides, the subject! . . .

- STENDHAL.

ST. GINGOUF, July 23, 1827.

# CHAPTER ONE

*It is old and plain*
*. . . It is silly sooth*
*And dallies with the innocence of love.*
TWELFTH NIGHT, Act II.

ON his twentieth birthday, Octave had just left the École Polytechnique. His father, the Marquis de Malivert, wished to keep his only son in Paris. As soon as Octave understood that this was the constant desire of a father whom he respected, and of his mother whom he loved with an almost passionate love, he abandoned his intention of entering the Artillery. He would have liked to spend a few years in a regiment, and then resign his commission until the next war, in which he was equally ready to serve as Lieutenant or with the rank of Colonel. This is typical of the eccentricities which made him odious to the common run of humanity.

Plenty of brains, a tall figure, refined manners, the handsomest great dark eyes in the world, would have assured Octave a place among the most distinguished young men in society, had not a certain sombre air, imprinted in those gentle eyes, led people to pity rather than to envy him. He would have created a sensation had he been in the habit of talking; but Octave desired

13

nothing, nothing appeared to cause him either pain or pleasure. Frequently ill in his childhood, ever since vital energy had assumed control of his organism he had always been observed to submit without hesitation to what seemed to him to be prescribed by duty; but it might have been thought that, if Duty had not made her voice heard, he would not have had, in himself, sufficient impulse to make him act. Perhaps some singular principle, deeply impressed upon his youthful heart, and incompatible with the events of real life, as he saw them develop round about him, led him to portray to himself in too sombre colours both his own future and his relations with his fellow men. Whatever the cause of his profound melancholy, Octave seemed to have turned misanthrope before his time. Commander de Soubirane, his uncle, said one day in his presence that the boy's nature alarmed him. "Why should I appear other than what I am?" was Octave's cold reply. "Your nephew will always keep to the line of reason." "But never rise above or fall below it," retorted the Commander with his Provençal vivacity; "from which I conclude that if you are not the Messiah expected by the Hebrews, you are Lucifer in person, come back to this world on purpose to worry me. What the devil are you? I can't make you out; you are duty *incarnate*." "How happy I should be never to fail in my duty!" said Octave; "how I wish I could render up my soul pure to my Creator, as I received it from Him!" "A miracle!" exclaimed the Commander; "in the last twelvemonth, this is the first wish I

14

have seen spring from a heart frozen stiff with purity."
And in order not to spoil the effect of this utterance,
the Commander hastily left the room.

Octave looked tenderly at his mother; she knew
whether his heart was indeed frozen. It might be said
of Madame de Malivert that she had remained young
although approaching her fiftieth birthday. It was not
only that she was still beautiful; she had, together with
an exceptionally sharp intellect, retained a keen and
active sympathy with her friends' interests, including
the joys and sorrows of young men. She entered naturally into their reasons for hope or fear; and soon
seemed to be hoping or fearing herself. This kind of
character has lost its charm now that public opinion
seems to have made it almost obligatory upon women
of a certain age who are not religious; but there was
never the least trace of affectation in Madame de
Malivert.

Her servants had observed for some time past that
she was in the habit of driving out in a hackney carriage; and often, when she came home, she was not
alone. Saint-Jean, an inquisitive old footman, who had
accompanied his employers during the emigration, tried
to discover who a certain man was whom Madame de
Malivert had more than once brought home with her.
On the first occasion, Saint-Jean lost sight of the
stranger in the crowd; at his second attempt, his curiosity was more successful; he saw the person whom he
was following pass into the Charity Hospital, where he

learned from the porter that the stranger was none
other than the famous Doctor Duquerrel. Madame de
Malivert's household discovered that their mistress was
bringing to the house in turn all the most eminent doctors in Paris, and almost always she found an excuse
for letting them see her son.

Struck by the eccentricities which she remarked in
Octave, she feared lest his lungs might be affected; but
she believed that, were she unfortunately to have
been right in her diagnosis, naming that cruel malady
would be tantamount to hastening its advance. Doctors, who were men of intelligence, assured Madame de
Malivert that her son was suffering from no malady
beyond that sort of dissatisfied and critical melancholy
characteristic of the young men of his generation and
position; but they warned her that she herself ought
to pay the closest attention to her lungs. These dread
tidings were divulged to the household by a régime
which had to be enforced; and M. de Malivert, from
whom a vain attempt was made to conceal the name
of the malady, foresaw the possibility of being left alone
in his old age.

Extremely rich and extravagant before the Revolution, the Marquis de Malivert, who had not set foot
again in France until 1814, in the train of his monarch,
found himself reduced by the confiscations to an income
of twenty or thirty thousand livres. He thought himself a beggar. The sole occupation of a mind that had
never been any too powerful was now to seek a bride

for Octave. But, being still more faithful to his code of honour than to the obsession that was tormenting him, the old Marquis de Malivert never failed to begin the overtures that he made in society with these words: "I can offer a good name, a *certain* pedigree from the Crusade of Louis the Young, and I know of but thirteen families in Paris that can hold up their heads and say that; but otherwise, I see myself reduced to starvation, to begging my bread; I am a pauper."

This view of life in an elderly man is not calculated to give rise to that meek and philosophic resignation which makes old age cheerful; and but for the outbursts of Commander de Soubirane, a slightly mad and distinctly malicious Southerner, the house in which Octave lived would have been conspicuous, even in the Faubourg Saint-Germain, for its gloom. Madame de Malivert, whom nothing could distract from her anxiety as to her son's health, not even the thought of her own peril, took advantage of the delicate state in which she found herself to cultivate the society of two famous doctors. She sought to win their friendship. As these gentlemen were, one the leader, the other one of the most fervent adherents, of two rival sects, their discussions, albeit of a subject so gloomy to any one who is not animated by an interest in science and in the solution of the problem that faces him, were sometimes amusing to Madame de Malivert, who had not lost a keen and curious mind. She led them on to talk, and thanks to them, now and again at least, voices were raised in the drawing-room, so nobly furnished and yet so sombre, of the Hôtel de Malivert.

Its hangings of green velvet, surcharged with gilded ornaments, seemed to have been put there on purpose to absorb all the light that might come in through two huge windows, the original panes of which had been replaced by plate glass. These windows gave upon a deserted garden, divided into irregular compartments by box hedges. A row of limes, trimmed regularly three times in the year, bounded its farther end, and their motionless shapes seemed a living image of the private lives of the family. The young Vicomte's bedroom, which stood above the drawing-room and had been sacrificed to the beauty of that essential apartment, was barely the height of a half-landing. This room was the bane of Octave's life, and a score of times, in his parents' hearing, he had sung its praises. He lived in dread lest some involuntary exclamation should betray him and reveal how intolerable this room and the whole house were to him.

He keenly regretted his little cell at the Ecole Polytechnique. His time there had been precious to him because it offered him the semblance of the retirement and calm of a monastery. For a long time Octave had had thoughts of withdrawing from the world and of consecrating his life to God. This idea had alarmed his family, especially the Marquis, who saw in the project the fulfilment of all his fears of the abandonment which he dreaded in his old age. But in seeking a closer knowledge of the truths of religion, Octave had been led to study the writers who for the last two centuries have tried to explain the nature of human thought and will, and his ideas had changed considerably; his father's had not changed at all. The Marquis, who had a horror of books and lawyers, was aghast to see this young man shew a passion for reading; he was constantly afraid of some scandal or other, and this was one of his principal reasons for wishing an early marriage for Octave.

While they were basking in the fine days of late autumn, which, in Paris, is like spring, Madame de Malivert said to her son: "You ought to go out riding." Octave saw nothing in this suggestion but an additional expense, and as his father's incessant lamentations made him suppose the family fortune to be far more reduced than it actually was, he held out for a long time. "What is the use, dear Mama," was his invariable reply; "I am quite a tolerable horseman, but riding gives me no pleasure." Madame de Malivert added to the stable a superb English horse, the youth and beauty of which formed a strange contrast to the pair of old Norman horses which for the last twelve years had sufficed for the needs of the household. Octave was embarrassed by this present; the next two days he spent in thanking his mother for it; but on the third, happening to be alone with her, when their conversation turned to the English horse: "I love you too well to thank you again," he said, taking Madame de Malivert's hand and pressing it to his lips. "Is your son, for once in his life, to be wanting in sincerity towards the person he loves most in the world? This horse is worth 4,000 francs; you are not rich enough to be able to spend so much money without feeling the want of it."

Madame de Malivert opened the drawer of a writing desk. "Here is my will," she said; "I have left you my diamonds, but upon the express condition that as long as the money you receive from the sale of them shall last, you shall have a horse which you are to ride now and again by my order. I have sold two of the diamonds secretly to give myself the pleasure of seeing you on a fine horse in my lifetime. One of the greatest sacrifices your father has imposed on me has been his making me promise not to part with these ornaments which become me so ill. He has some political expectation, which to my mind rests upon a very slender basis, and he would think himself twice as poor and twice as decayed on the day when his wife no longer had her diamonds."

A profound melancholy appeared on Octave's brow, and he replaced in the drawer of the desk that document the name of which reminded him of so painful, perhaps so imminent an event. He took his mother's hand again, and held it in both his own, a display of feeling which he rarely allowed himself. "Your father's plans," Madame de Malivert went on, "depend upon that Bill of Indemnity of which we have been hearing for the last three years." "I hope with all my heart that it may be rejected," said Octave. "And why," his mother went on, delighted to see him shew animation at anything and give her this proof of his esteem and affection, "why should you wish to see it rejected?" "In the first place, because, not being comprehensive, it seems to me to be scarcely just; secondly, because it will mean my marrying. I have the misfortune to have a peculiar nature, I did not create myself so; all that I have been able to do has been to know myself. Except at those moments when I have the happiness of being alone with you, my one pleasure in life consists in living in complete isolation, where not a living soul has the right to address me." "Dear Octave, this singular taste is the result of your inordinate passion for learning; your studies make me tremble; you will end like Goethe's Faust. Are you prepared to swear to me, as you did on Sunday, that your reading is not confined to very bad books?" "I read the books that you have indicated to me, dear Mama, at the same time as those which are called bad books." "Ah! There is something mysterious and sombre about you which makes me shudder; heaven only knows what you derive from all this reading!" "Dear Mama, I cannot refuse to believe in the truth of what seems to me to be true. How could an all-powerful and good Being punish me for placing my faith in the evidence of the organs with which He Himself has furnished me?" "Ah! I am always afraid of angering that terrible Being," said Madame de Malivert with tears in her eyes; "He may take you out of reach of my love. There are days when after reading Bourdaloue I am frozen with terror. I find in the Bible that that all-powerful Being is pitiless in His vengeance, and you are doubtless offending Him when you read the philosophers of the eighteenth century. I confess to you, the day before yesterday, I came out of Saint-Thomas d'Aquin in a state bordering on despair. Though the anger of the All-Powerful with impious books were but the tenth part of what M. l'Abbé Fay—— preaches, I might still be afraid of losing you. There is an abominable journal which M. l'Abbé Fay—— durst not even name in his sermon, and which you read every day, I am sure." "Yes, Mama, I do read it, but I am faithful to the promise I gave you; immediately afterwards I read the paper whose doctrine is diametrically opposed to it."

"Dear Octave, it is the violence of your passions that alarms me, and above all the course that they are secretly tracing in your heart. If I saw in you any of the tastes natural at your age, to provide a diversion from your singular ideas, I should be less alarmed. But you read impious books, and presently you will begin to doubt the very existence of God. Why reflect upon these terrible subjects? Do you recall your passion for chemistry? For eighteen months you refused to see anybody, you estranged by your absence our nearest relatives; you failed in the most essential duties." "My interest in chemistry," replied Octave, "was not a passion, it was a duty that I set myself; and heaven knows," he added with a sigh, "whether I should not have done better, by remaining faithful to that plan and making myself a man of learning withdrawn from the world, by following the example of Newton!"

That evening Octave remained with his mother until one o'clock. In vain had she urged him to go out to some social gathering, or at least to the play. "I stay where I feel most happy," said Octave. "There are moments when I believe you, and those are when I am with you," was his delighted mother's answer; "but if for two days on end I have seen you only with other people, my better judgment prevails. It is impossible that such solitude can be good for a boy of your age. I have diamonds here worth 74,000 francs lying idle, and likely to remain so for long, since you shew no intention of marrying; and indeed you are very young, twenty and five days!" here Madame de Malivert rose from her couch to kiss her son. "I have a good mind to sell these useless diamonds, I shall invest what I receive for them, and the interest I shall employ in increasing my expenditure; I should fix a day, and, on the plea of my feeble health, I should be at home to those people only to whom you had no objection." "Alas, dear Mama, the sight of all my fellow creatures depresses me equally; I care for no one in the world but you. . . ."

When her son had left her, notwithstanding the lateness of the hour, Madame de Malivert, troubled by sinister forebodings, was unable to sleep. She tried in vain to forget how dear Octave was to her, and to judge him as she would have judged a stranger. Invariably, instead of following a line of reason, her mind went astray among romantic suppositions as to her son's future; the Commander's saying recurred to her. "Certainly," she said, "I feel in him something superhuman; he lives like a creature apart, separated from the rest of mankind." Then reverting to more reasonable ideas, Madame de Malivert could not conceive her son's having the liveliest or at least the most exalted passions, and at the same time such an absence of inclination for everything that was real in life. One would have said that his passions had their source elsewhere and rested upon nothing that exists here below. Everything about Octave, even his noble features, alarmed his mother; his fine and tender eyes filled her with terror. They seemed at times to be gazing into heaven and reflecting the bliss that they saw there. A moment later, one read in them the torments of the damned.

One feels a modest reluctance to question a person whose happiness appears so fragile, and his mother often gazed at him without venturing to address him. In his calmer moments, Octave's eyes seemed to be dreaming of an absent happiness; you would have called him a tender heart kept at a great distance from the sole object of its affections. Octave was sincere in his answers to the questions with which his mother plied him, and yet she could not solve the mystery of that profound and often agitated distraction. From his fifteenth year, Octave had been like this, and Madame de Malivert had never thought seriously of any secret

24

passion. Was not Octave master of himself and of his fortune?

She constantly observed that the realities of life, so far from being a source of emotion to her son, had no other effect than to make him lose patience, as though they came to distract him and to tear him in an aggravating fashion from his beloved musings. Apart from the misfortune of this manner of life which seemed to alienate him from his whole environment, Madame de Malivert could not fail to recognise in Octave a strong and upright mind, spirited and honourable. But this mind knew very well the justice of its claim to independence and liberty, and his noble qualities formed a strange alliance with a profundity of dissimulation incredible in a boy of his age. This cruel reality destroyed in an instant all the dreams of happiness which had brought calm to Madame de Malivert's imagination.

Nothing was more irritating to her son, one might say, more odious, for he was incapable of loving or hating by halves, than the society of his uncle the Commander, and yet every one in the household believed that he liked nothing better than to be M. de Soubirane's adversary at chess, or to *saunter* with him on the boulevard. This was a favourite expression with the Commander, who for all his sixty years had still quite as many pretensions as in 1789; only the fatuity of argument and profundity had taken the place of the affectations of youth, which have at least the excuse of charm and gaiety. This instance of so ready a dissimulation frightened Madame de Malivert. "I have questioned my son as to the pleasure he finds in his uncle's company, and he has told me the truth; but," she said to herself, "who knows whether some strange design may not be lurking in that singular heart? And if I never put any questions to him about the matter, it will never occur to him to speak to me of it. I am a simple woman," Madame de Malivert told herself, "my vision extends only to a few trivial duties within my range. How could I ever dare to think myself capable of giving advice to so strong and singular a creature? I have no friend to consult, endowed with a sufficiently superior judgment; besides, how can I betray Octave's confidence; have I not promised him absolute secrecy?"

When these melancholy reflexions had disturbed her until daybreak, Madame de Malivert concluded, as was her custom, that she ought to employ such influence as she had over her son to make him go frequently to visit Madame la Marquise de Bonnivet. This was her intimate friend and cousin, a woman of the highest position, in whose drawing-room were constantly to be found all the most distinguished elements of society. "My business," Madame de Malivert told herself, "is to pay court to the persons of merit whom I meet at Madame de Bonnivet's, and so find out what they think of Octave." People went to this house to seek the pleasure of being numbered among Madame de Bonnivet's friends, and the support of her husband, a practised courtier burdened with years and honours, and almost as much prized by his master as was that delightful Admiral de Bonnivet, his ancestor, who made François I do so many foolish things and punished himself for them so nobly.[1]

[1] At the battle of Pavia, towards nightfall, seeing that all was lost, the Admiral cried: "Never shall it be said that I survived such a disaster"; and charging with raised visor into the midst of the enemy, had the consolation of killing a number of them before he himself fell pierced by many wounds (February 24, 1525).

# CHAPTER TWO

*Melancholy mark'd him for her own,*
*whose ambitious heart overrates the happi-*
*ness he cannot enjoy.*

MARLOW.[1]

T HE following morning, at eight o'clock, a
great upheaval occurred in the household of
Madame de Malivert. All the bells pealed at
once. Presently the old Marquis paid a visit to his
wife, who was still in bed; he himself had wasted no
time in dressing. He came and embraced her with tears
in his eyes. "My dear," he said to her, "we shall see
our grandchildren before we die," and the good old
man wept copious tears. "God knows," he added,
"that it is not the thought of ceasing to be a beggar
that makes me like this. . . . The Bill of Indemnity is
certain to pass, and you are to have two millions."
At this moment Octave, for whom the Marquis had sent,
knocked at the door; his father rose and flung himself
into his arms. Octave saw tears which he perhaps misinterpreted, for an almost imperceptible flush appeared

---

[1] The first of these lines is taken from the Epitaph in Gray's
*Elegy*, in the notes to which it is not shewn as an "Imitation."
The ascription of the whole passage to Marlow (*sic*) is probably,
therefore, one of Beyle's fantasies.—C. K. S. M.

on his pale cheeks. "Draw back the curtains; give me
daylight!" said his mother in a tone of vivacity. "Come
here, look at me," she added, in the same tone, and,
without replying to her husband, examined the imperceptible flush which was dyeing the upper part of
Octave's cheeks. She knew, from her conversations with
the doctors, that a circular patch of red on the cheeks
is a symptom of weak lungs; she trembled for her
son's health and gave no more thought to the two millions of the indemnity.

When Madame de Malivert was reassured, "Yes, my
son," the Marquis said at length, slightly out of patience with all this fuss, "I have just heard for certain
that the Bill of Indemnity is to be introduced, and we
can count upon 319 certain votes out of 420. Your
mother has lost a fortune which I reckon at more than
six millions, and whatever may be the sacrifices which
the fear of the Jacobins may impose upon the King's
justice, we may safely count upon two millions. And
so I am no longer a beggar, that is to say, you are no
longer a beggar, your fortune will once again be in
keeping with your birth, and I am now in a position
to seek, instead of begging a bride for you." "But,
my dear," said Madame de Malivert, "take care that
your haste to believe this great news does not expose
you to the petty criticisms of our cousin Madame la
Duchesse d'Ancre and her friends. She already has
all the millions that you promise us; don't count your
chickens before they are hatched." "For the last five
and twenty minutes," said the old Marquis, taking out

his watch, "I have been certain, yes, you may say *certain*, that the Bill of Indemnity will be passed."

The Marquis must have been right, for that evening, when the *impassive* Octave appeared in Madame de Bonnivet's drawing-room, he found a trace of eagerness in the welcome which he received on all sides. There was also a trace of pride in his manner of responding to this sudden interest; so at least the old Duchesse d'Ancre remarked. Octave's impression was one of aversion combined with scorn. He found himself greeted more warmly, *because of the prospect of two millions*, in Parisian society, and among the people with whom he had been on most intimate terms. His ardent spirit, as just and almost as severe towards others as towards himself, ended by extracting a profound melancholy from this sad truth. It was not that Octave's pride stooped to resentment of the people whom chance had brought together in this drawing-room; he was filled with pity for his own lot and for that of all mankind. "I am so little loved, then," he said to himself, "that two millions alter all the feelings that people had for me; instead of seeking to deserve their love, I ought to have tried to enrich myself by some form of trade." As he made these gloomy reflexions, Octave happened to be seated upon a divan, facing a little chair which was occupied by Armance de Zohiloff, his cousin, and by accident his eyes came to rest upon her. It occurred to him that she had not uttered a word to him all that evening. Armance was a niece, in reduced circumstances, of Mesdames de Bonnivet and

de Malivert, of about the same age as Octave, and as
these two young people were quite indifferent to one
another, they were in the habit of conversing with
entire frankness. For three-quarters of an hour Octave's heart had been steeped in bitterness, an idea now
struck him: "Armance pays me no compliment, she
alone of the people here is untouched by this increased
interest which I owe to money, she alone here has some
nobility of soul." And he found some consolation
merely in looking at Armance. "So here at last is a
creature worthy of respect," he said to himself, and as
the evening advanced, he saw with a pleasure equal to
the grief which at first had flooded his heart that she
continued to refrain from addressing him.

Once only, when a provincial, a member of the Chamber of Deputies, was paying Octave an ill-turned compliment with regard to the two millions which *he was
going to vote him* (these were the man's own words),
Octave caught a glance from Armance directed at himself. Her expression was one that it was impossible to
misinterpret; so at least Octave's judgment, more severe than could well be imagined, decided; this glance
was intended to study him, and (what gave him a per-
ceptible feeling of pleasure) seemed to expect to be
obliged to despise him. The Deputy who was preparing to vote millions received no quarter from Octave;
the young Vicomte's scorn was all too visible even to
a provincial. "They are all the same," said the Deputy
from the —— Department to Commander de Soubirane
whom he joined a moment later. "Ah, you fine noble-

31

men of the Court, if we could vote our own indemnities
without passing yours, you should not touch a penny,
begad, until you had given us guarantees. We have
no wish now, as in the old days, to see you colonels at
three and twenty and ourselves captains at forty. Of
the 319 Deputies who are on the right side, 212 of us
belong to that provincial nobility which was sacrificed
in the past. . . ." The Commander, highly flattered
at hearing such a complaint addressed to himself, began to make excuses for the people of quality. This
conversation, which M. de Soubirane in his self-importance called political, lasted for the rest of the
evening, and, notwithstanding the most piercing north
wind, took place in the bay of a window, the position
prescribed for talking politics.

The Commander deserted his post for a minute only,
after begging the Deputy to excuse him and to wait for
him there. "I must go and ask my nephew what he
has done with my carriage," and he went and whispered
to Octave: "Talk, people are remarking on your silence;
pride is the last thing you should shew at this change
of fortune. Remember that these two millions are a
restitution and nothing more. Keep your pride till the
King gives you a Blue Riband." And the Commander
returned to his window, running like a boy, and mutter-
ing to himself: "Ah! At half-past eleven, the carriage."

Octave began to talk, and if he did not arrive at the
ease and sprightliness which make for complete success,
his astonishing good looks and the intense earnestness
of his manner made a number of the women present

attach an uncommon value to what he said to them. It
is true that the noble simplicity with which he uttered
his words spoiled the effect of several piquant sallies;
it was only after a moment or two that his hearers
felt surprise. His proud nature never allowed him to
utter in an emphatic tone what he thought effective.
His was one of those minds which their natural pride
places in the position of a girl who appears without
rouge in a drawing-room where the use of rouge is
general; for the first few minutes her pallor makes her
appear sad. If Octave met with success, it was because
the place of the nimble wit and excitement which he
often lacked was filled that evening by a sentiment of
the bitterest irony.

This semblance of malice led the women of a certain
age to pardon him the simplicity of his manners, and the
fools whom he frightened made haste to applaud him.
Octave, delicately expressing all the contempt that was
devouring him, was tasting the only happiness that
society could give him, when the Duchesse d'Ancre came
up to the divan upon which he was seated and said,
not to him but for his benefit, and in the lowest of
tones, to her dearest friend Madame de la Ronze: "Look
at that little fool Armance, she has actually taken it
into her head to be jealous of the fortune that has fallen
from the clouds at M. de Malivert's feet. Lord! How
ill envy becomes a woman!" Her friend guessed the
Duchesse's meaning, and caught the fixed stare of
Octave who, while appearing to see nothing but the
venerable face of the Bishop of —— who was talking

to him at the moment, had heard all. In less than three minutes, Mademoiselle de Zohiloff's silence was explained, and she herself proved guilty, in Octave's mind, of all the base feelings of which she had been accused. "Great God," he said to himself, "there is no exception, then, to the baseness of feeling of all this set! And what grounds have I for supposing that other sets are in any way different? If people dare to flaunt such a worship of money in one of the most exclusive drawing-rooms in France, among people, none of whom can open the History of France without coming upon a hero of his own name, what can it be like among the wretched merchants, who are millionaires to-day, but whose fathers only yesterday were behind the counter? God, how vile men are!"

Octave fled from Madame de Bonnivet's drawing-room; the fashionable world filled him with horror. He left the family carriage for his uncle the Commander and returned home on foot. It was raining in torrents; the rain delighted him. Soon he had ceased to notice the regular tempest that was meanwhile flooding Paris. "The one resource against this general degradation," he thought, "would be to find a noble soul, not yet debased by the sham wisdom of the Duchesse d'Ancre and all her kind, to cling to her forever, to see no one but her, to live with her and solely for her and for her happiness. I should love her passionately. . . . *I should love her!* Wretch that I am!" At this moment a carriage turning at a gallop from the Rue de Poitiers into the Rue de Bourbon almost ran over Octave. The back wheel struck him violently in the chest and tore his waistcoat: he stood rooted to the ground; the vision of death had cooled his blood.

"God! Why was I not crushed out of existence?" he said, looking up to heaven. Nor did the rain that was falling in torrents make him bow his head; this cold rain did him good. It was only some minutes later that he proceeded on his way. He ran upstairs to his own room, changed his clothes, and inquired whether his mother were visible. But as she did not expect him she had gone early to bed. Left to his own company, he found everything tedious, even the sombre Alfieri, one of whose tragedies he attempted to read. For a long time he paced the floor of his vast and low apartment. Finally, "Why not make an end of it all?" he asked himself; "why this obstinate resistance to the fate that is crushing me? It is all very well my forming what are apparently the most reasonable plans of conduct, my life is nothing but a succession of griefs and bitter feelings. This month is no better than the last; this year is no better than last year. Why this obstinate determination to go on living? Can I be wanting in firmness? What is death?" he asked himself, opening his case of pistols and examining them. "A very small matter, when all is said; only a fool would be concerned about it. My mother, my poor mother, is dying of consumption; a little time, and I must follow her. I may even precede her if life is too bitter a grief for me. Were it possible to ask such a favour, she would grant it. . . . The Commander, my

35

father himself do not care for me; they value the name
I bear; they cherish in me an excuse for ambition. It is
a very minor duty that binds me to them. . . ." This
word *duty* came like a thunderbolt to Octave. "A *minor
duty!*" he cried, coming to a halt, "a duty of little importance! . . . Is it of little importance, if it is the
only duty I have left? If I do not overcome the
difficulties that chance presents to me here and now,
what right have I to assume that I am certain of con-
quering all those that it may one day present to me?
What! I have the pride to imagine myself superior
to every danger, to every sort of evil that may attack
a man, and yet I beg the grief that presents itself to
choose a form that will suit me, that is to say, to
diminish its force by half. What pettiness! And I
thought myself so strong! I was nothing but a pre-
sumptuous fool."

From seeing things in this new light to making a vow
to overcome the grief of living took only a moment.
Soon the disgust which Octave felt at everything became less violent, and he felt himself to be not such a
wretched creature. His heart, weighed down and dis-
organised to some extent by so prolonged an absence
of all happiness, regained a little life and courage with
the happiness of self-esteem. Ideas of another sort
presented themselves. The lowness of the ceiling of
his room displeased him intensely; he felt envious of the
magnificent saloon of the Hôtel de Bonnivet. "It is
at least twenty feet high," he said to himself, "how
freely I should breathe in it! Ah!" he exclaimed with

the glad surprise of a child, "there is a use for these millions. I shall have a magnificent saloon like the one in the Hôtel de Bonnivet; and only I shall set foot in it. Once a month, at the most, yes, on the first day of the month, a servant to dust it, but in my presence; he must not try to read my thoughts from my selection of books, nor to pry into what I write down for my soul's guidance in its moments of folly. . . . I shall carry the key always on my watch-chain, a tiny, invisible key of steel, smaller than the key of a portfolio. I shall choose for my saloon three mirrors, each seven feet high. I have always liked that sombre and splendid form of decoration. What is the size of the largest mirrors they make at Saint-Gobain?" And the man who, for the last three-quarters of an hour, had been thinking of ending his life, sprang at once upon a chair to look on his shelves for the price-list of the Saint-Gobain mirrors. He spent an hour in writing out an estimate of the cost of his saloon. He felt that he was behaving like a child; but went on writing all the more rapidly and seriously. This task performed, and the estimate checked, which brought up to 57,350 francs the cost of raising the ceiling of his bedroom and installing a saloon in its place. "If this be not counting one's chickens," he said to himself with a laugh, "I should like to know what is. . . . Oh, well! I am a miserable wretch!" he went on, striding up and down the room. "Yes, I am a miserable wretch; but I will be stronger than my misery. I shall measure my strength against it, and I shall be the master. Brutus sacrificed his children; that was the difficulty that faced him; as for me, I shall continue to live." He wrote down on a little tablet concealed in the secret drawer of his desk: "December 14th, 182—. *Pleasing effect of two m.—Increase of friendliness.—Envy on the part of Ar.—To make an end.—I will be the master.—Saint-Gobain mirrors.*"

This bitter reflexion was written down in Greek characters. Next he picked out on his piano a whole act of *Don Giovanni,* and those sombre chords of Mozart restored peace to his soul.

# CHAPTER THREE

*As the most forward bud*
*Is eaten by the canker ere it blow,*
*Even so by love the young and tender wit*
*Is turned to folly. . . .*
*. . . . So eating love*
*Inhabits in the finest wits of all.*
THE TWO GENTLEMEN OF VERONA, ACT I.

IT was not only at night and when alone that
Octave was seized by these fits of despair. An
extreme violence, an extraordinary spitefulness,
marked all his actions at such times, and doubtless, had
he been merely a poor law student without family or
friends, he would have been locked up as a madman.
But in that rank of society he would have had no opportunity of acquiring that elegance of manners which,
adding a final polish to so singular a character, made
him a being apart, even in court circles. Octave was
indebted to some extent for this extreme distinction to
the expression of his features; it was strong and
gentle, and not strong and hard, as we see in the
majority of men who are conscious of their good looks.
He was naturally endowed with the difficult art of com-
municating his thoughts, whatever they might be, without ever giving offence, or rather without ever giving
unnecessary offence, and thanks to this perfect re-

39

straint in the ordinary relations of life, the idea of his being mad never suggested itself.

It was less than a year since, seeing that a young footman, alarmed by the expression on his face, appeared to bar his way, one evening as he came running out of his mother's drawing-room, Octave in a fury had cried: "Who are you to stand up to me! If you are strong, shew your strength." And so saying he had seized him round the body and flung him out of the window. The footman landed upon a potted oleander in the garden, without serious injury to himself. For the next two months Octave appointed himself the man's body servant; in the end he gave him far too much money, and every day devoted several hours to his education. The whole family being anxious that this man should keep silence, presents were given him, and he found himself the object of excessive attentions which made him a nuisance who had to be sent back to his home with a pension. The reader can now understand Madame de Malivert's anxiety.

What had alarmed her most of all at the time of this unfortunate event was that Octave's repentance, albeit extreme, had not begun until the following day. That night, as he returned home, some one having happened to mention to him the danger the man had incurred: "He is young," had been his comment, "why did he not defend himself? When he tried to prevent me from passing, did I not tell him to defend himself?" Madame de Malivert thought she had discovered that

these furious outbursts came over her son at the very
moments in which he appeared to have most completely
forgotten those sombre musings which she could always
discern from his expression. It was, for instance, half-
way through the performance of a charade, when he
had been acting merrily for an hour with several young
men and five or six young persons with whom he was
intimately acquainted, that he had fled from the drawing-room and hurled the servant out of the window.

Some months before the evening of the two millions,
Octave had made almost as abrupt an exit from a ball
that Madame de Bonnivet was giving. He had figured
with remarkable grace in several country-dances and
valses. His mother was delighted with his success,
and he himself could not be unaware of it; a number
of women for whom their beauty had earned a great
celebrity in society, came up and spoke to him with
the most flattering air. His hair, of the most beautiful
gold, falling in heavy curls over a brow that was really
superb, had particularly impressed the celebrated
Madame de Claix. And in speaking of the fashions
followed by the young men of Naples, where she had
just been, she was paying him a marked compliment,
when suddenly Octave's face flushed a deep crimson,
and he left the room at a pace the swiftness of which
he sought in vain to hide. His mother, in alarm, went
after him but did not find him. She waited in vain for
him all night long; he appeared only the next morning,
and in a strange state; he had received three sabre-

cuts, which, to tell the truth, were not serious. The doctors were of opinion that this monomania was entirely *moral* (to use their expression), and must be due not to any physical cause, but to the influence of some singular idea. There was no warning signal of M. le Vicomte Octave's *migraines,* as they were called. These outbursts had been far more common during his first year at the École Polytechnique, and before he had thought of becoming a priest. His fellow-students, with whom he had frequent quarrels, thought him quite mad, and often this conception of him saved him from bodily hurt.

Confined to his bed by the slight injuries of which we have spoken, he had said to his mother, quite simply, as he said everything: "I was furious, I picked a quarrel with some soldiers who were staring at me and laughing, I fought with them, and got no more than I deserve," after which he had changed the subject. With Armance de Zohiloff, his cousin, he had entered into greater detail. "I am subject to moments of misery and fury which are not madness," he said to her one evening, "but which will make me be thought mad in society as I was at the École Polytechnique. It is unfortunate, that is all; but what I cannot face is the fear of finding myself suddenly burdened with some cause for everlasting regret, as nearly happened at the time of poor Pierre's accident." "You made a noble reparation for that, you gave him not only a pension but your time, and if he had had the least spark

of decent feeling in him you would have made his fortune. What more could you do?" "Nothing, I dare
say, once the accident had happened, or I should be a
monster not to have done it. But that is not all, these
fits of despondency which every one takes for madness,
seem to make me a creature apart. I see the poorest,
the most limited, the most wretched, outwardly, of the
young men of my generation each blessed with one or
two lifelong friends who share his joys and sorrows.
In the evening I see them go out and take the air together, and they tell one another everything that interests them; I and I only find myself isolated, without
a friend in the world. I have not, nor shall I ever
have any one to whom I can freely confide what is in
my mind. What outlet should I have for my feelings
if I had any of the sort that wring the heart! Am I
then fated to live always without friends, and with
barely an acquaintance! Am I an evil-doer?" he added,
with a sigh. "Certainly not, but you furnish the people
who do not like you with pretexts," Armance said to
him in the free, severe tone of friendship, and trying
to hide the all too real pity which his grief inspired in
her. "For instance, you who are so perfectly polite
towards everybody, why did you not shew yourself the
day before yesterday at Madame de Claix's ball?"
"Because it was her foolish compliments at the ball
six months ago that put me to the shame of being
worsted by two young peasants armed with sabres."
"That is all very well," Mademoiselle de Zohiloff re-

torted; "but pray observe that you always find reasons to excuse yourself from going into society. You must not go on to complain of the isolation in which you live." "Ah, it is friends that I need, and not society. Is it among the drawing-rooms that I shall find a friend?" "Yes, since you did not succeed in finding one at the École Polytechnique." "You are right," Octave replied after a long silence; "I see your point of view for the moment, and to-morrow, when it is a question of acting, I shall act in a manner the opposite of that which seems reasonable to me to-day, and entirely from pride! Ah, if heaven had made me the son of a linen-draper, I should have worked in the counting-house from the age of sixteen; instead of which all my occupations have been mere luxury; I should be less proud and more happy. . . . Ah! how I detest myself! . . ."

These complaints, albeit apparently selfish, interested Armance; Octave's eyes expressed such possibilities of love, and were at times so tender!

She, without clearly explaining it to herself, felt that Octave was the victim of that sort of unreasoning sensibility which makes men wretched and worthy to be loved. A passionate imagination led him to exaggerate the happiness which he could not enjoy. Had he received from heaven a dry, cold, reasoning heart, had he been born at Geneva; then, with all the other advantages which he did possess, he might have been quite happy. All that he lacked was an ordinary nature.

It was only in the company of his cousin that Octave ventured now and again to express his thoughts aloud. We see now why he had been so painfully affected on discovering that this charming cousin's sentiments had changed with his change of fortune.

On the morning after the day on which Octave had longed for death, he was awakened with a start at seven o'clock by his uncle the Commander, who entered his room making as much noise as possible. The man was never free from affectation. Octave's anger at this noise lasted for barely a few seconds; a sense of duty recurred to him, and he greeted M. de Soubirane in the light and pleasant tone which seemed best suited to his mood.

This vulgar soul who, before or after good birth, could think of nothing in the world but money, explained at length to the noble Octave that he must not go altogether out of his mind with joy when he passed from an income of twenty-five thousand livres to the prospect of one hundred thousand. This philosophical and almost Christian discourse ended with the advice to speculate on 'Change as soon as he should have secured a twentieth part of his two millions. The Marquis would not fail to place part of this increased fortune at Octave's disposal; but he was on no account to operate on 'Change save by the Commander's advice; the latter knew Madame la Comtesse de ——, and they could speculate in the Funds *with certainty*. These last words made Octave start. "Yes, my boy," said the Commander, who mistook this movement for a sign of doubt, *"with certainty.* I have rather neglected the Comtesse since her absurd behaviour with M. le Prince de S——; still, we are more or less related, and I shall leave you now to go and find our friend in common, the Duc de ——, who will bring us together again."

# CHAPTER FOUR

*Half a dupe, half duping,*
*The first deceived perhaps by her deceit*
*And fair words, as all these philosophers.*
*Philosophers they say? Mark this, Diego,*
*The devil can cite scripture for his purpose.*
*Oh, what a goodly outside falsehood hath!*
MASSINGER.[1]

THIS fatuous invasion by the Commander almost plunged Octave back in his misanthropy of overnight. His disgust with the rest of mankind had risen to a climax when his servant appeared carrying a stout volume very carefully wrapped in English tissue paper. The seal it bore had been beautifully engraved, but the blazon itself was somewhat repellent: sable, two bones in saltire. Octave, whose taste was perfect, admired the accuracy of outline of this pair of *tibias* and the perfection of the engraver's skill. "It is the School of Pikler," he said to himself; "this must be one of my cousin, the devout Madame de C——'s follies." This suspicion proved unfounded when he saw inside the parcel a magnificent

---

[1] This motto is printed in the French editions as prose. The last two lines are taken from *The Merchant of Venice*, Act I, Scene III, where Antonio says: "Mark you this, Bassanio, The devil," etc. The ascription to Massinger need not be taken too seriously. Compare *Scarlet and Black*, Chapter XLVI.—C. K. S. M.

47

copy of the Bible, bound by Thouvenin. "Devout Catholics do not give one the Bible," said Octave as he opened the accompanying letter; but he sought in vain for the signature; there was none, and he tossed the letter unread into the grate. A moment later, his servant, old Saint-Jacques, entered the room with an air of cunning. "Who sent me this parcel?" said Octave. "It is a mystery, they are trying to keep it secret from M. le Vicomte; but it was simply old Perrin who left it with the porter and made off like a pick-pocket." "And who is old Perrin?" "One of Madame la Marquise de Bonnivet's servants whom she pretended to dismiss and now uses for secret errands." "Do you mean that people suspect Madame de Bonnivet of a love-affair?" "Good heavens, no, Sir. The secret errands are for the new religion. It is a Bible, perhaps, that Madame la Marquise has sent to Monsieur as a great secret. Monsieur perhaps recognized the writing of Madame Rouvier, Madame la Marquise's confidential maid." Octave looked in the grate and made the man give him back the letter which had fallen behind the fire and was not burned. He saw with surprise that the writer knew quite well that he read Helvetius, Bentham, Bayle and other bad books. "The most spotless virtue would not be safe," he said to himself; "as soon as people form a sect, they stoop to the use of intrigue and employ spies. It is evidently since the Bill of Indemnity was introduced that I have become worthy that people should take an interest in my salvation and the influence that I may one day wield."

Throughout that day, the conversation of the Marquis de Malivert, the Commander and two or three trusted friends who were invited to dine was an almost incessant allusion, in distinctly bad taste, to Octave's marriage and to his new position. Being still affected by the spiritual crisis through which he had passed during the night, he was less frigid than usual. His mother thought him paler, and he made it his duty, if not to be gay, at least to appear to be occupying himself only with ideas that gave rise to pleasing pictures; he set himself to the task with so much energy that he succeeded in taking in every one in the room. Nothing could deter him, not even the Commander's pleasantries touching the prodigious effect produced by two millions on the mind of a philosopher. Octave took advantage of his feigned bewilderment to say that, were he a Prince, he would not marry before he was twenty-six, this being the age at which his father had married. "It is evident that the fellow is nourishing the secret ambition of becoming a Bishop or a Cardinal," said the Commander as soon as Octave had left the room; "his birth and sound doctrine will carry him to the Hat." This speech, which made Madame de Malivert smile, caused the Marquis great uneasiness. "You may say what you please," he replied to his wife's smile, "my son's only intimate relations are with churchmen or young scholars of the same way of thinking, and, a thing that is quite unknown in my family, he shews a marked dislike for officers of his own age." "There is something strange about that young man," M. de

Soubirane went on. At this reflexion it was Madame de Malivert's turn to sigh.

Octave, overcome by the boredom with which the obligation to talk had filled him, left this group of old people and went at an early hour to the Gymnase: he could not endure the wit of M. Scribe's amusing plays. "Still," he told himself, "nothing else has had so genuine a success, and to despise a thing without knowing it is an absurdity too common in our society for me to acquire any credit by avoiding it." It was in vain that he prolonged the experiment through two of the most charming sketches given at the Théâtre de Madame. The wittiest and most amusing lines seemed to him to be tainted with vulgarity, and the handing over of the key in the second act of *Le Mariage de Raison* drove him from the theatre. He entered a restaurant and, faithful to the mystery which enveloped all his actions, called for candles and a plate of soup: when the soup was put before him, he locked the door, read with interest two newspapers which he had bought outside, burned them with the greatest care in the grate, paid his bill and left. He went home and changed his clothes, and found himself almost eager that evening to put in an appearance at Madame de Bonnivet's. "How can I be certain," he wondered, "that that wicked Duchesse d'Ancre was not slandering Mademoiselle de Zohiloff? My uncle is convinced that my head has been turned by those two millions." This idea, which had been suggested to Octave by something of no importance that he had read in one of his newspapers, restored his happiness. He thought still of Armance, but as of his only friend, or rather the only person who was almoșt a friend to him.

He was far from imagining himself to be in love, he had a horror of that sentiment. He had sworn to himself a thousand times in the last four years that he would never love. This obligation to refrain from love was the mainspring of his whole conduct and the chief occupation of his life. This evening, his soul strengthened by virtue and misery, and become merely virtue and strength, felt simply the fear of having too lightly condemned *a friend*.

On reaching Madame de Bonnivet's drawing-room, Octave did not once look at Armance; but throughout the evening his eyes did not miss a single one of her movements. He began, upon entering the room, by paying marked attention to the Duchesse d'Ancre; he spoke to her with a deference so profound that the lady had the pleasure of supposing him to be converted to the respect due to her rank. "Now that he has the prospect of becoming rich, this philosopher is one of us," she murmured to Madame de la Ronze.

Octave wished to make certain of the extent of this woman's perversity; if he found that she was really wicked, that would be to some extent an admission that Mademoiselle de Zohiloff was innocent. He observed that the feeling of hatred alone retained some animation in the withered heart of Madame d'Ancre; whereas, on the other hand, only things that were generous and noble inspired her with revulsion. One would have said

that she felt the need to be avenged on them. Ignoble
and base sentiments, but ignobility clothed in the most
elegant expressions, had alone the privilege of making
the Duchesse's little eyes sparkle.

Octave was thinking of how to free himself from the
interest with which she was listening to him when he
heard Madame de Bonnivet call for her chessmen.
These were a little masterpiece of carved ivory which
M. l'Abbé Dubois had brought from Canton. Octave
seized the opportunity to leave Madame d'Ancre, and
asked his cousin to entrust him with the key of the
desk in which her fear of her servants' clumsiness made
her keep these magnificent chessmen. Armance was no
longer in the room; she had gone out a few moments
earlier with Méry de Tersan, her bosom friend; had
not Octave asked for the key of the desk, the absence
of Mademoiselle de Zohiloff would have given rise to
unfavourable comment, and on her return she might
perhaps have had to endure several hostile glances, perfectly restrained, but distinctly harsh. Armance was
penniless; she was only eighteen, and Madame de Bonnivet was thirty and more; she was still quite a beautiful
woman, but Armance, too, was beautiful.

The two friends had stopped by the chimneypiece of
a large boudoir that opened out of the drawing-room.
Armance had wished to shew Méry a portrait of Lord
Byron a proof of which Mr. Phillips, the English
painter, had recently sent to her aunt. Octave could
hear quite distinctly as he passed along the passage
by the door of the boudoir: "What can you expect? He

is like all the rest! A soul that I thought so noble overpowered by the prospect of two millions!" The accent in which these flattering words, *that I thought so noble,* were uttered, fell on Octave like a bolt from the blue; he stood rooted to the ground. When he moved on, his tread was so light that the sharpest ear could not have caught it. As he passed again by the boudoir with the chessmen in his hand, he stopped for a moment; immediately he blushed at his indiscretion and returned to the drawing-room. The words which he had just overheard were by no means decisive in a world in which envy is capable of assuming every imaginable form; but the accent of candour and honesty in which they had been uttered echoed in his heart. That was not the tone of envy.

Having handed the Chinese chessmen to his cousin, Octave felt that he needed time for reflexion; he took up a position in a corner of the room behind a whist-table, and there his imagination repeated to him a score of times the sound of the words he had just overheard. This profound and delicious meditation had long absorbed him, when the voice of Armance came to his ear. He had not yet thought what means to employ to regain his cousin's esteem; he was still lost in ecstatic enjoyment of the bliss of having forfeited it. As he rejoined the group that surrounded Madame de Bonnivet, and came away from the remote corner occupied by the tranquil whist-players, Armance noticed the expression in his eyes; they rested upon her with that sort of tenderness and weariness which, after intense joys, makes the eyes seem almost incapable of unduly rapid movements.

Octave was not to find happiness a second time that evening; he could not address a single word to Armance. "Nothing could be harder than to justify myself," he said to himself while pretending to be listening to the exhortations of the Duchesse d'Ancre who, being with him the last to leave the drawing-room, insisted upon taking him home. The night was cold and dry with a brilliant moon; on reaching home, Octave called for his horse and rode for some miles along the new boulevard. On his return, about three o'clock in the morning, without knowing what he was doing or why, he passed before the Hôtel de **Bonnivet**.

# CHAPTER FIVE

*Her glossy hair was cluster'd o'er a brow*
*Bright with intelligence, and fair, and*
*smooth;*
*Her eyebrows' shape was like th' aërial bow,*
*Her cheek all purple with the beam of youth,*
*Mounting, at times, to a transparent glow,*
*As if her veins ran lightning. . . .*
DON JUAN, I, 61.

"HOW am I to prove to Mademoiselle de Zohiloff, by deeds and not by vain words, that the pleasure of seeing my father's fortune multiplied fourfold has not absolutely turned my head?" The search for an answer to this question was Octave's sole occupation during the next twenty-four hours. For the first time in his life, he had lost his heart without knowing it.

For many years past, he had always been conscious of his own sentiments, and had confined their attention to the objects that seemed to him reasonable. Now, on the other hand, it was with all the impatience of a boy of twenty that he waited for the hour at which he was to meet Mademoiselle de Zohiloff. He had no longer the slightest doubt as to the possibility of speaking to a person whom he saw twice almost every day; he was embarrassed only over the selection of the words

55

best fitted to convince her. "For, really," he said, "I cannot within twenty-four hours perform an action that will prove in a decisive manner that I am above the pettiness of which in her heart of hearts she accuses me, and I must be allowed to protest first of all in words." And indeed an abundance of words presented themselves to him in turn; some seemed to him to be over-emphatic; at other moments he was afraid of treating too lightly so serious an imputation. He had not in the least decided what he ought to say to Mademoiselle de Zohiloff when eleven struck, and he arrived among the first visitors in the drawing-room of the Hôtel de Bonnivet. But what was his astonishment when he discovered that Mademoiselle de Zohiloff, who spoke to him several times in the course of the evening, and apparently quite in her ordinary tone, deprived him nevertheless of any opportunity of saying a word to her which no one else might hear! Octave was greatly vexed, the evening passed in a flash.

On the following day he was equally unfortunate; next day again, and for many days after that, he was prevented from speaking to Armance. Each day he hoped to find an opportunity of saying the words that were so essential to his honour, and each day, without there being the slightest sign of affectation in Mademoiselle de Zohiloff's behaviour, he saw his hope vanish. He was losing the friendship and esteem of the one person who seemed to him worthy of his own, because he was suspected of sentiments the opposite to those that he actually held. Nothing really could have been more flattering, but at the same time nothing was more annoying.  Octave was intensely preoccupied in what was happening to him; it took him several days to grow accustomed to his new position of disfavour with Armance.  Quite unconsciously, he who had so loved silence acquired the habit of talking volubly whenever Mademoiselle de Zohiloff was within earshot.  In truth, it mattered little to him though he seemed odd or inconsequent.  Whatever brilliant or eminent lady he might be addressing, he spoke really to Mademoiselle de Zohiloff alone, and for her benefit.

This real misfortune distracted Octave from his black misery, he forgot his habit of seeking always to estimate the amount of happiness that he was enjoying at the moment.  He was losing his one friend; he saw himself refused an esteem which he was so certain that he deserved; but these misfortunes, cruel as they might be, did not go so far as to inspire in him that profound distaste for life which he had felt a fortnight earlier.  He asked himself: "What man is there who has not been slandered?  The severity with which I am treated is an earnest of the eagerness with which the injury will be repaired when the truth shall at last be known."

Octave could see an obstacle that kept him from happiness, but he could also see happiness, or at least the end of his suffering and of a suffering that completely absorbed his thoughts.  His life had a new object, he longed passionately to reconquer the esteem of Armance; it was no easy undertaking.  The girl had a strange nature.  Born on the outskirts of the

Russian Empire near the Caucasian frontier, at Sebastopol where her father was in command, Mademoiselle de Zohiloff concealed beneath an apparent meekness a firm will, worthy of the rugged clime in which she had spent her childhood. Her mother, who was closely related to Mesdames de Bonnivet and de Malivert, had when attached to the Court of Louis XVIII at Mitau, married a Russian colonel. M. de Zohiloff came of a family which for the last hundred years had obtained the highest preferments; but the father and grandfather of this officer, having had the misfortune to attach themselves to favourites who were shortly afterwards banished to Siberia, had seen their fortune rapidly diminish.

Armance's mother died in 1811; shortly afterwards she lost General de Zohiloff, her father, who was killed at the battle of Montmirail. Madame de Bonnivet, on learning that she had a relative living alone and friendless in a small town in the heart of Russia, with no fortune beyond an income of one hundred louis, did not hesitate to invite her to France. She spoke of her as a niece and reckoned upon marrying her by obtaining some pension from the Court; Armance's maternal great-grandfather had worn the Blue Riband. We see that, though barely eighteen, Mademoiselle de Zohiloff had already had sufficient experience of misfortune. This perhaps was why the minor events of life seemed to glide over her, leaving her unmoved. Now and again it was not impossible to read in her eyes that she was capable of being deeply affected, but one could see that nothing vulgar would succeed in touching her. This perfect serenity, which it would have been so gratifying to make her forget for a moment, was combined in her with the subtlest intellect, and entitled her to a consideration beyond her years.

She was indebted to this singular nature, and above all to the enchanting gaze of a pair of large, deep blue eyes, for the friendship of all the most eminent ladies in Madame de Bonnivet's circle; but Mademoiselle de Zohiloff had also a number of enemies. In vain had her aunt tried to force her out of her sheer incapacity to bestow her attention upon people whom she did not like. It was all too evident that in speaking to them she was thinking of something else. There were, moreover, any number of little tricks of speech and behaviour which Armance would not have ventured to condemn in other women; possibly it never occurred to her to forbid herself the use of them; but had she allowed herself that liberty, for long afterwards she would have blushed whenever she thought of them. In her childhood, her feelings with regard to childish trifles had been so violent that she had strongly reproached herself for them. She had formed the habit of criticising herself with reference not to the effect she produced on others but to her sentiments at the moment, the memory of which next day might be the bane of her life.

People found something Asiatic in the features of this girl, as in her gentleness and a carelessness which seemed to belie her age, so childish was it. None of her actions gave any direct indication of an exaggerated sense of what a woman owes to herself, and yet a certain graceful charm, an enchanting reserve, was diffused round about her. Without seeking in any way to attract attention, and letting opportunities of success escape her at every moment, the girl was interesting. One could see that Armance did not allow herself a whole crowd of things which custom has authorised and which are to be observed every day in the conduct of the most distinguished women. In short, I have no doubt that, but for her extreme gentleness and her youth, Mademoiselle de Zohiloff's enemies would have accused her of being a prude.

Her education abroad, and her belated arrival in France, served as a further excuse for whatever slight oddity the eye of malice might have discovered in her manner of being impressed by events, and indeed in her behaviour generally.

Octave spent his life among the enemies which this unusual nature had created for Mademoiselle de Zohiloff; the marked favour which she enjoyed with Madame de Bonnivet was a grievance which the friends of that lady, so important a figure in society, could not forgive her. It was above all things her unswerving honesty that alarmed them. As it is far from easy to attack the actions of a young girl, they attacked her beauty. Octave was the first to admit that his young cousin might easily have been far better looking. She was remarkable for what I might perhaps venture to call Russian beauty: this was a combination of features which, while expressing to a marked degree a simplicity and piety no longer to be found among over-civilised races, offered, one must confess, a singular blend of the purest Circassian beauty with certain German forms somewhat prematurely developed. There was nothing common in the outline of those features, so profoundly serious, but a little too full of expression, even in repose, to correspond exactly to the idea generally held in France of the beauty becoming to a young girl.

It is a great advantage, with generous natures, to the people who are accused in their hearing, that those people's faults should be pointed out first of all by the lips of an enemy. When the hatred of Madame de Bonnivet's bosom friends deigned to stoop to open jealousy of the poor little existence of Armance, they never ceased to mock at the bad effect produced by the too prominent brow and by features which, seen in full face, were perhaps a little too strongly marked.

The only real grounds for attack which the expression of Armance's countenance could offer to her enemies was a singular look which she had at times when her mind was most detached. This fixed and profound gaze was one of extreme attention; there was nothing in it, certainly, that could shock the most severe delicacy; it suggested neither coquetry nor assurance; but no one could deny that it was singular, and, in that respect, out of place in a young person. Madame de Bonnivet's flatterers, when they were sure of being noticed, would sometimes imitate this look, in discussing Armance among themselves; but these vulgar spirits robbed it of an element that they had never thought of noticing. "It is with such eyes," Madame de Malivert said to them one day, out of patience with their malevolence, "that a pair of angels exiled among men and obliged to disguise themselves in mortal form, would gaze at one another in mutual recognition."

It will be admitted that with a character so steadfast in its beliefs and so frank as was that of Armance, it was no easy matter to justify oneself against a grave charge by adroit hints. Octave would have required, to be successful, a presence of mind and above all a degree of assurance which were beyond his years.

Unconsciously Armance allowed him to see, by a casual utterance, that she no longer looked upon him as an intimate friend; his heart was wrung, he remained speechless for a quarter of an hour. He was far from discovering in the form of Armance's speech a pretext for replying to it in an effective manner and so recovering his rights. Now and again he attempted to speak, but it was too late, and his reply was no longer appropriate; still, it did shew that he was concerned. While seeking in vain for a way of justifying himself in face of the accusation which Armance brought against him in secret, Octave let it be seen, quite unconsciously, how deeply it affected him; this was perhaps the most skilful method of winning her forgiveness.

Now that the course to be adopted with regard to the Bill of Indemnity was no longer a secret, even from society as a whole, Octave, greatly to his surprise, found that he had become a sort of personage. He saw himself made an object of attention by serious people. He was treated in quite a novel fashion, especially by very great ladies who might see in him a possible match for their daughters. This mania of the mothers of the period, to be constantly in pursuit of a son-in-law, shocked Octave to a degree which it is difficult to express. The Duchesse de ——, to whom he had the honour to be distantly related, thought it necessary to apologise to him for not having kept him a place in a box which she had engaged at the Gymnase for the following evening. "I know, my dear cousin," she said to him, "how unfair you are to that charming theatre, the only one that I find amusing." "I admit my error," said Octave, "the dramatists are right, and their witty speeches are not tainted with vulgarity; but the object of this retractation is by no means to beg you for a place. I admit that I am not made for society, nor for that kind of play which, evidently, is the most lifelike copy of it." This misanthropic tone, in so handsome a young man, appeared highly ridiculous to the Duchesse's two grand-daughters, who made fun of him for the rest of the evening, but nevertheless on the following day treated Octave with *perfect simplicity*. He observed this change and shrugged his shoulders.

Astounded by his successes, and even more by their requiring so little effort on his part, Octave, who was very strong on the theory of life, expected to have to meet the attacks of envy; "for unquestionably," he told himself, "this Indemnity must procure me that pleasure also." He had not long to wait; a few days later, he was informed that some young officers of Madame de Bonnivet's circle were only too ready to mock at his change of fortune. "What a misfortune for that poor Malivert," said one, "these two millions falling on his head like a chimney-can! He won't be able to become a priest now! It is hard!" "One fails to conceive," put in a second, "that in this age when the nobility is so savagely attacked, a man can dare to bear a title and yet shrink from his baptism of blood." "Still, that is the only virtue which the Jacobin party has not yet thought of calling hypocritical," added a third.

Fired by these remarks, Octave began to go about more, appeared in all the ballrooms, was very haughty and even, so far as it lay in his power, impertinent to other young men; but this produced no effect. Greatly to his astonishment (he was only twenty), he found that people respected him all the more for this attitude. As a matter of fact, it was generally decided that the Indemnity had absolutely turned his head; but most of the women went on to say: "The only thing he lacked was that proud, independent air!" It was the name which they were pleased to give to what seemed to him insolence, which he would never have allowed himself to display had he not been told of the ill-natured remarks that were being made about him. Octave enjoyed the surprising welcome which he received in society and which went so well with that tendency to hold himself aloof which was natural to him. His success pleased him most of all on account of the happiness which he discerned in his mother's eyes; it was in answer to repeated pressure from Madame de Malivert that he had abandoned his beloved solitude. But the most usual effect of the attentions of which he saw himself made the object was to remind him of his disfavour with Mademoiselle de Zohiloff. This seemed to increase day by day. There were moments when this disfavour almost bordered upon incivility, it was at all events the most decided aloofness, and was all the more marked inasmuch as the new existence which Octave owed to the Indemnity was nowhere more evident than at the Hôtel de Bonnivet.

Now that he might one day find himself the host in an influential drawing-room, the Marquise was absolutely determined to wean him from that arid philosophy of *utility*. This was the name which she had given for some months past to what is ordinarily called the philosophy of the eighteenth century. "When will you throw on the fire," she said to him, "the books of those gloomy writers which you alone, of all the young men of your age and rank, still read?"

It was to a sort of German mysticism that Madame de Bonnivet hoped to convert Octave. She deigned to examine him, to see whether he possessed the *sense of religion*. Octave reckoned this attempt at conversion among the strangest of the things that had happened to him, since his emerging from the solitary life.

"Here is one of the follies," he thought, "which no one could ever foresee."

Madame la Marquise de Bonnivet might be reckoned one of the most remarkable women in society. Features of a perfect regularity, very large eyes, with the most imposing gaze, a superb figure and manners that were distinctly noble, a little too noble, perhaps, placed her in the highest rank wherever she might be found. Rooms of a certain vastness were especially favourable to Madame de Bonnivet; for instance, on the day of the opening of the final session of the Chambers, she had been the first to be mentioned among the most brilliant women present. Octave saw with pleasure the effect that would be created by her researches into his *sense of religion.* This creature, who imagined himself to be so free from shams, could not restrain a start of pleasure at the sight of a sham which the world would shortly be placing to his credit.

Madame de Bonnivet's exalted virtue was beyond the reach of slander. Her imagination was occupied exclusively with God and the Angels, or at the lowest with certain intermediary beings between God and man, who, according to the most modern German philosophers, hover a few feet above our heads. It is from this elevated though not remote station that they *magnetise our souls,* etc., etc. These visions, in a woman so highly esteemed, were most distressing to His Grace the Archbishop. "The reputation for wisdom which Madame de Bonnivet has enjoyed, upon such good grounds, since her entry into society, and which all the cunning innuendo of the Jesuits in lay clothing has been powerless to assail, she is going to risk for my sake," Octave told himself, and the pleasure of attracting in a marked fashion the attention of so important a woman made him endure with patience the long explanations which she deemed necessary to his conversion.

Presently, among his new acquaintance, Octave was marked down as the inseparable companion of that Marquise de Bonnivet, so famous in a certain section of society, and (or so she thought) creating a sensation at Court when she deigned to appear there. Although the Marquise was a very great lady in the height of the fashion, and moreover was still very good looking, these advantages made no impression upon Octave; unfortunately he detected a trace of affectation in her manner, and whenever he observed this defect anywhere, his natural instinct was only to deride it. But this sage of twenty summers was far from penetrating the true cause of the pleasure which he found in letting himself be converted. He, who so many times had taken vows against love, that one might say that hatred of that passion was the main object of his life, went with pleasure to the Hôtel de Bonnivet because invariably that Armance who despised him, who hated him perhaps, was stationed within a few feet of her aunt. Octave was quite free from presumption; the principal flaw in his character was indeed that he exaggerated his own disadvantages, but if he did admire himself at all, it was in respect of his honesty and stoutness of heart. He had rid himself, without the least ostentation or weakness, of a number of opinions, ridiculous but agreeable enough in themselves, which are guiding principles to the majority of young men of his class and age.

These victories which he could not conceal from himself, that for instance over his love of a military career, independent of any ambition for military rank and promotion, these victories, I repeat, had inspired him with great confidence in his own firmness. "It is from cowardice and not from want of enlightenment that we do not read in our own hearts," he was in the habit of saying, and with the help of this fine principle, he relied a little too much on his own perspicacity. A chance word informing him that one day he might be in love with Mademoiselle de Zohiloff would have made him leave Paris immediately: but in his present position such an idea never occurred to him. He esteemed Armance highly and so to speak exclusively; he saw himself scorned by her, and he esteemed her precisely on account of her scorn. Was it not quite natural to wish to regain her esteem? There was, underlying this, no suspicious desire to attract the girl. What was calculated to prevent the very birth of the slightest suspicion of love for her was that when Octave found himself among Mademoiselle de Zohiloff's enemies he was the first to admit her defects. But the state of uneasiness and hope, doomed to incessant disappointment, in which his cousin's silent treatment of him kept him plunged prevented him from seeing that none of the faults with which she was reproached in his hearing amounted to anything serious in his mind.

One day, for instance, they were attacking Armance's predilection for hair cut short and falling in thick curls round the head, as worn in Moscow. "Mademoiselle de Zohiloff finds the fashion convenient," said one of the Marquise's flatterers; "she does not wish to sacrifice too much time to her toilet." Octave's malicious spirit noticed with pleasure the success which this argument achieved among society women. They let it be understood that Armance did right to sacrifice everything to the duties which her devotion to her aunt imposed upon her; and their eyes seemed to be saying: "to sacrifice everything to her duties as paid companion." Octave's pride was far from thinking of replying to this insinuation. While they in their malice enjoyed it, he yielded in silence and delight to a little start of passionate admiration. He felt, without expressing it to himself: "This woman who is attacked thus by all the rest is nevertheless the only one here who is worthy of my esteem! She is as poor as these other women are rich; and she alone might be permitted to exaggerate the importance of money. And yet she despises it, she who has not a thousand crowns a year; and it is solely and basely adored by these women, all of whom are living in the greatest comfort."

# CHAPTER SIX

*Cromwell, I charge thee, fling away ambition;*
*By that sin fell the angels, how can man then,*
*The image of his Maker, hope to win by't?*
                    KING HENRY VIII, Act III.

ONE evening, after the tables had been arranged and the great ladies arrived for whom Madame de Bonnivet put herself out, she talked to Octave with an unusual interest: "I do not understand your nature," she repeated for the hundredth time. "If you will swear to me," he replied, "never to betray my secret, I will confide in you; and no one else has ever known it." "What! Not even Madame de Malivert?" "My respect for her forbids me to distress her." Madame de Bonnivet, in spite of all the idealism of her faith, was by no means insensible of the charm of knowing the great secret of one of the men who, in her eyes, came nearest to perfection; besides, this secret had never been confided to any one.

Upon Octave's requesting an eternal discretion, Madame de Bonnivet left the drawing-room and after a while returned, wearing upon the gold chain of her watch a singular ornament: this was a sort of cross of iron made at Königsberg; she held it in her left hand and said to Octave in a low and solemn tone: "You ask me for eternal secrecy; in all circumstances, towards every one in the world. With no mental reservation or Jesuitical pretermission, *I declare to you by Jehovah*, yes, I will keep your secret."

"Very well, Madame," said Octave, amused by this little ceremony and by the sacramental air of his noble cousin, "what often clouds my soul with darkness, what I have never confided to any one, is this horrible misfortune: I have no *conscience*. I find in myself no trace of what you call the *intimate sense*, no *instinctive* revulsion from crime. If I abhor vice, it is quite vulgarly by force of reason and because I find it harmful. And what proves to me that there is absolutely nothing divine or *instinctive* in my nature, is that I can always recall all the elements of the reasoning by dint of which I find vice to be horrible." "Ah, how I pity you, my dear cousin! You distress me," said Madame de Bonnivet in a tone that revealed the keenest pleasure; "yours is precisely what we call the *rebellious nature.*"

At this moment, her interest in Octave was plain to the eyes of several malicious watchers; for they were being watched. Her gestures shed all their affectation and became passionate and genuine; her eyes darted a mild flame as she listened to this handsome young man; still more, when she commiserated him. Madame de Bonnivet's good friends, who were watching her from a distance, indulged in the most rash judgments, whereas she was merely transported by the pleasure of having at last found a *rebellious nature*. Octave

71

promised her a memorable victory if she succeeded in awakening in him conscience and the *intimate sense.* A celebrated Doctor of the last century, summoned to the bedside of a great nobleman, his friend, after examining the symptoms of the disease, slowly and in silence, exclaimed in a sudden transport of joy: "Ah! Monsieur le Marquis, it is a disease that has been lost for centuries! Vitreous phlegm! A superb disease, absolutely fatal. Ah! I have discovered it, I have discovered it!" Such was the joy of Madame de Bonnivet; it was in a sense the joy of an artist.

Since she had been engaged in spreading the new Protestantism, which is to take the place of Christianity, the latter being now a thing of the past, and, as we know, on the point of undergoing its fourth metamorphosis, she had heard mention of *rebellious natures;* they form the solitary objection to the system of German mysticism, founded upon the existence of the intimate consciousness of good and evil. She now had the good fortune to have discovered one; she alone in the world knew his secret. And this *rebellious nature* was perfect; for his moral conduct being strictly honourable, no suspicion of personal interest could taint the purity of his *diabolism.*

I shall not repeat any of the sound reasons which Madame de Bonnivet advanced that evening to Octave to persuade him that he had an *intimate sense.* The reader has not, perhaps, the good fortune to be seated within a few feet of a charming cousin who despises him with all her heart and whose friendship

72

he is burning to reconquer. This intimate sense, as its name implies, cannot manifest itself by any outward sign; but nothing could be simpler or easier to understand, said Madame de Bonnivet; "you are a *rebellious nature*," etc., etc. "Do you not see, do you not feel, that, apart from space and time, there is nothing real here below?"

Throughout the course of these sound arguments, a joy that was really almost diabolical sparkled in the glance of the Vicomte de Malivert; and Madame de Bonnivet, who for that matter was a most perspicacious woman, exclaimed: "Ah, my dear Octave, *rebellion* is evident in your eyes." It must be admitted that those great dark eyes, which as a rule shewed such discouragement, and whose darting flames escaped through the curls of the most beautiful golden hair in the world, were quite touching at that moment. They had that charm better felt perhaps in France than anywhere else: they revealed a soul which has been thought frozen for years past and which all of a sudden becomes animated, but for you, and for you *alone*. The electrical effect produced in Madame de Bonnivet by this instant of perfect beauty and the natural tone full of feeling which it imparted to her accents made her truly seductive. At that moment, she would have gone to the scaffold to assure the triumph of her new religion; generosity and devotion shone in her eyes. What a triumph for the malice that was watching her.

And these two people, the most remarkable in the room, in which, all unconsciously, they were providing a spectacle, had no thought of their own pleasure; nothing was farther from their minds. This is what would have seemed perfectly incredible to Madame la Duchesse d'Ancre and her neighbours, the most refined women in France. Thus it is that matters of sentiment are judged in society.

Armance had remained perfectly consistent in her attitude towards her cousin. Several months had passed without her addressing a word to him upon personal matters. Often she did not speak to him throughout an evening, and Octave was beginning to note the days upon which she had deigned to be aware of his presence.

Being careful not to appear disconcerted by Mademoiselle de Zohiloff's hatred, Octave was no longer remarkable in society for his invincible silence nor for the singular and perfectly noble air with which, in the past, those fine eyes of his had seemed to shew their boredom. He talked freely and without the least regard for the absurdities into which he might be led. In this way he became, unconsciously, one of the most fashionable of the male visitors to the drawing-rooms which in a sense were dependent upon Madame de Bonnivet's. He was indebted to the perfect want of interest with which he approached everything for a real superiority over his rivals; he arrived without pretensions among a crowd of people who were devoured by them. His *fame*, descending from the drawing-room of the illustrious Marquise de Bonnivet into social spheres in which that lady was envied, had placed him without the least effort in a most agreeable position. Without having as yet done anything, he saw himself, from his first entry into society, classed as a being apart. There was nothing about him, not even the disdainful silence with which he was at once inspired by the presence of people whom he thought incapable of understanding exalted feelings, that was not accepted as a striking singularity. Mademoiselle de Zohiloff observed this success and was amazed by it. In the last three months, Octave was no longer the same man. It was not surprising that his conversation, so brilliant to every one else, had a secret charm for Armance; the sole object of that conversation was to give her pleasure.

Towards midwinter, Armance thought that Octave was going to make a brilliant marriage, and it was easy to estimate the social position to which a few months had sufficed to raise the young Vicomte de Malivert. There appeared now and again in Madame de Bonnivet's drawing-room a very great nobleman indeed who had all his life been on the watch for things or people that were going to become the fashion. His mania was to attach himself to these, and to this strange idea he was indebted for a considerable social success; a man of the commonest mould, he had raised himself far above his level. This great nobleman, as servile towards Ministers as any clerk, was on the best of terms with them, and he had a grand-daughter, his sole heir, to whose husband he would be able to convey the highest honours and the greatest benefits that it is in the power of the Monarchy to bestow. All this winter he had appeared to have his eye upon Octave, but no one as yet dreamed of the heights to which the young Vicomte was to rise. M. le Duc de —— was giving a great stag-hunt in his forests in Normandy. To be admitted to these parties was a distinction; and for the last thirty years he had not issued an invitation for which skilful commentators could not divine a reason.

Suddenly, and without a word of warning, he wrote a charming note to the Vicomte de Malivert, inviting him to come and hunt with him.

It was decided in Octave's family circle, perfectly acquainted with the ways and character of the old Duc de ——, that if his visit to the Château de Ranville should prove a success, they would one day see him a Duke and a Peer of France. He set off loaded with good advice by the Commander and the rest of the household; he had the honour to see a stag and four excellent hounds fling themselves into the Seine from a rock one hundred feet high, and on the third day he was back in Paris.

"You are evidently mad," Madame de Bonnivet said to him before Armance. "Does the young lady displease you?" "I scarcely examined her," he replied with great coolness, "she seems to me quite pleasant; but when the hour struck at which I always come here I felt my soul plunged in darkness."

The religious discussions waxed warmer than ever after this fine piece of philosophy. Octave seemed to

Madame de Bonnivet an astonishing creature. At length, the instinct of the conventions, if I dare venture upon such an expression, or certain intercepted smiles gave the fair Marquise to understand that a drawing-room in which one hundred persons assemble every evening is not precisely the most appropriate place in the world in which to *investigate rebellion.* She told Octave one evening to come to the house next day at noon, after breakfast. This was an invitation for which Octave had long been waiting.

The day following was one of the most brilliant of the month of April. The presence of spring in the air was revealed by a delicious breeze and gusts of warmth. Madame de Bonnivet decided to transport her theological conference into the garden. She was confident of finding in the *always novel* spectacle of nature some striking argument in support of one of the fundamental ideas of her philosophy: *"What is really beautiful must always be true."* The Marquise had indeed been talking extremely well and for a considerable time, when a maid came in search of her to remind her to pay her respects to a foreign Princess. This was an engagement which she had made a week earlier; but the interest of the new religion, of which it was hoped that Octave would one day be the Saint Paul, had banished every other thought from her mind. As the Marquise felt herself in the mood for discussion, she asked Octave to wait for her. "Armance will keep you company," she added.

As soon as Madame de Bonnivet had left them: "Do

you know, cousin, what my *conscience* tells me?" Octave went on at once without the least timidity, for timidity is begotten of the love that knows itself and makes pretensions; "It tells me that for the last three months you have been despising me as a vulgar fellow whose head has been absolutely turned by the hope of an increase of fortune. I have long sought to justify myself to you, not by vain words but by actions. I can think of none that would be decisive; I, too, can have recourse only to your *intimate sense*. Well, this is what has happened to me. While I am talking, look in my eyes and see whether I am lying." And Octave began to relate to his young kinswoman, with great wealth of detail and with the most perfect simplicity, the whole sequence of sentiments and endeavours of which the reader has been informed. He did not forget the speech addressed by Armance to her friend Méry de Tersan, which he had overheard when going to fetch the Chinese chessmen. "Those words determined the course of my life; from that moment I have thought of nothing but how to regain your esteem." This memory touched Armance deeply, and silent tears began to trickle down her cheeks.

She did not once interrupt Octave; when he had finished speaking, she still remained silent for a long time. "You think me guilty!" said Octave, extremely touched by this silence. She did not answer. "I have forfeited your esteem," he cried, and the tears trembled on his eyelids. "Tell me of any single action in the world by which I can reconquer the place I once held in your heart, and in an instant it will be performed." These last words, uttered with a restrained and deep-rooted energy, were too much for Armance's courage to endure; it was no longer possible for her to pretend, her tears overpowered her, and she wept openly. She was afraid lest Octave might go on and say something that would increase her discomfiture, and make her lose what little self-control she still retained. Above all, she was afraid to speak. She made haste to offer him her hand; and making an effort to speak, and to speak only as a friend: "You have all my esteem," she told him. She was greatly relieved to see a maid approaching in the distance; the necessity of concealing her tears from the girl furnished her with an excuse for leaving the garden.

# CHAPTER SEVEN

*But passion most dissembles, yet betrays*
*Even by its darkness; as the blackest sky*
*Foretells the heaviest tempest, it displays*
*Its workings through the vainly guarded eye,*
*And in whatever aspect it arrays*
*Itself, 'tis still the same hypocrisy;*
*Coldness or anger, even disdain or hate,*
*Are masks it often wears, and still too late.*
Don Juan, I, 73.

OCTAVE remained motionless, his eyes brimming with tears, and not knowing whether he ought to rejoice or to mourn. After so long a period of waiting, he had at last been able to give battle, that battle for which he had so longed; but had he lost or won it? "If it is lost," he told himself, "there is nothing more for me in this direction. Armance thinks me so reprehensible that she pretends to be satisfied with the first excuse that I offer her, and does not deign to enter upon an explanation with a man so little worthy of her friendship. What is the meaning of those brief words: *You have all my esteem?* Could anything be colder? Is that a complete return to our old intimacy? Is it a polite way of cutting short a disagreeable explanation?" The departure, so abruptly, of Armance seemed to him to be an especially evil omen.

While Octave, a prey to a profound astonishment, was seeking to recall exactly what had happened to him, trying to forecast the consequences, and trembling lest, amid his efforts to reason fairly, he should suddenly arrive at some decisive revelation which would make an end of all uncertainty by proving to him that his cousin found him unworthy of her esteem, Armance was being racked by the most intense grief. Her tears choked her; but they were tears of shame and no longer of happiness.

She hastened to shut herself up in her own room. "Great God," she said to herself in the intensity of her confusion, "what on earth will Octave think after seeing me in this state? Has he understood my tears? Alas! Can I doubt it? Since when has a simple admission of friendship made a girl of my age burst into tears? Oh, God! After such humiliation how can I venture to face him again? The only thing wanting to complete the horror of my situation was to have deserved his contempt. But," Armance said to herself, "it was something more than a simple admission; for three months I avoided speaking to him; it is a sort of reconciliation between friends who have quarrelled, and people say that one sheds tears at reconciliations of that sort;—yes, but one does not run away, one is not plunged in the most intense confusion.

"Instead of shutting myself up and crying in my bedroom, I ought to be out in the garden and to go on talking to him, happy in the simple happiness of friendship. Yes," Armance told herself, "I ought to go back to the garden; perhaps Madame de Bonnivet has not yet returned." As she rose, she looked at herself in the glass and saw that she was not in a fit state to let herself be seen by a man. "Ah!" she cried, letting herself sink down in despair upon a chair, "I am a poor wretch who has forfeited her honour, and in whose eyes? In Octave's." Her sobs and her despair prevented her from thinking.

"What!" she said to herself, after an interval, "so peaceful, so happy even, in spite of my fatal secret, half an hour ago, and now ruined! Ruined for ever, without remedy! A man of such intelligence as his must have seen the whole extent of my weakness, and it is one of the weaknesses that must be most offensive to his stern judgment." Armance was stifled by her tears. This violent state continued for some hours; it produced a slight touch of fever which won for Armance the permission not to leave her room that evening.

The fever increased, presently an idea came to her: "I am only half despicable, for after all I did not confess in so many words my fatal secret. But after what has happened, I cannot answer for anything. I must erect an eternal barrier between Octave and myself. I must enter religion, I shall choose the order that allows most solitude, a convent situated among high mountains, with a picturesque view. There I shall never hear his name spoken. This is the voice of *duty*," the unhappy Armance told herself. From that moment the sacrifice was made. She did not say it to herself, she felt (to express it in detail would have been tantamount to doubting it), she felt this truth: "From the moment when I perceived my *duty*, not to follow it immediately, blindly, without argument, is to act in a vulgar spirit, is to be unworthy of Octave. How often has he told me that this is the secret sign by which one can recognise a noble spirit! Ah! I will submit to your decree, my noble friend, my dear Octave!" Her fever emboldened her to utter his name in a whisper, and she found happiness in repeating it.

Presently Armance was picturing herself as a nun. There were moments in which she was astonished at the mundane ornaments which decorated her little room. "That fine engraving of the Sistine Madonna which Madame de Malivert gave me, I too must give it away," she said to herself; "it was chosen by Octave, he preferred it to the Marriage of the Madonna, Raphael's first painting. Even then I remember that I argued with him over the soundness of his choice, solely that I might have the pleasure of hearing him defend it. Was I in love with him then without knowing it? Have I always loved him? Ah! I must tear that dishonourable passion from my heart." And the unhappy Armance, trying to forget her cousin, found his memory blended with all the events of her life, even the most insignificant. She was alone, she had sent her maid away, to be able to weep without constraint. She rang the bell and had her engravings carried into the next room. Soon the little room was stripped bare and adorned only with its pretty wallpaper of a lapis-lazuli blue. "Is a nun allowed," she wondered, "to have a wallpaper in her cell?" She pondered for long over this difficulty; her spirit needed to form an exact idea of the state to which she would be reduced in her cell; her uncertainty in this matter surpassed all other evils, for it was her imagination that was engaged in portraying them. "No," she said to herself at length, "papers cannot be allowed, they were not invented in the days of the foundresses of the religious orders; these orders come from Italy; Prince Touboskin told us that a white wall, washed every year with lime, is the only ornament of many beautiful monasteries. Ah!" she went on in her delirium, "I ought perhaps to go and take the veil in Italy; I should make my health an excuse.

"Oh, no. Let me at least not leave Octave's native land, let me at least always hear his tongue spoken." At this moment Méry de Tersan entered the room; the bareness of the walls caught her eye; she turned pale as she approached her friend. Armance, exalted by her fever and by a certain virtuous enthusiasm which was also another way of being in love with Octave, sought to bind her by a confidence. "I wish to become a nun," she said to Méry. "What! Has the sereness of a certain person's heart gone so far as to wound your delicacy?" "Oh, Lord, no, I have no fault to find with Madame de Bonnivet; she is as fond of me as she can be of a penniless girl who has no position in society. Indeed, she is loving to me when things vex her, and could not be kinder to any one than she is to me. I should be unjust, and be shewing a spirit worthy of my position, if I reproached her in the slightest degree." One of the final phrases of this reply drew tears from Méry, who was rich and had the noble sentiments that distinguish her illustrious family. Without conversing save by their tears and the pressure of one another's hand, the friends spent a great part of the evening together. Finally, Armance told Méry all her reasons for retiring to a convent, with one exception: what was to become socially of a penniless girl, who after all could not be given in marriage to a small shopkeeper round the corner? What fate was in store for her? In a convent one is bound only by the rule. If there are not those distractions which we owe to the arts and to the intelligence of people in society, distractions which she enjoyed with Madame de Bonnivet, there is never either the absolute necessity of attracting one person in particular, with humiliation if one does not succeed. Armance would have died of shame sooner than utter the name of Octave. "This is the climax of my misery," she thought, weeping and throwing herself into Méry's arms. "I cannot ask advice even of the most devoted, the most virtuous friendship."

While Armance was weeping in her room, Octave, yielding to an impulse which, for all his philosophy, he was far from explaining to himself, knowing that throughout the evening he would not set eyes on Mademoiselle de Zohiloff, engaged in talk with the women whom as a rule he neglected for the religious arguments of Madame de Bonnivet. For many months now Octave had found himself pursued by advances which were extremely polite and all the more irritating in consequence. He had become misanthropical and soured; soured like Alceste, on the subject of marriageable daughters. As soon as any one spoke to him of a woman in society whom he did not know, his first remark was: "Has she a daughter to marry?" Latterly, indeed, his prudence had taught him not to be satisfied with an initial reply in the negative. "Madame So-and-So has no daughter to marry," he would say, "but are you sure there isn't some niece or other?"

While Armance was being racked by delirium, Octave, who was seeking distraction from the uncertainty in which the incident of the afternoon had plunged him, not only talked to all the women who had nieces, but even tackled several of those redoubtable mothers who have as many as three daughters. Perhaps this display of courage had been rendered easy to him by the sight of the little chair on which Armance generally sat, near Madame de Bonnivet's armchair; it had just been taken by one of the young ladies de Claix, whose fine German shoulders, benefiting by the lowness of Armance's little seat, took the opportunity to display all their freshness. "What a difference!" thought or rather felt Octave; "how ashamed my cousin would be of what constitutes the triumph of Mademoiselle de Claix! For her, it is no more than permissible coquetry; it is not even a fault; of this, too, one can say: *Noblesse oblige.*" Octave set to work to pay court to Mademoiselle de Claix. It would have required some

personal motive for trying to understand him or greater
familiarity with the habitual simplicity of his expression
to detect all the bitterness and scorn that underlay
his pretended gaiety. His listeners were kind enough
to discover wit in what he said to them; to himself
the remarks that received most applause seemed quite
commonplace and sometimes even tainted with vulgarity. As he had not once stopped to talk to Madame
de Bonnivet during the evening, when she passed by him
she scolded him in a whisper, and Octave apologised
for his desertion of her in a speech which the Marquise
thought charming. She was highly pleased with the
intelligence of her future proselyte, and the self-pos-
sessed air which he assumed in society.

She sang his praises with the artless candour of innocence (if the word *candour* does not blush to see itself
employed with reference to a woman who could adopt
such charming poses in her *bergère* and whose eyes
were so picturesque when raised to heaven). It must be
confessed that at times, when she gazed fixedly at a
gilded ornament on the ceiling of her drawing-room,
she would actually say to herself: "There, in that empty
space, in that air, there is a Spirit who hears me,
magnetises my soul and imparts to it the singular and
really quite spontaneous sentiments which I express at
times with such eloquence." That evening, Madame
de Bonnivet, highly pleased with Octave and with the
thought of the position to which her disciple might one
day rise, said to Madame de Claix: "Indeed, the only
thing wanting to the young Vicomte was the assurance

that is given by wealth. Even if I were not in love with that excellent Law of Indemnity, because it is so fair to our poor *émigrés*, I should love it for the new spirit it has given my cousin." Madame d'Ancre shot a glance at Madame de Claix and Madame la Comtesse de la Ronze; and as Madame de Bonnivet left these ladies, in order to greet a young Duchesse who was entering the room: "It seems to me to be all quite clear," she said to Madame de Claix. "All too clear," the latter replied: "we shall be having a scandal; only a little more friendliness on the part of the *astounding* Octave, and our dear Marquise will be unable to resist the temptation to take us altogether into her confidence." "That is always the way," went on Madame d'Ancre, "that I have seen these people of pronounced virtue end, who go in for laying down the law about religion. Ah! my dear Marquise, blessed is the woman who just listens meekly to her parish priest and offers the holy bread!" "It is certainly better than having Bibles bound by Thouvenin," put in Madame de Claix.

But all Octave's feigned friendliness had vanished in the twinkling of an eye. He had just caught sight of Méry, who had come down from Armance's bedroom because her mother had sent for her carriage, and Méry's face was woebegone. She left so hurriedly that Octave had no opportunity of speaking to her. He himself left immediately after her. It would have been impossible for him from that moment to address a word to any one. The distressed air of Mademoiselle de Tersan told him that something out of the common was happening; perhaps Mademoiselle de Zohiloff was about to leave Paris to escape him. What is truly remarkable is that our philosopher had not the slightest idea that he was genuinely in love with Armance. He had bound himself by the strongest vows to resist that passion, and as what he lacked was penetration rather than character, he would probably have kept his vows.

# CHAPTER EIGHT

*What shall I do the while? where bide? how*
*live?*
*Or in my life what comfort, when I am*
*Dead to him?*

CYMBELINE, Act III.

ARMANCE was far from being under any such
illusion. It was now a long time since to see
Octave had become her one interest in life.
When an unexpected turn of fortune had altered her
young kinsman's position in society, how her heart had
been torn by inward conflicts! What excuses had she
not invented for the sudden change that had become
apparent in Octave's behaviour! She asked herself incessantly: "Has he a vulgar soul?"

When at length she had succeeded in proving to herself that Octave was capable of feeling other forms of
happiness than those arising from money and vanity,
a fresh cause of distress seized her attention. "I
should be doubly scorned," she said to herself, "were
any one to suspect my feelings for him; I, the most
penniless of all the girls who come to Madame de Bonnivet's drawing-room." This utter misery which threatened her from every side, and which ought to have
set her to curing herself of her passion, had no effect,
but, by inducing in her a profound melancholy, that of

90

abandoning her more blindly than ever to the sole pleasure that remained to her in the world, the pleasure of thinking of Octave.

Every day she saw him for some hours, and the petty incidents of each day affected her mental attitude towards her cousin; how could she possibly be cured? It was from fear of betraying herself and not from scorn that she had taken such good care never to have any intimate conversation with him.

On the day following the explanation in the garden, Octave called twice at the Hôtel de Bonnivet, but Armance did not appear. This strange absence greatly increased his uneasiness as to the favourable or disastrous effect of the step he had ventured to take. That evening, he read his sentence in his cousin's absence and had not the heart to seek distraction in the sound of vain words; he could not bring himself to speak to any one.

Whenever the door of the drawing-room opened, he felt that he was about to die of hope and fear combined; at length one o'clock struck, and it was time to go. As he left the Hôtel de Bonnivet, the hall, the street-front, the black marble lintel of the door, the crumbling wall of the garden, all these things, common enough in themselves, seemed to him to wear a new and special aspect, derived from Armance's anger. Their familiar forms became precious to Octave, owing to the melancholy which they inspired in him. Dare I say that they rapidly acquired in his eyes a sort of tender nobility? He shuddered when next day he detected a resemblance between the old wall of his father's garden, crowned with a few yellow wall-flowers in blossom, and the enclosing wall of the Hôtel de Bonnivet.

On the third day after his venturing to speak to his cousin, he called upon the Marquise, firmly convinced that he had been for ever relegated to the category of mere acquaintance. What was his dismay on catching sight of Armance at the piano? She greeted him in a friendly fashion. He thought her pale and greatly altered. And yet—and this astonished him greatly and almost restored a glimpse of hope—he thought he could detect in her eyes a certain trace of happiness.

The weather was perfect, and Madame de Bonnivet wished to take advantage of one of the most beautiful mornings of spring to make some long excursion. "Will you be one of us, cousin?" she said to Octave. "Yes, Madame, if it is not to be the Bois de Boulogne, nor the Bois de Mousseaux." Octave knew that Armance disliked both places. "The King's Garden, if we go by the boulevard; will that find favour in your sight?" "It is more than a year since I was last there." "I have never seen the baby elephant," said Armance, jumping for joy, as she went to put on her hat. They set off gaily. Octave was almost beside himself; Madame de Bonnivet drove along the boulevard in an open carriage with her good-looking Octave. This was how the men of their circle who saw them spoke of them. Those whose livers were out of order gave utterance to melancholy reflexions as to the frivolity of great ladies, who were reverting to the ways of the

Court of Louis XV. "In the serious events towards which we are marching," these poor creatures went on to say, "it is a great mistake to let the Third Estate and the working classes have the advantage of regularity of morals and decent behaviour. The Jesuits are perfectly right to make a point of severity."

Armance said that her aunt's bookseller had just sent three volumes entitled *History of* ———. "Do you recommend the book?" the Marquise asked Octave. "It is so blatantly praised in the newspapers that I am distrustful of it." "You will find it very well written, all the same," Octave told her; "the author knows how to tell a story and he has not yet sold himself to any party." "But is it amusing?" said Armance. "Plaguily dull," replied Octave. The talk turned to historical certainty, then to monuments. "Did you not tell me, the other day," said Madame de Bonnivet, "that there is nothing certain except ancient monuments?" "Yes, for the history of the Romans and Greeks, who were rich people and built monuments; but the libraries contain thousands of manuscripts dealing with the middle ages, and it is only from pure laziness on the part of our so-called scholars that we do not make use of them." "But those manuscripts are written in such vile Latin," Madame de Bonnivet went on. "Barely intelligible perhaps to our scholars, but not so bad. You would be highly pleased with the Letters of Heloise to Abelard." "Their tomb used to be, I have heard, in the Musée Français," said Armance, "what has become of it?" "It has been set up in Père-Lachaise."

"Let us go and look at it," said Madame de Bonnivet, and a few minutes later they arrived in that English garden, the only garden of real beauty as a site that exists in Paris. They visited the tomb of Abelard, the obelisk erected to Masséna; they looked for the grave of Labédoyère. Octave saw the spot where rests the young B——, and made her an oblation of tears.

Their conversation was serious, grave, but touching in its intensity. Their true feelings came boldly to the surface. As a matter of fact, they touched only upon subjects that were hardly likely to compromise them, but the heavenly charm of candour was none the less keenly felt by the party, when they saw advancing upon them a group the presiding deity of which was the clever Comtesse de G——. She came to the place in search of inspiration, she informed Madame de Bonnivet.

At this speech, our friends could barely help smiling; never had the commonness and affectation that underlay the words seemed to them so shocking. Madame de G——, like all vulgar French people, exaggerated her impressions in order to create an effect, and the people whose conversation she was interrupting modified their sentiments slightly when they expressed them, not from insincerity but from a sort of instinctive modesty which is unknown among common people, however intelligent they may be.

After a few words of general conversation, as the path was extremely narrow, Octave and Armance found themselves left in the rear.

"You were unwell the day before yesterday," said Octave; "indeed, your friend Méry's pallor, when she came down from your room, made me afraid that you must be feeling very ill."

"I was not ill at all," said Armance in a tone the lightness of which was a trifle marked, "and the interest which your old friendship takes in all that concerns me, to speak like Madame de G——, makes it my duty to tell you the cause of my little disturbance. For some time past there has been a question of my marriage; the day before yesterday, it was on the point of being broken off, and that is why I was a little upset in the garden. But I beg of you absolute secrecy," said Armance in alarm as Madame de Bonnivet began to move towards them. "I rely upon eternal secrecy, even from your mother, and especially from my aunt." This avowal greatly astonished Octave; Madame de Bonnivet having again withdrawn: "Will you permit me to ask one question," he went on. "Is it purely a marriage of convenience?"

Armance, to whose cheeks the fresh air and exercise had brought the most vivid colours, suddenly turned pale. When forming her heroic project overnight, she had not foreseen this very simple question. Octave saw that he had been indiscreet, and was trying to think of some way of turning the conversation with a jest, when Armance said to him, making an effort to subdue her grief: "I hope that the person in question will deserve your friendship; he has all mine. But, if you please, let us not say any more about this arrangement, which

is still perhaps far from complete." Shortly afterwards, they returned to the carriage, and Octave, who
could think of nothing more to say, asked to be set
down at the Gymnase.

# CHAPTER NINE

*Now, peace be here,*
*Poor house, that keep'st thyself!*
            CYMBELINE, Act III.[1]

O
N the evening before this, after a terrible day
of which we can at the most form a feeble
idea by thinking of the state of a poor wretch
wholly devoid of courage who is preparing to undergo
a surgical operation that often proves fatal, an idea
had occurred to Armance: "I am on sufficiently intimate
terms with Octave to tell him that an old friend of my
family is thinking of marrying me.  If my tears betrayed me, this confession will re-establish me in his
esteem.  My approaching marriage and the anxiety it
must be causing me, will make him set my tears down to
some allusion a trifle too direct to the position in which
I am placed.  If he takes any interest in me, alas! he
will be cured of it, but at least I can still be his friend;
I shall not be banished to a convent and condemned
never to set eyes on him again, never once even, for the
rest of my life."

[1]Beyle ascribes this motto, which he quotes in French, to Burns,
thinking possibly of various phrases in the lines *To a Field
Mouse*.  In *Henri Brulard* he again quotes the passage, as from
*Cymbeline*, but gives the speech to Imogen instead of Belarius.—
C. K. S. M.

Armance realised, during the days that followed, that Octave was seeking to discover who the favoured suitor might be. "It will have to be some one whom he knows," she said to herself with a sigh; "my painful duty extends to that also. It is only on those terms that I may still be permitted to see him."

She thought of the Baron de Risset, who had been a leader in the Vendée, a heroic character, who appeared not infrequently in Madame de Bonnivet's drawing-room, but only to remain silent.

The very next evening, Armance spoke to the Baron of the *Memoirs* of Madame de Rochejaquelein. She knew that he was jealous of their success; he spoke of them very critically and at great length. "Is Mademoiselle de Zohiloff in love with a nephew of the Baron," Octave asked himself, "or can it be possible that the old General's gallant deeds have made her forget his fifty-five years?" It was in vain that Octave tried to draw the taciturn Baron, who was more silent and suspicious than ever now that he saw himself made the object of these singular attentions.

Some pieces of politeness unduly marked, addressed to Octave by a mother of marriageable daughters, aroused his misanthropy and made him say to his cousin, who was praising the young ladies in question, that even although they had a more eloquent sponsor, he had, thank God, forbidden himself all exclusive admiration until he should reach the age of six and twenty. This unexpected utterance came like a bolt from the blue to Armance; never in all her life had she felt so happy.

Ten times perhaps since his change of fortune, Octave
had spoken in her hearing of the time at which he would
think of marrying. From the surprise which her
cousin's words caused her, she realised that she had forgotten all about it.

This moment of happiness was exquisite. Wholly absorbed the day before in the intense pain that is caused
by a great sacrifice which must be made to duty, Armance had entirely forgotten this admirable source of
comfort. It was forgetfulness of this sort which made
her be accused of want of intelligence by those people
in society whom the emotions of their hearts leave with
the leisure to think of everything. As Octave was
just twenty, Armance might hope to be his best friend
for six years still, and to be so *without remorse.* "And
who knows," she said to herself, "but I may have the
good fortune to die before the end of those six years?"

A new mode of existence began for Octave. Authorised by the confidence which Armance placed in him,
he ventured to consult her as to the petty incidents of
his life. Almost every evening he had the happiness of
being able to talk to her without being actually overheard by the people near them. He observed with delight that his confidences, however trivial they might be,
were never burdensome. To give courage to her diffi-
dence, Armance too spoke to him of her troubles, and a
very singular intimacy sprang up between them.

The most blissful love has its storms; one may even
say that it lives as much by its terrors as by its felici-
ties. Neither storms nor any uneasiness ever disturbed

99

the friendship of Armance and Octave. He felt that he had no claim upon his cousin; there was nothing that he could have complained of.

Far from exaggerating the gravity of their relations, these delicate natures had never uttered a word on the subject; the word friendship even had never been spoken by either since the confession of her proposed marriage, made by the tomb of Abelard. As, though they met continually, they were rarely able to converse without being overheard, they had always in their brief moments of entire freedom so many things to learn, so many facts to communicate rapidly to one another, that all vain delicacy was banished from their speech.

It must be admitted that Octave would have had difficulty in finding grounds for complaint. All the sentiments that the most exalted, the tenderest, the purest love can bring to life in a woman's heart, Armance felt for him. The hope of death, in which the whole prospect of that love terminated, gave indeed to her speech something heavenly and resigned, quite in keeping with Octave's character.

The tranquil and perfect happiness with which Armance's gentle affection filled him, was felt by him so keenly that he hoped to change his own nature.

Since he had made peace with his cousin, he had never again relapsed into moments of despair, as when he regretted that he had not been killed by the carriage which turned at a gallop into the Rue de Bourbon. He said to his mother: "I am beginning to think that I shall no longer have those fits of rage which made you fear for my reason."

Octave was happier, and became more intelligent. He was astonished to notice in society many things which had never before struck him, though they had long been before his eyes. The world seemed to him less hateful, and, above all, less intent upon doing him harm. He told himself that, except among the class of pious or plain women, everybody thought far more about himself, and far less about doing harm to his neighbour, than he had supposed at a time when he imagined a world which he did not yet know.

He realised that an incessant frivolity makes any consecutive reasoning impossible; he discovered at last that this world, which, in his insensate pride, he had believed to be arranged in a manner *hostile to himself*, was simply nothing more than ill arranged. "But," he said to Armance, "such as it is, one must take it or leave it. One must either end everything swiftly and without delay with a few drops of prussic acid, or else take life gaily." In speaking thus, Octave was trying to convince himself far more than he was expressing a conviction. His heart was beguiled by the happiness that he owed to Armance.

His confidences were not always free from peril for the girl. When Octave's reflexions took on a sombre hue; when he was made wretched by the prospect of isolation in time to come, Armance had the greatest difficulty in concealing from him how wretched it would have made her to imagine that she might ever for an instant in her life be parted from him.

"When a man is without friends at my age," Octave said to her one evening, "can he still hope to acquire any? Does one love according to plan?" Armance, who felt that her tears were about to betray her, was obliged to leave him abruptly. "I see," she said to him, "that my aunt wishes to speak to me."

Octave, his face pressed to the window, continued by himself the course of his sombre reflexions. "It does not do to scowl at the world," he said to himself at length. "It is so spiteful that it would not deign to notice that a young man, shut up under lock and key on a second floor in the Rue Saint-Dominique, hates it with passion. Alas! One creature alone would notice that I was missing from my place, and her *friendship* would be distressed"; and he began to gaze across the room at Armance; she was sitting on her little chair beside the Marquise, and seemed to him at that moment ravishingly beautiful. All Octave's happiness, which he imagined to be so solid and so well assured, depended nevertheless upon the one little word *friendship* which he had just uttered. It is difficult to escape from the prevailing disease of one's generation: Octave imagined himself to be philosophical and profound.

Suddenly Mademoiselle de Zohiloff came towards him with an air of uneasiness and almost of anger: "My aunt has just been told," she said to him, "a strange slander at your expense. A serious person, who has never before shewn himself your enemy, came and told her that often at midnight, when you leave this house, you go and end the evening in strange places which are nothing more than gambling rooms.

"And that is not all; in these places, in which the most degrading tone prevails, you distinguish yourself by excesses which astonish their oldest frequenters. Not only are you seen surrounded by women the mere sight of whom is a scandal; but you talk, you hold the ball in their conversation. She went so far as to say that you shine in those places, and by pleasantries, the bad taste of which passes all belief. The people who take an interest in you, for there are such to be found even in those houses, did you the honour at first to take your utterances for *acquired* wit. 'The Vicomte de Malivert is young,' they said to themselves; 'he must have heard these pleasantries used at some vulgar gathering to stimulate attention and make pleasure sparkle in the eyes of a few coarse men.' But your friends have observed with pain that you take the trouble to invent your most revolting speeches for the occasion. In short, the incredible scandal of your alleged conduct seems to have earned you an unfortunate celebrity among the young men of the worst tone that are to be found in Paris.

"The person who slanders you," continued Armance, whom Octave's obstinate silence was beginning somewhat to disconcert, "ended by giving details which only my aunt's astonishment prevented her from contradicting."

Octave observed with delight that Armance's voice

began to tremble during this long speech. "Everything that you have been told is true," he said to her at length, "but it shall never happen again. I will not appear any more in those places in which your friend ought never to have been seen."

Armance's astonishment and distress were intense. For an instant she felt a sentiment akin to contempt. But next day, when she saw Octave again, her attitude towards what is fitting in the conduct of a young man had quite altered. She found in her cousin's noble confession, and still more in that simple promise made to herself, a reason for loving him all the more. Armance thought that she was being sufficiently severe with herself when she made a vow to leave Paris and never to see Octave again, should he reappear in those houses that were so unworthy of him.

# CHAPTER TEN

*O conoscenza! non è senza il suo perchè che il*
*fedel prete ti chiamò: il più gran dei mali.*
*Egli era tutto disturbato, e però non dubi-*
*tava ancora, al più al più, dubitava di esser*
*presto sul punto di dubitare. O conoscenza!*
*tu sei fatale a quelli, nei quali l'oprar segue*
*da vicino il credo.*

IL CARDINAL GERDIL.

NEED it be said that Octave was faithful to his promise? He abandoned the pleasures proscribed by Armance.

The need for action and the desire to acquire novel experiences had driven him to frequent bad company, often less tedious than good. Now that he was happy, a sort of instinct led him to mix with men; he wished to dominate them.

For the first time, Octave had caught a glimpse of the tedium of too perfect manners and of the excess of cold politeness: bad tone allows a man to talk about himself, in and out of season, and he feels less isolated. After punch had been served in those brilliant saloons at the end of the Rue de Richelieu, which foreigners mistake for good company, one no longer has the sensation: "I am alone in a wilderness of people." On the contrary, he can imagine that he has a score of intimate friends, whose names are unknown to him. May

we venture to say, at the risk of compromising at one
and the same time both our hero and ourself: Octave
thought with regret of several of his supper companions.

The part of his life that had elapsed before his intimacy with the inhabitants of the Hôtel de Bonnivet
was beginning to strike him as foolish and marred by
misunderstanding. "It rained," he would say to himself
in his original and vivid manner; "instead of taking an
umbrella, I used foolishly to lose my temper with the
state of the sky, and in moments of enthusiasm for what
was beautiful and right, which were after all nothing
but fits of madness, I used to imagine that the rain was
falling on purpose to do me an ill turn."

Charmed with the possibility of talking to Mademoiselle de Zohiloff of the observations he had made,
like a second Philibert, in certain highly elegant ballrooms: "I found it a little unexpected," he would say
to her. "I no longer find such pleasure in that pre-
eminently good society, of which I was once so fond.
It seems to me that beneath a cloak of clever talk it
proscribes all energy, all originality. If you are not
a *copy*, people accuse you of being ill-mannered. And
besides, good society usurps its privileges. It had in
the past the privilege of judging what was *proper*, but
now that it supposes itself to be attacked, it condemns
not what is coarse and disagreeable without compensation, but what it thinks harmful to its interests."

Armance listened coldly to her cousin, and said to
him finally: "From what you think to-day, it is only a
step to Jacobinism." "I should be in despair," Oc-

tave sharply retorted. "In despair at what? At knowing the truth," said Armance. "For obviously you would not let yourself be converted by a doctrine that was marred by falsehood." Throughout the rest of the evening, Octave could not help seeming lost in meditation.

Now that he saw society in a rather truer light, Octave was beginning to suspect that Madame de Bonnivet, for all her supreme pretension of never thinking about the world and of despising success, was the slave of an ambition which made her long for an unbounded success in society.

Certain calumnies uttered by the Marquise's enemies, which chance had brought to his hearing, and which had seemed to him unspeakably horrible a few months earlier, were now nothing more in his eyes than exaggerations, treacherous or in bad taste. "My fair cousin is not satisfied," he said to himself, "with illustrious birth, an immense fortune. The splendid existence which her irreproachable conduct, her prudent mind, her wise benevolence assure her is perhaps only a means to her and not an end.

"Madame de Bonnivet requires power. But she is very particular as to the nature of that power. The respect which one obtains from a great position in society, from a welcome at court, from all the advantages that are to be enjoyed under a monarchy no longer means anything to her, she has enjoyed it too long. When one is King, what more can one want? To be God.

"She is satiated with the pleasure that comes from calculated respect, she needs a respect from the heart. She requires the sensation which Mahomet feels when he talks to Seïde, and it seems to me that I have come very near to the honour of being Seïde.[1]

"My fair cousin cannot fill her life with the sensibility that she lacks. She needs, not touching or sublime illusions, not the devotion and passion of one man alone, but to see herself regarded as a Prophetess by a crowd of initiates, and above all, if one of them rebels, to be able to crush him immediately. She has too positive a nature to be content with illusions; she requires the reality of power, and, if I continue to talk to her with an open heart about various things, one day that absolute power may be brought into action against me.

"It is inevitable that she must soon be besieged by anonymous letters; people will reproach her with the frequency of my visits. The Duchesse d'Ancre, irritated by my neglect of her own drawing-room, will perhaps allow herself to make a direct charge. My position is not strong enough to withstand this twofold danger. Very soon, while scrupulously maintaining all the outward forms of the closest friendship, and heaping reproaches on me for the infrequency of my visits, Madame de Bonnivet would put me under the obligation to make them very infrequent indeed.

"For instance, I give the impression of being half

[1] A slave of Mahomet in Voltaire's tragedy.

converted to this German mysticism; she will ask me
to make some public and utterly ridiculous exhibition.
If I submit to that, out of friendship for Armance,
very soon she will suggest to me something that is
quite impossible."

# CHAPTER ELEVEN

*Somewhat light as air.*
*There's language in her eye, her cheek, her lip,*
*Nay, her foot speaks; her wanton spirits look*
*out*
*At every joint and motive of her body.*
*O! These encounterers, so glib of tongue,*
*That give a coasting welcome ere it comes.*
TROILUS AND CRESSIDA, Act IV.[1]

THERE were few pleasant drawing-rooms pertaining to that section of society which three times in the year pays its respects to the King in which Octave was not warmly welcomed. He observed the celebrity of Madame la Comtesse d'Aumale. She was the most brilliant and perhaps the cleverest coquette of the day. An ill-humoured foreigner has said that the women of high society in France have a cleverness akin to that of an old Ambassador. It was a childish simplicity that shone in the manners of Madame d'Aumale. The artlessness of her repartees and the wild gaiety of her actions, always inspired by the circumstances of the moment, were the despair of her rivals. She had caprices of a marvellous unexpectedness, and how is any one to imitate a caprice?

[1] The first half-line, which is not in *Troilus and Cressida*, is perhaps a reminiscence of *Othello:* "Trifles light as air."—C. K. S. M.

110

The natural and unexpected were by no means the most brilliant element in Octave's behaviour. He was compact of mystery. Never any sign of thoughtlessness in him, unless occasionally in his conversations with Armance. But he needed to be certain that he would not be interrupted unexpectedly. No one could reproach him with falseness; he would have scorned to tell a lie, but he never went straight towards his goal. Octave took into his service a footman who had come from Madame d'Aumale; this man, an old soldier, was ambitious and cunning. Octave used to make him ride with him on long excursions of seven or eight leagues which he made through the forests round Paris, and there were moments of evident boredom in which the man was allowed to talk. It was barely a matter of weeks before Octave had the most definite information as to Madame d'Aumale's conduct. This young woman, who had compromised herself deeply by an unbounded thoughtlessness, was really entitled to all the esteem which certain people no longer gave her.

Octave calculated, pencil in hand, the amount of time and trouble which Madame d'Aumale's society would require of him, and hoped, without undue effort, to be able before long to pass as a lover of this brilliant woman. He arranged matters so well that it was Madame de Bonnivet herself who, in the course of a party that she was giving at her country house at Andilly, presented him to Madame d'Aumale, and the manner of the presentation was picturesque and impressive for the giddy young Comtesse.

With the object of enlivening a stroll that the party were taking, by night, among the charming woods that crown the heights of Andilly, Octave suddenly appeared disguised as a magician, and was seen in a glare of Bengal lights, cunningly concealed behind the trunks of forest trees. Octave was looking his best that evening, and Madame de Bonnivet, quite unconsciously, spoke of him with a sort of exaltation. Less than a month after this first encounter, people began to say that the Vicomte had succeeded M. de R—— and all the rest of them in the post of intimate friend to Madame d'Aumale.

This most frivolous of women, of whom neither she herself nor any one else could ever say what she would be doing in a quarter of an hour, had noticed that a drawing-room clock, when it struck twelve, sent home the majority of the bores in the room, people of regular habits; and so entertained from midnight until two o'clock. Octave was always the last to leave Madame de Bonnivet's drawing-room, and would kill his horses to hasten his arrival at Madame d'Aumale's, in the Chaussée d'Antin. There he found a woman who thanked heaven for her exalted birth and her fortune, solely because of the privilege they conferred on her, to do at every minute of the day whatever she might be inspired to do by the caprice of the moment.

In the country, at midnight, when every one went up to bed, did Madame d'Aumale remark, as she crossed the hall, a fine night and a pleasing moon, she would take the arm of the young man who, that evening, seemed to her to be the most amusing, and go roaming through the woods. Should some fool offer to accompany her on her stroll, she would beg him without ceremony to choose another path; but next day, should her companion overnight have proved boring, she did not speak to him again. It must be confessed that in the presence of so lively an intelligence, employed in the service of so unbalanced a head, it was very difficult not to seem a trifle dull.

This was what made Octave's fortune; the amusing element of his nature was completely invisible to the people who before taking action always think of a model to be copied and of the conventions. No one, on the other hand, could be more conscious of this than the prettiest woman in Paris, always in pursuit of some novel idea which might enable her to pass the evening in an exciting way. Octave accompanied Madame d'Aumale everywhere, as for instance to the Italian theatre.

During the two or three final performances given by Madame Pasta, to which the cult of fashion had brought the whole of Paris, he took the trouble to converse aloud with the young Comtesse, and in such a way as to spoil the whole of the show. Madame d'Aumale, amused by what he was saying to her, was delighted by the simple air with which he displayed his impertinence.

Nothing could have seemed in worse taste to Octave; but he was beginning to acquire a mastery of foolish conduct. The twofold attention which, when he took some ridiculous liberty, he gave unconsciously to the impertinence that he was committing and to the sober conduct for which he substituted it, kindled a certain fire in his eyes which amused Madame d'Aumale. Octave took pleasure in hearing it said on all sides that he was madly in love with the Comtesse, and in never saying anything to this young and charming woman, with whom he spent all his time, that in the remotest degree suggested love.

Madame de Malivert, astonished at her son's conduct, went now and again to the drawing-rooms in which he was to be seen in the train of Madame d'Aumale. One evening, as she left Madame de Bonnivet's, she asked her to let her have Armance for the whole of the next day. "I have a number of papers to arrange, and I need the eyes of my Armance."

On the following morning, at eleven o'clock, before luncheon, as had been arranged, Madame de Malivert's carriage went to fetch Armance. The ladies took luncheon by themselves. When Madame de Malivert's maid was leaving them, "remember," her mistress told her, "that I am at home to nobody, neither to Octave nor to M. de Malivert." She carried her precautions so far as to bolt the door of her outer room herself.

When she was comfortably settled in her *bergère*, with Armance on her little chair facing her: "My child," she said to her, "I am going to speak to you of a matter which I have long ago decided. But unfortunately my most firm desire is not enough to bring about a result which would be the joy of my life. You

have but a hundred louis a year, that is all that my
enemies can say against the passionate desire that I
feel to make you marry my son." So saying, Madame
de Malivert threw herself into Armance's arms. This
was the happiest moment in the poor girl's life; tears
of joy bathed her cheeks.

# CHAPTER TWELVE

Estavas, linda Ignez, posta em socego
De teus annos colhendo doce fruto
Naquelle engano da alma ledo e cego
Que a fortuna, naô deixa durar muito.
                                    Os Lusiadas, III.

"BUT, dear Mama," said Armance, after a long
pause, and when they were once more able
to talk seriously, "Octave has never told me
that he was attached to me as it seems to me that a husband ought to be to his wife." "If I had not to rise
from my chair to take you in front of a mirror," replied Madame de Malivert, "I should let you see how
your eyes are sparkling with joy at this moment, and
should ask you to repeat to me that you are not sure
of Octave's heart. I am quite sure of it myself, though
I am only his mother. However, I am under no illusion
as to the faults that my son may have, and I do not
ask for your answer before at least a week has passed."

I cannot say whether it was to the Slavonic blood
that flowed in her veins, or to her early experience of
misfortune that Armance owed her faculty of perceiv-
ing in a flash all the consequences that a sudden change
in her life might involve. And whether this new state
of things were deciding her own fate or that of some

116

one to whom she was indifferent, she saw the outcome
with the same clarity of vision. This strength of character or of mind entitled her at once to the daily confidences and to the reprimands of Madame de Bonnivet.
The Marquise consulted her readily as to her own most
private arrangements; and at other times would say to
her: "A mind like yours is never becoming in a girl."

After the first moment of happiness and profound
gratitude, Armance decided that she ought not to say
anything to Madame de Malivert of the untrue statement she had made to Octave with regard to a proposal of marriage. "Madame de Malivert has not consulted her son," she thought, "or else he has concealed
from her the obstacle in the way of his plan." This
second possibility made Armance extremely sombre.

She wished to believe that Octave felt no love for
her; every day she had need of this certainty to justify
in her own eyes any number of attentions which her
tender affection allowed her to pay him, and yet this
terrible proof of her cousin's indifference, which came to
her thus suddenly, crushed her heart under an enormous weight, and deprived her of the power of speech.

With what sacrifices would not Armance have paid
at that moment for the right to weep freely! "If
my cousin surprises a tear in my eyes," she said to
herself, "what decisive conclusion will she not feel herself entitled to draw from it? For all I can tell, in
her eagerness for this marriage, she may mention my
tears to her son, as a proof of my response to his supposed affection." Madame de Malivert was not at all

surprised at the air of profound abstraction which
dominated Armance at the end of this day.

The ladies returned together to the Hôtel de Bonnivet, and although Armance had not set eyes on her
cousin all day, even his presence, when she caught sight
of him in the drawing-room, was powerless to wrest her
from her black melancholy. She could barely answer
him; she had not the strength to speak. Her preoccupation was plain to Octave, no less than her indifference towards him; he said to her sadly: "To-day
you have not time to remember that I am your friend."

Armance's only answer was to gaze at him fixedly,
and her eyes assumed, unconsciously, that serious and
profound expression which had earned her such fine
moral lectures from her aunt.

These words from Octave pierced her to the heart.
"So he knows nothing of his mother's intervention, or
rather he took no interest in it, and wished only to
be a friend." When, after seeing the guests depart and
receiving Madame de Bonnivet's confidences as to the
state of all her various plans, Armance was at length
able to seek the solitude of her little room, she found
herself a prey to the most sombre grief. Never had
she felt so wretched; never had the act of living so
hurt her. With what bitterness did she reproach herself for the novels among whose pages she sometimes
allowed her imagination to stray! In those happy moments, she ventured to say to herself: "If I had been
born to a fortune, and Octave could have chosen me
as his companion in life; according to what I know of

his character, he would have found greater happiness
with me than with any other woman in the world."

She was paying dearly now for these dangerous suppositions. Armance's profound grief did not grow any
less in the days that followed; she could not abandon
herself for a moment to meditation, without arriving
at the most entire disgust with everything, and she had
the misfortune to feel her state keenly. The external
obstacles in the way of a marriage to which, upon any
assumption, she would never have consented, seemed to
be smoothed away; but Octave's heart alone was not
on her side.

Madame de Malivert, having seen the dawn of her
son's passion for Armance, had been alarmed by his
assiduous courtship of the brilliant Comtesse d'Aumale.
But she had only had to see them together to discern
that this relation was a duty which her son's odd
nature had imposed on him; Madame de Malivert knew
quite well that if she questioned him on the subject,
he would tell her the truth; but she had carefully ab-
stained from asking even the most indirect questions.
Her rights did not seem to her to extend so far. Out
of regard for what she thought due to the dignity of
her sex, she had wished to speak of this marriage to
Armance before opening the subject with her son, of
whose passion she was sure.

Having disclosed her plan to Mademoiselle de Zohiloff, Madame de Malivert arranged her time so that she
spent hours on end in Madame de Bonnivet's drawing-
room. She thought she could see that something

strange was occurring between Armance and her son.
Armance was evidently very unhappy. "Can it be
possible," Madame de Malivert asked herself, "that
Octave, who adores her and sees her incessantly, has
never told her that he is in love with her?"

The day upon which Mademoiselle de Zohiloff was to
give her answer had arrived. Early in the morning
Madame de Malivert sent round her carriage with a
little note in which she invited her to come and spend
an hour with her. Armance arrived with the face of a
person who is recovering from a long illness; she would
not have had the strength to come on foot. As soon
as she was alone with Madame de Malivert, she said
to her in the gentlest of tones, beneath which could
be seen that firmness which comes of despair: "My
cousin has a strain of originality in his character;
his happiness requires, and perhaps mine also," she
added, blushing deeply, "that my darling Mama shall
never speak to him of a plan which her extreme interest in myself has inspired in her." Madame de
Malivert affected to grant with great reluctance her
consent to what was asked of her. "I may die sooner
than I think," she said to Armance, "and then my son
will never win the only woman in the world who can
mitigate the despondency of his nature. I am sure that
it is the thought of money that has led to your decision," she said at other moments; "Octave, who has
always something to confide in you, cannot have been
such a fool as not to confess to you a thing of which I
am certain, namely, that he loves you with all the

passion of which he is capable, which is saying a great deal, my child. If certain moments of excitement, which become rarer every year, may furnish grounds for sundry objections to the character of the husband I offer you, you will have the comfort of being loved as few women are loved to-day. In the stormy times that may come upon us, firmness of character in a man will mean a great probability of happiness for his family.

"You yourself know, my Armance, that the external obstacles which crush down common men are nothing to Octave. If his soul is at peace, the whole world banded together against him would not give him a quarter of an hour of unhappiness. Well, I am certain that the peace of his soul hangs upon your consent. Judge for yourself of the ardour with which I ought to plead for him; on you depends my son's happiness. For four years I thought day and night of how to assure it, I could find no way; at last he fell in love with you. As for myself, I shall be the victim of your exaggerated delicacy. You do not wish to incur the reproach of having married a husband far richer than yourself, and I shall die with the utmost anxiety as to Octave's future, and without having seen my son united to the woman whom, in my whole life, I have most highly esteemed."

These assurances of Octave's love were excruciating to Armance. Madame de Malivert remarked, underlying her young relative's answers, irritation and wounded pride. That evening, at Madame de Bonnivet's, she observed that her son's presence did not at all relieve Mademoisele de Zohiloff of that sort of misery which springs from the fear of not having shewn sufficient pride towards the person whom one loves, and of having perhaps thus lowered herself in his esteem. "Is a poor girl with no family," Armance was saying to herself, "the person to be so forgetful?"

Madame de Malivert herself was extremely anxious. After many sleepless nights, she at length arrived at a curious idea, probable however in view of her son's strange character, that really, just as Armance had said, he had never uttered a word to her of his love.

"Is it possible," thought Madame de Malivert, "that Octave can be so timid as that? He is in love with his cousin; she is the one person in the world who can ensure him against those fits of melancholy which have made me tremble for him."

After careful reflexion, she decided upon her course; one day she said to Armance in an indifferent tone: "I cannot think what you have done to my son, to discourage him; but while he admits to me that he has the most profound attachment to you, the most entire esteem, and that to win your hand would be in his eyes the greatest of blessings, he adds that you present an insuperable obstacle to his most cherished ambitions, and that certainly he would not be indebted for you to the persecutions to which we might subject you on his behalf."

# CHAPTER THIRTEEN

*Ay! que ya siento en mi cuidoso pecho*
*Labrarme poco a poco un vivo fuego*
*Y desde alli con movimiento blando*
*Ir por venas y huesos penetrando.*
ARAUCANA, XXII.

THE extreme happiness that shone in Armance's eyes consoled Madame de Malivert, who was beginning to feel some remorse at having introduced a tiny falsehood into so serious a negotiation. "After all," she said to herself, "what harm can there be in hastening the marriage of two charming but rather proud children, who feel a passion for each other such as we rarely see in this world? To preserve my son's reason, is not that my paramount duty?"

The singular course which Madame de Malivert had decided to adopt had delivered Armance from the most profound grief that she had ever felt in her life. A little while since, she had longed for death; and now these words, which she supposed to have been uttered by Octave, placed her on a pinnacle of happiness. She was quite determined never to accept her cousin's hand; but this charming speech allowed her once again to hope for many years of happiness. "I shall be able to love him in secret," she told herself, "during the six years that must pass before he marries; and I shall

123

be fully as happy, and perhaps far happier than if
I were his partner. Is it not said that marriage is the
grave of love; that there may be agreeable marriages
but never one that is really delightful? I should be
terrified of marrying my cousin; if I did not see that
he was the happiest of men, I should myself be in the
depths of despair. If, on the other hand, we continue
to live in our pure and holy friendship, none of the
petty concerns of life can ever reach the high level
of our feelings to wound them."

Armance weighed in her mind with all the calm of
happiness the reasons which she had given herself in
the past for never accepting Octave's hand. "I should
be regarded in society as a paid companion who had
seduced the son of the house. I can hear Madame la
Duchesse d'Ancre saying so, and indeed the most
honourable women, such as the Marquise de Seyssins,
who looks on Octave as a husband for one of her
daughters.

"The loss of my reputation would be all the more
rapid, from my having lived in the company of several
of the most unimpeachable women in Paris. They can
say anything they like about me; their word will be
believed. Heavens! Into what an abyss of shame they
can hurl me! And Octave might at any time withdraw
his esteem from me; for I have no means of defence.
What drawing-room is there in which I could make
my voice heard? Where are my friends? And besides,
after the evident baseness of such an action, what justification would be possible? Even if I had a family, a

brother, a father, would they ever believe that, if Octave was in my position and I extremely rich, I should be as devoted to him as I am at this moment?"

Armance had a reason for feeling keenly the kind of indelicacy which money involves. Only a few days earlier, Octave had said to her, speaking of a certain majority vote which had made a stir: "I hope, when I have taken my place in public life, that I shall not allow myself to be bought like those gentlemen. I can live upon five francs a day; and, under an assumed name, it is open to me to earn twice that amount in any part of the world, as a chemist employed in some factory."

Armance was so happy that she did not shrink from examining any objection, however perilous it might be to discuss it. "If Octave preferred me to a fortune and to the support which he is entitled to expect from the family of a wife of his own rank, we might go and live somewhere in retirement. Why not spend ten months of every year on that charming estate Malivert, in Dauphiné, of which he often speaks? The world would very soon forget us.—Yes; but I myself, I should not forget that there was a place on earth where I was despised, and despised by the noblest souls.

"To see love perish in the heart of a husband whom she adores is the greatest of all misfortunes for a young person born to wealth; well, that terrible misfortune would be as nothing to me. Even if he continued to cherish me, every day would be poisoned by the fear that Octave might come to think that I had chosen him

because of the difference in our fortunes. That idea
will not come to him spontaneously, I am sure; anonymous letters, like those that are sent to Madame de
Bonnivet, will bring it to his notice. I shall tremble
at every mail that he receives. No, whatever happens,
I must never accept Octave's hand; and the course
that honour prescribes is also the most certain to
assure our happiness."

On the morrow of the day that made Armance
so happy, Mesdames de Malivert and de Bonnivet went
to stay in the charming house that the Marquise owned
near Andilly. Madame de Malivert's doctors had
recommended exercise on horseback and on foot; and
on the morning after her arrival she decided to try a
pair of charming little ponies which she had procured
from Scotland for Armance and herself. Octave accompanied the ladies on their first ride. They had
scarcely gone a quarter of a league before he thought
he noticed a slight increase of reserve in his cousin's
attitude towards himself, and especially a marked tendency to gaiety.

This discovery gave him much food for thought; and
what he observed during the rest of the ride confirmed
his suspicions. Armance was no longer the same to
him. It was clear that she was going to be married;
he was going to lose the only friend that he had in
the world. As he was helping Armance to dismount,
he found an opportunity to say to her, without being
overheard by Madame de Malivert: "I am sorely afraid
that my fair cousin is soon going to change her name;

that event will deprive me of the only person in the world who has been kind enough to shew me some friendship." "Never," said Armance, "will I cease to feel for you the most devoted and most exclusive friendship." But while she was rapidly uttering these words, there was such a look of happiness in her eyes, that Octave, forewarned, saw in them the confirmation of all his fears.

The good nature, the air almost of intimacy with which Armance treated him during their ride on the following day, succeeded in robbing him of all peace of mind: "I see," he said to himself, "a decided change in Mademoiselle de Zohiloff's manner; she was extremely agitated a few days ago, now she is extremely happy. I am ignorant of the cause of this change; therefore it can only be to my disadvantage.

"Who was ever such a fool as to choose for his intimate friend of a girl of eighteen? She marries, and all is over. It is my cursed pride that makes me prepared to die a thousand deaths rather than venture to say to a man the things that I confide in Mademoiselle de Zohiloff.

"Work might offer some resource; but have I not abandoned every reasonable occupation? To tell the truth, for the last six months, has not the effort to make myself agreeable in the eyes of a stupid and selfish world been my only task?" So as to devote himself at any rate to this useful form of boredom, every day, after his mother's outing, Octave left Andilly and went to pay calls in Paris. He sought new habits to fill the void that would be left in his life by this charming cousin when she withdrew from society to go with her husband; this idea put him in need of violent exercise.

The more his heart was wrung by misery, the more he spoke and sought to please; what he most feared, was finding himself left alone; and, above all, the prospect of the future. He repeated incessantly to himself: "It was childish of me to choose a girl as my friend." This statement, by its self-evident truth, soon became a sort of proverb in his eyes, and prevented him from proceeding farther with his exploration of his own heart.

Armance, who saw his misery, was moved by it, and often reproached herself for the false admission she had made to him. Not a day passed but, as she saw him set off for Paris, she was tempted to tell him the truth. "But that falsehood is my one weapon against him," she said to herself; "if I so much as admit to him that I am not engaged, he will implore me to yield to his mother's wishes, and how am I to resist? And yet, never and upon no pretext must I consent; no, this pretended marriage with a stranger is my sole defence against a happiness that would destroy us both."

To dissipate the sombre thoughts of this beloved cousin, Armance allowed herself to indulge in the little pleasantries of the most tender friendship. There was such charm, such an artless gaiety in the assurances of undying friendship given him by this girl, so natural in all her actions, that often Octave's dark misanthropy was disarmed by them. He was happy in spite of himself; and at such moments nothing was wanting either to complete Armance's happiness.

"How pleasant it is," she said to herself, "to do one's duty! If I were Octave's wife, I, a penniless girl with no family, should I be as well pleased? A thousand cruel suspicions would assail me without ceasing." But, after these moments in which she was satisfied with herself and with the rest of the world, Armance ended by treating Octave more kindly than she intended. She kept a careful watch over her speech; and never did her speech convey anything but the most holy friendship. But the tone in which certain words were uttered! The glance that sometimes accompanied them! Any one but Octave would have been able to read in them an expression of the warmest passion. He enjoyed without understanding them.

As soon as he had granted himself permission to think incessantly of his cousin, his thoughts no longer rested with passion upon anything else in the world. He became once more fair and even indulgent; and his happiness made him abandon his harsh judgments of many things: fools no longer seemed to him anything more than people who had been unlucky from birth.

"Is it a man's fault if he has black hair?" he said to Armance. "But it rests with me carefully to avoid the man if the colour of his hair annoys me."

Octave was considered malicious in certain sections of society, and fools had an instinctive fear of him;

at this period they became reconciled with him. Often he took with him into society all the happiness that he owed to his cousin. He was less feared, his affability was felt to be more youthful. It must be admitted that in all his actions there was a trace of that intoxication which springs from that form of happiness which a man does not admit even to himself; life passed rapidly for him and delightfully. His criticisms of himself no longer bore the imprint of that inexorable, harsh logic, taking pleasure in its own harshness, which in his boyhood had controlled all his actions. Beginning often to speak without knowing how his sentence would end. he talked far better than before.

# CHAPTER FOURTEEN

*Il giovin cuore o non vede affatto i difetti di
chi li sta vicino o li vede immensi. Error
comune ai giovinetti che portano fuoco
nell' interno dell' anima.*

LAMPUGNANI.

ONE day Octave learned in Paris that one of
the men whom he saw most often and took
most pleasure in seeing, one of his friends,
as the word is used in society, owed the handsome fortune which he spent with such grace to what in Octave's
eyes was the basest of actions (legacy hunting). Mademoiselle de Zohiloff, to whom he made haste, immediately
on his return to Andilly, to impart this painful discovery, felt that he bore it very well. He underwent no
attack of misanthropy, shewed no desire to quarrel
openly with the man.

Another day, he returned quite early from a country
house in Picardy, where he was to have spent the evening. "How dull all that talk is!" he said to Armance.
"Always hunting, the beauty of the country, Rossini's
music, the fine arts! Not only that, but they are
lying when they pretend to be interested. These people
are foolish enough to be frightened, they imagine they
are living in a beleaguered city and forbid themselves

131

to discuss the news of the siege. What a miserable race! And how angry it makes me to belong to it!" "Very well! Go and visit the besiegers," said Armance; "their absurdities will help you to endure those of the army in which your birth has enrolled you." "It is a serious question," Octave went on. "Heaven knows what I feel when I hear in one of our drawing-rooms one of our friends give voice to some opinion that is absurd or cruel; still, I can remain honourably silent. My regret remains invisible. But if I let myself be taken to see the banker Martigny . . ." "There you are," said Armance, "a man so refined as he is, so clever, such a slave to his vanity, will receive you with open arms." "Doubtless; but for my part, however moderate, however modest, however silent I try to make myself, I shall end by expressing my opinion about somebody or something. A moment later, the door of the drawing-room is flung open; the butler announces Monsieur So-and-so, manufacturer at ——, who in stentorian tones shouts from the threshold: 'Would you believe it, my dear Martigny, there are *ultras*, fools enough, stupid enough, idiotic enough to say that . . .' Whereupon the worthy manufacturer repeats, word for word, the little scrap of opinion which I have just announced in all modesty. What am I to do?" "Pretend not to have heard him." "That is what I should like. I was not put into this world to correct coarse manners or wrong judgments; still less do I wish to give the man, by speaking to him, the right to shake hands with me in the street when next we meet. But in that drawing-room I have the misfortune not to be just like any one else. Would to God that I might find there the *equality* of which all those gentlemen make so much. For instance, what would you have me do with the title that I bear when I am announced at M. de Martigny's?" "But it is your intention to discard the title if you can manage to do so without offending your father." "Doubtless; but to forget the title, in giving my name to M. de Martigny's servant, might seem, might it not, an act of cowardice? Like Rousseau, who called his dog *Turc* instead of *Duc*, because there was a Duke in the room." [1]

"But there is no such hatred of titles among the Liberal bankers," said Armance. "The other day Madame de Claix, who goes everywhere, happened to go to the ball at M. Montange's, and you remember how she made us laugh that evening by pretending that they are so fond of titles that she had heard some one announced as 'Madame la Colonelle.'"

"Now that the steam engine rules the world, a title is an absurdity, still I am dressed up in this title. It will crush me if I do not support it. The title attracts attention to myself. If I do not reply to the thunder-

[1] Like Rousseau, poor Octave is fighting against phantoms. He would have passed unnoticed in any drawing-room in Paris, notwithstanding the prefix to his name. There prevails, moreover, in his sketch of a section of society which he has never seen, an absurd tone of animosity which he will correct in time. Fools are to be found in every class. If there were a class which rightly or wrongly was accused of coarseness, it would very soon be distinguished by a great prudery and solemnity of manners.

ing voice of the manufacturer who shouts from the door that what I have just said is asinine, how they will all stare at me. That is the weak point in my nature: I cannot simply twitch my ears and laugh at them, as Madame d'Aumale would suggest.

"If I intercept their stare, all my pleasure is gone for the rest of the evening. The discussion that will then begin in my mind, as to whether they meant to insult me, is capable of destroying my peace of mind for three days."

"But are you quite certain," said Armance, "of this alleged coarseness of manners which you so generously attribute to the other side? Did not you see the other day that Talma's children are boarding at the same school as the sons of a Duke?" "It is the men of forty-five, who became rich during the Revolution, who hold the ball in our drawing-rooms, not the school-fellows of Talma's children." "I would wager that they have more intelligence than many of us. Who is the man who shines in the House of Peers? You yourself made that painful observation the other day."

"Oh! If I were to give my fair cousin lessons in logic, how I should tease her! What is a man's intelligence to me? It is his manners that may make me unhappy. The most foolish of our men, M. de ——, for instance, may be highly ridiculous, but he is never offensive. The other day I was talking at the Aumales' of my visit to Liancourt; I was talking of the latest machinery which the worthy Duke has imported from

Manchester. A man who was in the room said suddenly: 'It's not so, that's not true.' I was quite sure that he did not mean to contradict me; but his rudeness kept me silent for an hour."

"And this man was a banker?" "He was not one of us. The amusing thing is, that I wrote to the foreman of the mills at Liancourt, and it appears that my friend who contradicted me was quite wrong." "I don't find that M. Montange, the young banker who comes to see Madame de Claix, has rude manners." "His are honeyed; it is a form that rude manners take, when they are frightened."

"I think their women very pretty," Armance went on. "I should like to know whether their conversation is marred by that note of hatred or of dignity that is afraid of being wounded, which appears at times among us. Oh, how I wish that a good judge like my cousin could tell me what goes on in those drawing-rooms! When I see the bankers' ladies in their boxes, at the Théâtre-Italien, I am dying with longing to hear what they say and to join in their conversation. If I catch sight of a pretty one, and some of them are charming, I long to throw my arms round her neck. All this will seem childish to you; but to you, master philosopher, who are so strong in logic, I will say this: how are you to know mankind if you see only one class? And the class that is least energetic because it is the farthest removed from any real needs!"

"And the class that has most affectation, because it

thinks that people are watching it. You must admit that it is amusing to see a philosopher supply his adversary with arguments," said Octave, laughing. "Would you believe that yesterday, at the Saint-Imiers', M. le Marquis de ——, who, the other day, in this house, made such fun of the little newspapers, and pretended not to know of their existence, was in the seventh heaven, because *l'Aurore* had printed a vulgar joke about his enemy, M. le Comte de ——, who has just been made a Privy Councillor? He had the paper in his pocket." "It is one of the drawbacks of our position, to have to listen to fools telling the most ridiculous lies and not be able to say: 'A fine disguise, I know you.'" "We are obliged to deny ourselves the best jokes, because they might make the other side laugh if they heard them."

"I know the bankers," said Armance, "only from our silvery Montange and that charming comedy *Le Roman;* but I doubt whether, as far as the worship of money is concerned, they are any worse than some of our own people. You know that it is a hard task to maintain the perfection of a whole class. I shall say no more of the pleasure it would give me to know more about their ladies. But, as the old Duc de —— said at Petersburg, when he had the *Journal de l'Empire* sent to him at such expense, and at the risk of offending the Tsar Alexander: 'Ought one not to read what the other side has to say?'" "I will go a great deal farther, *but in confidence,* as Talma says so perfectly in *Polyeucte:* You and I, in our hearts, do not, certainly, wish to live among these people; but on many questions we think as they do." "And it is sad at our age," Armance put in, "to have to resign ourselves to being for the rest of our lives on the defeated side."

"We are like the priests of the heathen idols, at the time when the Christian religion was beginning to triumph. We still persecute to-day, we still have the police and the budget on our side, but to-morrow, perhaps, we shall be persecuted by public opinion." "You do us a great honour when you compare us to those worthy priests of paganism. I see something even more false in our position, yours and mine. We belong to our party only to share its misfortunes." "That is all too true, we see its absurdities without daring to laugh at them, and its advantages are a burden to us. How does the antiquity of my name help me? It would be a nuisance to me to derive any benefit from that advantage."

"The conversation of the young men of your sort makes you sometimes want to shrug your shoulders, and, afraid of yielding to the temptation, you are always in a hurry to speak of Mademoiselle de Claix's beautiful album or of Madame Pasta's singing. On the other hand, your title and the manners, which are slightly rough perhaps, of the people who think like you on most questions prevent you from seeing them."

"Ah, how I should love to command a gun or a steam engine! How glad I should be to be a chemist employed in some factory; for rude manners are nothing to me, one grows accustomed to them in a week." "Apart from the fact that you are by no means so certain that they are so rude," said Armance. "Were they ten times more so," replied Octave, "there is the excitement of trying a foreign language; but one would have to be called M. Martin or M. Lenoir." "Could you not find a man of sense who had made a tour of discovery in the Liberal drawing-rooms?" "Many of my friends go there to dance, they say that the ices there are perfect, and that is all. One fine day I may venture there myself, for there is nothing so foolish as to think for a year on end of a danger which perhaps does not exist."

In the end, Armance extracted the admission that he had thought of a way of appearing in those circles in which it is wealth that confers precedence and not birth: "Well, yes, I have found a way," said Octave; "but the remedy would be worse than the disease, for it would cost me several months of my life, which I should have to spend away from Paris."

"What is your way?" said Armance, growing suddenly quite serious. "I should go to London, I should see there, naturally, all the most distinguished elements of society. How can one go to England and not be introduced to the Marquess of Lansdowne, Mr. Brougham, Lord Holland? These gentlemen will talk to me of our famous men in France; they will be surprised to hear that I do not know them; I shall express

deep regret; and, on my return, I shall have myself
introduced to all the most popular people in France.
My action, if they do me the honour to mention it at
the Duchesse d'Ancre's, will not seem in the least an
abandonment of the ideas which they may suppose to
be inseparable from my name: it would be simply the
quite natural desire to know the superior people of the
age in which we live. I shall never forgive myself for
not having met General Foy." Armance remained
silent.

"Is it not humiliating," Octave went on, "that all
our supporters, even the *monarchist* writers whose duty
it is to preach every morning in the newspaper the
advantages of birth and religion, are furnished us by
that class which has every advantage, except that of
birth?" "Ah, if M. de Soubirane were to hear you!"
"Do not attack me upon the greatest of all my misfortunes, that of being obliged to lie all day long. . . ."

The tone of perfect intimacy allows endless paren-
theses, which give pleasure because they are a proof of
an unbounded confidence, but may easily bore a third
person. It is enough for us to have shewn that the
brilliant position of the Vicomte de Malivert was far
from being a source of unmixed pleasure to him.

It is not without danger that we have been faithful
chroniclers. The intrusion of politics into so simple a
narrative may have the effect of a pistol shot in the
middle of a concert. Moreover, Octave is no philosopher, and has characterised most unfairly the two
shades of opinion which, in his day, bisect society. How

scandalous that Octave does not reason like a sage of fifty.[2]

[2] We are not sufficiently grateful to the Villèle Ministry. The Three Per Cents, the Law of Primogeniture, the Press Laws have brought about a fusion of parties. The inevitable relations between the Peers and the Deputies began this reconciliation which Octave could not have foreseen, and fortunately the ideas of this proud and timid young man are even less true to-day than they were a few months ago; but this is how he was bound to see things, given his character. Must we leave unfinished the sketch of an eccentric character because he is unfair to every one? It is precisely this unfairness that is his misfortune.

## CHAPTER FIFTEEN

*How am I glutted with conceit of this!*
*Shall I make spirits fetch me what I please,*
*Resolve me of all ambiguities,*
*Perform what desperate enterprise I will?*
                              DOCTOR FAUSTUS.

OCTAVE was so much in the habit of leaving Andilly to visit Madame d'Aumale in Paris, that one day a slight feeling of jealousy began to quench Armance's gaiety. On her cousin's return, that evening, she exercised her authority. "Do you wish to oblige your mother in a matter which she will never mention to you?" "Of course." "Very well, for the next three months, that is to say for ninety days, do not refuse any invitation to a ball, and do not come away from a ball until you have danced."

"I should prefer a fortnight's imprisonment." "You are easily satisfied," Armance went on, "but do you promise me, or do you not?" "I promise anything except to keep my promise for three months. Since you all tyrannise over me here," said Octave with a laugh, "I shall run away. There is an old idea of mine which quite spontaneously kept coming into my mind throughout the evening yesterday, at M. de ——'s sumptuous party, at which I danced as though I had guessed your orders. If I were to leave Andilly for six months

141

I have two plans more amusing than that of going to England.

"One is to assume the name of M. Lenoir ; under that fine name, I should go into the country and give lessons in arithmetic, in geometry applied to the arts, anything they want to learn. I should make my way by Bourges, Aurillac, Cahors ; I should easily procure letters from any number of Peers who are Members of the Institute, recommending to the Prefects the learned royalist Lenoir, and so forth.

"But the other plan is better still. In my capacity as a teacher, I should see only a lot of enthusiastic and volatile young fellows who would soon bore me, and various intrigues by the *Congregation.*

"I hesitate to reveal to you the better plan of the two ; I should assume the name of Pierre Gerlat, I should start at Geneva or Lyons by becoming valet to some young man who is destined to play a part more or less identical with my own in society. Pierre Gerlat would be provided with excellent testimonials from the young Vicomte de Malivert, whose faithful servant he had been for six years. In a word, I should assume the name and identity of that poor Pierre whom I once threw out of the window. Two or three men of my acquaintance will oblige me with testimonials. They will seal these with their arms upon huge lumps of wax, and in that way I hope to find a place with some young Englishman, either very rich or the son of a Peer. I shall take care to stain my hands with an acid solution. I have learned how to clean boots from the servant I have now, the gallant Corporal Voreppe. In the last three months I have stolen all his talents."

"One evening your master, when he comes home tipsy, will start kicking Pierre Gerlat."

"Were he to throw me out of the window, I am prepared for that. I shall defend myself, and give him notice the next day, and bear him no grudge whatever."

"You would be guilty of an abuse of confidence which would be very wrong indeed. A man exposes the defects of his nature to a young peasant who is incapable of understanding his most salient eccentricities, but he would take good care, I am sure, not to act thus before a man of his own class." "I shall never repeat what I have seen or heard. Anyhow, a *master*, to talk like Pierre Gerlat, always runs the risk of hitting upon a rascal, mine will only find curiosity. Realise what I am suffering," Octave went on. "My imagination is so foolish at certain moments, and so far exaggerates what I owe to my position, that, without being a Sovereign Prince, I long for an incognito. I am supreme in misery, in absurdity, in the extreme importance that I attach to certain things. I feel a compelling need to see another Vicomte de Malivert in my place. Since, unfortunately, I have embarked on this career, since, to my great and sincere regret, I cannot be the son of the chief foreman of M. de Liancourt's carding mill, I require six months of domestic service to cure the Vicomte de Malivert of various weaknesses.

"This is the only way; my pride raises a wall of

adamant between myself and my fellow men. Your presence, my dear cousin, makes this unsurmountable wall disappear. In conversation with you, I should take nothing in ill part, such serenity does your presence give to my soul, but unfortunately I have not the magic carpet to take you everywhere with me. I cannot see you as a third person when I go riding in the Bois de Boulogne with one of my *friends*. Soon after our first meeting, there is none of them who is not *estranged* by my talk. When, after a year, and in spite of anything I can do, they understand me thoroughly, they wrap themselves up in the closest reserve, and would rather (I really believe) that their secret thoughts and actions were known to the devil than to me. I would not swear that many of them do not take me for *Lucifer himself* (as M. de Soubirane says, in fact, it is one of his favourite remarks) *brought into the world on purpose to torment them.*"

Octave imparted these strange ideas to his cousin as they strolled in the woods of Moulignon, in the wake of Mesdames de Bonnivet and de Malivert. These oddities distressed Armance deeply. Next day, after her cousin had left for Paris, her free and lively air which often became quite unrestrained gave way to that fixed and tender gaze from which Octave, when he was present, could not tear his own.

Madame de Bonnivet invited a number of guests, and Octave no longer had such frequent reasons for going to Paris, for Madame d'Aumale came to stay at Andilly. With her there arrived seven or eight women at the height of the fashion, and mostly remarkable for the brilliance of their wit or for the influence that they had obtained in society. But their affability only enhanced the triumph of the charming Comtesse; her mere presence in a drawing-room aged her rivals.

Octave was too intelligent not to feel this, and Armance's spells of musing became more frequent. "Of whom have I the right to complain?" she asked herself. "Of no one, and of Octave least of all. Have I not told him that I prefer another man? And there is too much pride in his nature to be content with the second place in a heart. He is attached to Madame d'Aumale; she is a brilliant beauty, spoken of everywhere, and I am not even pretty. Anything that I can say to Octave can be but faintly interesting, I am certain that often I bore him, or am interesting only as a sister. Madame d'Aumale's life is gay, unusual; things never flag where she is to be found, and it seems to me that I should often be bored in my aunt's drawing-room if I listened to what people say there." Armance wept, but her noble soul did not so far debase itself as to feel hatred for Madame d'Aumale. She observed every action of that charming lady with a profound attention which ended often in moments of keen admiration. But each act of admiration was like a dagger thrust in her heart. Her peaceful happiness vanished, Armance was a prey to all the anguish of the passions. Finally, Madame d'Aumale's presence disturbed her more than that of Octave himself. The torture of

145

jealousy is most unbearable when it is rending hearts to which their natural inclination as well as their social position forbid every way of appeal that is at all dangerous.

# CHAPTER SIXTEEN

*Let Rome in Tiber melt, and the wide arch*
*Of the rang'd empire fall! Here is my space.*
*Kingdoms are clay; our dungy earth alike*
*Feeds beast as man: the nobleness of life*
*Is to love thus.*
ANTONY AND CLEOPATRA, Act I.

ONE evening after a day of stifling heat, they were strolling quietly amid the handsome groves of chestnuts that crown the heights of Andilly. Sometimes during the day these woods are spoiled by the intrusion of strangers. On this charming night, bathed in the calm light of a summer moon, these deserted slopes were an enchantment to the eye. They assumed a certain grandeur, the dark shadows cast by a brilliant moon eliminated their details. A soft breeze was playing among the trees, and completed the charms of this delicious evening. From some caprice or other, Madame d'Aumale was determined, on this occasion, to keep Octave by her side; she reminded him coaxingly and without the slightest regard for her male escort, that it was in these woods that she had seen him for the first time: "You were disguised as a magician, and never was a first meeting more prophetic," she went on, "for you have never bored me, and there is no other man of whom I can say that."

147

Armance, who was walking with them, could not help feeling that these memories were very affectionate. Nothing could be so pleasant as to hear this brilliant Comtesse, so gay as a rule, deigning to speak in serious tones of the great interests of life and of the courses that one must follow to find any happiness here below. Octave withdrew from Madame d'Aumale's group, and, finding himself presently alone with Armance some little way from the rest of the party, began to relate to her in the fullest detail the whole of the episode of his life in which Madame d'Aumale had been involved. "I sought that brilliant connexion," he told her, "in order not to offend Madame de Bonnivet, who, but for some such precaution, might easily have finished by banishing me from her society." So tender a confidence as this was made without any mention of love, but it was exactly attuned to Armance's jealousy.

When Armance was able to hope that her voice would not betray the extreme distress in which this confession had plunged her: "I believe, my dear cousin," she said to him, "I believe, as I am bound to believe, everything that you tell me; your word to me is as the Gospel. I observe, however, that you have never until now waited, before taking me into your confidence about any of your enterprises, until it was so far advanced." "To that, I have my answer ready. Mademoiselle Méry de Tersan and you take the liberty sometimes of laughing at my success: one evening, for instance, two months ago, you almost accused me of fatuity. I might easily, even then, have confessed to you the decided feeling

that I have for Madame d'Aumale; but I should have
had to be treated kindly by her in your presence. Before I had succeeded, your malicious wit would not
have failed to deride my feeble efforts. To-day, the
presence of Mademoiselle de Tersan is the only thing
lacking to complete my happiness."

There was in the profound and almost tender accents
with which Octave uttered these vain words, such an incapacity to love the somewhat bold charms of the
pretty woman of whom he was speaking, and so passionate a devotion to the friend in whom he was confiding that she had not the courage to resist the
happiness of seeing herself so dearly loved. She leaned
upon Octave's arm, and listened to him as though in an
ecstasy. All that her prudence could obtain of her
was to refrain from speaking; the sound of her voice
would have revealed to her companion the whole extent
of the passion by which she was torn. The gentle rustle
of the leaves, stirred by the night breeze, seemed to
lend a fresh charm to their silence.

Octave gazed into Armance's open eyes which were
fastened on his own. Suddenly they became aware
of a certain sound which for some minutes had reached
their ears without attracting their attention. Madame
d'Aumale, surprised at Octave's absence, and feeling
the need of his company, was calling to him at the top
of her voice. "Some one is calling you," said Armance,
and the broken accents in which she uttered these simple
words would have enlightened any one but Octave as
to the passion that she felt for himself. But he was

so astonished by what was going on in his heart, so
disturbed by Armance's shapely arm, barely veiled by
a light gauze, which he was pressing to his bosom, that
he could pay no attention to anything. He was beside
himself, he was tasting the pleasures of the most blissful love, and almost admitted as much to himself. He
looked at Armance's hat, which was charming, he gazed
into her eyes. Never had Octave found himself in a
position so fatal to his vows to refrain from love. He
had meant to speak lightly to Armance, as usual, and
his light speech had suddenly taken a grave and unexpected turn. He felt himself led away, he was incapable of reason, he was raised to the pinnacle of
happiness. It was one of those rapid instants which
chance accords now and again, in compensation for
so many hardships, to natures that are created to feel
with energy. Life becomes pressing in the heart, love
makes us forget everything that is not divine like itself,
and we live more fully in a few moments than in long
periods.

They could still hear from time to time Madame
d'Aumale's voice calling: "Octave!" and the sound of
that voice succeeded in destroying all poor Armance's
prudence. Octave felt that it was time to let go the
fair arm that he was pressing gently to his bosom; he
must part from Armance; on leaving her he could
hardly refrain from taking her hand and pressing it
to his lips. Had he permitted himself this token of
love, Armance was so disturbed at the moment, that

she would have let him see and would perhaps have admitted all that she felt for him.

They rejoined the rest of the party. Octave walked a little way ahead. As soon as Madame d'Aumale caught sight of him, she said to him with a trace of vexation, not loud enough for Armance to hear: "I am surprised to see you so soon, how could you leave Armance for me? You are in love with that pretty cousin, do not attempt to deny it; I know." The last words were uttered in a loud voice in contrast to her previous tone.

Octave had not yet recovered from the intoxication that had overpowered him; he still saw Armance's beautiful arm pressed to his bosom. Madame d'Aumale's speech fell on him like a thunderbolt, for it came with the force of truth. He felt the shock of its impact.

That frivolous voice seemed to him a pronouncement of fate, falling on him from the clouds. The sound of it seemed to him extraordinary. This startling speech, by revealing to Octave the true state of his heart, dashed him from a pinnacle of bliss into a frightful, hopeless misery.

# CHAPTER SEVENTEEN

> *What is a man,*
> *If his chief good and market of his time*
> *Be but to sleep, and feed? a beast, no more.*
> *. . . Rightly to be great*
> *Is not to stir without great argument,*
> *But greatly to find honour in a straw*
> *When honour's at the stake.*
>
> HAMLET, Act IV.

AND so he had been so weak as to violate the oaths he had so often sworn! A single moment had upset the work of his whole life. He had forfeited all right to his own esteem. Henceforward the world of men was closed to him; he was not worthy to inhabit it. Nought remained to him but solitude and a hermit's abode in some wilderness. The intensity of the grief that he felt and its suddenness might well have caused some disturbance in the stoutest heart. Fortunately Octave saw at once that if he did not reply quickly and with the calmest air to Madame d'Aumale, Armance's reputation might suffer. He spent all his time with her, and Madame d'Aumale's speech had been seized upon by two or three people who detested him as well as Armance.

"I, in love!" he said to Madame d'Aumale. "Alas! That is a privilege which heaven has evidently denied me; I have never felt it so plainly nor so keenly regretted it. I see every day, though less often than I could wish, the most attractive woman in Paris; to win her favour is doubtless the most ambitious project that a man of my age can entertain. Doubtless she would not have accepted my devotion; still, I have never felt myself moved to the degree of enthusiasm which would make me worthy to offer it to her. Never, in her presence, have I lost the most complete self-possession. After such a display of savagery and insensibility, I despair of ever going out of my depth with any woman."

Never had Octave spoken to such effect. This almost diplomatic explanation was skilfully protracted and received with a corresponding eagerness. There were present two or three men who were naturally attractive, and who often imagined that they saw in Octave a fortunate rival. He was delighted to overhear several sharp comments. He spoke volubly, continued to alarm their self-esteem, until he felt himself justified in hoping that no one would pay any further attention to the all too true observation which Madame d'Aumale had let fall.

She had uttered it with an air of conviction; Octave felt that he must force her to think of herself. Having proved to her that he was incapable of loving her, for the first time in his life he allowed himself to address to Madame d'Aumale allusions that were almost affectionate; she was amazed.

Before the evening ended, Octave was so confident

of having banished all suspicions that he began to have time to think of himself. He dreaded the moment when the party would break up, and he would be free to look his misery in the face. He began to count the hours as they sounded from the clock in Andilly; midnight had long since struck, but the night was so fine that they preferred to remain out of doors. One o'clock struck, and Madame d'Aumale dismissed her retinue.

Octave had still a momentary respite. He must go and find his mother's footman and tell him that he was going to sleep in Paris. This duty performed, he returned to the woods, and here words fail me if I am to give any idea of the grief that overpowered the poor wretch. "I am in love," he said to himself in stifled accents. "I, in love! Great God!" and with throbbing heart, parched throat, staring eyes raised to heaven, he stood motionless, as though horror-stricken; presently he began to walk at a headlong pace. Unable to hold himself erect, he let himself fall against the trunk of an old tree that barred his way, and in that moment of repose seemed to see more clearly than ever the whole extent of his misery.

"I had nothing but my own self-esteem," he said to himself; "I have forfeited it." The confession of his love which he made in the plainest terms and without finding any way of denying it was followed by transports of rage and inarticulate cries of fury. Spiritual agony can go no farther.

An idea, the common resource of the wretched who have still some courage, soon occurred to him; but he said to himself: "If I take my life, Armance will be compromised; the whole of society for the next week will be nosing out every trifling detail of what occurred this evening. Armance will be in despair, her despair will be noticed, and each of the gentlemen who was present will be authorised to furnish a different account."

Nothing selfish, no attachment to the vulgar interests of life, could be found in this noble spirit to resist the transports of the frightful grief which was rending it. This absence of all common interest, capable of providing a diversion at such moments, is one of the punishments which heaven seems to take pleasure in inflicting upon lofty spirits.

The hours glided rapidly by without diminishing Octave's despair. Remaining motionless at times for several minutes, he felt that fearful anguish which completes the torment of the greatest criminals: an utter contempt for himself.

He could not weep. The hatred of which he felt himself so deserving prevented him from having any pity for himself, and dried his tears. "Ah!" he cried, in one of those agonising moments, "if I could make an end!" and he gave himself leave to taste the ideal happiness of ceasing to feel. With what pleasure would he have put himself to death, as a punishment of his weakness and to retrieve in a sense his lost honour! "Yes," he told himself, "my heart deserves contempt because it has committed an action which I had forbidden myself on pain of death, and my mind is, if possible, even more contemptible than my heart. I have failed to see what was self-evident: I love Armance, and I have loved her ever since I submitted to listening to Madame de Bonnivet's dissertations upon German philosophy.

"I was foolish enough to imagine myself a philosopher. In my idiotic presumption, I regarded myself as infinitely superior to the futile arguments of Madame de Bonnivet, and I failed to see in my heart what the weakest of women would have seen in hers: a strong, obvious passion, which for long has destroyed all the interest that I used to take in the things of life.

"Everything that cannot speak to me of Armance is to me as though it did not exist. I criticised myself incessantly, and failed to see this! Ah, how contemptible I am!"

The voice of duty which was beginning to prevail ordered Octave to shun Mademoiselle de Zohiloff from that instant; but out of her presence he could think of no action that justified the effort of living. Nothing seemed to him worthy to inspire the least interest in him. Everything appeared to him to be equally insipid, the noblest action and the most vulgarly useful occupation alike: to march to the aid of Greece and to seek death by the side of Fabvier, as to make obscure agricultural experiments in some remote Department.

His imagination ran swiftly over the scale of possible actions, to fall back afterwards with an intenser grief into the most profound despair, the most hopeless, the worthiest of his name; ah, how pleasant would death have been at those moments!

Octave uttered aloud things that were foolish and in bad taste, the bad taste and folly of which he observed with interest. "What use in shutting my eyes to the facts," he exclaimed suddenly, while he was occupied in enumerating to himself certain agricultural experiments that might be made among the peasants of Brazil. "What use in being so cowardly as to shut my eyes to the facts? To complete my misery, I can say to myself that Armance feels some affection for me, and my duty is all the stricter in consequence. Why, if Armance were engaged, would the man to whom she had promised her hand permit her to spend all her time with me? And her joy, outwardly so calm, but so deep and true, when I revealed to her last night the secret plan of my conduct with Madame d'Aumale, to what must it be ascribed? Is it not a proof positive, as plain as daylight? And I was blind to it! Can I have been a hypocrite with myself? Can I have been treading the path which the vilest scoundrels have followed? What! Last night, at ten o'clock, I failed to perceive a thing which this morning seems as plain as possible? Ah, how weak and contemptible I am!

"I have all the pride of a child, and never in my whole life have I risen to perform one manly action; not only have I wrought my own undoing, I have dragged down into the abyss her who was dearer to me than any one in the world. Oh, heavens! How could any one, even if he tried, be viler than I?" This thought left him almost delirious. Octave felt his brain melt in the fiery heat of his head. At each step that his mind advanced, he discovered a fresh variety of misery, a fresh reason for despising himself.

The instinct of self-preservation which exists in every man, even in the most painful moments, even at the foot of the scaffold, made Octave try to prevent himself from thinking. He clasped his head in his hands, making almost a physical effort not to think.

Gradually everything lost its importance for him, except the memory of Armance whom he must evermore avoid, and never see again upon any pretext whatsoever. Even filial love, so deeply rooted in his heart, had vanished from it.

He had now only two ideas, to leave Armance and never allow himself to set eyes on her again; to support life on these conditions for a year or two until she were married or society had forgotten him. After which, as people would then have ceased to think of him, he would be free to put an end to himself. Such was the last conscious thought of this spirit exhausted by suffering. Octave leaned against a tree and fell in a swoon.

When he regained consciousness, he felt an unusual sense of cold. He opened his eyes. Day was beginning to dawn. He found that he was receiving the attentions of a peasant who was trying to restore his consciousness by deluging him with cold water which he fetched in his hat from a neighbouring spring. Octave was confused for a moment, his ideas were not clearly defined: he found himself lying upon the bank of a ditch, in the middle of a clearing, in a wood; he saw great rounded masses of mist pass rapidly before his eyes. He could not tell where he was.

Suddenly the thought of all his misfortunes recurred to his mind. People do not die of grief, or he would have been dead at that moment. A groan or two escaped him which frightened the peasant. The man's alarm recalled Octave to a sense of duty. It was essential that this peasant should not talk. Octave took out his purse to offer him some money; he said to the man, who seemed to feel some compassion for his state, that he found himself in the woods at that hour in consequence of a rash wager, and that it was most important to him that it should not be known that the cold night air had upset him.

The peasant appeared not to understand. "If the others hear that I fainted," said Octave, "they will make fun of me." "Ah, I understand," said the peasant, "count on me not to breathe a word, it shall never be said that I made you lose your wager. It is lucky for you all the same that I happened to pass, for, upon my soul, you looked half dead." Octave, instead of replying, was gazing at his purse. This was a further grief, the purse was a present from Armance; he found a pleasure in feeling with his fingers each of the little steel beads that were stitched to the dark tissue.

As soon as the peasant had left him, Octave broke off a branch of a chestnut tree, with which he made a hole in the ground; he allowed himself to bestow a kiss

159

on the purse, Armance's present, and buried it beneath
the very spot on which he had fainted. "There," he
said to himself, "my first virtuous action. Farewell,
farewell for life, dear Armance! God knows that I
loved thee!"

# CHAPTER EIGHTEEN

*On her white breast a sparkling Cross she*
*wore,*
*Which Jews might kiss, and Infidels adore.*

POPE.[1]

AN instinctive movement impelled him towards the
house. He felt confusedly that to reason with
himself was the greatest misfortune possible;
but he had seen where his duty lay, and hoped to find
the necessary courage to perform such actions as fell
to his lot, whatever they might be. He found an excuse
for his return to the house, which was prompted by his
horror of loneliness, in the idea that some servant might
arrive from Paris and report that he had not been
seen in the Rue Saint-Dominique, which might lead
to the discovery of his foolish conduct, and cause his
mother some uneasiness.

Octave was still some way from the house: "Ah,"
he said to himself as he walked home through the woods,
"only yesterday there were boys here shooting; if a
careless boy, firing at a bird from behind a hedge, were
to kill me, I should have no complaint to make.
Heavens! How delightful it would be to receive a

[1] Beyle quotes this motto in French, and attributes it to
Schiller.—C. K. S. M.

bullet in this burning brain! How I should thank him before I died, if I had time!"

We can see that there was a trace of madness in Octave's attitude this morning. The romantic hope of being killed by a boy made him slacken his step, and his mind, with a slight weakness of which he was barely conscious, refused to consider whether he were justified in so doing. At length he arrived at the house by the garden gate, and twenty yards from that gate, at a turn in a path, saw Armance. He stood rooted to the ground, the blood froze in his veins, he had not expected to come upon her so soon. As soon as she caught sight of him, Armance hastened towards him smiling; she had all the airy grace of a bird; never had she seemed to him so pretty; she was thinking of what he had said to her overnight about his intimacy with Madame d'Aumale.

"So I am beholding ner for the last time!" Octave said to himself, and gazed at her hungrily. Armance's wide-brimmed straw hat, her light and supple form, the long ringlets that dangled over her cheeks in charming contrast to a gaze so penetrating and at the same time so gentle, he sought to engrave all these upon his heart. But her smiling glances, as Armance approached him, soon lost all their joy. She felt there was something sinister in Octave's manner. She noticed that his clothes were wringing wet.

She said to him in a voice ᴊremulous with emotion: "What is the matter, cousin?" As she uttered this simple speech, she could hardly restrain her tears, so strange was the expression she discerned in his gaze. "Mademoiselle," he replied with a glacial air, "you will permit me to be not unduly sensible of an interest which attaches itself to me so as to deprive me of all freedom. It is true, I have come from Paris; and my clothes are wet: if this explanation does not satisfy your curiosity, I shall go into details. . . ." Here Octave's cruelty came to a standstill in spite of himself.

Armance, whose features had assumed a deathly pallor, seemed to be making vain efforts to withdraw; she was shaking visibly, and seemed to be on the point of falling. He stepped forward to offer her his arm; Armance gazed at him with lifeless eyes, which moreover seemed incapable of receiving any idea.

Octave seized her hand none too gently, placed it beneath his arm and strode towards the house. But he felt that his strength too was failing; on the point of falling himself, he yet had the courage to say to her: "I am going away, I have to start on a long voyage to America; I shall write; I rely upon you to comfort my mother; tell her that I shall certainly return. As for you, Mademoiselle, people have said that I am in love with you; I am far from making any such pretension. Indeed, the old ties of friendship that bound us should have been sufficient, to my mind, to resist the birth of love. We know each other too well to feel for each other that sort of sentiment, which always implies a certain amount of illusion."

At that moment Armance found herself incapable of walking; she raised her drooping eyes and looked at

Octave; her pale and trembling lips seemed to be trying to speak. She attempted to lean upon the tub of an orange tree, but had not the strength to support herself; she slipped to the ground by the side of the orange tree, completely unconscious.

Without offering her any assistance, Octave stood motionless and gazed at her; she was in a dead faint, her lovely eyes were still half open, the lines of that charming mouth retained an expression of profound grief. All the rare perfection of her delicate body was revealed beneath a simple morning gown. Octave noticed a small cross of diamonds which Armance was wearing that day for the first time.

He was so weak as to take her hand. All his philosophy had evaporated. He saw that the tub of the orange tree concealed her from the curiosity of the people in the house; he fell on his knees by her side: "Pardon me, O my dear angel," he said in a low murmur, covering her frozen hand with kisses, "never have I loved thee more!"

Armance stirred slightly; Octave rose to his feet, almost with a convulsive effort: soon Armance was able to walk, and he escorted her to the house without venturing to look at her. He reproached himself bitterly for the shameful weakness into which he had let himself be drawn; had Armance noticed it, all the deliberate cruelty of his words became useless. She hastily took leave of him on entering the house.

As soon as Madame de Malivert was visible, Octave asked if he might see her and threw himself into her arms. "Dear Mama, give me leave to travel, it is the one course open to me if I am to avoid an abhorrent marriage without failing in the respect I owe to my father." Madame de Malivert, greatly astonished, tried in vain to extract from her son any more positive information as to this alleged marriage.

"What!" she said to him, "neither the young lady's name, nor who are her family, I am to know nothing? But this is madness." Soon Madame de Malivert no longer dared to employ that word, which seemed to her to be too true. All that she could extract from her son, who seemed determined to start that day, was that he would not go to America. The goal of his journey was a matter of indifference to Octave, he had thought only of the pain of departure.

As he was talking to his mother, and trying, in order not to alarm her, to moderate his feelings, a plausible reason for his action suddenly occurred to him: "Dear Mama, a man who bears the name of Malivert and who has the misfortune to have done nothing in the first twenty years of his life, ought to begin by going on the Crusade like our ancestors. I beg you to allow me to go to Greece. If you wish, I shall tell my father that I am going to Naples; from there, quite by chance, curiosity will lead me on to Greece, and what more natural than that a gentleman should visit that country sword in hand? By announcing my itinerary in this way I shall strip it of any air of pretension. . . ."

This plan caused Madame de Malivert the greatest uneasiness; but there was a certain nobility in it and it was in accordance with her idea of duty. After a conversation lasting for two hours, which was a momentary respite for Octave, he obtained his mother's consent. Clasped in the arms of that tenderest of friends, he enjoyed for a brief moment the bliss of being able to weep freely. He agreed to conditions which he would have refused when he entered the room. He promised her that, if she wished it, twelve months from the day of his landing in Greece, he would come and spend a fortnight with her.

"But, dear Mama, to spare me the annoyance of seeing my return announced in the newspaper, consent to receive my visit at your place, Malivert, in Dauphiné." Everything was arranged as he wished, and loving tears sealed the terms of this sudden departure.

On leaving his mother's presence, after performing his duty with regard to Armance, Octave found himself sufficiently calm to pay a visit to the Marquis. "Father," he said when he had embraced him, "allow your son to ask you a question: what was the first action of Enguerrand de Malivert, who flourished in 1147, under Louis the Young?"

The Marquis threw open his desk and drew from it a handsome roll of parchment which always lay ready to his hand: it was the pedigree of his family. He saw with intense pleasure that his son's memory had not failed him. "My dear boy," said the old man as he took off his spectacles, "Enguerrand de Malivert started in 1147 on the Crusade with his King." "He was then nineteen, was he not?" Octave went on. "Nineteen exactly," said the Marquis, with growing pleasure in the respect which the young Vicomte shewed for the family tree.

When Octave had given his father's pleasure time to develop and to establish itself firmly in his heart, "Father," he said to him in a firm tone, *"noblesse oblige.* I am now twenty, I have spent time enough with my books. I have come to ask your blessing, and your leave to travel in Italy and Sicily. I shall not conceal from you, but it is to you alone that I am making this admission, that from Sicily I shall be tempted to proceed to Greece; I shall try to take part in a battle and shall return to you, a little more worthy perhaps of the fine name that you have handed down to me."

The Marquis, gallant as he was, had not at all the spirit of his ancestors in the days of Louis the Young; he was a father and a loving father of the nineteenth century. He was left speechless by Octave's sudden resolve; he would gladly have had a son who was less heroic. Nevertheless, this son's austere air, and the firm resolve indicated by his manner made an impression upon him. Strength of character had never been one of his qualities and he dared not refuse a consent that was asked of him with an air of indifference to his possible refusal.

"You pierce me to the heart," said the worthy old man as he returned to his desk; and without waiting for his son to ask for it, with a trembling hand he wrote out a draft for a considerable sum upon a notary who held funds in his name. "Take this," he said to Octave, "and pray God it be not the last money that I shall give you!"

The bell rang for luncheon. Fortunately Mesdames d'Aumale and de Bonnivet had gone to Paris; and the members of this sad family were not obliged to conceal their grief with meaningless words.

Octave, somewhat fortified by the consciousness that he had done his duty, found courage to continue. He had thought of starting before luncheon; he felt that it was better to behave as though nothing had happened. The servants might talk. He took his seat at the small luncheon-table, facing Armance.

"It is the last time in my life that I shall see her," he told himself. Armance managed fortunately to burn herself quite seriously while making tea. This accident would have furnished an excuse for her distress, if any one in that small room had been in a fit state to observe it. M. de Malivert's voice was tremulous; for the first time in his life, he could think of nothing pleasant to say. He was wondering whether some pretext compatible with the solemn words *"Noblesse oblige!"* which his son had so aptly quoted, might not furnish him with the means of delaying his son's departure.

# CHAPTER NINETEEN

*He unworthy you say?*
*'Tis impossible. It would*
*Be more easy to die.*

DECKAR.[1]

OCTAVE thought he observed that Mademoiselle de Zohiloff looked at him now and again quite calmly. In spite of his peculiar sense of honour, which formally forbade him to dwell upon relations that no longer existed, he could not help thinking that this was the first time that he had seen her since his admission to himself that he loved her; that morning, in the garden, he had been disturbed by the need for action. "So this," he told himself, "is the impression a man feels at the sight of a woman whom he loves. But it is possible that Armance feels no more than friendship for me. Last night it was only

[1] This motto and that prefixed to Chapter XXII are quoted by Beyle in English, which makes it seem probable that by Deckar he meant the voluminous writer Thomas Dekker, the "Mr. Dickers" of Henslowe's *Diary*, the author of *Satiromastix* and *The Honest Whore* and the *Gull's Horn-book* and the *Witch of Edmonton;* but this quotation, which the French editors religiously print in three lines, imagining it to be a specimen of English poetry, bears the marks of Beyle's composition.— C. K. S. M.

a piece of presumption on my part that made me think otherwise."

Throughout this distressing meal, not a word was uttered on the subject that was filling every heart. While Octave was with his father, Madame de Malivert had sent for Armance to inform her of this strange plan of foreign travel. The poor girl felt a need of sincerity; she could not help saying to Madame de Malivert: "Ah, well, Mama, you see now what foundation there was for your ideas!"

These two charming women were plunged in the bitterest grief. "What is the reason for this sudden departure?" Madame de Malivert repeated, "for it cannot be an insane freak; you have cured him of that." It was agreed that they should not say a word to any one of Octave's travels, not even to Madame de Bonnivet. It would never do to bind him to his plan, "and perhaps," said Madame de Malivert, "we may still be allowed to hope. He will abandon an intention so suddenly conceived. It is the reaction from some distressing occurrence."

This conversation made Armance's grief more acute, were that possible, than before; ever loyal to the eternal secrecy which she felt to be due to the sentiment that existed between her cousin and herself, she paid the penalty of her discretion. The words uttered by Madame de Malivert, so prudent a friend and one who loved her so tenderly, since they related to facts of which she was but imperfectly aware, offered no consolation to Armance.

And yet, how sorely she needed the counsels of a woman friend as to the several reasons, any one of which, it seemed to her, might equally well have led to this strange conduct on her cousin's part! But nothing in the world, not even the intense grief that was lacerating her heart, could make her forget the respect that a woman owes to herself. She would have died of shame rather than repeat the words which the man of her choice had addressed to her that morning. "If I made such a disclosure," she told herself, "and Octave were to hear of it, he would cease to respect me."

After luncheon, Octave made hasty preparations to start for Paris. He acted precipitately; he had ceased to account to himself for his movements. He was beginning to feel all the bitterness of his plan of departure and was in dread of the danger of finding himself alone with Armance. If her angelic goodness was not irritated by the frightful harshness of his conduct, if she deigned to speak to him, could he promise himself that he would not be swayed by emotion in bidding farewell to so beautiful, so perfect a cousin?

She would see that he loved her; he must nevertheless leave immediately after, and with the undying remorse of not having done his duty even in that supreme moment. Were not his most sacred duties towards the creature who was dearer to him than any one in the world, and whose tranquillity he had perhaps endangered?

Octave drove out of the courtyard with the feelings

of a man going to his death; and in truth he would have been glad to feel no more than the grief of a man who is being led to execution. He had dreaded the loneliness of the journey, he was scarcely conscious of it; he was amazed at this momentary respite which he owed to misery.

He had just received a lesson in modesty too severe for him to attribute this tranquillity to that vain philosophy which had been his pride in the past. In this respect misery had made a new man of him. His strength was exhausted by so many violent efforts and feelings; he was no longer capable of feeling. Scarcely had he come down from Andilly upon the plain before he fell into a lethargic slumber, and he was astonished, on reaching Paris, to find himself being driven by the servant who, when they started, had been at the back of his cabriolet.

Armance, hidden in the attic of the house, behind the shutters, had watched every incident of his departure. When Octave's cabriolet had passed out of sight behind the trees, standing motionless at her post, she had said to herself: "All is over, he will not return."

Towards evening, after a long spell of weeping, a question that occurred to her caused her some distraction from her grief. "How in the world could Octave, who is so distinguished for his exquisite manners, and was so attentive, so devoted, perhaps even so tender a friend," she added with a blush, "last night, when we were strolling together, adopt a tone that was so harsh, so insulting, so out of keeping with his character, at an interval of a few hours? Certainly he can have heard nothing about me that could offend him."

Armance sought to recall every detail of her own conduct, with the secret desire to come upon some fault which might justify the odd tone that Octave had adopted towards her. She could find nothing that was reprehensible; she was in despair at not seeing herself in the wrong, when suddenly an old idea came to her mind.

Might not Octave have felt a recurrence of that frenzy which in the past had led him to commit many strange acts of violence? This memory, albeit painful at first, shed a ray of light in her mind. Armance was so wretched that every argument which she was capable of advancing very soon proved to her that this explanation was the most probable. The conviction that Octave had not been unfair, whatever excuse he might have, was to her an extreme consolation.

As for his madness, if he was mad, it only made her love him more passionately. "He will need all my devotion, and never shall that devotion fail him," she added with tears in her eyes, and her heart throbbed with generous courage. "Perhaps at this moment Octave exaggerates the obligation that compels a young gentleman who has done nothing hitherto to go to the aid of Greece. Was not his father anxious, some years ago, to make him assume the Cross of Malta? Several members of his family have been Knights of Malta.

Perhaps, since he inherits their fame, he thinks him-self obliged to keep the vows which they took to fight the Turks?"

Armance recalled that Octave had said to her on the day on which the news came of the fall of Misso-longhi: "I cannot understand the calm tranquillity of my uncle the Commander, he who has taken vows, and, before the Revolution, enjoyed the stipend of a con-siderable Commandery. And we hope to be respected by the Industrial Party!"

By dint of pondering this comforting way of account-ing for her cousin's conduct, Armance said to herself: "Perhaps some personal motive came to reinforce this general obligation by which it is quite possible that Octave's noble soul believes itself to be bound?

"The idea of becoming a priest which he once held, before the success of one section of the clergy, has per-haps been responsible for some recent criticism of him. Perhaps he thinks it more worthy of his name to go to Greece and to shew there that he is no degenerate scion of his ancestors than to seek in Paris some obscure quarrel the grounds of which would always be difficult to explain and might leave a stain?

"He has not told me, because things of that sort are not mentioned to a woman. He is afraid that his habit of confiding in me may lead him to confess it; that accounts for the harshness of his words. He did not wish to be led on to confide in me something that was not proper. . . ."

Thus it was that Armance's imagination strayed

174

among suppositions that were consoling, since they portrayed an Octave innocent and generous. "It is only from excess of virtue," she told herself, with tears in her eyes, "that so generous a being can have the appearance of being in the wrong."

# CHAPTER TWENTY

*"A fine woman! a fair woman! a sweet woman!"*
*"Nay, you must forget that."*
*"... O, the world hath not a sweeter creature."*
OTHELLO, Act IV.

WHILE Armance was walking by herself in a part of the woods of Andilly that was screened from every eye, Octave was in Paris occupied with preparations for his departure. He was alternating between a sort of tranquillity, which he was surprised to feel, and moments of the most poignant despair. Shall we attempt to record the different kinds of grief that marked every moment of his life? Will not the reader weary of these melancholy details?

He seemed to hear a continual sound of voices speaking close to his ear, and this strange and unexpected sensation made it impossible for him to forget his misery for an instant.

The most insignificant objects reminded him of Armance. So great was his distraction that he could not see at the head of an advertisement or on a shop sign an A or a Z without being violently compelled to think of that Armance de Zohiloff whom he had vowed to himself that he would forget. This thought fastened upon him like a destroying fire and with all that attrac-

176

tion of novelty, all the interest he would have felt in it, if for ages past the idea of his cousin had never occurred to his mind.

Everything conspired against him; he was helping his servant, the worthy Voreppe, to pack his pistols; the garrulous talk of the man, enchanted to be going off alone with his master and to be in charge of all the arrangements, was some distraction. Suddenly he caught sight of the words engraved in abbreviated characters on the mounting of one of the pistols: "Armance tried to fire this weapon, September 3rd, 182—."

He took up a map of Greece; as he unfolded it, there fell out one of the pins decorated with a tiny red flag with which Armance had marked the Turkish positions at the time of the siege of Missolonghi.

The map of Greece slipped from his hands. He stood paralysed by despair. "It is forbidden me, then, to forget!" he cried, raising his eyes to heaven. In vain did he endeavour to stiffen his resistance. Everything round about him was stamped with some memory of Armance. The abbreviated form of that beloved name, followed by some significant date, was everywhere inscribed.

Octave wandered aimlessly about his room; he kept giving orders which he instantly countermanded. "Ah! I do not know what I want," he told himself in a paroxysm of grief. "O heavens! What suffering can be greater than this?"

He found no relief in any position. He kept making the strangest movements. If he derived from them a certain surprise and some physical pain, for half an hour, the image of Armance ceased to torment him. He tried to inflict on himself a physical pain of some violence whenever his thoughts turned to Armance. Of all the remedies that he could imagine, this was the least ineffectual.

"Ah!" he said to himself at other moments, "I must never see her any more! That is a grief which outweighs all the rest. It is a whetted blade the point of which I must employ to pierce my heart."

He sent his servant to purchase something that would be required on the journey; he needed to be rid of the man's presence; he wished for a few moments to abandon himself to his frightful grief. Constraint seemed to envenom it more than ever.

The servant had not been out of the room for five minutes before it seemed to Octave that he would have found some relief in being able to speak to him; to have to suffer in solitude had become the keenest of torments. "And suicide is impossible!" he cried. He went and stood by the window in the hope of seeing something that would occupy his mind for a moment.

Evening came, intoxication proved powerless to help him. He had hoped to derive a little help from sleep, it only maddened him.

Alarmed by the ideas that came to him, ideas which might make him the talk of the household and indirectly compromise Armance: "it would be better," he told himself, "to give myself leave to make an end of things," and he turned the key in his door.

Night had fallen; standing motionless on the balcony of his window, he gazed at the sky. The slightest sound attracted his attention; but gradually, every sound ceased. This perfect silence, by leaving him entirely to himself, seemed to him to add yet more to the horror of his position. Did his extreme exhaustion procure him an instant of partial repose, the confused hum of human speech which he seemed to hear sounding in his ear made him awake with a start.

Next morning, when his door opened, the mental torment which urged him to take action was so atrocious that he felt a desire to throw his arms round the neck of the barber who was cutting his hair, and to tell the man how greatly he was to be pitied. It is by a wild shriek that the wretch who is being tortured by the surgeon's bistouri thinks to relieve his pain.

In his least unendurable moments, Octave felt the need to make conversation with his servant. The most childish trivialities seemed to absorb his whole attention, which he applied to them with a marked assiduity.

His misery had endowed him with an exaggerated modesty. Did his memory recall to him any of those little differences of opinion which arise in society, he was invariably astonished at the positively discourteous emphasis which he had displayed; it seemed to him that his adversary had been entirely in the right and himself in the wrong.

The picture of each of the misfortunes which he had encountered in his life presented itself to him with a painful intensity; and because he was not to see Ar-

179

mance again, the memory of that swarm of minor
evils which a glance from her eyes would have made
him forget, revived now with greater bitterness than
ever before. He who had so detested boring visitors
began now to long for them. A fool who came to see
him was his benefactor for the space of an hour. He
had to write a polite letter to a distant relative; this
lady was tempted to regard it as a declaration of love,
with such sincerity and profundity did he speak of himself, so plain was it from his words that the writer
stood in need of pity.

Between these painful alternatives, Octave had
reached the evening of the second day after his parting
with Armance; he was coming away from his saddler's.
All his preparations would at last be completed during
the night, and by the following morning he would be
free to start.

Ought he to return to Andilly? This was the question that he was inwardly debating. He perceived with
horror that he no longer loved his mother, for she had
no place in the reasons that he advanced for visiting
Andilly again. He dreaded the sight of Mademoiselle
de Zohiloff, all the more because at certain moments he
said to himself: "But is not the whole of my conduct
an act of deception?"

He dared not answer: "Yes," whereupon the voice of
the tempter said: "Is it not a sacred duty to visit my
poor mother whom I promised that I would see again?"
"No, wretch," cried conscience; "that answer is a mere
subterfuge; you no longer love your mother."

At this agonizing moment his eyes came to rest mechanically upon a playbill, he saw there the word *Otello* printed in bold characters. This word recalled to him the existence of Madame d'Aumale. "Perhaps she has come to Paris for *Otello;* in that event, it is my duty to speak to her once again. I must make her regard my sudden departure as the idea of a man who is suffering from boredom. I have long kept this plan from my friends; but for many months my departure has been delayed only by pecuniary difficulties of a sort of which a man cannot speak to his wealthy friends."

# CHAPTER TWENTY-ONE

*Durate, et vosmet rebus servate secundis.*
VIRGIL.[1]

OCTAVE entered the Théâtre-Italien; there he
did indeed find Madame d'Aumale and in her
box a certain Marquis de Crêveroche; he was
one of the fops who especially besieged that charming
woman; but being less intelligent or more self-satisfied
than the rest, he fancied himself to enjoy some distinction. As soon as Octave appeared, Madame d'Aumale
had no eyes for any one else, and the Marquis de
Crêveroche, mad with jealousy, left the box without
their so much as noticing his departure.

Octave took his place in the front of the box, and,
from force of habit, for, this evening, he was far from
seeking any sort of affectation, began to talk to
Madame d'Aumale in a voice which sometimes drowned
those of the singers. We must confess that he slightly
exceeded the amount of impertinence which is tolerated,
and, if the audience in the stalls of the Théâtre-Italien
had been such as is to be found in the other playhouses,
he would have had the distraction of a public scene.

In the middle of the second act of *Otello*, the boy

[1] This line, taken from the *Æneid* (I, 207), is inadvertently
ascribed by Beyle to Horace.—C. K. S. M.

messenger who sells the *libretti* of the opera, and proclaims them in nasal accents, came to him with a note couched as follows:

"I am, Sir, naturally contemptuous of all affectations; one comes upon so many in society, that I take notice of them only when they annoy me. You are annoying me by the racket you are making with the little d'Aumale. Hold your tongue.

"I have the honour to be, etc.,

"Le marquis de Crêveroche.

"Rue de Verneuil, no. 54."

Octave was profoundly astonished by this note which recalled him to the sordid concerns of life; he was at first like a man who has been drawn up for a moment from hell. His first thought was to feign the joy which soon flooded his heart. He decided that M. de Crêveroche's opera-glass must be directed at Madame d'Aumale's box, and that this would give his rival an advantage, if she appeared to be less amused after the delivery of his note.

This word *rival* which he employed in his unspoken thoughts made him laugh aloud; there was a strange look in his eyes. "Why, what is the matter?" asked Madame d'Aumale. "I am thinking of my rivals. Can there be anywhere in the world a man who tries to do more to win your favour than I?" This touching reflexion was more precious to the young Comtesse than the most impassioned notes of the sublime Pasta.

Late that night, after escorting home Madame
183

d'Aumale, who wished to sup, Octave, once more master of himself, was calm and cheerful. What a difference from the state in which he had been since the night he spent in the forest!

It was by no means easy for him to find a second. His manner created such a barrier and he had so few friends that he was greatly afraid of being indiscreet should he ask one of his boon companions to accompany him to M. de Crêveroche's. At last he remembered a M. Dolier, an officer on half-pay, whom he saw but seldom, but who was his cousin.

At three o'clock in the morning he sent a note to M. Dolier's porter; at half-past five he called in person, and shortly afterwards the two presented themselves at the house of M. de Crêveroche, who received them with a politeness that was somewhat mannered but adhered strictly to the forms. "I have been expecting you, gentlemen," he said to them in a careless tone; "I was in hopes that you would be so kind as to do me the honour of taking tea with my friend, M. de Meylan, whom I have the honour to present to you, and myself."

They drank tea. As they rose from table, M. de Crêveroche mentioned the forest of Meudon.

"This gentleman's affected politeness is beginning to make me lose my temper, too," said the officer of the old army as he stepped into Octave's cabriolet. "Let me drive, you must not tire your wrist. How long is it since you were last in a fencing school?" "Three or four years," said Octave, "as far as I can remember." "When did you last fire a pistol?" "Six months ago,

perhaps, but I never dreamed of fighting with pistols."
"The devil!" said M. Dolier, "six months! This is
beginning to be serious. Hold out your arm. You
are trembling like a leaf." "That is a weakness I
have always had," said Octave.

M. Dolier, greatly annoyed, said not another word.
The silent hour that they spent in driving from Paris
to Meudon was to Octave the pleasantest moment he
had known since his disaster. He had in no way provoked this duel. He meant to defend himself keenly;
still, should he be killed, he would be in no way to blame.
Situated as he then was, death was for him the greatest
good fortune possible.

They arrived at a secluded spot in the forest of
Meudon; but M. de Crêveroche, more affected and more
of a dandy than ever, offered absurd objections to two
or three places. M. Dolier could barely contain himself; Octave had the greatest difficulty in controlling
him. "Let me at least talk to the second," said
M. Dolier; "I intend to let him know what I think of
the pair of them." "Let them wait till to-morrow,"
Octave checked him in a severe tone; "bear in mind
that to-day you have had the privilege of promising to
do me a service."

M. de Crêveroche's second chose pistols without making any mention of swords. Octave thought this in bad
taste and made a sign to M. Dolier who at once agreed.
Finally, it was time to fire. M. de Crêveroche, a skilled
marksman, scored the first hit; Octave was wounded
in the thigh; his blood flowed in streams. "I have the

right to fire," he said coolly; and M. de Crêveroche received a graze on the leg. "Bandage my thigh with my handkerchief and your own," Octave said to his servant; "the blood must not flow for some minutes." "Why, what is your idea?" said M. Dolier. "To continue," Octave replied. "I do not feel at all weak, I am just as strong as when we came here; I should carry through any other business, why not make an end of this?" "But it seems to me to be more than finished," said M. Dolier. "And your anger of ten minutes ago, what is become of that?" "The man had no thought of insulting us," replied M. Dolier; "he is merely a fool."

The seconds met in conference; both were emphatically opposed to a continuation of the duel. Octave had observed that M. de Crêveroche's second was an inferior creature whom his valour had perhaps thrust into social prominence, but who at heart lived in a state of perpetual adoration of the Marquis; he addressed a few stinging words to the latter. M. de Meylan was reduced to silence by a firm rebuke from his friend, and Octave's second could not in decency open his lips. As he spoke, Octave was perhaps happier than he had ever been in his life. I cannot say what vague and criminal hope he was founding upon a wound that would keep him prisoner for some days in his mother's house, and at no great distance, therefore, from Armance. Finally, M. de Crêveroche, purple with rage, and Octave the happiest of men, succeeded after a quarter of an hour in making their seconds reload their pistols.

M. de Crêveroche, made furious by the fear of not being able to dance for some weeks, owing to the graze on his leg, suggested in vain their firing at one another point blank; the seconds threatened to leave their principals on the ground with their servants and to take the pistols from them if they moved one pace nearer. Luck was once again with M. de Crêveroche; he took a careful aim and wounded Octave severely in the right arm. "Sir," Octave called to him, "you are bound to await my fire, allow me to have my arm bandaged." This operation having been rapidly performed, and Octave's servant, an old soldier, having soaked the handkerchief in brandy which made it cling tightly to the arm; "I feel quite strong," Octave told M. Dolier. He fired, M. de Crêveroche fell, and a minute or two later, died.

Octave, leaning upon his servant's arm, walked back to his cabriolet, into which he climbed without uttering a single word. M. Dolier could not help expressing his pity for the handsome young fellow who lay dying, and whose limbs they could see growing rigid only a few yards away. "It only means one fop the less," said Octave calmly.

Twenty minutes later, although the cabriolet was going at a walking pace, "My arm is hurting me badly," Octave said to M. Dolier, "the handkerchief is too tight," and all of a sudden he fainted. He recovered consciousness only an hour later, in the cottage of a gardener, a kind-hearted fellow whom M. Dolier had taken the precaution of paying liberally as soon as he entered the cottage.

"You know, my dear cousin," Octave said to him, "my mother's delicate health; leave me, go to the Rue Saint-Dominique; if you do not find my mother in Paris, be so extremely kind as to go out to Andilly; tell her, with every possible precaution, that I have had a fall from my horse and have broken a bone in my right arm. Not a word about duels or bullets. I have reason to hope that certain circumstances, about which I shall tell you later, may prevent my mother from being distressed by this slight wound; say nothing about a duel unless to the police, if necessary, and send me a surgeon. If you go on to the mansion house of Andilly, which is five minutes' walk from the village, ask for Mademoiselle Armance de Zohiloff, she will prepare my mother for the story you have to tell her."

The sound of Armance's name revolutionised Octave's situation. So he dared to utter that name, a luxury he had so often forbidden himself! He would not be parted from her for another month, perhaps. It was an exquisite moment.

While the duel was in progress, the thought of Armance had many times occurred to Octave, but he banished it sternly. After mentioning her name, he ventured to think of her for a moment; a little later, he felt very weak. "Ah! If I were to die," he said to himself with joy, and allowed himself to think of Armance as in the days before the fatal discovery of his love for her. Octave observed that the peasants who stood round him appeared greatly alarmed; their evident anxiety diminished his remorse for the liberty he was allowing himself in thinking of his cousin. "If my wounds prove serious," he said to himself, "I shall be allowed to write to her; I have treated her most cruelly."

No sooner had the idea of writing to Armance occurred to him than it took entire possession of Octave's mind. "If I feel better," he said to himself at length, to hush the reproachful voice of conscience, "I shall still be at liberty to burn my letter." Octave was in great pain; his head had begun to ache violently. "I may die at any moment," he told himself cheerfully, making an effort to recall a few scraps of anatomical science. "Ah, surely I am entitled to write!"

In the end he was weak enough to call for pen, paper and ink. There was no difficulty in providing him with a sheet of coarse essay paper and a bad pen; but there was no ink in the house. Dare we confess it? Octave was so childish as to write with his own blood, which continued to ooze from the bandage on his right arm. He wrote with his left hand, and found this less difficult than he had supposed:

"MY DEAR COUSIN:

"I have just received two wounds, each of which may confine me to the house for a fortnight. As you are, next to my mother, the person whom I venerate most in the world, I write these lines to give you the above information. Were I in any danger, I should tell you. You have made me accustomed to the proofs of your tender affection; would you be so kind as to pay a call, as though by chance, upon my mother, whom M. Dolier is going to inform of a mere fall from my horse and a fracture of my right arm. Are you aware, my dear Armance, that we have two bones in the part of the arm next to the hand? It is one of those bones that is broken. Of all the injuries that confine one to the house for a month, it is the simplest that I can think of. I do not know whether it will be proper for you to come and see me during my illness; I am afraid not. I intend to do something rash: because of the narrow stair to my room, they will perhaps suggest placing my bed in the sitting-room through which one has to pass to reach my mother's bedroom, and I shall agree. I beg you to burn this letter. . . . I have just fainted, it is the natural and in no way dangerous effect of a hæmorrhage; you see, I am already using scientific terms. You were my last thought as I lost consciousness, my first upon coming to myself. If you think it quite proper, come to Paris before my mother; in the transport of a wounded man, even when it is merely a flesh-wound, there is always something sinister which she must be spared. One of your misfortunes, dear Armance, is that you have lost your parents; if I by any chance (though it is most improbable) die, you will be parted from one who loved you more dearly than a father loves his daughter. I pray to God that He will grant you the happiness that you deserve. That is saying a great, great deal.

"OCTAVE."

"*P.S.* Forgive my harsh words, which were necessary at the time."

The idea of death having come to Octave, he asked for a second sheet of paper, upon which, in the middle, he wrote:

"I bequeath absolutely everything that I now possess to Mademoiselle Armance de Zohiloff, my cousin, as a trifling token of my gratitude for the care which I am sure that she will take of my mother when I am no longer here.

"Signed at Clamart, the ................, 182..
"OCTAVE DE MALIVERT."

And he made two witnesses attest, the nature of his ink leaving him in some doubt as to the validity of the deed.

191

# CHAPTER TWENTY-TWO

*To the dull plodding man whose vulgar soul
is awake only to the gross and paltry interests of every-day life, the spectacle of a
noble being plunged in misfortune by the
resistless force of passion, serves only as an
object of scorn and ridicule.*

DECKAR.[1]

AS the witnesses completed their attestation, he
fainted again; the peasants, greatly concerned,
had gone in search of their parish priest.
Finally two surgeons arrived from Paris and pronounced Octave's condition to be serious. These gentlemen realised what a nuisance it would be for them to
come every day to Clamart, and decided that the
patient should be removed to Paris.

Octave had sent his letter to Armance by an oblig-
ing young peasant who engaged a horse from the post
and promised to be, within two hours, at the mansion
of Andilly. This letter outstripped M. Dolier, who
had been kept for some time in Paris looking for
surgeons. The young peasant succeeded admirably in
having himself admitted to Mademoiselle de Zohiloff's
presence without making any stir in the house. She

[1] Compare the motto prefixed to Chapter XIX. This, like the
other, is presumably of Beyle's composition.

192

read the letter. She had barely the strength to ask
a few questions. Her courage had completely deserted
her.

The receipt of these dreadful tidings induced in her
that tendency to discouragement which is the sequel
to great sacrifices, made at the call of duty but with
no immediate effect save tranquillity and inertia. She
was trying to accustom herself to the thought that she
would never see Octave any more, but the idea of his
dying had never once occurred to her. This final
blow of fortune took her unprepared.

As she listened to the highly alarming details which
the young peasant was giving her, she began to sob
convulsively, and Mesdames de Bonnivet and de Malivert were in the next room! Armance shuddered at
the thought of their hearing her and of having to meet
their gaze in the state in which she then was. Such a
sight would have been the death of Madame de Malivert, and, in due course, Madame de Bonnivet would
have worked it into a tragic and touching anecdote,
extremely unpleasant for its heroine.

Mademoiselle de Zohiloff could not, in any case, allow an unhappy mother to see this letter written in
the blood of her son. She settled upon the plan of
going to Paris, accompanied by her maid. The woman
encouraged her to take the young peasant in the carriage with her. I shall pass over the painful details
that were repeated to her during the drive. They
reached the Rue Saint-Dominique.

She shuddered as the carriage came in sight of the house in a bedroom in which Octave was perhaps drawing his last breath. As it happened, he had not yet arrived; Armance's last doubt vanished, she was sure that he was lying dead in the peasant's cottage at Clamart. Her despair made her incapable of giving the simplest orders; finally she was able to say that a bed must be made ready in the drawing-room. The astonished servants did not understand, but obeyed.

Armance had sent out for a hackney carriage, and her one thought was of how to find an excuse that would allow her to go to Clamart. Everything, it seemed to her, must give way to the obligation to succour Octave in his last moments if he still lived. "What is the world to me, or its vain judgments?" she asked herself. "I considered it only for his sake; besides, if people are reasonable, they must approve of my conduct."

Just as she was about to start, she realised, from a clattering sound at the carriage entrance, that Octave was arriving. The exhaustion caused by the motion of the journey had made him relapse into a state of complete unconsciousness. Armance, drawing open a window that overlooked the court, saw, between the shoulders of the peasants who were carrying the litter, the pale face of Octave in a dead faint. The spectacle of that lifeless head, keeping time with the motion of the litter and swaying from side to side on its pillow, was too painful for Armance who sank upon the window-sill and lay there motionless.

When the surgeons, after a preliminary dressing of his injuries, came to report to her upon their patient's condition, as to the one member of the family that was in the house, they found her speechless, staring fixedly at them, incapable of replying, and in a state which they judged to be bordering upon insanity.

She listened incredulously to all that they said to her; she believed what her own eyes had seen. This most rational young person had lost all her self-control. Choked by her sobs, she read Octave's letter over and over again. Carried away by her grief, she dared, in the presence of a maid, to raise it to her lips. At last, as she re-read the letter, she saw the injunction to burn it.

Never was any sacrifice more painful; so she must part with all that remained to her of Octave; still, it was his wish. Notwithstanding her sobs, Armance set to work to copy the letter; she broke off at every line, to press it to her lips. Finally she had the courage to burn it on the marble top of her little table; she gathered up the ashes with loving care.

Octave's servant, the faithful Voreppe, was sobbing by his master's bedside; he remembered that he had a second letter written by his master: it was the will. This document reminded Armance that she was not the only sufferer. It was incumbent on her to return to Andilly, to carry news of Octave to his mother. She passed by the bed of the wounded man, whose extreme pallor and immobility seemed to indicate the

approach of death; he was still breathing, however.
To abandon him in this state to the care of the servants
and of a humble surgeon of the neighbourhood, whom
she had called in, was the most painful sacrifice of all.

On reaching Andilly, Armance found M. Dolier who
had not yet seen Octave's mother; Armance had forgotten that the whole party had gone off together
that morning on an excursion to the Château d'Écouen.
They had a long time to wait before the ladies returned, and M. Dolier was able to relate what had
occurred that morning: he did not know the motive of
the quarrel with M. de Crêveroche.

Finally they heard the horses enter the courtyard.
M. Dolier decided to withdraw and to appear only in
in the event of M. de Malivert's desiring his presence.
Armance, trying to look as little alarmed as possible,
announced to Madame de Malivert that her son had
had a fall from his horse while out riding that morning and had broken a bone in his right arm. But her
sobs, which after the first sentence she was incapable
of controlling, gave the lie to every word of her story.

It would be superfluous to speak of Madame de Malivert's despair; the poor Marquis was dumbfounded.
Madame de Bonnivet, deeply moved herself, and absolutely insisting upon going with them to Paris, failed
completely to restore his courage. Madame d'Aumale
had made off at the first word of Octave's accident and
went at a gallop along the road to the Clichy barrier;
she reached the Rue Saint-Dominique long before the

family, learned the whole truth from Octave's servant
and vanished when she heard Madame de Malivert's
carriage stop at the door.

The surgeons had said that in the state of extreme weakness in which their patient lay every strong
emotion must be carefully avoided. Madame de Malivert took her stand behind her son's bed so that she
could watch him without his seeing her.

She sent in haste for her friend, the famous surgeon
Duquerrel; on the first day, that able man pronounced
favourably upon Octave's injuries; the household began to hope. As for Armance, she had been convinced
from the first moment, and was never under the slightest illusion. Octave, not being able to speak to her
before so many witnesses, tried once to press her hand.

On the fifth day tetanus appeared. In a moment
in which an increase of fever gave him strength, Octave
begged M. Duquerrel very seriously to tell him the whole
truth.

This surgeon, a man of true courage, who had himself been wounded more than once upon the field of
battle by a Cossack lance, answered him: "Sir, I shall
not conceal from you that there is danger, but I have
seen more than one wounded man in your condition
survive tetanus." "In what proportion?" Octave
went on.

"Since you are determined to end your life like a
man," said M. Duquerrel, "the odds are two to one
that in three days you will have ceased to suffer; if
you have to make your peace with heaven, now is your

time." Octave remained pensive after this announcement but presently his reflexions gave place to a feeling of joy and an emphatic smile. The excellent Duquerrel was alarmed by this joy, which he took to be the first signs of delirium.

# CHAPTER TWENTY-THREE

*Tu sei un niente, o morte! Ma sarebbe mai
dopo sceso il primo gradino della mia tomba,
che mi verrebbe dato di veder la vita come
ella è realmente?*

GUASCO.

UNTIL that moment Armance had not seen her
cousin save in his mother's presence. That
day, after the surgeon had left, Madame de
Malivert thought she could detect in Octave's eyes an
unusual access of strength coupled with a wish to
talk to Mademoiselle de Zohiloff. She asked her young
relative to take her place for a moment by her son's
bedside, while she herself went to the next room where
she was obliged to write a letter.

Octave followed his mother with his eyes; as soon as
she was out of sight: "Dear Armance," he said, "I am
going to die; there are certain privileges attached to
such a moment, and you will not take offence at what
I am now going to say to you for the first time in my
life; I die as I have lived, loving you with passion; and
death is sweet to me, because it enables me to make you
this confession."

Armance was too much overcome to reply; tears
welled into her eyes, and strange to relate, they were

199

tears of happiness. "The most devoted, the tenderest friendship," she said at length, "binds my destiny to yours." "I hear you," Octave replied, "I am doubly glad to die. You bestow on me your friendship, but your heart belongs to another, to that happy man who has received the promise of your hand."

Octave's accents were too eloquent of misery; Armance had not the heart to distress him at this supreme moment. "No, my dear cousin," she said to him, "I can feel nothing more for you than friendship; but no one upon earth is dearer to me than you are." "And the marriage of which you spoke to me?" said Octave. "In all my life I have allowed myself to tell but that one lie, and I implore you to forgive me. I saw no other way of opposing a plan suggested to Madame de Malivert by her extreme interest in my welfare. Never will I be her daughter, but never shall I love any one more than I love you; it is for you, cousin, to decide whether you desire my friendship at such a price." "Were I fated to live, it would make me happy." "I have still a condition to make," Armance went on. "So that I may venture without constraint to enjoy the happiness of being perfectly sincere with you, promise me that, if heaven grants us your life, there shall never be any question of marriage between us." "What a strange condition!" said Octave. "Are you prepared to swear to me again that you are not in love with any one?" "I swear to you," Armance replied with tears in her eyes, "that never in my life have I loved any one but Octave, and that he is by far the dearest person in the world to me; but I can feel nothing stronger for him than friendship," she added, blushing a deep red at this speech, "and I shall never be able to place any confidence in him unless he gives me his word of honour that, whatever may happen, he will never as long as he lives make any direct or indirect attempt to obtain my hand." "I swear it," said Octave, profoundly astonished . . . "but will Armance permit me to speak to her of my love?" "It will be the name that you will give to our friendship," said Armance with a bewitching glance. "It is only for the last few days," Octave went on, "that I have known that I love you. This is not to say that, for a very long time back, never have five minutes passed without the memory of Armance arising to determine whether I ought to deem myself fortunate or unfortunate; but I was blind.

"A moment after our conversation in the woods of Andilly, a pleasantry which Madame d'Aumale let fall proved to me that I love you. That night, I tasted the most cruel torments of despair, I felt that I ought to shun you, I made a vow to forget you and to go away. Next morning, as I returned from the forest, I came upon you in the garden, and spoke to you harshly, in order that your righteous indignation at such atrocious behaviour on my part might arm me with strength to resist the sentiment that was keeping me in France. Had you addressed to me but a single one of those tender words which you have said to me at times in the past, had you looked me in the face,

I should never have found the courage that I required to make me go. Do you forgive me?" "You have made me very unhappy, but I had forgiven you before the confession you have just made me."

An hour followed during which Octave for the first time in his life tasted the happiness of speaking of his love to the beloved.

A single utterance had at once altered the whole situation between Octave and Armance; and as for a long time past every moment of the life of each had been occupied in thinking of the other, an astonishment that was full of charm made them forget the approach of death; they could not utter a word to one another without finding fresh reasons for loving one another.

More than once Madame de Malivert had come, on tiptoe, to the door of her own room. She had remained unobserved by two creatures who had forgotten everything, even the cruel death that was waiting to part them. In the end she became afraid that Octave's agitation might increase the peril; she went up to them and said, almost with a laugh: "Are you aware, children, that you have been chattering for more than an hour and a half, it may send up his temperature." "Dear Mama, I can assure you," replied Octave, "that I have not felt so well for four days." He said to Armance: "There is one thing that worries me when my fever is very high. That poor Marquis de Crêveroche had a very fine dog which seemed to be greatly attached to him. I am afraid the poor beast may

202

be neglected now that his master is no more. Could not Voreppe dress up as a gamekeeper and go and buy that fine sporting dog. I should like at least to be certain that it is being well treated. I hope to see it. In any case, I give it to you, my dear cousin."

After this day of agitation, Octave fell into a deep sleep, but on the morrow the tetanus reappeared. M. Duquerrel felt it his duty to speak to the Marquis, and the whole household was plunged in despair. Notwithstanding the stiffness of his nature, Octave was beloved by the servants; they admired his firmness and sense of justice.

As for him, albeit suffering at times the most agonising torments, happier than he had ever yet been in the whole course of his life, the approaching end of that life made him judge of it at last in a rational manner which intensified his love for Armance. It was to her that he was indebted for the few happy moments which he could perceive amid that ocean of bitter sensations and misfortunes. Acting upon her advice, instead of shunning the world, he had acted, and was cured of many false judgments which had increased his misery. Octave was in constant pain, but, greatly to the astonishment of the worthy Duquerrel, he still lived, he had even some strength.

It took him a whole week to renounce the vow never to fall in love which had been the principal motive of his whole life. The approach of death obliged him first of all to forgive himself with sincerity for having violated his oath. "People die as and how they must," he told himself, "but I am dying on the pinnacle of happiness; fortune owed me perhaps this compensation after dooming me continually to such misery.

"But I may live," he thought, and was then more embarrassed than before. At length he arrived at the conclusion that, in the unlikely event of his surviving his injuries, the sign of weakness of character would be in his keeping the rash vow made in early youth and not in breaking it. "For after all the pledge was given solely in the interests of my own happiness and honour. Why, if I live, may I not continue to enjoy in Armance's company the delights of that tender affection which she has sworn for me? Is it within my power not to feel the passionate love that I have for her?"

Octave was astonished to find himself alive; when at length, after a week of inward struggle, he had solved all the problems that were troubling his spirit, and had entirely resigned himself to accepting the unexpected pleasure which heaven was sending him, in twenty-four hours there was a complete change in his condition, and the most pessimistical of the doctors ventured to answer to Madame de Malivert for her son's life. Shortly afterwards, the fever ceased, and he sank into a state of extreme weakness, barely able to speak.

On returning to life, Octave was seized with a lasting astonishment; everything was altered in his eyes. "It seems to me," he said to Armance, "that before that accident I was mad. Every moment I dreamed

204

of you, and managed to extract unhappiness from that charming thought. Instead of making my behaviour conform to the incidents which I encountered in life, I had made myself an *a priori* rule anterior to all experience." "There is bad philosophy," said Armance with a laugh, "that is why my aunt was so determined to convert you. You are really mad from excess of pride, you learned gentlemen; I cannot think why we choose you, for you are far from merry. For my own part, I despise myself for not having formed a friendship with some quite inconsequent young man who talks of nothing but his tilbury."

When he was in full possession of his faculties, Octave continued to reproach himself with having broken his word; he had fallen slightly in his own estimation. But the happiness of being able to say everything to Armance, even the remorse that he felt for loving her with passion, created, for a person who had never in his life confided in any one, a state of bliss so far exceeding anything that he had expected that he never had any serious intention of returning to his old moods and prejudices.

"When I promised myself that I would never fall in love, I was setting myself a task beyond human capacity; that is why I have always been miserable. And that violation of nature lasted for five years! I have found a heart the like of which I never had the slightest idea could exist anywhere on earth. Fortune, outwitting my folly, plants happiness in my way, and I take offence at it, I almost fly into a passion!

In what respect am I breaking the law of honour? Who is there that knew of my vow to reproach me with breaking it? But it is a contemptible habit, this of forgetting one's promises; is it nothing to have to blush in one's own sight? But this is a vicious circle; have I not furnished myself with excellent reasons for breaking that rash vow made by a boy of sixteen? The existence of a heart like Armance's excuses everything."

Anyhow, such is the force of habit, Octave found perfect happiness only with his cousin. He needed her presence.

An uncertainty crept in now and again to trouble Armance's happiness. She felt that Octave had not taken her completely into his confidence as to the motives that had led him to avoid her society and to leave France after the night he had spent in the woods of Andilly. She considered it beneath her dignity to ask questions, but she did say to him one day, indeed with a distinct air of severity: "If you wish me to give way to the inclination which I feel in myself to become your great friend, you must give me assurances against the fear of being abandoned at any moment, at the prompting of some odd fancy that may have entered your head. Promise me that you will never leave the place in which I am with you, Paris or Andilly or wherever it may be, without telling me *all* your reasons." Octave promised.

On the sixtieth day after his injury, he was able to rise, and the Marquise, who felt keenly the absence

of Mademoiselle de Zohiloff, reclaimed her from Madame
de Malivert, who was almost pleased to see her go.

People are less self-conscious in the intimacy of
family life and during the anxiety of a great sorrow.
The dazzling varnish of an extreme politeness is then
less in evidence, and the true qualities of the heart regain their proper proportions. The want of fortune
of this young relative and her foreign name, which
M. de Soubirane was always careful to mispronounce,
had led the Commander, and even M. de Malivert himself at times, to address her almost as they would have
addressed a paid companion.

Madame de Malivert was trembling lest Octave should
perceive this. The respect which sealed his lips with
regard to his father, would have made him all the
more insolent towards M. de Soubirane, and the Commander's easily irritated vanity would not have failed
to take its revenge in some discreditable anecdote
which he would put in circulation at Mademoiselle de
Zohiloff's expense.

These rumours might come to Octave's ears, and,
knowing the violence of his nature, Madame de Malivert anticipated the most painful scenes, the most
impossible, perhaps, to conceal. Fortunately nothing
of all that her somewhat vivid imagination had pictured
did occur. Octave had noticed nothing. Armance had
turned the tables on M. de Soubirane with a few veiled
epigrams on the ferocity of the war which, in recent
years, the Knights of Malta had waged upon the Turks,

while the Russian officers, with names unknown in history, were taking Ismailoff.

Madame de Malivert, thinking in anticipation of her daughter-in-law's interests, and of the immense disadvantage of entering society without either a fortune or a name, imparted to a few intimate friends confidences intended to discredit beforehand anything that wounded vanity might inspire in M. de Soubirane. These extreme precautions had perhaps not been out of place; but the Commander, who had been gambling on 'Change since his sister's indemnity, and gambling on *certainties*, lost quite a considerable sum, which made him forget all the niceties of his hatred.

After Armance's departure, Octave, who saw her now only in Madame de Bonnivet's presence, began to nourish dark thoughts; his mind dwelt once again upon his old vow. As the wound in his arm gave him constant pain, and even fever at times, the doctors suggested sending him to take the waters at Barèges; but M. Duquerrel, who was intelligent enough not to prescribe the same treatment for all his patients, declared that any air that was at all keen would·suffice for his patient's convalescence, and ordered him to spend the autumn on the slopes of Andilly.

This was a spot dear to Octave; by the following day he had removed there. Not that he had any hope of finding Armance there; Madame de Bonnivet had long been speaking of an expedition into the heart of Poitou. She was having restored at great expense the ancient castle in which Admiral de Bonnivet had had the honour, in times past, to entertain François **I**, and Mademoiselle de Zohiloff was to accompany her.

But the Marquise had had secret information of an approaching list of promotion to the Order of the Holy Spirit. The late King had promised the Blue Riband to M. de Bonnivet. Consequently, the Poitevin architect soon wrote to say that Madame's presence would be superfluous at that moment, since they were short of workmen, and, a few days after Octave's arrival, Madame de Bonnivet came and settled at Andilly.

# CHAPTER TWENTY-FOUR

IN case the noise made by the servants in moving about their attic quarters should disturb Octave, Madame de Bonnivet transferred them to a peasant's house near at hand. It was in what one might call material considerations of this sort that the Marquise's genius triumphed; she brought an exquisite grace to bear upon what she was doing, and was most skilful in employing her wealth to enhance her reputation for cleverness.

The core of her little world was composed of people who for the last forty years had never done anything that was not strictly conventional, the people who set the fashions and are then surprised at them. These declared that, since Madame de Bonnivet was deliberately sacrificing the prospect of a visit to her estates in the country, and was going instead to spend the autumn at Andilly, in order to keep her dear friend Madame de Malivert company, it was the bounden duty of every one with a heart in his bosom to go out and share her solitude.

So popular was this solitude that the Marquise was obliged to take rooms in the little village down the hill in order to accommodate all the friends who came crowding to see her. She put in wallpapers and beds.

Soon half the houses in the village had been decorated under her guidance and were occupied. It became the correct thing to come out from Paris and keep this admirable Marquise, who was looking after that poor Madame de Malivert, company, and Andilly was as thronged with fashion throughout the month of September as any watering-place. This new fashion threatened even to invade the Court. "If we had a score of clever women like Madame de Bonnivet," some one was heard to say, "we might risk going to live at Versailles." And M. de Bonnivet's Blue Riband appeared certain.

Never had Octave been so happy. The Duchesse d'Ancre felt this happiness to be quite natural. "Octave," she said, "may well regard himself as being in a sense the centre of all this movement to Andilly: in the mornings every one sends to inquire after his health; what could be more flattering at his age? That young man is extremely fortunate," the Duchesse went on to say. "He is getting to know the whole of Paris, and it will make him more impertinent than ever." This, however, was not the true reason for Octave's happiness.

He saw that beloved mother, to whom he had given so much cause for anxiety, perfectly happy. She was overjoyed at the brilliant manner in which her son was making his entry into society. Since his triumph, she had begun not to conceal from herself that this kind of distinction was too original and too little copied from recognised types not to need the support of the all-powerful influence of fashion. Failing that reinforcement, it would have passed unnoticed.

One of the things that gave Madame de Malivert great pleasure about this time was a conversation that she had with the famous Prince de R——, who came to spend a night at Andilly.

This most outspoken of courtiers, whose word moreover was law in society, appeared to be taking notice of Octave. "Have you observed, as I have, Madame," he said to Madame de Malivert, "that your son never utters a syllable of that *rehearsed wit* which is the curse of our age? He scorns to appear in a drawing-room armed with his tablets, and his wit varies with the feelings that may be aroused in him. That is why the fools are sometimes so cross with him and withhold their support. When any one succeeds in interesting the Vicomte de Malivert, his wit appears to spring at once from his heart or from his character, and that character seems to me to be one of the strongest. Don't you agree with me, Madame, that character is an organ which has grown obsolete among the men of to-day? Your son seems to me to be destined to play an exceptional part. He is bound to enjoy the very highest reputation among his contemporaries: he is the most solid, and the most obviously solid man that I know. I should like to see him enter the peerage early in life, or to see you get him made Maître des Requêtes."
"But," put in Madame de Malivert, almost breathless with the pleasure she felt at the praise of so good a judge, "Octave's success is anything but general."

"All the better," M. de R—— went on with a smile; "it will take the imbeciles of this country three or four years, perhaps, to understand Octave, and you will be able, before any jealousy appears, to push him almost to his proper place; I ask one thing only: restrain your son from appearing in print, he is too well born for that sort of thing."

The Vicomte de Malivert had still a long way to go before he should be worthy of the brilliant horoscope that had been drawn for him; he had still many prejudices to overcome. His distaste for his fellow men was deeply rooted in his heart; were they prosperous, they filled him with revulsion; wretched, the sight of them was more burdensome still. It was only rarely that he had been able to attempt to cure himself of this distaste by a course of good actions. Had he succeeded in this, his unbounded ambition would have thrust him into their midst and into places where fame is purchased with the most costly sacrifices.

At the time of which we are speaking, Octave was far from any thought of a brilliant destiny for himself. Madame de Malivert had had the good sense not to speak to him of the singular future which M. le Prince de R—— predicted for him; it was only with Armance that she ventured to indulge in the blissful discussion of this prophecy.

Armance possessed in a supreme degree the art of banishing from Octave's mind all the annoyances that society caused him. Now that he ventured to confess these to her, she was more and more astonished at the revelation of his singular character. There were still days upon which he would draw the most sinister conclusions from the most casual utterances. There was much talk of him at Andilly. "You are tasting the immediate fruits of celebrity," Armance told him; "people are saying all sorts of foolish things about you. Do you expect a fool, simply because he has the honour to be speaking about you, to find witty things to say?" This was a severe test for a man inclined to take offence.

Armance insisted upon his making her a full and immediate report of all the speeches offensive to himself that he might hear uttered in society. She had no difficulty in proving to him that they had been uttered without any reference to himself, or that they contained only that amount of malice which every one feels towards every one else.

Octave's self-esteem had nothing now to keep secret from Armance, and these two young hearts had arrived at that unbounded confidence which is perhaps the most charming thing about love. They could not discuss anything under the sun without secretly comparing the charm of their present taste of mutual confidence with the constraint by which they had been bound a few months earlier when they spoke of the same subjects. And this constraint itself, the memory of which was so strong, and in spite of which they were already, at this period, so happy, was a proof of the old and lasting nature of their friendship.

Next day, on reaching Andilly, Octave was not with-

out some hope that Armance would come there also;
he announced that he was ill and kept the house. A
few days later, Armance did indeed arrive with Madame
de Bonnivet. Octave so arranged that his first outing
might take place precisely at seven o'clock in the morning. Armance met him in the garden, where he led her
up to an orange tree planted beneath his mother's windows. There, some months earlier, Armance, her heart
wrung by the strange words that he was addressing
to her, had fallen to the ground in a momentary faint.
She recognised the spot, smiled, and leaned against
the tub of the orange tree, shutting her eyes. But for
the absence of pallor, she was almost as beautiful
as upon the day when she had fainted for love of
him. Octave felt keenly aware of the change in their
relations. He recognised the little diamond cross which
Armance had received from Russia and which was a
relic of her mother. As a rule it was hidden, it was
now brought to light by the movement which Armance
made. Octave for a moment lost his senses; he seized
her hand, as upon the day when she had fainted, and
his lips ventured to brush her cheek. Armance drew
herself up quickly and blushed a deep red. She reproached herself bitterly for this flirtation. "Do you
wish to make me angry?" she asked him. "Do you wish
to force me never to leave the house without a maid?"

A breach that lasted for some days was the immediate result of Octave's indiscretion. But between two
people who felt a perfect attachment to one another,
occasions for quarrelling were rare: whatever Octave

might have occasion to do, before considering whether
it would be agreeable to himself, he would seek to discover whether Armance would be able to see in it a fresh
proof of his devotion.

In the evening, when they were at opposite ends of
the immense drawing-room in which Madame de Bonnivet assembled all the most remarkable and influential
people in the Paris of the day, if Octave had to answer
a question, he would make use of some word which
Armance had just employed, and she could see that the
pleasure of repeating this word made him oblivious of
the interest he might otherwise have felt in what he
was saying. Without any deliberate intention, there
grew up thus for the two of them, amid the most
delightful and animated society, not so much a habit
of private conversation as a sort of echo which, without
expressing anything distinctly, seemed to speak of a
perfect friendship and an unbounded affection.

May we venture to reproach with a trace of stiffness the extreme politeness which the present generation thinks itself to have inherited from that blissful
eighteenth century when there was nothing to hate?

In the midst of this advanced civilisation which for
every one of our actions, however trivial it may be,
insists upon furnishing us with a pattern which we
must copy or state our case against it, this sentiment
of sincere and unbounded devotion comes very near to
creating perfect happiness.

Armance never found herself alone with her cousin
save in the garden, beneath the windows of the mansion,

216

the ground floor of which was occupied, or in Madame
de Malivert's bedroom and in her presence.  But this
room was very large, and often the frail state of
Madame de Malivert's health obliged her to lie down
for a little; she would then ask her children (for thus
it was that she always spoke of them) to go over to the
bay of the window overlooking the garden, so as not
to disturb her rest with the sound of their voices.
This tranquil, entirely intimate life in the morning
hours gave place in the evening to the life of the highest
society.

In addition to the people staying in the village,
many carriages would come out from Paris, returning
after supper.  These cloudless days passed rapidly.
It never occurred to either of these two young hearts
to admit that they were enjoying one of the rarest
forms of happiness that is to be met with here below;
on the contrary they supposed that they had still many
unsatisfied desires.  Having no experience of life, they
did not see that these fortunate moments could only
be of very brief duration.  At most, this happiness,
wholly sentimental and deriving nothing from vanity
or ambition, might have survived in the bosom of some
poor family who never saw any strangers.  But they
were living in society, they were but twenty years old,
they were spending all their time together, and, what
was the height of imprudence, they let it be guessed
that they were happy, and had an air of caring singularly little what society might think.  It was bound to
have its revenge.

Armance gave no thought to this peril. The only thing that troubled her from time to time was the necessity of renewing her private vow never to accept her cousin's hand, whatever might happen. Madame de Malivert, for her part, was quite calm; she had not the least doubt that her son's present way of life was bringing about an event for which she passionately longed.

Notwithstanding the happy days with which Armance was filling the life of Octave, in her absence there were darker moments in which he pondered the destiny in store for him, and he arrived at the following conclusion: "The most favourable impression of myself reigns in Armance's heart. I might confess to her the strangest things about myself, and, so far from despising me, or taking a horror of me, she would pity me."

Octave told his friend that in his boyhood he had had a passion for stealing. Armance was appalled by the terrible details into which his imagination was pleased to enter as to the lamentable consequences of this strange weakness. This admission overturned her whole existence; she sank into a profound abstraction for which she was scolded; but, before a week had passed since this strange confession, she was pitying Octave and more tender to him, were that possible, than ever before. "He needs my consolation," she told herself, "to make him pardon himself."

Octave, assured by this experience of the unbounded devotion of her whom he loved, and no longer having to conceal his dark thoughts, became far more affable in society; before the confession of his love, induced by the approach of death, he had been an extremely witty and remarkable, rather than an affable young man; he appealed especially to serious people. These thought they could detect in him the *every-day* side of a man destined to do great things. The idea of duty was too much in evidence in his manner, and went the length at times of giving him an English expression. His misanthropy was interpreted as pride and ill-humour by the older element of society, and shunned the effort to conquer it. Had he been a peer at this date, he would have won a reputation.

It is the want of the hard school of misfortune that often mars the perfection of the young men who were created to be the most charming. In a day, Octave had been formed by the lessons of that terrible master. It may be said that, at the period of which we are speaking, nothing was wanting to the personal beauty of the young Vicomte, or to the brilliant existence which he enjoyed in society. His praises were sung there without ceasing by Mesdames d'Aumale and de Bonnivet and by the older men.

Madame d'Aumale was justified in saying that he was the most attractive man she had ever met, "for he never bores one," was her foolish explanation. "Until I knew him, I had never even dreamed of such a recom- mendation, and the great thing, after all, is to be amused." "And I," thought Armance as she listened to this artless speech, "I refuse this man who is so welcome everywhere else the permission to clasp my hand; it is a duty," she went on, with a sigh, "and never shall I fail to observe it." There were evenings on which Octave indulged in the supreme happiness of not talking, and of watching the spectacle of Armance, as presented before his eyes. These moments did not pass unobserved, either by Madame d'Aumale, vexed that any one should neglect to provide her with amusement, or by Armance, delighted to see the man she adored occupied exclusively with herself.

The list of promotions in the Order of the Holy Spirit appeared to have been delayed; it was a question of Madame de Bonnivet's departure for the old castle situated in the heart of Poitou, which had given its name to the family. A new personage was to join the expedition, namely, M. le Chevalier de Bonnivet, the youngest of the sons that the Marquis had had by a former marriage.

# CHAPTER TWENTY-FIVE

*Totus mundus stult.*
HUNGARIÆ R——.

ABOUT the time of Octave's wound, a fresh person had arrived from Saint-Acheul to join the Marquise's party. This was the Chevalier de Bonnivet, her husband's third son.

Had the old order been still in existence, he would have been destined for Episcopal rank, and, albeit many things have now changed, a sort of family tradition had persuaded everybody, himself included, that he ought to belong to the Church.

This young man, who was barely twenty, was supposed to be very clever; his chief characteristic was a wisdom beyond his years. He was a little creature, very pale; he had a plump face, and, taking him all round, a somewhat priestly air.

One evening the *Étoile* was brought in. The single paper band that is used to wrap this newspaper happened to be displaced; it was evident that the porter had read it. "And this paper, too!" was the Chevalier de Bonnivet's impulsive exclamation, "simply to save the cost of a second band of grey paper, folded across the other, it is not afraid of running the risk of letting the lower orders read it, as though the lower orders were intended to read! As though the lower orders were capable of distinguishing good from evil! What are we to expect of the Jacobin papers when we see the Monarchist sheets behave like this?"

This burst of spontaneous eloquence greatly enhanced the Chevalier's reputation. It at once brought over to his side the elderly people and every one who in Andilly society had more pretensions than wit. The taciturn Baron de Risset, whom the reader may perhaps remember, rose gravely and crossed the room to embrace the Chevalier without uttering a word. This action cast an air of solemnity over the room for some minutes and amused Madame d'Aumale. She called the Chevalier to her side, tried to make him talk, and took him to some extent under her wing.

All the young women followed in her wake. They made the Chevalier a sort of rival to Octave, who had already been wounded and was confined to the house, in Paris.

But presently they began to find that the Chevalier de Bonnivet, young as he was, gave them a sense of revulsion. He was felt to be singularly wanting in sympathy with all the things in which people are interested. The young man had a future of his own. There might be detected in him an element of deeply rooted treachery towards every one in the world.

On the day following that on which he had shone at the expense of the *Etoile*, the Chevalier de Bonnivet, who saw Madame d'Aumale from an early hour, opened the ball with her on the lines of Tartufe when he offers a handkerchief to Dorine so that she may cover "things which ought not to be seen." He read her a serious lecture upon some frivolous remark which she had just made about a procession.

The young Comtesse retorted sharply, brought him repeatedly back to the charge, and was in ecstasies at his absurdity. "He is just like my husband," she thought. "What a pity poor Octave is not here, how we should laugh!"

The Chevalier de Bonnivet was shocked more than by anything else by the sort of renown that clung to the Vicomte de Malivert, whose name he heard upon every tongue. Octave came to Andilly and reappeared in society. The Chevalier supposed him to be in love with Madame d'Aumale, and, with this idea in his head, formed the plan of developing a passion for the pretty Comtesse, with whom he was most affable.

The Chevalier's conversation was a perpetual and very clever string of allusions to the masterpieces of the great writers and poets of French and Latin literature. Madame d'Aumale, whose knowledge was scanty, made him explain the allusions to her, and nothing amused her more. The Chevalier's really astounding memory did him good service; he repeated without hesitation the lines of Racine or the passages from Bossuet to which he had referred, and indicated clearly and elegantly the bearing of the allusion he had intended to make upon the subject of their conversation. All this had the charm of novelty in the eyes of Madame d'Aumale.

One day the Chevalier said: "A single short article in *La Pandore* is enough to spoil all the pleasure that we derive from power." This was considered very deep.

Madame d'Aumale greatly admired the Chevalier; but after a very few weeks had passed he had begun to alarm her. "You have the effect upon me," she told him, "of a venomous animal encountered in some solitary spot in the heart of the forest. The cleverer you are, the more capable you become of doing me harm."

Another day she said to him that she would wager that he had of his own initiative discovered the great principle: that speech was given to man to enable him to conceal his thoughts.

The Chevalier had been highly successful with the rest of society. For instance, although separated from his father for the last eight years, which he had spent at Saint-Acheul, Brig, and elsewhere, often without the Marquis's even knowing where he was, once he had returned and was living with him, in less than two months he succeeded in acquiring a complete domination over the mind of the old man, one of the shrewdest courtiers of the time.

M. de Bonnivet had always been afraid of seeing the French Restoration end like the English; but for the last year or so this fear had made a regular miser of him. Society was therefore greatly astonished to see him give thirty thousand francs to his son the Chevalier, as a contribution to the foundation of certain houses of Jesuits.

Every evening, at Andilly, the Chevalier used to recite prayers, together with the forty or fifty servants in attendance upon the people who were staying in the mansion or in the peasants' houses that had been secured for the Marquise's friends. These prayers were followed by a short exhortation, improvised and very well expressed.

The elderly women began to make their way to the orangery, where these evening exercises were held. The Chevalier had it decorated with charming flowers, constantly renewed, for which he sent to Paris. Soon this pious and severe exhortation began to arouse a general interest; it was in marked contrast to the frivolous manner in which the rest of the evening was spent.

Commander de Soubirane declared himself one of the warmest supporters of this method of leading back to good principles all the subordinates who of necessity surround important persons and who, he would add, shewed such cruelty the moment the reign of terror began. This was a favourite expression with the Commander, who went about everywhere announcing that within ten years, unless we re-established the Knights of Malta and the Jesuits, we should have a second Robespierre.

Madame de Bonnivet had not failed to send to her son-in-law's pious exercises those of her own people whom she could trust. She was greatly astonished to learn that he made doles of money to the servants who came to confide to him in private that they were in want.

The list of promotions in the Order of the Holy Spirit being apparently delayed, Madame de Bonnivet announced that her architect had written to her from Poitou that he had managed to collect a sufficient number of workmen. She made her preparations for the journey, as did Armance. She was none too well pleased when the Chevalier de Bonnivet announced his intention of accompanying her to Bonnivet, in order, he said, to see once more the old castle, the cradle of his race.

The Chevalier saw quite well that his presence annoyed his mother-in-law; all the more reason for him to accompany her on this expedition. He hoped to impress Armance by recalling the glories of his ancestors; for he had noticed that Armance was friends with the Vicomte de Malivert, and intended to take her from him. These projects, long under consideration, became apparent only at the moment of their execution.

No less successful with the young people than with the more serious element of society, before leaving Andilly, the Chevalier de Bonnivet had managed artfully to fill Octave with jealousy. After the departure of Armance, Octave even began to think that this Chevalier de Bonnivet, who boasted an esteem and a respect for her that were unbounded, might well be that mysterious suitor whom an old friend of her mother had found for her.

On taking leave of one another, Armance and her cousin were alike tormented by dark suspicions. Armance felt that she was leaving Octave with Madame d'Aumale; but she did not think that she could allow herself to write to him.

During this cruel separation, Octave could do nothing but address to Madame Bonnivet two or three letters, quite charming but couched in a singular tone. Had any one who was a stranger to their society seen these letters, he would have thought that Octave was madly in love with Madame de Bonnivet and dared not confess his love to her.

In the course of this month of absence, Mademoiselle de Zohiloff, whose good sense was no longer troubled by the bliss of being under the same roof as her friend and of seeing him thrice daily, made some severe reflexions. Albeit her behaviour had been perfectly proper, she could not blind herself to the fact that it must be easy to read the expression in her eyes when she looked at her cousin.

The promiscuity of travel was the cause of her overhearing a conversation among Madame de Bonnivet's maids which drew many tears from her eyes. These women, like every one who is connected with persons of importance, seeing nothing anywhere but pecuniary interests, set down to this motive the appearance of passion which Armance was assuming, they said, in order to become Vicomtesse de Malivert; no small matter to a penniless girl of such obscure birth.

The idea of her being slandered to such a degree had never occurred to Armance. "I am a ruined girl," she said to herself; "my feeling for Octave has passed beyond suspicion, and even that is not the worst of my supposed offences. I live under the same roof as he, and it is not possible for him to marry me. . . ." From that instant, the thought of the slanders that were being uttered against her, resisting every argument that Armance could advance, poisoned her life.

There were moments in which she fancied that she had forgotten even her love for Octave. "Marriage is not intended for a girl in my position. I shall not marry him;" she thought; "and I shall have to live far more apart from him. If he forgets me, as is highly probable, I shall go and end my days in a convent; that will be a very proper asylum, and greatly to be desired, for the rest of my existence. I shall think of him, I shall hear of his triumphs. People in society will be able to recall many examples of lives similar to that which I shall be leading."

These precautions were sound; but the thought, terrible for a girl, that she might, with some appearance of justice, be exposed to the slander of a whole household, and that the household in which Octave was living, cast a shadow over Armance's life which nothing could dissipate. Did she endeavour to escape from the memory of her misdeeds, for this was the name she gave to the sort of life she had led at Andilly, she would begin to think of Madame d'Aumale, whose attractions she would unconsciously exaggerate. Chevalier de Bonnivet's company made her regard as even more irremediable than they actually are all the harm that society can do us when we have offended it. Towards the end of her stay at the old Château de Bonnivet,

228

Armance spent every night in weeping. Her aunt noticed this melancholy, and did not conceal from the girl how angry it made her.

It was during her stay in Poitou that Armance learned of an event which affected her but little. She had three uncles in the Russian service; these young men perished by suicide during the troubles in that country. Their death was kept secret; but finally, after many months, some letters which the police had not succeeded in intercepting were delivered to Mademoiselle de Zohiloff. She had succeeded to a comfortable fortune, which would make her a suitable match for Octave.

This event was not calculated to appease the anger of Madame de Bonnivet, to whom Armance was necessary. The poor girl had to listen to some very sharp comments on the preference that she shewed for Madame de Malivert's drawing-room. Great ladies are no more spiteful than the average rich woman; but one acquires in their society a greater susceptibilty, and feels more profoundly and, if I may venture to use the expression, more irremediably, their unpleasant remarks.

Armance supposed that nothing was wanting to complete her misery, when the Chevalier de Bonnivet informed her, one morning, with the indifferent air which people assume in repeating a piece of news which is already stale, that Octave was again far from well, and that the wound in his arm had opened and was causing anxiety. Since Armance had left him, Octave, who had become hard to please, was often bored with his mother's drawing-room. He was guilty of acts of

imprudence when shooting, which had serious consequences. He had had the idea of using a little gun,
very light, which he fired with his left hand; his success with this weapon encouraged him.

One day, as he was going after a winged partridge,
he jumped a ditch and hit his arm against a tree, which
brought back his fever. During this fever and the
state of weakness that followed it, the artificial happiness, so to speak, which he had enjoyed in the company of Armance, seemed to have become as unsubstan-
tial as a dream.

Mademoiselle de Zohiloff returned at length to Paris,
and the following day, at Andilly, the lovers met once
more; but they were very sad, and this sorrow was of
the worst possible kind: it sprang from a mutual doubt.
Armance did not know what tone to adopt with her
cousin; and they barely spoke to one another the first
day.

While Madame de Bonnivet was indulging in the
pleasure of building gothic towers in Poitou and imagining that she was reconstructing the twelfth century,
Madame d'Aumale had taken decisive action to ensure
the great triumph which came at last to crown the long-
nourished ambition of M. de Bonnivet. She was the
heroine of Andilly. In order not to have to part with
so valuable a friend, during her own absence, Madame
de Bonnivet had made the Comtesse d'Aumale agree
to occupy a little apartment in the highest part of
the mansion, close to Octave's room. And Madame
d'Aumale seemed to every one to be perfectly well aware

that it was in a sense for her sake that Octave had received the wound which was causing his fever. It was in extremely bad taste to remind people of the affair, which had cost the Marquis de Crêveroche his life; Madame d'Aumale could not, however, refrain from making frequent allusions to it: the fact is that the way of the world is to natural delicacy pretty much what science is to the mind. Her character, entirely on the surface and not at all romantic, was impressed first and foremost by realities. Armance had not been more than a few hours at Andilly before this constant recurrence to the same topics, by a mind that as a rule was so frivolous, struck her forcibly.

Armance arrived there very sad and greatly discouraged; she felt for the second time in her life the assault of a sentiment that is terrifying, especially when it coincides in a single heart with an exquisite sense of the proprieties. Armance imagined that she had serious fault to find with herself in this respect. "I must keep a strict watch over myself," she said to herself as she turned away her gaze, which was resting on Octave, to examine the brilliant Comtesse d'Aumale. And each separate charm of the Comtesse was for Armance the occasion of an excessive act of humility. "How could Octave fail to give her the preference?" she said to herself; "I myself feel that she is adorable."

Such painful sentiments, combined with the remorse which Armance was feeling, wrongly no doubt, but none the less painfully for that, made her far from affable to Octave. On the morning after her arrival, she did not come down betimes to the garden; this had been her habit in the past, and she knew very well that Octave was waiting for her there.

In the course of the day, Octave spoke to her two or three times. An extreme shyness which seized her, with the thought that everybody was watching them, paralysed her, and she barely answered him.

That day, at dinner, mention was made of the fortune which chance had just brought to Armance; and she observed that the news seemed to give little pleasure to Octave, who did not say a single word to her about it. The word that was not uttered, had her cousin addressed it to her, would not have given birth in her heart to a pleasure equivalent to one hundredth part of the grief which his silence caused her.

Octave was not listening; he was thinking of the singular manner that Armance had adopted towards him since her return. "No doubt she no longer cares for me," he was saying to himself, "or she has made some definite engagement with the Chevalier de Bonnivet." Octave's indifference to the news of Armance's fortune opened for the poor girl a fountain of sorrows both new and deep. For the first time, she thought long and earnestly of this inheritance which had come to her from the North, and which, had Octave loved her, would have made her a more or less suitable match for him.

Octave, to obtain an excuse for writing her a page, had sent to her, in Poitou, a short poem about Greece which had just been published by Lady Nelcombe, a young Englishwoman who was a friend of Madame de Bonnivet. In the whole of France there were but two copies of this poem, which was greatly discussed. Had the copy which had made the journey to Poitou appeared in the drawing-room, a score of indiscreet attempts would have been made to intercept it; Octave begged his cousin to have it sent to his room. Armance, greatly intimidated, could not summon up courage to entrust such a mission to her maid. She went up to the second floor of the mansion and placed the little English poem on the handle of Octave's door, so that he could not enter his room without noticing it.

Octave was greatly troubled; he saw that Armance was definitely reluctant to speak to him. Feeling himself by no means in the humour to speak to her, he left the drawing-room before ten o'clock. He was agitated by a thousand sinister thoughts. Madame d'Aumale was soon bored with the drawing-room: they were talking politics, and in a depressing tone; she pleaded a headache, and by half-past ten had retired to her own apartment. Probably Octave and Madame d'Aumale were taking a stroll together; this idea, which occurred to every one, made Armance turn pale. Whereupon she reproached herself with her very grief as an impropriety which made her less worthy of her cousin's esteem.

Next morning, at an early hour, Armance was with Madame de Malivert, who needed a particular hat. Her maid had gone to the village; Armance hurried to the room in which the hat was; she was obliged to pass by the door of Octave's room. She stood as though

thunderstruck on catching sight of the little English
poem balanced upon the handle of the door, exactly
as she had left it overnight. It was evident that Octave
had not gone to his own room.

This was the absolute truth. He had gone out shooting, notwithstanding the recent accident to his arm;
and, so as to be able to rise betimes and unobserved,
had spent the night in the game-keeper's cottage. He
intended to return to the house at eleven, when the bell
rang for luncheon, and thus to escape the reproaches
which would have been heaped on him for his imprudence.

On returning to Madame de Malivert's room, Armance found herself obliged to say that she was unwell.
From that moment she was a different person. "I am
bearing a fit punishment," she told herself, "for the
false position in which I have placed myself, and which
is so improper in a young person. I have come to the
stage of sufferings which I cannot admit even to myself."

When she saw Octave again, Armance had not the
courage to put to him any question as to the accident
which had prevented him from seeing the little English
poem; she would have felt that she was wanting in
everything that she owed to herself. This third day
was even more sombre than those that had gone before.

# CHAPTER TWENTY-SIX

OCTAVE, aghast at the alteration which he noticed in Armance's manner, thought that, even as a mere friend, he might hope that she would confide in him the cause of her anxiety; for that she was unhappy he could have no doubt. It was equally clear to him that the Chevalier de Bonnivet was seeking to rob them of every opportunity of exchanging a word in private which chance might offer them on a walk or in the drawing-room.

The hints which Octave threw out now and again met with no response. If she were to confess her grief and abandon the systematic restraint to which she had subjected herself, Armance would first have had to be profoundly moved; Octave was too young and too wretched himself to make this discovery or to profit by it.

Commander de Soubirane had come to dine at Andilly; there was a storm that evening, it rained in torrents. The Commander was invited to stay the night, and was given a room next to the one into which Octave had recently moved, on the second floor. That evening Octave had set himself to revive a little of Armance's gaiety; he wanted to see her smile; he would have seen in that smile a presentment of their old friendship. His gaiety failed completely, and greatly annoyed Armance. As she did not answer him, he was obliged to address his fine speeches to Madame d'Aumale, who was one of the circle and laughed constantly, while Armance preserved a grim silence.

Octave ventured to put a question to her which seemed to require a fairly long answer: he was answered in two words, most drily. In desperation at this proof of his disgrace, he left the room immediately. As he took the air in the garden, he met the game-keeper, and told him that he would be going out shooting early next morning.

Madame d'Aumale, seeing only serious people in the drawing-room whose conversation she found burdensome, decided to retire and did so. This second assignation seemed plain as daylight to the wretched Armance. Furious above all at the duplicity of Octave, who, only that evening, as they passed from one room to the next, had murmured a few very tender words in her ear, she went up to her own room to fetch a volume which she intended to balance, like the little English poem, upon the handle of Octave's door. As she advanced along the corridor which led to her cousin's room, she heard a sound from within; his door stood ajar, and he was priming his gun. There was a small closet which served as a second entrance to the room that had been prepared for the Commander, and the door of this closet opened upon the corridor. As ill luck would have it, this door was open. Octave came to the door of his room as Armance approached, and made a movement as though of emerging into the passage. It would

236

have been frightful for Armance to be discovered by Octave at that moment. She had barely time to fling herself behind the open door that offered a way of escape. "As soon as Octave has gone," she said to herself, "I shall arrange the book." She was so troubled by the thought of the liberty she was allowing herself to take, which was a great sin, that she was barely capable of reasoning connectedly.

Octave did indeed come out of his room; he passed by the open door of the little closet in which Armance was hiding; but he went no farther than the end of the corridor. He leaned out of one of the windows and whistled twice, as though to give a signal. As the game-keeper, who was drinking in the servants' hall, did not reply, Octave remained at the window. The silence that reigned in this part of the house, the guests being assembled in the drawing-room on the ground floor and the servants in the basement, was so profound that Armance, whose heart was beating violently, dared not move a muscle. Besides, poor Armance could not blind herself to the fact that Octave had given a signal; and, however unsuited it might be to a lady, it seemed to her that it was one that Madame d'Aumale might very well have arranged.

The window from which Octave was leaning was at the head of the little stair leading down to the first floor, it was impossible for her to pass him. Octave whistled a third time as the clock finished striking eleven; the game-keeper, who was with the others in the servants' hall, did not answer. About half-past eleven, Octave returned to his room.

Armance, who had never in her life been engaged in any enterprise for which she need blush, was so much upset that she found herself unable to walk. It was evident that Octave was giving a signal; either some one would answer or presently he would come out of his room again. The third quarter sounded from the stable clock, then midnight. The lateness of the hour increased Armance's misgivings; she decided to leave the closet which had given her shelter, and as the last of the twelve strokes sounded she stepped forth. She was so much upset that she, whose step was usually light, made quite a loud noise.

As she moved along the corridor, she caught sight of a figure in the darkness, by the window at the head of the stair, outlined against the sky, and at once recognised M. de Soubirane. He was waiting for his servant to bring him a candle, and, as Armance stood motionless gazing at the face of the Commander whom she had just recognised, the light of the candle, which was now being carried upstairs, appeared upon the ceiling of the corridor.

Had she kept her head Armance might have attempted to hide behind a big cupboard which stood in the corner of the corridor, near the stair, and might thus have been saved. Rooted to the ground with terror, she lost a moment or two, and, as the servant reached the head of the stair, the light of the candle shone full upon her, and the Commander recognised her.  A hideous smile appeared on his lips.  His suspicions of the understanding between Armance and his nephew were confirmed, while at the same time he had found a way to ruin them for ever. "Saint-Pierre," he said to his servant, "is not that Mademoiselle Armance de Zohiloff standing there?"  "Yes, Sir," said the servant, greatly confused.  "Octave is better, I hope, Mademoiselle?" said the Commander in a coarse, bantering tone, and walked past her.

## CHAPTER TWENTY-SEVEN

ARMANCE, in despair, saw herself at once disgraced for ever and betrayed by her lover. She sat down for a moment on the landing of the stair. She decided to go and knock at the door of Madame de Malivert's maid. The girl was asleep and did not answer. Madame de Malivert, with a vague fear that her son might be ill, took her nightlight and came to the door of her own room; she was alarmed by the expression on Armance's face. "What has happened to Octave?" cried Madame de Malivert. "Nothing, Madame, nothing at all to Octave, it is only I who am in distress and miserable at having disturbed your sleep. My idea was to speak to Madame Dérien and to ask for you only if I was told that you were still awake." "My child, you increase my alarm with all these *Madames*. Something strange has happened. Is Octave ill?" "No, Mama," said Armance and burst into tears, "it is only that I am a ruined girl."

Madame de Malivert took her into her bedroom, and there Armance told her what had just happened to her, concealing nothing and passing nothing over in silence, not even her own jealousy. Her heart, crushed by all her miseries, had not the strength to keep anything back.

Madame de Malivert was appalled. Suddenly she exclaimed: "There is no time to be lost, give me my pelisse, my poor child, my dear child," and she kissed her again and again with all the passion of a mother. "Light my candle, and do you stay here." Madame de Malivert ran to her son's room; fortunately the door was not locked; she entered quietly, awoke Octave and told him what had occurred. "My brother may ruin us," said Madame de Malivert, "and, to judge by appearances, he will not miss the opportunity. Rise, go to his room, tell him that I have had a sort of seizure in your room. Can you think of anything better?" "Yes, Mama, to marry Armance to-morrow, if that angel will still have me."

This unexpected speech was a fulfilment of Madame de Malivert's dearest wish; she embraced her son, but added, on second thoughts: "Your uncle does not like Armance, he may talk; he will promise to keep silence, but he has his servant who will talk by his order, and whom he will then dismiss for having talked. I stick to my idea of a seizure. This make-believe will keep us painfully busy for three days, but your wife's honour is more precious than anything else. Remember to appear greatly alarmed. As soon as you have told the Commander, go down to my room, tell Armance of our plan. When the Commander passed her on the stair, I was in your room, and she was going to fetch Madame Dérien." Octave hastened to tell his uncle, whom he found wide awake. The Commander looked at him with a derisive expression which turned all his emotion to anger. Octave left M. de Soubirane to fly to his mother's room: "Is it possible," he said to Armance, "that you have not been in love with the Chevalier de Bonnivet, and that he is not the mysterious husband of whom you spoke to me once, long ago?" "I have a horror of the Chevalier. But you, Octave, are not you in love with Madame d'Aumale?" "Never as long as I live will I see her again or give her another thought," said Octave. "Dear Armance, deign to say that you accept me as a husband. Heaven is punishing me for having kept you in the dark as to my shooting expeditions, I was whistling for the keeper, who did not answer." Octave's protestations had all the warmth but not all the delicacy of true passion; Armance thought she could make out that he was performing a duty while his thoughts were elsewhere. "You are not in love with me just now," she said to him. "I love you with all my heart and soul, but I am mad with rage at that ignoble Commander, vile man, upon whose silence we cannot count." Octave renewed his solicitations. "Are you sure that it is love that is speaking," Armance said to him, "perhaps it is only generosity, and you are in love with Madame d'Aumale. You used to have a horror of marriage, this sudden conversion seems to me suspicious." "In heaven's name, dear Armance, do not let us waste any more time; all the rest of my life shall answer to you for my love." He was so far convinced of the truth of what he was saying that he ended by convincing her also. He hastened upstairs and found the Commander with his mother, whom her joy at the prospect of Octave's marriage had given the courage to play her part admirably. Nevertheless, the Commander did not seem to be at all convinced of his sister's seizure. He ventured upon a pleasantry with regard to Armance's nocturnal roamings. "Sir, I have still one sound arm," cried Octave, springing to his feet and throwing himself upon him; "if you say one word more, I shall fling you out of that window." Octave's restrained fury made the Commander blench, he remembered in time his nephew's mad outbursts and saw that he was worked up to the pitch of committing a crime.

Armance appeared at that moment, but Octave could think of nothing to say to her. He could not even look lovingly at her, this calm after the storm left him powerless. The Commander, to make the best of a bad business, having tried to say something light and pleasant, Octave was afraid of his wounding Mademoiselle de Zohiloff's feelings. "Sir," he said to him, gripping his arm tightly. "I must ask you to withdraw at once to your own room." As the Commander hesitated, Octave seized him by the arm, carried him off to his room, flung him inside, locked the door, and put the key in his pocket.

When he rejoined the ladies he was furious. "If I do not kill that base and mercenary creature," he cried, as though talking to himself, "he will dare to speak evil of my wife. A curse upon him!"

"As far as I am concerned, I like M. de Soubirane," said Armance in her alarm, seeing the distress that

Octave was causing his mother. "I like M. de Soubirane, and if you go on being furious I may think that
you are cross because of a certain rather sudden engagement which we have just announced to him."

"You do not believe it," Octave interrupted her, "I
am sure of that. But you are right, as you always
are. When all is said and done, I ought to be thankful
to that base creature;" and gradually his wrath sub-
sided. Madame de Malivert had herself carried to her
room, keeping up admirably the pretence of a seizure.
She sent to Paris for her own Doctor.

The rest of the night passed charmingly. The gaiety
of this happy mother infected Octave and his mistress.
Led on by Madame de Malivert's merry speeches, Armance, who was still greatly upset and had lost all self-
control, ventured to let Octave see how dear he was to
her. She had the intense pleasure of seeing him jealous
of the Chevalier de Bonnivet. It was this fortunate
sentiment which accounted in a manner so gratifying
to her for his apparent indifference during the last
few days. Mesdames d'Aumale and de Bonnivet, who
had been awakened in spite of Madame de Malivert's
orders to the contrary, did not appear until the night
was far spent, and the whole party retired to bed as
dawn was breaking.

# CHAPTER TWENTY-EIGHT

*This is the state of man: to-day he puts forth*
*The tender leaves of hope; to-morrow blos-*
*    soms,*
*And bears his blushing honours thick upon*
*    him;*
*The third day comes a frost, a killing frost;*
*. . . And then he falls—see his character.*[1]
                    KING HENRY VIII, Act III.

EARLY on the following morning Madame de Malivert proceeded to Paris to lay the plan of Octave's marriage before her husband. All day long he held out against it; "not that you are to suppose," said the Marquis, "that I have not long been expecting this stupid proposal. I cannot pretend to be surprised. Mademoiselle de Zohiloff is not absolutely penniless, I agree; her Russian uncles have died at a very opportune moment for her. But her fortune is no greater than what we might find elsewhere, and—what is of the greatest importance to my son—there is no family connexion in this alliance; I can see nothing in it but a deplorable similarity of character. Octave has not enough relatives in society, and his reserved manner makes him no friends. He will be a Peer when

---

[1] The last three words are added by Beyle. The source is cited in all the editions as *King Henry III.*—C. K. S. M.

his cousin and I are gone, that is all, and, as you know very well, my dear, in France, the value of a title depends on the man who bears it. I belong to the older generation, as these insolent fellows say; I shall soon pass away, and with me all the ties that can connect my son with society; for he is an instrument in the hands of our dear Marquise de Bonnivet, rather than an object of her pursuit. We ought, in seeking a wife for Octave, to put social support above fortune even. I grant him, if you like, the sort of exceptional merit which succeeds by itself. I have always observed that these sublime beings require to have their virtues preached, and my son, so far from flattering the people who make or mar reputations, seems to take a malicious pleasure in defying them to their faces. That is not the way to achieve success. With a numerous connexion, well established, he would have passed in society as a worthy candidate for ministerial office; he has no one to sing his praises, he will be regarded as merely an original."

Madame de Malivert protested volubly against this expression. She could see that some one had been *buttonholing* her husband.

His eloquence increased: "Yes, my dear, I would not swear that the readiness to take offence which Octave shews, and his passion for what are called *principles*, now that the Jacobins have changed all our customs including our language, may not lead him one day into the worst excess of folly, into what you call the *opposition*. The one outstanding man whom your op-

246

position could boast, the Comte de Mirabeau, ended by selling himself; that is an ugly ending, and one that I should not care to see my son make." "Nor need you have any fear of his doing so," Madame de Malivert parried him boldly. "No, it is over the other precipice that my son's fortunes will be engulfed. This marriage will only make him a bumpkin, buried in the heart of the country, within the four walls of his manor. His sombre nature makes him too much inclined as it is to that sort of life. Our dear Armance has an odd way of looking at things; so far from attempting to alter what I find reprehensible in Octave, she will encourage him in his plebeian habits, and by this marriage you will destroy our family." "Octave will one day be summoned to the House of Peers, he will be a noble representative of the youth of France, and will win personal consideration by his eloquence." "There is too much competition. All these young Peers lay claim to eloquence. Why, good lord, they will be in their Chamber what they are in society, perfectly well mannered, highly educated, and that is all. All these young representatives of the youth of France will be the most bitter enemies of Octave, who has at least a point of view of his own."

Madame de Malivert returned late in the day to Andilly, with a charming letter for Armance, in which M. de Malivert besought her hand for his son.

Tired as she was by the exertions of the day, Madame de Malivert hastened to find Madame de Bonnivet, who must learn of the marriage from her lips alone. She let her see M. de Malivert's letter to Armance; she was only too glad to take this precaution against the people who might make her husband change his mind. This action was, moreover, necessary, the Marquise being in a sense Armance's guardian. This position sealed her lips. Madame de Malivert was grateful for the affection which Madame de Bonnivet shewed for Octave without at all seeming to approve personally of the marriage. The Marquise took refuge in enthusiastic praise of Mademoiselle de Zohiloff's character. Madame de Malivert did not forget to mention the overtures that she had made to Armance some months earlier, and the noble refusal made by the young orphan, who was then still penniless.

"Ah, it is not about Armance's noble qualities that my affection for Octave needs to be reassured," said the Marquise. "Any that she may have come from us. These family marriages are suitable only among the rich and powerful bankers; as their principal object is money, they are certain of finding it without trouble."

"We are coming to a time," replied Madame de Malivert, "when favour at Court, unless he chooses to purchase it by incessant personal services, will be merely a secondary object for a man of high birth, a Peer of France with a great fortune. Look at our friend Lord N——; his immense influence in his own country springs from the fact that he nominates eleven Members of the House of Commons. He never even sees his King."

It was in similar terms that Madame de Malivert met the objections raised by her brother, whose opposition was far stronger. Furious at the last night's scene and fully determined not to let the opportunity pass of making a great show of indignation, he wished, when he should allow his wrath to be appeased, to place his nephew under a burden of undying gratitude.

Octave, by himself, he would have forgiven, for after all he must either forgive him or abandon those dreams of wealth which had been occupying his thoughts, to the exclusion of all else, for the last year. As for the midnight scene, his vanity would have had the consolation, among his intimate friends, of Octave's well-known mania for throwing his mother's footmen out of windows.

But the thought of Armance reigning with absolute power over the heart of a husband who loved her to madness drove M. de Soubirane to declare that never again would he shew his face at Andilly. They were all very happy at Andilly, they took him more or less at his word, and, after offering him all sorts of apologies and invitations, proceeded to forget him.

Since he had seen his position strengthened by the arrival of the Chevalier de Bonnivet, who furnished him with good arguments and, at a pinch, with ready-made phrases, his antipathy towards Mademoiselle de Zohiloff had turned to hatred. He could not forgive her allusions to Russian bravery as displayed beneath the walls of Ismailoff, while the Knights of Malta, *sworn* enemies of the Turks, sat idly upon their rock. The Commander might have forgotten an epigram provoked by himself; but the fact is that there was *money* at the bottom of all this anger with Armance. The Commander's head, never at any time too strong, was absolutely turned by the idea of making a vast fortune on 'Change. As is universal among commonplace natures, about the age of fifty, the interest that he used to take in the things of this world had died away, and boredom had made its appearance; as might also be expected, the Commander had aspired successively to be a man of letters, a political intriguer and a patron of the Italian opera. Only some mischance had prevented his being a lay Jesuit.

Finally, the sport of gambling on 'Change had appeared and had proved a sovereign remedy for a vast boredom. And to gamble on 'Change he had all the requirements save only funds and credit. The indemnity had turned up at a most opportune moment, and the Commander had vowed that he would have no difficulty in controlling his nephew, who was a mere philosopher. He fully intended to invest on 'Change a good share of the sum that Octave would receive from his mother's indemnity.

At the height of his passion for millions, Armance had presented herself as an insuperable obstacle in the Commander's path. Now her adoption into the family destroyed forever his hold over his nephew and with it all his castles in the air crumbled. The Commander did not waste any time in Paris, but went about fulminating against his nephew's marriage in the houses of Madame la Duchesse de C——, the head of the family, Madame la Duchesse d'Ancre, Madame de la Ronze, Madame de Claix, whom he visited daily. All these friends of the family soon decided that the marriage was most unsuitable.

In less than a week the young Vicomte's intended marriage was common knowledge and was no less commonly deplored. The great ladies who had marriageable daughters were furious.

"Madame de Malivert," said the Comtesse de Claix, "has the cruelty to force that poor Octave into marrying her companion, evidently to save the salary she would have to pay the girl; it's a shame."

In the midst of all this the Commander felt that he was forgotten in Paris, where he was bored to death. The general outcry against Octave's marriage could be no more permanent than anything else. He must take advantage of this universal storm while it still lasted. A marriage once arranged can be broken off only by prompt action.

Finally all these sound arguments and, more than they, his own boredom brought it to pass that one fine morning the Commander was seen to arrive at Andilly, where he resumed his old room and his ordinary life as though nothing had occurred.

Every one was most polite to the newcomer, who did not fail to make the most cordial overtures to his niece

251

to be. "Friendship has its illusions no less than love," he said to Armance, "and if I found fault at first with certain proposals, it was because I too am passionately devoted to Octave."

# CHAPTER TWENTY-NINE

*Ses maux les plus cruels sont ceux qu'il se
fait lui-même.*          BALZAC.[1]

**A**RMANCE might perhaps have been taken in
by these polite overtures, but she did not stop
to think about the Commander; she had other
grounds for anxiety.

Now that there was no longer any obstacle in the
way of his marriage, Octave was given to fits of sombre
ill-temper which he found difficulty in concealing; he
pleaded a series of violent headaches, and would go out
riding by himself in the woods of Écouen and Senlis.
He would sometimes cover seven or eight leagues at a
gallop. These symptoms appeared ominous to Armance; she remarked that at certain moments he gazed
at her with eyes in which suspicion was more evident
than love.

It was true that these fits of sombre ill-temper ended
as often as not in transports of love and in a passionate abandonment which she had never observed in
him *in the days of their happiness.* It was thus that
she was beginning to describe, in her letters to Méry

[1] This quotation is presumably from the seventeenth century
letter writer, Guez de Balzac, whom Beyle in *Henri Brulard* com-
pares with Chateaubriand.—C. K. S. M.

253

de Tersan, the time that had passed between Octave's injury and her own fatal act of imprudence in hiding in the closet by the Commander's room.

Since the announcement of her marriage, Armance had had the consolation of being able to open her heart to her dearest friend. Méry, brought up in a far from united family which was always being torn asunder by fresh intrigues, was quite capable of giving her sound advice.

During one of these long walks which she took with Octave in the garden of the mansion, beneath Madame de Malivert's windows, Armance said to him one day: "There is something so extraordinary in your sadness that I, who love you and you alone in the world, have found it necessary to seek the advice of a friend before venturing to speak to you as I am going now to speak. You were happier before that cruel night when I was so imprudent, and I have no need to tell you that all my own happiness has vanished far more rapidly than yours. I have a suggestion to make to you: let us return to a state of perfect happiness and to that pleasant intimacy which was the delight of my life, after I knew that you loved me, until that fatal idea arose of our marriage. I shall take upon myself entire responsibility for so odd a change. I shall tell people that I have made a vow never to marry. They will condemn the idea, it will impair the good opinion that some of my friends are kind enough to hold of me; what do I care? Public opinion is after all important to a girl with money only so long as she thinks of marrying; and I certainly shall never marry." Octave's only answer was to take her hand, while tears streamed from his eyes in abundance. "Oh, my dear angel," he said to her, "how far superior you are to me!" The sight of these tears on the face of a man not ordinarily subject to that weakness combined with so simple a speech to destroy all Armance's resolution.

At length she said to him with an effort: "Answer me, my friend. Accept a proposal which is going to restore my happiness. We shall continue to spend our time together just as much as before." She saw a servant approaching them. "The luncheon bell is going to ring," she went on in some distress, "your father will be arriving from Paris, afterwards I shall not have another opportunity of speaking to you, and if I do not speak to you I shall be unhappy and agitated all day, for I shall be a little doubtful of you." "You! Doubtful of me!" said Octave gazing at her in a way which for a moment banished all her fears.

After walking for some minutes in silence: "No, Octave," Armance went on, "I am not doubtful of you; if I doubted your love, I hope that God would grant me the blessing of death; but after all you have been less happy since your marriage was settled." "I shall talk to you as I should to myself," said Octave impetuously. "There are moments in which I am far more happy, for now at last I have the certainty that nothing in the world can separate me from you; I shall be able to see you and to talk to you at every hour of the day, *but*," he went on . . . and fell into one of those moods of gloomy silence which filled Armance with despair.

The dread of hearing the luncheon bell, which was going to separate them for the rest of the day perhaps, gave her for the second time the courage to break in upon Octave's musings: "But what, dear?" she asked him, "tell me all; that fearful *but* is making me a hundred times more wretched than anything you could add to it."

"Very well!" said Octave stopping short, turning to face her and gazing fixedly at her, no longer with the gaze of a lover but so as to be able to read her thoughts, "you shall know all; death itself would be less painful to me than the story which I have to tell you, but also I love you far more than life. Do I need to swear to you, no longer as your lover" (and at that moment his eyes were indeed no longer the eyes of a lover) "but as an honourable man and as I should swear to your father, if heaven in its mercy had spared him to us, do I need to swear to you that I love you and you only in the world, as I have never loved before and shall never love again? To be parted from you would be death to me and a hundred times worse than death; but I have a fearful secret which I have never confided to any one, this secret will explain to you my fatal vagaries."

As he stammered rather than spoke these words, Octave's features contracted, there was a hint of madness in his eyes; one would have said he no longer saw Armance; his lips twitched convulsively. Armance,

256

more wretched than he, leaned upon the tub of an orange tree; she shuddered on recognising that fatal orange tree by which she had fainted when Octave spoke harshly to her after the night he had spent in the forest. Octave had stopped and stood facing her as though horror-stricken and not daring to continue. His startled eyes gazed fixedly in front of him as though he beheld a vision of a monster.

"Dear friend," said Armance, "I was more unhappy when you spoke cruelly to me by this same orange tree months ago; at that time I doubted your love. What am I saying?" she corrected herself with passion. "On that fatal day I was certain that you did not love me. Ah! my friend, how far happier I am to-day!"

The accent of truth with which Armance uttered these last words seemed to moderate the bitter, angry grief to which Octave was a prey. Armance, forgetful of her customary reserve, clasped his hand passionately and urged him to speak; her face came for a moment so close to his that he could feel her warm breath. This sensation moved him to tenderness; speech became easy to him.

"Yes, dear friend," he said to her, gazing at length into her eyes, "I adore you, you need not doubt my love; but what is the man who adores you? He is a *monster*."

With these words, Octave's tenderness seemed to forsake him; all at once he flew into a fury, tore himself from the arms of Armance who tried in vain to hold

257

him back, and took to his heels. Armance remained motionless. At that instant the bell rang for luncheon. More dead than alive, she had only to shew her face before Madame de Malivert to obtain leave not to remain at table. Octave's servant came in a moment later to say that a sudden engagement had obliged his master to set off at a gallop for Paris.

The party at luncheon was silent and chilly; the only happy person was the Commander. Struck by this simultaneous absence of both the young people, he detected tears of anxiety in his sister's eyes; he felt a momentary joy. It seemed to him that the affair of the marriage was no longer going quite so well: "marriages have been broken off later than this," he said to himself, and the intensity of his preoccupation prevented him from making himself agreeable to Mesdames d'Aumale and de Bonnivet. The arrival of the Marquis, who had come from Paris, notwithstanding a threatening of gout, and shewed great annoyance at not finding Octave whom he had warned of his coming, increased the Commander's joy. "The moment is auspicious," he told himself, "for making the voice of reason heard." As soon as luncheon was over, Mesdames d'Aumale and de Bonnivet went upstairs to their rooms; Madame de Malivert disappeared into Armance's room, and the Commander was animated, that is to say happy, for an hour and a quarter, which he employed in trying to shake his brother-in-law's determination in the matter of Octave's marriage.

There was a strong vein of honesty underlying everything that the old Marquis said in reply. "The indemnity belongs to your sister," he said; "I myself am a pauper. It is this indemnity which makes it possible for us to think of establishing Octave in life; your sister is more anxious than he, I think, for this marriage with Armance, who, for that matter, has some fortune of her own; in all this I can do nothing, as a man of honour, but express my opinion; it would be impossible for me to speak with authority; I should have the air of wishing to deprive my wife of the pleasure of spending the rest of her life with her dearest friend."

Madame de Malivert had found Armance greatly agitated but scarcely communicative. Urged by the call of affection, Armance spoke in the vaguest terms of a trifling quarrel, such as occurs at times between people who are most fervently in love. "I am sure that Octave is to blame," said Madame de Malivert as she rose to go, "otherwise you would tell me all;" and she left Armance to herself. This was doing her a great service. It soon became plain to her that Octave had committed some serious crime, the dread consequences of which he might perhaps have exaggerated, and that as a man of honour he would not allow her to unite her destiny with that of one who was perhaps a murderer, without letting her know the whole truth.

Dare we say that this explanation of Octave's eccentricity restored his cousin to a sort of tranquillity? She went down to the garden, half hoping to find him there. She felt herself at that moment entirely rid of the profound jealousy which Madame d'Aumale had inspired in her; she did not, it is true, admit to herself that this might account for the state of blissful emotion in which she found herself. She felt herself transported by the most tender and most generous pity. "If we have to leave France," she said to herself, "and go into banishment far away, were it even in America, well, away we shall go," she said to herself with joy, "and the sooner the better." And her imagination began to wander, picturing a life of complete solitude on a desert island, ideas too romantic and, what is more, too familiar on the pages of novels to be recorded here. Neither on that day nor on the next did Octave put in an appearance: only on the evening of the second day Armance received a letter dated from Paris. Never had she been so happy. The most burning, the most abandoned passion glowed in this letter. "Ah! If he had been here at the moment when he wrote, he would have told me all." Octave let it be understood that he was detained in Paris because he was ashamed to tell her his secret. "It is not at every moment," the letter went on, "that I shall have the courage to utter that fatal word, even to you, for it may destroy the sentiments which you deign to feel for me and which are everything to me. Do not press me upon this subject, dear friend." Armance made haste to reply to him by a servant who was waiting. "Your greatest crime," she told him, "is your remaining away from us," and she was no less surprised than joyful when, half an hour after writing to him, she saw Octave appear, he having come out to await her answer at Labarre near Andilly.

The days that followed were days of unbroken happiness. The illusions induced by the passion that was animating Armance were so strange that presently she found herself quite accustomed to the idea of being in love with a murderer. It seemed to her that it must at the very least be murder, this crime of which Octave hesitated to admit himself guilty. Her cousin spoke too carefully to exaggerate his ideas, and he had used these very words: "I am a monster."

In the first love letter that she had ever written to him or to any one, she had promised him that she would not ask him questions; this vow was sacred in her eyes. Octave's letter to her in reply she treasured. She had read it a score of times, she formed the habit of writing every evening to the man who was to be her husband; and as it would have made her blush to speak his name to her maid, she concealed her first letter in the tub of that orange tree which Octave had good reason to know.

She informed him of this in a word one morning as they were sitting down to luncheon. He left the room with the excuse that he had to give an order, and Armance had the indescribable pleasure, when he returned a quarter of an hour later, of reading in his eyes the expression of the keenest happiness and tenderest gratitude.

A day or two after this, Armance found the courage to write to him: "I believe you to be guilty of some great crime; it shall be our lifelong duty to atone for it, if atonement be possible; but the strange thing is that I am perhaps even more tenderly devoted to you than before this confidence.

"I feel how much this avowal must have cost you, it is the first great sacrifice that you have ever made for me, and, let me tell you, it is only from that moment that I have been cured of an ugly sentiment which I too scarcely dared confess to you. I imagine the worst. And so it seems to me that you need not make me a more detailed confession before a certain ceremony is performed. You will not have deceived me, I swear to you. God pardons the penitent, and I am sure that you are exaggerating your offence; were it as grave as it can be, I, who have seen your anxieties, forgive you. You will make me a full confession in a year from now, perhaps you will then be less afraid of me. . . . I cannot, however, promise to love you more dearly."

A number of letters written in this strain of angelic goodness had almost made Octave decide to confide in writing to his mistress the secret that she was entitled to learn; but the shame, the embarrassment of writing such a letter still held him back.

He went to Paris to consult M. Dolier, the relative who had acted as his second. He knew that M. Dolier was a man of honour, endowed with a straightforward mind and not clever enough to compound with his duty or to indulge in illusions. Octave asked him whether he was absolutely bound to confide in Mademoiselle de Zohiloff a fatal secret, which he would not have hesitated to disclose, before his marriage, to her father or guardian. He went so far as to shew M. Dolier the part of Armance's letter which we have quoted above.

"You can have no excuse for not speaking," was the gallant officer's reply, "it is your bounden duty. You must not take advantage of Mademoiselle de Zohiloff's generosity. It would be unworthy of you to deceive any one, and it would be even more beneath the noble Octave to deceive a poor orphan who has perhaps no friend but himself among all the men of her family."

Octave had told himself all this a thousand times, but it acquired an entirely new force when it issued from the lips of a firm and honourable man.

Octave thought he heard the voice of destiny speaking.

He took his leave of M. Dolier vowing that he would write the fatal letter in the first café that he should find on his right hand after leaving his cousin's house; he kept his word. He wrote a letter of ten lines and addressed it to Mademoiselle de Zohiloff, at the Château de ——, by Andilly.

On leaving the café, he looked about him for a letter-box; as luck would have it, there was none to be seen. Presently a remnant of that awkward feeling which urged him to postpone such a confession as long as possible, succeeded in persuading him that a letter of such importance ought not to be entrusted to the post, that it was better that he should place it himself in the tub of the orange tree in the garden at Andilly. Octave had not the intelligence to see in the idea of this postponement a lingering illusion of a passion that was barely conquered.

The essential thing, in his situation, was for him not to give way an inch to the repugnance which M. Dolier's stern advice had helped him to overcome. He mounted his horse to carry his letter to Andilly.

Since the morning on which the Commander had had a suspicion of some misunderstanding between the lovers, the natural frivolity of his character had given way to an almost incessant desire to do them an injury.

He had taken as confidant the Chevalier de Bonnivet. All the time that the Commander had formerly employed in dreaming of speculations on 'Change and in jotting down figures in a pocket-book, he now devoted to seeking a way in which to break off his nephew's engagement.

His proposals at first were none too reasonable; the Chevalier de Bonnivet regularised his plan of attack. He suggested to him that he should have Armance followed, and, by spending a few louis, the Commander made spies of all the servants in the house. They told him that Octave and Armance were corresponding, and that they concealed their letters in the tub of an orange tree bearing a certain number.

Such imprudence appeared incredible to the Chevalier de Bonnivet. He left the Commander to think over it. Seeing at the end of a week that M. de Soubirane had progressed farther than the obvious idea of reading the amorous expressions of a pair of lovers, he skilfully reminded him that, among a score of different foibles, he had had, for six months, a passion for autograph letters; the Commander had employed at that time a very clever copyist. This idea penetrated that thick skull but produced no effect. It had the company there, however, of a burning hatred.

The Chevalier hesitated long before risking himself with such a man. The sterility of his associate's mind was discouraging. Moreover, at the first check, he might confess everything. Fortunately, the Chevalier remembered a vulgar novel in which the villain has the lovers' handwriting copied and fabricates forged letters. The Commander read scarcely anything, but had at one time worshipped fine bindings. The Chevalier decided to make a final attempt; should this prove unsuccessful, he would abandon the Commander to all the aridity of his own methods. One of Thouvenin's men, lavishly paid, worked day and night and clothed in a superb binding the novel in which the trick of forging letters occurred. The Chevalier took this sumptuous book, brought it out to Andilly and stained with coffee the page on which the substitution of the forged letters was described.

"I am in despair," he said one morning to the Commander as he entered his room. "Madame de ———, who is mad about her books, as you know, has had this miserable novel bound in the most beautiful style. I was ass enough to pick it up in her house, and have stained one of the pages. Now you have collected or invented the most astounding secrets for doing everything, could not you shew me how to forge a new page?" The Chevalier, having discoursed at great length and used the expressions *most akin* to the idea that he wished to suggest, left the volume in the Commander's room.

He mentioned it to him at least ten times before it occurred to M. de Soubirane to hatch a quarrel between the lovers by means of forged letters.

He was so proud of this idea that at first he was inclined to exaggerate its importance; he spoke of it in this light to the Chevalier, who was horrified at so immoral an action and left that evening for Paris. A couple of days later the Commander, in the course of conversation with him, returned to his idea. "To substitute a forged letter would be atrocious," cried the Chevalier. "Is your love for your nephew so strong that *the end justifies the means?*"

But the reader is doubtless no less tired than ourselves of these sordid details; details in which we see the cankered fruit of the new generation competing with the frivolity of the old.

The Commander, still full of pity for the Chevalier's innocence, proved to him that, in an almost hopeless cause, the most certain way to be defeated was to attempt nothing.

M. de Soubirane boldly rescued from his sister's hearth a number of scraps of Armance's handwriting, and easily obtained from his penman copies which it was hard to distinguish from their originals. He had already begun to base his hopes of a breach of Octave's engagement upon the most definite anticipations of the intrigues of the coming winter, the distractions of the ballroom, the advantageous offers which he would be able to have made to the family. The Chevalier de Bonnivet was filled with admiration for his character. "Why is not this man a Minister," he said to himself, "the highest offices would be mine. But with this cursed Charter, public debates, the liberty of the press, never could such a man become a Minister, however noble his birth." Finally, after he had waited patiently for a fortnight, it occurred to the Commander to compose a letter from Armance to Méry de Tersan, her dearest friend. The Chevalier was for the second time on the point of throwing up the sponge. M. de Soubirane had spent two days in drafting a model letter sparkling with wit and overloaded with delicate fancies, a reminiscence of the letters he himself used to write in 1789.

"Our generation is more serious than that," the Chevalier told him, "you should aim at being pedantic, grave, boring. . . . Your letter is charming; the Chevalier de Laclos would not have disowned it, but it will not take in any one to-day." "Always to-day, to-day!" retorted the Commander, "your Laclos was nothing but a fool. I do not know why all you young men

267

model yourselves on him. His characters drivel like barbers," etc., etc.

The Chevalier was enchanted with the Commander's hatred for Laclos; he put up a stout defence of the author of *Les liaisons dangereuses,* was completely routed, and finally obtained a model letter, not nearly emphatic or German enough for his purpose, but still quite reasonable. The model letter drafted after so stormy a discussion was presented by the Commander to his copier of autographs who, thinking that it was merely a question of epistolary gallantry, raised only the objections necessary to secure ample payment for himself, and produced a lifelike imitation of Mademoiselle de Zohiloff's hand. Armance was supposed to be writing her friend Méry de Tersan a long letter about her approaching marriage to Octave.

As he returned to Andilly with the letter written according to M. Dolier's suggestions, the predominant thought in Octave's mind throughout his ride had been that he must make Armance promise not to read his letter until they had parted for the night. Octave intended to leave the following morning at daybreak; he was quite certain that Armance would write in reply. He hoped thus somewhat to diminish the awkwardness of a first meeting after such a confession. He had made up his mind to this course only because he discerned an element of heroism in Armance's attitude. For a long time past he had never surprised her at any moment in her life when she was not dominated by the happiness or grief arising from the sentiment that united them. Octave had no doubt that she felt a violent passion for himself. Arriving at Andilly he sprang from the saddle, ran to the garden and there, as he was hiding his letter beneath some leaves in the corner of the orange-tree tub, found one from Armance.

## CHAPTER THIRTY

HE withdrew rapidly to the shelter of a lime alley to be able to read it without interruption. He saw from the opening lines that this letter was intended for Mademoiselle Méry de Tersan (it was the letter composed by the Commander). But the opening lines had so disturbed him that he went on, and read: "I do not know how to reply to your reproaches. You are right, my kind friend, I am mad to complain. This arrangement is, from every point of view, far better than anything a poor girl, who has woken up to find herself rich, and has no family to establish and protect her, could expect. He is a man of parts and of the highest virtue: perhaps he has too much virtue for me. Shall I confess it to you? The times have indeed changed; what would have been the height of bliss for me a few months ago is no more now than a duty; has heaven withheld from me the power to love constantly? I am completing an arrangement that is reasonable and advantageous, as I repeat to myself incessantly, but my heart no longer knows those sweet transports that I used to feel at the sight of the most perfect man, in my eyes, to be found anywhere upon earth, the one being worthy to be loved. I see to-day that his mood is inconstant, or rather

270

why accuse him? It is not he that has changed; my whole misfortune is that there is inconstancy in my heart. I am about to contract a marriage that is advantageous, honourable, in every sense; but, dear Méry, I blush to confess it to you; I am no longer marrying the person whom I loved above all; I find him serious and at times barely entertaining, and it is with him that I am going to spend my life! Probably in some lonely manor house in the depths of the country where we shall promote the spread of pupil-teaching and vac‧cination. Perhaps, dear friend, I shall look back with regret upon Madame de Bonnivet's drawing-room; who would have said so six months ago? This strange fickleness in my character is what distresses me most. Is not Octave the most remarkable young man we have seen this winter? But I have had so miserable a girl-hood! I should like an amusing husband. Farewell. The day after to-morrow *I am to be allowed* to go to Paris; at eleven I shall be at your door."

Octave stood horror-stricken. All at once he awoke as though from a dream and ran to retrieve the letter which he had just left in the tub of the orange tree: he tore it up furiously, and put the fragments in his pocket.

"I needed," he said to himself coldly, "the wildest and profoundest passion if I was to be pardoned for my fatal secret. In defiance of all reason, in defiance of every vow I had made to myself throughout my life, I thought I had met with a creature above the rest of humanity. To deserve such an exception, I should

271

have had to be pleasant and gay, and those are the qualities that I lack. I have been mistaken; there is nothing left for me but to die.

"It would doubtless be an offence against the laws of honour not to make a confession, were I involving for all time the destiny of Mademoiselle de Zohiloff. But I can leave her free within a month. She will be a young widow, rich, very beautiful, no doubt greatly sought after; and the name of Malivert will be of greater use to her in finding an *amusing husband* than the still unfamiliar name of Zohiloff."

It was in this frame of mind that Octave entered his mother's room, where he found Armance who was talking of him and longing for his return; soon she was as pale and almost as unhappy as himself, and yet he had just said to his mother that he could not endure the delays that kept postponing the date of his marriage. "There are plenty of people who would be glad to mar my happiness," he had gone on to say; "I am certain of it. Why do we need all these preparations? Armance is richer than I am, and it is not likely that she will ever want for clothes or jewels. I venture to hope that before the end of the second year of our marriage she will be gay, happy, enjoying all the pleasures of Paris, and that she will never repent of the step she is now about to take. I am sure that she will never be buried in the country in an old manor house."

There was something so strange in the sound of Octave's words, so little in keeping with the aspiration that they expressed, that almost simultaneously Ar-

mance and Madame de Malivert felt their eyes fill with
tears. Armance could barely find strength to reply:
"Ah, dear friend, how cruel you are!"

Greatly vexed that he had not managed to assume
an air of happiness, Octave left the room abruptly. His
determination to end his marriage by death imparted a
certain harshness and cruelty to his manner.

Having deplored with Armance what she called her
son's madness, Madame de Malivert came to the conclusion that solitude was of no avail to a character
that was naturally sombre. "Do you love him still
in spite of this defect from which he is the first to
suffer?" said Madame de Malivert; "consult your heart,
my child, I have no wish to make you unhappy, everything may yet be broken off." "Oh, Mama, I believe
that I love him even more than ever, now that I no
longer think him so perfect." "Very well, my pet," replied Madame de Malivert, "I shall have you married in
a week from now. Until then, be indulgent to him,
he loves you, you cannot doubt that. You know what
he feels about his duty to his family, and yet you saw
his fury when he thought you were being made the butt
of my brother's wicked tongue. Be kind and good, my
dear child, with this creature who is being made
wretched by some odd prejudice against marriage."
Armance, to whom these words spoken at random presented so true a meaning, increased her attentions and
tender devotion to Octave.

The following day, at dawn, Octave came to Paris,
and spent a very considerable sum, almost two-thirds

of what he had at his disposal, in buying costly jewelry which he included among the wedding presents.

He called upon his father's lawyer and made him insert in the marriage contract certain clauses extremely advantageous to the bride to be, which, in the event of her widowhood, assured her the most ample independence.

It was with business of this sort that Octave occupied the ten days that elapsed between the discovery of Armance's supposed letter and his marriage. These days were for Octave more tranquil than he could have dared to hope. What makes misery so cruel to tender hearts is a little ray of hope which sometimes lingers.

Octave had no hope. His course was decided, and for a stout heart, however hard the part he may have to play, it dispenses him from reflecting upon his fate, and asks no more of him than the courage to perform it scrupulously; which is a small matter.

What most impressed Octave, when the necessary preparations and business of all sorts left him to himself, was a prolonged astonishment: What! So Mademoiselle de Zohiloff no longer meant anything to him! He was so far accustomed to believe firmly in the eternity of his love and of their intimate relation, that at every moment he kept forgetting that all was changed, he was incapable of imagining life without Armance. Almost every morning, he was obliged when he awoke to remind himself of his misery. It was a cruel moment. But presently the thought of death came to console him and to restore calm to his heart.

At the same time, towards the end of this interval of ten days, Armance's extreme tenderness caused him some moments of weakness. During their solitary walks, thinking herself authorised by the imminence of their marriage, Armance allowed herself on more than one occasion to take Octave's hand, which was beautifully shaped, and to raise it to her lips. This increase of tender attentions of which Octave was quite well aware, and, in spite of himself, extremely sensible, often made keen and poignant a grief which he believed himself to have overcome.

He pictured to himself what those caresses would have been coming from a person who really loved him, coming from Armance as, on her own admission, in the fatal letter to Méry, she had still been two months since. "And my want of friendliness and gaiety has been able to kill her love," said Octave bitterly to himself. "Alas! It was the art of making myself welcome in society that I ought to have studied instead of abandoning myself to all those useless sciences! What good have they done me? What good have I had from my success with Madame d'Aumale? She would have loved me had I wished it. I was not made to please those whom I respect. Evidently a wretched shyness makes me sad, wanting in friendliness, just when I am passionately anxious to please.

"Armance has always alarmed me. I have never approached her without feeling that I was appearing before the ruler of my destiny. I ought to have derived from my experience, and from what I could see going on round about me, a more accurate idea of the effect produced by a pleasant man who seeks to interest a girl of twenty. . . .

"But all that is useless now," said Octave, breaking off with a melancholy sigh: "my life is ended. *Vixi et quem dederat fortuna sortem peregi.*" [1]

In certain moments of sombre humour, Octave went so far as to interpret Armance's tender manner, so little in keeping with the extreme reserve which was so natural to her, as the performance of a disagreeable duty which she had set herself. Nothing then could be comparable to his rudeness, which really had almost the appearance of insanity.

Less wretched at other moments, he allowed himself to be touched by the seductive grace of this girl who was to be his bride. It would indeed have been difficult to imagine anything more touching or more noble than the caressing ways of a girl who was ordinarily so reserved, doing violence to the habits of a lifetime in the attempt to restore a little calm to the man whom she loved. She believed him to be the victim of remorse and yet felt a violent passion for him. Now that the main occupation of Armance's life was no longer to conceal her love and to reproach herself for it, Octave had become dearer to her than ever.

One day, on a walk in the direction of the woods of

---

[1] When dying, abandoned by Æneas, Dido exclaims: "I have lived and have run the course which fortune appointed for me." [Octave shows a certain indifference here to the laws of prosody. Virgil's line (*Æneid* IV, 653), runs: *Vixi et quem dederat cursum fortuna peregi.*—C. K. S. M.]

Ecouen, carried away herself by the tender words which she was venturing to utter, Armance went so far as to say to him, and at the moment she meant what she was saying: "I sometimes think of committing a crime equal to yours so as to deserve that you shall no longer fear me." Octave, charmed by the accents of true passion, and understanding all that was in her mind, stopped short to gaze fixedly at her, and in another moment might have given her the letter containing his confession, the fragments of which he still carried on his person. As he thrust his hand into the pocket of his coat, he felt the finer paper of the false letter addressed to Méry de Tersan, and his good intention froze.

# CHAPTER THIRTY-ONE

*If he be turn'd to earth, let me but give him
one hearty kiss, and you shall put us both
into one coffin.* WEBSTER.[1]

OCTAVE was involved in endless conciliations of important relatives whom he knew to disapprove strongly of his marriage. In ordinary circumstances, nothing would have annoyed him more. He would have come away wretched and almost disgusted with his prospective happiness from the mansions of his illustrious kinsfolk. Greatly to his surprise he found, as he performed these duties, that nothing caused him any annoyance; because nothing now interested him any more. He was dead to the world.

Since the revelation of Armance's fickleness, men were for him creatures of an alien species. Nothing had power to move him, neither the misfortunes of virtue nor the prosperity of crime. A secret voice said to him: these wretches are less wretched than you.

Octave carried through with admirable indifference all the idiotic formalities that modern civilisation has piled up to mar a happy day. The marriage was celebrated.

[1] From *Vittoria Corombona*, Act IV. Cornelia finds her son Marcello killed by his brother Flamineo.—C. K. S. M.

278

Taking advantage of what is now becoming an established custom, Octave set off at once with Armance for the domain of Malivert, situated in Dauphiné; and in the end took her to Marseilles. There he informed her that he had made a vow to go to Greece, where he would shew that, notwithstanding his distaste for military ways, he knew how to wield a sword. Armance had been so happy since her marriage that she consented without undue regret to this temporary separation. Octave himself, being unable to conceal from himself Armance's happiness, was guilty of what was in his eyes the very great weakness of postponing his departure for a week, which he spent in visiting with her the Holy Balm, the Château Borelli and other places in the neighbourhood of Marseilles. He was greatly touched by the happiness of his young bride. "She is playing a part," he said to himself, "her letter to Méry is a clear proof of it; but she plays it so well!" He underwent moments of self-deception when Armance's perfect felicity succeeded in making him happy. "What other woman in the world," Octave asked himself, "even by the most sincere sentiments, could give me such happiness?"

At length it was time for them to part; once on board the ship, Octave paid dearly for his moments of self-deception. For some days he could no longer summon up courage to die. "I should be the lowest of mankind," he said to himself, "and a coward in my own eyes, if after hearing my sentence uttered by the wise Dolier, I do not speedily give Armance back her

freedom. I lose little by departing from this life,"
he added with a sigh; "if Armance plays the lover so
gracefully, it is merely a reminiscence, she is recalling
what she felt for me in the past. Before long I should
have begun to bore her. She respects me, no doubt,
but has no longer any passionate feeling for me, and
my death will distress her without plunging her in
despair." This painful certainty succeeded in making
Octave forget the heavenly beauty of an Armance in-
toxicated with love, and *swooning* in his arms on the
eve of his departure. He regained courage, and from
the third day at sea, with his courage there reappeared
tranquillity. The vessel happened to be passing the
Island of Corsica. The memory of a great man who
had died so pitiably occurred vividly to Octave and
began to restore his firmness of purpose. As he thought
of him incessantly, he almost had him as a witness to
his conduct. He feigned a mortal malady. Fortunately, the only medical officer that they had on
board was an old ship's carpenter who claimed to understand fever, and he was the first to be taken in by
Octave's alarming state and by his ravings. By dint
of playing his part for a few moments now and again,
Octave saw at the end of a week that they despaired
of his recovery. He sent for the captain in what was
called one of his lucid intervals, and dictated his will,
which was witnessed by the nine persons composing the
crew.

Octave had taken care to deposit a similar will with
a lawyer at Marseilles. He bequeathed everything

that was at his disposal to his wife, on the strange condition that she should remarry within twenty months of his death. If Madame Octave de Malivert did not think fit to comply with this condition, he begged his mother to accept his fortune.

Having signed his testament in the presence of the entire crew, Octave sank into a state of extreme weakness and asked for the prayers for the dying, which several Italian sailors repeated by his bedside. He wrote to Armance, and enclosed in his letter the other which he had had the courage to write to her from a café in Paris, and the letter to her friend Méry de Tersan which he had intercepted in the tub of the orange tree. Never had Octave so fallen under the spell of the most tender love as at this supreme moment. Except for the nature of his death, he gave himself the happiness of telling Armance everything. Octave continued to languish for more than a week, every day he gave himself the fresh pleasure of writing to his beloved. He entrusted his letters to various sailors, who promised him that they would convey them in person to his lawyer at Marseilles.

A ship's boy, from the crow's nest, cried: "Land !" It was the shores of Greece and the mountains of the Morea that had come into sight on the horizon. A fresh breeze bore the vessel rapidly on. The name of Greece revived Octave's courage: "I salute thee," he murmured, "O land of heroes !" And at midnight, on the third of March, as the moon was rising behind Mount Kalos, a mixture of opium and digitalis prepared by himself delivered Octave peacefully from a life which had been so agitated. At break of day, they found him lying motionless on the bridge, leaning against a coil of rope. A smile was on his lips, and his rare beauty impressed even the sailors who gave him burial. The manner of his death was never suspected in France save by Armance alone. Shortly afterwards, the Marquis de Malivert having died, Armance and Madame de Malivert took the veil in the same convent.

**THE END**

*The Shorter Novels
of Stendhal*

---

## VOLUME II

## CONTENTS

# THE ABBESS OF CASTRO

## I

WE have so often been shewn in melodrama the Italian brigands of the sixteenth century, and so many people have spoken of them without any real knowledge, that we have come to hold the most erroneous ideas of what they were like. Speaking generally, one may say that these brigands were the *Opposition* to the vile governments which, in Italy, took the place of the mediaeval Republics. The new tyrant was, as a rule, the wealthiest citizen of the defunct Republic, and, to win over the populace, would adorn the town with splendid churches and fine pictures. Such were the Polentini of Ravenna, the Manfredi of Faenza, the Riario of Imola, the Cani of Verona, the Bentivoglio of Bologna, the Visconti of Milan, and lastly, the least bellicose and most hypocritical of all, the Medici of Florence. Among the historians of these little States none has dared to relate the countless poisonings and assassinations ordered by the fear that used to torment these petty tyrants; these grave historians were in their pay. When you consider that each of these tyrants was personally acquainted with each of the Republicans by whom he knew himself to be execrated (the Tuscan Grand Duke Cosimo, for instance, knew Strozzi), and that several of these tyrants died by the hand of the assassin, you will understand the profound hatreds, the eternal distrust which gave so much spirit and courage to the Italians of the sixteenth century, and such genius to their artists. You will see these profound passions preventing the birth of that

[ 11 ]

really rather absurd prejudice which was called *honour* in the days of Madame de Sévigné, and consists first and foremost in sacrificing one's life to serve the master whose subject one is by birth, and to please the ladies. In the sixteenth century, a man's activity and his real worth could not be displayed in France, nor win admiration, except by bravery on the field of battle or in duels; and, as women love bravery, and above all daring, they became the supreme judges of a man's worth. Then was born the *spirit of gallantry*, which led to the destruction, one after another, of all the passions, including love, in the interests of that cruel tyrant whom we all obey: namely, vanity. Kings protected vanity, and with good reason, hence the power of the riband.

In Italy, a man distinguished himself by *all forms* of merit, by famous strokes with the sword as by discoveries in ancient manuscripts: take Petrarch, the idol of his time; and a woman of the sixteenth century loved a man who was learned in Greek as well as, if not more than she would have loved a man famous for his martial valour. Then one saw passions, and not the habit of gallantry. That is the great difference between Italy and France, that is why Italy has given birth to a Raphael, a Giorgione, a Titian, a Correggio, while France produced all those gallant captains of the sixteenth century, so entirely forgotten to-day, albeit each of them had killed so vast a number of enemies.

I ask pardon for these homely truths. However it be, the atrocious and *necessary* acts of vengeance of the petty Italian tyrants of the middle ages won over the hearts of their peoples to the brigands. The brigands were hated when they stole horses, corn, money, in a word everything that was necessary to support life; but, in their heart of hearts, the people were for them, and the village girls preferred to all the rest the boy who once in his life had been obliged *andare alla macchia*, that is to say to flee to the woods and take refuge among the brigands, in consequence of some over-rash action.

And even in our own day everyone dreads, unquestionably, an encounter with brigands; but when they are caught and punished everyone is sorry for them. The fact is that this people, so shrewd, so cynical, which laughs at all the publications issued under the official censure of its masters, finds its favourite reading in little poems which narrate with ardour the lives of the most renowned brigands. The heroic element that it finds in these stories thrills the artistic vein that still survives in the lower orders, and besides, they are so weary of the official praise given to certain people, that everything of this sort which is not official goes straight to the heart. It must be explained that the lower classes in Italy suffer from certain things which the traveller would never observe, were he to live ten years in the country. For instance, fifteen years ago, before governments in their wisdom had suppressed the brigands,[1] it was not uncommon to see certain of their exploits punish the iniquities of the *Governors* of small towns. These Governors, absolute magistrates whose emoluments do not amount to more than twenty scudi monthly, are naturally at the disposal of the most important family of the place, which by this simple enough method oppresses its enemies. If the brigands did not always succeed in punishing these despotic little Governors, they did at least make fools of them, and defy their authority, which is no small matter in the eyes of this quick-witted race. A satirical sonnet consoles them for all their mis-

[1] Gasparone, the last of the brigands, made terms with the Government in 1826; he was confined in the citadel of Civita-Vecchia with thirty-two of his men. It was the want of water on the heights of the Apennines, where he had taken refuge, that obliged him to make terms. He was a man of spirit, with a face that is not easily forgotten.

fortunes, and never do they forget an injury. That is another fundamental difference between the Italian and the Frenchman.

In the sixteenth century, had the Governor of a township sentenced to death a poor inhabitant who had incurred the hatred of the leading family, one often found brigands attacking the prison in an attempt to set free the victim; on the other hand the powerful family, having no great faith in the nine or ten soldiers of the government who were set to guard the prison, would raise at its own expense a troop of temporary soldiers. These latter, who were known as *bravi*, would install themselves in the neighbourhood of the prison, and make it their business to escort to the place of execution the poor devil whose death had been bought. If the powerful family included a young man, he would place himself at the head of these improvised soldiers.

This state of civilisation makes morality groan, I admit; in our day we have the duel, dulness, and judges are not bought and sold; but these sixteenth century customs were marvellously well adapted to create men worthy of the name.

Many historians, praised even to-day in the hack literature of the academies, have sought to conceal this state of affairs, which, about the year 1550, was forming such great characters. At the time, their prudent falsehoods were rewarded with all the honours which the Medici of Florence, the Este of Ferrara, the Viceroys of Naples and so forth had at their disposal. One poor historian, named Giannone, did seek to raise a corner of the veil, but as he ventured only to tell a very small part of the truth, and even then only by using ambiguous and obscure expressions, he made himself extremely tedious, which did not prevent him from dying in prison at the age of eighty-two, on March 7th, 1758.

The first thing to be done, then, if one wishes to learn the history of Italy, is on no account to read the authors generally commended; nowhere has the value of a lie been better appreciated, nowhere has lying been better rewarded.[1]

The earliest histories to be written in Italy, after the great wave of barbarism in the ninth century, make mention already of the brigands, and speak of them as though they had existed from time immemorial. (See Muratori's collection.) When, unfortunately for the general welfare, for justice, for good government, but fortunately for the arts, the mediaeval Republics were overthrown, the most energetic among the Republicans, those who loved freedom more than the majority of their fellow-citizens, took refuge in the forests. Naturally a populace harassed by the Baglioni, the Malatesta, the Bentivoglio, the Medici, etc., loved and respected their enemies. The cruelties of the petty tyrants who succeeded the first usurpers, the cruelties, for instance, of Cosimo, the first Duke of Florence, who had the Republicans who had fled to Venice, and even to Paris, slain, furnished recruits to these brigands. To speak only of the times in which our heroine lived, about the year 1550, Alfonso Piccolomini, Duca di Monte Mariano, and Marco Sciarra led with success armed bands which, in the neighbourhood of Albano, used to brave the Pope's soldiers, who at that time were very brave indeed. The line of operations of these famous chiefs, whom the populace still admire, extended from

[1] Paolo Giovio, Bishop of Como, Aretino, and a hundred others less amusing, whom the dulness that they diffuse has saved from disrepute, Robertson, Roscoe are full of lies. Guicciardini sold himself to Cosimo I, who treated him with contempt. In our time, Coletta and Pignotti have told the truth, the latter with the constant fear of being disgraced, although he refused to allow his work to be printed until after his death.

[ 15 ]

the Po and the marshes of Ravenna as far as the woods that then covered Vesuvius. The forest of la Faggiola, rendered so famous by their exploits, and situated five leagues from Rome, on the way to Naples, was the head-quarters of Sciarra, who, during the Pontificate of Gregory XIII, had often several thousands of men under his command. The detailed history of this illustrious brigand would appear incredible to the present generation, for the reason that no one would ever be able to understand the motives of his actions. He was not defeated until 1592. When he saw that his affairs were in a desperate state, he made terms with the Venetian Republic, and transferred himself to its service, with the most devoted, or most criminal (as you please) of his men. At the request of the Roman Government, Venice, which had signed a treaty with Sciarra, had him put to death, and sent his brave soldiers to defend the Isle of Candia against the Turks. But Venice in her wisdom knew well that a deadly plague was raging in Candia, and in a few days the five hundred soldiers whom Sciarra had brought to the service of the Republic were reduced to sixty-seven.

This forest of la Faggiola, whose giant trees screen an extinct volcano, was the final scene of the exploits of Marco Sciarra. Every traveller will tell you that it is the most impressive spot in that marvellous Roman Campagna, whose sombre aspect appears made for tragedy. It crowns with its dusky verdure the summit of Monte Albano.

It is to a volcanic eruption centuries earlier than the foundation of Rome that we owe this splendid mountain. At an epoch before any of the histories, it rose in the midst of the vast plain which at one time extended from the Apennines to the sea. Monte Cavi, which rises surrounded by the dusky shade of la Faggiola, is its culminating point: it is visible from all sides, from Terracina and

Ostia as well as from Rome and Tivoli, and it is the mountain of Albano, covered now with palaces, which closes to the south that Roman horizon so familiar to travellers. A convent of Blackfriars has taken the place, on the summit of Monte Cavi, of the temple of Jupiter Feretrius, where the Latin peoples came to sacrifice in common and to confirm the bonds of a sort of religious federation. Protected by the shade of magnificent chestnuts, the traveller arrives after some hours at the enormous blocks which mark the ruins of the temple of Jupiter; but beneath this dark shade, so delicious in that climate, even to-day, the traveller peers anxiously into the depths of the forest; he is afraid of brigands. On reaching the summit of Monte Cavi, we light a fire in the ruins of the temple, to prepare our meal. From this point, which commands the whole of the Roman Campagna, we perceive, to the west of us, the sea, which seems to be within a stone's throw, although three or four leagues away; we can distinguish the smallest vessels; with the least powerful glass, we can count the people who are journeying to Naples on board the steamer. To all the other points of the compass, the view extends over a magnificent plain, which is bounded on the east by the Apennines above Palestrina, and to the north by Saint Peter's and the other great buildings of Rome. Monte Cavi being of no great height, the eye can make out the minutest details of this sublime landscape, which might well dispense with any historical association, and yet every clump of trees, every fragment of ruined wall, catching the eye in the plain or on the slopes of the mountain, recalls one of those battles, so admirable for their patriotism and their valour, which Livy has put on record.

And we to-day can still follow, on our way to the enormous blocks, the remains of the temple of Jupiter Feretrius, which serve as a wall to the garden of the

Blackfriars, the *triumphal road* travelled long ago by the
first Kings of Rome. It is paved with stones cut with
great regularity; and, in the middle of the forest of la
Faggiola, we come upon long sections of it.

On the lip of the crater which, filled now with clear
water, has become the charming lake of Albano, five or
six miles in circumference, so deeply embedded in its
socket of lava, stood Alba, the mother of Rome, which
Roman policy destroyed in the days of the first kings.
Its ruins, however, still exist. Some centuries later, a
quarter of a league from Alba, on the slope of the mountain that faces the sea, arose Albano, the modern city;
but it is divided from the lake by a screen of rocks which
hide the lake from the city and the city from the lake.
When one sees it from the plain, its white buildings stand
out against the dark, profound verdure of the forest so
dear to the brigands and so often made famous, which
crowns the volcanic mountain on every side.

Albano, which numbers to-day five or six thousand inhabitants, had not three thousand in 1540, when there
flourished, in the highest rank of the nobility, the powerful family of Campireali, whose misfortunes we are about
to relate.

I translate this story from two bulky manuscripts, one
Roman, the other Florentine. At great risk to myself,
I have ventured to reproduce their style, which is more
or less that of our old legends. So fine and restrained
a style as is fashionable at the present day would, I feel,
have been too little in keeping with the events recorded,
and less still with the reflexions of the writers. They
wrote about the year 1598. I crave the reader's indulgence as well for them as for myself.

## II

"HAVING committed to writing so many tragic histories," says the author of the Florentine manuscript, "I shall conclude with that one which, among them all, it most pains me to relate. I am going to speak of that famous Abbess of the Convent of the Visitation at Castro, Elena de' Campireali, whose trial and death caused so great a stir in the high society of Rome and of Italy. As far back as 1555, brigands reigned in the neighbourhood of Rome, the magistrates were sold to the powerful families. In the year 1572, which was that of the trial, Gregory XIII, Buoncompagni, ascended the Throne of Saint Peter. This holy pontiff combined all the apostolic virtues but has been blamed for a certain weakness in his civil government: he was unable either to select honest judges or to suppress the brigands; he burdened his soul with crimes which he could not punish. He felt that, in inflicting the death penalty, he was taking upon himself a terrible responsibility. The result of this attitude was to people with an almost innumerable host of brigands the roads that lead to the eternal city. To travel with any security, one had to be a friend of the brigands. The forest of la Faggiola, lying astride of the road that runs to Naples by Albano, had long been the headquarters of a government unfriendly to that of His Holiness, and on several occasions Rome was obliged to treat, as one power with another, with Marco Sciarra, one of the kings of the forest. What gave these brigands their strength was that they had endeared themselves to their peasant neighbours.

# THE ABBESS OF CASTRO

"This charming town of Albano, so close to the brigand headquarters, witnessed the birth, in 1542, of Elena de' Campireali. Her father was reckoned the wealthiest patrician of the district, and in this capacity had married Vittoria Carafa, who owned a large estate in the Kingdom of Naples. I could name several old men still living who knew both Vittoria Carafa and her daughter quite well. Vittoria was a model of prudence and sense; but despite all her cleverness she could not avert the ruin of her family. And this is curious: the terrible misfortunes which are to form the melancholy subject of my story cannot, it seems to me, be ascribed especially to any of the actors whom I am going to present to the reader: I see people who are unfortunate, but truly I cannot find any that are to be blamed. The extreme beauty and tender heart of the young Elena were two great perils for her, and form an excuse for Giulio Branciforte, her lover, just as the absolute want of sense of Monsignor Cittadini, Bishop of Castro, may excuse him also up to a certain point. He had owed his rapid advancement in the scale of ecclesiastical dignities to the honesty of his conduct, and above all to the most noble bearing and most regularly handsome features that one could hope to meet. I find it written of him that one could not set eyes on him without loving him.

"As I do not wish to flatter anyone, I shall make no attempt to conceal the fact that a holy friar of the Convent of Monte Cavi, who had often been surprised, in his cell, floating at a height of several feet from the ground, like Saint Paul, when nothing but divine grace could maintain him in that extraordinary posture,[1] had prophesied

---

[1] Even to-day, this singular position is regarded by the populace of the Roman Campagna as a sure sign of sanctity. About the year 1826, a monk of Albano was seen many times raised from the ground by divine grace. Many miracles were ascribed

[ 20 ]

to Signor de' Campireali that his family would be extinguished with him, and that he would have but two children, each of whom was to perish by a violent death. It was on account of this prophecy that he could find no one to marry in the district, and went to seek his fortune at Naples, where he was lucky enough to find great possessions and a wife capable, by her intelligence, of averting his evil destiny, had such a thing been possible. This Signor de' Campireali was considered a most honourable man, and dispensed charity lavishly; but he lacked spirit, which meant that gradually he withdrew from the annual visit to Rome, and ended by passing almost the whole year in his palazzo at Albano. He devoted himself to the cultivation of his estates, situated in that rich plain which extends from the city to the sea. On the advice of his wife, he caused the most splendid education to be given to his son Fabio, a young man extremely proud of his birth, and his daughter Elena, who was a marvel of beauty, as may be seen to this day from her portrait, which is preserved in the Farnese collection. Since I began to write her history I have gone to the palazzo Farnese to consider the mortal envelope which heaven had bestowed upon this woman, whose grim destiny caused so much stir in her own time, and even now still finds a place in human memory. The shape of the head is an elongated oval, the brow is very large, the hair of a dark gold. Her general air is on the whole one of gaiety; she had large eyes with a profound expression, and chestnut eyebrows that formed a perfectly traced arch. The lips are very thin, and you would say that the lines of her mouth had been drawn by the famous painter Correggio. Viewed

to him; people came from a radius of twenty leagues to receive his blessing; women, belonging to the highest ranks of society, had seen him floating in his cell three feet from the ground. Suddenly he vanished.

amid the portraits which hang on either side of hers in the Farnese gallery, she has the air of a queen. It is very seldom that an air of gaiety is found in combination with majesty.

"Having spent eight whole years as a boarder in the Convent of the Visitation in the town of Castro, now destroyed, to which, in those days, the majority of the Roman princes sent their daughters, Elena returned to her home, but did not leave the convent without first making an oblation of a splendid chalice to the high altar of the church. No sooner had she returned to Albano than her father summoned from Rome, at a considerable salary, the celebrated poet Cecchino, then a man of great age; he enriched Elena's mind with the finest passages of the divine Virgil, and of Petrarch, Ariosto and Dante, his famous disciples."

Here the translator is obliged to omit a long dissertation on the varying degrees of fame which the sixteenth century assigned to these great poets. It would appear that Elena knew Latin. The poetry that she was made to learn spoke of love, and of a love that would seem to us highly ridiculous, were we to come across it in 1839; I mean the passionate love that feeds on great sacrifices, that can exist only when wrapped in mystery, and borders always on the most dreadful calamities.

Such was the love that was inspired in Elena, then barely seventeen, by Giulio Branciforte. He was one of her neighbours, and very poor; he lived in a wretched house built on the side of the mountain, a quarter of a league from the town, amid the ruins of Alba, and on the edge of the precipice of one hundred and fifty feet, screened with foliage, which surrounds the lake. This house, which stood within the sombre and splendid shade of the forest of la Faggiola, was afterwards demolished, when the convent of Palazzuola was built. The poor

young man had no advantages beyond his lively and light-
hearted manner and the unfeigned indifference with which
he endured his misfortunes. The most that could be said
in his favour was that his face was expressive without
being handsome. But he was understood to have fought
gallantly under the command of Prince Colonna, and
among his *bravi,* in two or three highly dangerous enterprises. Despite his poverty, despite his want of good
looks, he possessed nevertheless, in the eyes of all the
young women of Albano, the heart that it would have
been most gratifying to win. Well received everywhere,
Giulio Branciforte had made none but the easiest con-
quests, until the moment when Elena returned from the
convent of Castro. "When, shortly afterwards, the great
poet Cecchino moved from Rome to the palazzo Campireali,
to teach the girl literature, Giulio, who knew him, sent
him a set of Latin verses on the good fortune that had
befallen him in his old age, in seeing so fine a pair of eyes
fastened upon his own, and so pure a heart become perfectly happy when he deigned to bestow his approval upon
its thoughts. The jealousy and disgust of the girls to
whom Giulio had been paying attention before Elena's return soon rendered vain every precaution that he might
take to conceal a dawning passion, and I must confess
that this affair between a young man of two and twenty
and a girl of seventeen was carried on in a fashion of which
prudence could not approve. Three months had not gone
by before Signor de' Campireali observed that Giulio
Branciforte was in the habit of passing unduly often beneath the windows of his palazzo (which is still to be seen
about half way along the high road that leads up to the
lake)."

Freedom of speech and rudeness, natural consequences
of the liberty which Republics tolerate, and the habit of
giving way to passions not yet subdued by the manners of

a monarchy appear unconcealed in the first steps taken by
Signor de' Campireali. On the very day on which he had
taken offence at the frequent appearance of young Branciforte, he addressed him in these terms:

"How is it you dare loiter about like this all day in front
of my house, and have the impertinence to stare up at my
daughter's windows, you who have not even a coat to your
back? Were I not afraid that such an action might be
misinterpreted by my neighbours, I should give you three
gold sequins, and you would go to Rome and buy yourself a more decent jacket. At any rate my eyes and my
daughter's would not be offended any more by the sight of
your rags."

Elena's father no doubt exaggerated: young Branciforte's clothes were by no means rags; they were made of
the plainest materials; but, although spotlessly clean and
often brushed, it must be admitted that their appearance
betokened long wear. Giulio was so cut to the heart by
Signor Campireali's reproaches that he ceased to appear
by day outside his house.

As we have said, the two lines of arches, remains of an
ancient aqueduct, which formed the main walls of the
house built by Branciforte's father and left by him to his
son, were no more than five or six hundred yards from
Albano. In coming down from this higher ground to the
modern city, Giulio was obliged to pass by the palazzo
Campireali. Elena soon remarked the absence of the singular young man who, her friends told her, had abandoned
all other society in order to consecrate himself wholly to
the pleasure which he appeared to find in gazing at her.

One summer evening, towards midnight, Elena's window
stood open, the girl herself was enjoying the sea breeze
which makes itself felt quite distinctly on the hillside of
Albano, albeit the town is divided from the sea by a plain
three leagues in width. The night was dark, the silence

profound; one could have heard a leaf fall to the ground. Elena, leaning upon her window sill, may have been thinking of Giulio, when she caught sight of something like the soundless wing of a nocturnal bird which passed gently to and fro close to her window. She drew back in alarm. It never occurred to her that this object might be being held up by some passer-by: the second storey of the palazzo, from which her window looked, was more than fifty feet from the ground. Suddenly she thought she identified a bunch of flowers in this strange article which amid a profound silence kept passing to and fro outside the window on the sill of which she was leaning; her heart beat violently. These flowers appeared to her to be fastened to the extremity of two or three of those *canne,* a large kind of reed not unlike the bamboo, which grow in the Roman Campagna, and send up shoots to a height of twenty or thirty feet. The flexibility of the reeds and the strength of the breeze made it difficult for Giulio to keep his nosegay exactly opposite the window from which he supposed that Elena might be looking out, and besides, the night was so dark that from the street one could make out nothing at that height. Standing motionless inside her window, Elena was deeply stirred. To take these flowers, would not that be an admission? Not that she experienced any of the feelings to which an adventure of this sort would give rise, in our day, in a girl of the best society prepared for life by a thorough education. As her father and her brother Fabio were in the house, her first thought was that the least sound would be followed by a shot from an arquebus aimed at Giulio; she was moved to pity by the risk which that poor young man was running. Her second thought was that, although she as yet knew him very slightly, he was nevertheless the person she loved best in the world after her own family. At length, after hesitating for some minutes, she took the

nosegay, and, as she touched the flowers in the intense
darkness, could feel that a note was tied to the stem of
one of them; she ran to the great staircase to read this
note by the light of the lamp that burned before the image
of the Madonna. "How rash!" she said to herself when
the opening lines had made her blush with joy; "If anyone
sees me, I am lost, and my family will persecute that poor
young man for ever." She returned to her room and
lighted the lamp. This was an exquisite moment for
Giulio, who, ashamed of his action and as though to hide
himself even in the pitch darkness, had flattened himself
against the enormous trunk of one of those weirdly shaped
evergreen oaks which are still to be seen opposite the
palazzo Campireali.

In his letter Giulio related with the most perfect simplicity the crushing reprimand that had been addressed
to him by Elena's father. "I am poor, it is true," he went
on, "and you would find it hard to imagine the whole extent of my poverty. I have only my house which you may
have observed beneath the ruins of the Alban aqueduct;
round the house is a garden which I cultivate myself, and
live upon its produce. I also possess a vineyard which is
leased at thirty scudi a year. I do not know, really, why
I love you; certainly I cannot suggest that you should
come and share my poverty. And yet, if you do not love
me, life has no further value for me; it is useless to tell
you that I would give it a thousand times over for you. And
yet, before your return from the convent, that life was by
no means wretched; on the contrary, it was filled with the
most dazzling dreams. So that I can say that the sight
of happiness has made me unhappy. To be sure, no one
in the world would then have dared to say the things to
me with which your father lashed me; my dagger would
have done him prompt justice. Then, with my courage and
my weapons, I reckoned myself a match for anyone; I

wanted nothing. Now it is all altered: I have known **fear**. I have written too much; perhaps you despise me. If, on the other hand, you have any pity for me, in spite of the poor clothes that cover me, you will observe that every night, when twelve strikes from the Capuchin convent at the top of the hill, I am hiding beneath the great oak, opposite the window at which I never cease to gaze, because I suppose it to be that of your room. If you do not despise me as your father does, throw me down one of the flowers from your nosegay, but take care that it is not caught on one of the cornices, or on one of the balconies of your palazzo."

This letter was read many times; gradually Elena's eyes filled with tears; she tenderly examined this splendid nosegay, the flowers of which were tied together with a strong silken cord. She tried to pull out a flower, but failed; then she was seized with remorse. Among Roman girls, to pull out a flower, to damage in any way a nosegay given in love, means risking the death of that love. Fearing lest Giulio might be growing impatient, she ran to her window; but, on reaching it, suddenly reflected that she was too easily visible, the lamp flooding the room with light. Elena could not think what signal she might allow herself to give; it seemed as though there were none that did not say a great deal too much.

Covered with shame, she ran back into her room. But time was flying; suddenly an idea occurred to her which threw her into unspeakable confusion: Giulio would think that, like her father, she despised his poverty! She saw a little specimen of a precious marble lying on her table, tied it in her handkerchief and threw the handkerchief down to the foot of the oak opposite her window. She then made a sign that he was to go; she heard Giulio obey her; for, as he went away, he no longer sought to muffle the sound of his step. When he had reached the summit

[ 27 ]

of the girdle of rocks which separates the lake from the
last houses of Albano, she heard him singing words of
love; she made him signals of farewell, this time less timid,
then began to read his letter again.

The following evening, and every evening after this
there were similar letters and assignations; but as everything is observed in an Italian village, and as Elena was
by far the greatest heiress in the place, Signor de' Campireali was informed that every evening, after midnight,
a light was seen in his daughter's room; and, what was far
more extraordinary, the window was open, and indeed
Elena stood there as though she were in no fear of *zanzare*
(an extremely troublesome kind of midge, which greatly
spoils the fine evenings in the Roman Campagna. Here
I must once again crave the reader's indulgence. When
one is trying to understand the ways of foreign countries,
one must expect to find very grim ideas, very different
from our own). Signor de' Campireali made ready his
own arquebus and his son's. That evening, as the clock
struck a quarter to twelve, he called Fabio, and the two
stole out, making as little sound as possible, on to a great
stone balcony which projected from the first floor of the
palazzo immediately beneath Elena's window. The massive pillars of the stone balustrade gave them breast-high
cover from the fire of any arquebus that might be aimed
at them from without. Midnight struck; father and son
could hear quite distinctly a slight sound from beneath
the trees which bordered the street opposite their palazzo;
but, and this filled them with surprise, no light appeared
at Elena's window. This girl, so simple until then, and
to all appearances a child, from the spontaneity of her
movements, had changed in character since she had been
in love. She knew that the slightest imprudence jeopard-
ised her lover's life; if a gentleman of the importance
of her father killed a poor man like Giulio Branciforte, he

could clear himself by disappearing for three months, which he would spend at Naples; during that time, his friends in Rome would settle the matter, and all would be ended with the offer of a silver lamp costing some hundreds of scudi to the altar of the Madonna in fashion at the moment. That day, at luncheon, Elena had read on her father's features that he had some grave cause for anger, and, from the way in which he watched her when he thought that he was not observed, she concluded that she herself was largely responsible for this anger. She went at once and sprinkled a little dust on the stocks of the five splendid arquebuses which her father kept hanging by his bed. She covered also with a fine layer of dust his swords and daggers. All day she shewed a wild gaiety, running incessantly from top to bottom of the house; at every moment she went to the windows, quite determined to make Giulio a negative signal, should she be so fortunate as to catch sight of him. But there was no chance of that: the poor fellow had been so profoundly humiliated by the onslaught made on him by the rich Signor de' Campireali, that by day he never appeared in Albano; duty alone brought him there on Sundays to the parochial mass. Elena's mother, who adored her and could refuse her nothing, went out with her three times that day, but all in vain: Elena saw no sign of Giulio. She was in despair. What were her feelings when, on going towards nightfall to examine her father's weapons, she saw that two arquebuses had been loaded, and that almost all the swords and daggers had been handled. She was distracted from her mortal anxiety only by the extreme care she took to appear to suspect nothing. On retiring to bed at ten o'clock, she turned the key in the door of her room, which opened into her mother's ante-room, then remained glued to her window, leaning upon the sill in such a way as not to be visible from without. One may judge of the anxiety

with which she heard the hours strike: it was no longer
a question of the reproaches which she often heaped on
herself for the rapidity with which she had attached herself to Giulio, which might render her less worthy in his
eyes of love. This day did more to strengthen the young
man's position than six months of constancy and protestations. "What is the use of lying?" Elena said to herself.
"Do I not love him with all my heart and soul?"

At half past eleven she saw quite plainly her father and
brother ambush themselves on the great stone balcony beneath her window. A minute or two after midnight had
sounded from the Capuchin convent, she heard quite plainly
also the step of her lover, who stopped beneath the great
oak; she noticed with joy that her father and brother
seemed to have heard nothing: it required the anxiety of
love to distinguish so faint a sound.

"Now," she said to herself, "they are going to kill me,
but at all costs they must not intercept this evening's letter, they would persecute my poor Giulio for ever." She
made the sign of the Cross, and, holding on with one hand
to the iron balcony of her window, leaned out, thrusting
herself as far forward as possible over the street. Not
a quarter of a minute had passed when the nosegay, fastened as usual to a long cane, came brushing against her
arms. She seized the nosegay, but, as she wrenched it
vigorously from the cane to the end of which it was tied,
she caused the said cane to strike against the stone balcony. At once two arquebus shots rang out, followed by
complete silence. Her brother Fabio, not knowing, in the
darkness, whether what was tapping violently against the
balcony might not be a cord with the help of which Giulio
was climbing down from his sister's room, had fired at her
balcony; next day she found the mark of the bullet, which
had flattened itself against the iron. Signor de' Campireali
had fired into the street, beneath the stone balcony, for

THE ABBESS OF CASTRO

Giulio had made some noise in catching the cane as it fell.
Giulio, for his part, hearing a noise above his head, had
guessed what would follow, and had taken cover beneath
the projection of the balcony.

Fabio quickly reloaded his arquebus, and, heedless of
anything that his father might say, ran to the garden of
the house, quietly opened a little door which gave on one
of the adjoining streets and stole out on tiptoe to see for
himself who the people were that were walking beneath
the balcony of the palazzo. At that moment Giulio who,
this evening, was well escorted, was within twenty paces
of him, flattened against a tree. Elena, leaning from her
balcony and trembling for her lover, at once began a conversation at the top of her voice with her brother, whom
she could hear moving in the street; she asked him if
he had killed the robbers.

"Do not imagine that I am taken in by your wicked
tricks!" he called up to her from the street which he was
exploring in every direction, "but prepare your tears, I
am going to kill the insolent wretch who dares to approach
your window."

No sooner had these words been uttered than Elena
heard her mother knock at the door of her room.

She made haste to open it, saying that she could not
conceive how the door had come to be locked.

"No make-believe with me, my dear angel," her mother
told her; "your father is furious, and will perhaps kill
you: come and lie down with me in my bed; and, if you have
a letter, give it to me, I will hide it."

Elena said to her:

"Here is the nosegay; the letter is hidden among the
flowers."

Scarcely were mother and daughter in bed, when Signor de' Campireali entered his wife's room; he came from
her oratory, to which he had paid a visit, overturning

everything in it. What impressed Elena was that her father, pale as a spectre, was acting in a slow, deliberate fashion, like a man who has entirely made up his mind. "I am as good as dead!" she said to herself.

"We rejoice that we have children," said her father as he passed by his wife's bed on his way to his daughter's room, trembling with rage, but affecting a perfect calm; "we rejoice that we have children, we ought rather to shed tears of blood when those children are girls. Great God! Is it indeed possible! Their loose conduct is capable of destroying the honour of a man who in sixty years has never given anyone the slightest hold over him."

So saying, he passed into his daughter's room.

"I am lost," Elena told her mother, "the letters are beneath the pedestal of the crucifix, beside the window."

At once the mother sprang out of bed and ran after her husband; she shouted out to him the most senseless things imaginable, to stimulate his anger; in this she was entirely successful. The old man became furious, he broke everything in his daughter's room; but the mother was able to remove the letters unobserved. An hour later, when Signor de' Campireali had returned to his own room next door to his wife's, and all was quiet in the house, the mother said to her daughter:

"Here are your letters, I have no wish to read them, you see what they might have cost us! If I were you, I would burn them. Good night, kiss me."

Elena returned to her own room, dissolved in tears; it seemed to her that, after these words from her mother, she no longer loved Giulio. Then she made ready to burn his letters; but, before destroying them, could not refrain from reading them again. She read them so carefully and so often that the sun was already high in the heavens when at length she determined to listen to the voice of reason.

[ 32 ]

On the following day, which was a Sunday, Elena walked to the parish church with her mother; fortunately, her father did not follow them. The first person on whom her eyes fell in church was Giulio Branciforte. A glance at him assured her that he was not injured. Her happiness knew no bounds; the events of the night were a million leagues away from her memory. She had prepared five or six little notes scribbled on old scraps of paper stained with a mixture of earth and water, such as might naturally be found lying on the floor of a church; each of these notes contained the same warning:

*"They have discovered all, except his name. He must not appear again in the street; a certain person will come here often."*

Elena let fall one of these scraps of paper; a glance was sufficient to warn Giulio, who picked it up and vanished. On her return home, an hour later, she found on the great staircase of the palazzo a fragment of paper which attracted her attention by its exact resemblance to those of which she had made use that morning. She took possession of it, without even her mother's noticing anything; and read:

*"In three days he will return from Rome, where he is forced to go. There will be singing by daylight, on market-days, above the din made by the peasants, about ten o'clock."*

This departure for Rome seemed to Elena strange. "Does it mean that he is afraid of my brother's arquebus?" she asked herself sadly. Love pardons everything, except a deliberate absence; that being the worst of tortures. Instead of passing in a delightful dream and being wholly occupied in weighing the reasons that one has for loving one's lover, life is then agitated by cruel doubts. "But, after all, can I believe that he no longer loves me?" Elena asked herself during the three long days of Branciforte's

[ 33 ]

absence. Suddenly her grief gave way to a wild joy: on the third day, she saw him appear in the full light of noon, strolling in the street in front of her father's palazzo. He was wearing new, almost grand clothes. Never had the nobility of his bearing and the gay and courageous simplicity of his features shone to better advantage; never either, before that day, had there been so much talk in Albano of Giulio's poverty. It was the men, the young men especially, who repeated that cruel word; the women, and especially the girls, never wearied in their praises of his fine appearance.

Giulio spent the whole day walking about the town; he appeared to be making up for the months of seclusion to which his poverty had condemned him. As befits a man in love, Giulio was well armed beneath his new tunic. Apart from his dirk and dagger, he had put on his *giacco* (a sort of long waistcoat of chain mail, extremely uncomfortable to wear, but a cure, to these Italian hearts, for a sad malady, the piercing attacks of which were incessantly felt in that age, I mean the fear of being killed at the street corner by one of the enemies one knew oneself to have). On the day in question, Giulio hoped for a glimpse of Elena, and moreover felt some repugnance at the thought of being left to his own company in his lonely house: for the following reason. Ranuccio, an old soldier of his father, after having served with him in ten campaigns in the troops of various *condottieri,* and finally in those of Marco Sciarra, had followed his captain when the latter's wounds forced him to retire. Captain Branciforte had reasons for not living in Rome: he was exposed there to the risk of meeting the sons of men whom he had killed; even at Albano, he was by no means anxious to place himself entirely at the mercy of constituted authority. Instead of buying or leasing a house in the town, he preferred to build one so situated that its occupant could see visitors approaching a long way off. He found amid the ruins of Alba an admirable site: one could, unobserved by indiscreet visitors, slip away into the forest where ruled his old friend and patron, Prince Fabrizio Colonna. Captain Branciforte gave no thought to his son's future. When he retired from the service, only fifty years old, but riddled with wounds, he calculated that he had still some ten years of life, and, having built his house, spent every year a tenth part of what he had collected in the lootings of towns and villages in which he had had the honour to take part.

He purchased the vineyard which brought in a rental of thirty scudi to his son as a retort to the sneer of a burgess of Albano, who had said to him, one day when he was disputing hotly over the interests and honour of the town, that it was evidently right and proper for so rich a proprietor as himself to give advice to the *anziani* of Albano. The captain bought the vineyard, and announced that he would buy any number more: then, meeting his critic in a solitary place, killed him with a pistol shot.

After eight years of this sort of life, the captain died; his supporter Ranuccio adored Giulio; nevertheless, weary of idleness, he took service once again in Prince Colonna's band. He often came to see *his son Giulio,* for so he called him, and, on the eve of a perilous assault which the Prince was about to face in his fortress of la Petrella, he had taken Giulio with him to fight. Finding him to be extremely brave:

"You must be mad," he told him, "and very easily satisfied, to be living on the outskirts of Albano like the humblest and poorest of its inhabitants, when with what I have seen you do and your father's name you might be a brilliant soldier of fortune among us, and, what is more, make your fortune."

Giulio was tormented by these words; he knew the

Latin that had been taught him by a priest, but, as his father had always laughed at everything that the priest said apart from his Latin, he had absolutely no education. At the same time, despised for his poverty, isolated in his lonely house, he had acquired a certain commonsense which, by its boldness, would have astonished men of learning. For instance, before falling in love with Elena, and without knowing why, he loved war, but he felt a repugnance towards pillage, which, in the eyes of his father the captain and of Ranuccio, was like the short play intended to raise a laugh which follows the noble tragedy. Since he had been in love with Elena, this commonsense, the fruit of his solitary reflexions, had been torturing Giulio. So light-hearted before, he now dared not consult anyone as to his doubts, his heart was full of passion and misery. What would not Signor de' Campireali say if he knew him to be a soldier of fortune? This time, his reproaches would not be without foundation! Giulio had always reckoned upon the military profession, as a sure resource when he should have spent the price of the gold chains and other jewels which he had found in his father's strong-box. If Giulio had no scruple as to carrying off (he, so poor) the daughter of the rich Signor de' Campireali, it was because in those days fathers disposed of their property after their death as they pleased, and Signor de' Campireali might very well leave his daughter a thousand scudi as her entire fortune. Another problem kept Giulio's imagination closely occupied: first of all, in what city should he install young Elena after he had married her and carried her off from her father? Secondly, with what money was he to support her?

When Signor de' Campireali addressed to him that stinging reproach which he had felt so keenly, Giulio remained for two days a victim to the most violent rage and grief: he could not make up his mind either to kill the insolent

old man, or to let him live. He passed whole nights in
tears; at length he decided to consult Ranuccio, the one
friend that he had in the world; but would that friend
understand him? It was in vain that he sought for
Ranuccio throughout the forest of la Faggiola, he was
obliged to take the road to Naples, past Velletri, where
Ranuccio was in command of an ambuscade: he was waiting there, with a large company, for Ruiz d'Avalos, a
Spanish General, who was proceeding to Rome by land,
forgetting that, not long since, before a large audience, he
had spoken with contempt of the soldiers of fortune of the
Colonna band. His chaplain reminded him most oppor-
tunely of this little circumstance, and Ruiz d'Avalos decided to charter a vessel and to approach Rome by sea.

As soon as Captain Ranuccio had heard Giulio's story:
"Describe to me exactly," he said to him, "the person
of this Signor de' Campireali, that his imprudence may not
cost the life of some worthy inhabitant of Albano. As soon
as the business that is keeping us here is brought to an
end one way or the other, you will take yourself off to
Rome, where you will take care to shew yourself in the
inns and other public places at all hours of the day; you
must not let anyone suspect you, on account of your love
for the daughter."

Giulio had great difficulty in calming the anger of his
father's old comrade. He was obliged to lose his temper.
"Do you suppose that I am asking you for your sword?"
he said finally. "Surely I have a sword, myself! I ask
you for good advice."

Ranuccio ended every speech with these words:
"You are young, you have no wounds; the insult was
public: a man who has lost his honour is despised, even
by women."

Giulio told him that he desired time for further reflexion as to what his heart wished, and despite the protesta-

tions of Ranuccio, who was quite determined that he should take part in the attack upon the Spanish General's escort, where, he said, there would be honour to be won, not to mention the doubloons, Giulio returned alone to his little house. It was there that, the day before that on which Signor de' Campireali fired an arquebus at him, he had entertained Ranuccio and his corporal, who had come there from the neighbourhood of Velletri. Ranuccio employed force to open the little iron strong box in which his patron, Captain Branciforte, used to lock up the gold chains and other jewels which he did not choose to convert into cash immediately after an expedition. He found in it two scudi.

"I advise you to become a monk," he said to Giulio, "you have all the necessary virtues: love of poverty, here is a proof of it; humility, you allow yourself to be black-guarded in the public street by a rich townsman of Albano; you want only hypocrisy and gluttony."

Ranuccio insisted on putting fifty doubloons into the iron box.

"I give you my word," he said to Giulio, "that if within a month from to-day Signor de' Campireali is not buried with all the honours due to his nobility and wealth, my corporal here present will come with thirty men to pull down your little house and burn your wretched furniture. Captain Branciforte's son must not cut a poor figure in this world, on the strength of being in love."

When Signor de' Campireali and his son fired the two shots from their arquebuses, Ranuccio and the corporal had taken up their position beneath the stone balcony, and Giulio had the greatest possible difficulty in restraining them from killing Fabio, when that young man made an imprudent sally through the garden, as we have already related. The argument that calmed Ranuccio was as follows: it is not right to kill a young man who may grow

up and become of use in the world, while there exists an
aged sinner more guilty than he, and fit only to fill a grave.

The day after this adventure, Ranuccio disappeared into
the forest, and Giulio set out for Rome. The joy which
he felt in buying fine clothes with the doubloons which
Ranuccio had given him, was cruelly marred by an idea
quite extraordinary for that time, and one that foreboded
the exalted destiny that was in store for him: he kept
saying to himself: "Elena must be told who I am." Any
other man of his age and period would have thought only
of enjoying his love and carrying off Elena, without asking himself for a moment what was to become of her in
six months' time, any more than what opinion she would
form of himself.

On his return to Albano, and on the afternoon of the
day on which he displayed before the eyes of all the town
the fine clothes that he had brought back from Rome,
Giulio learned from old Scotti, his friend, that Fabio had
left the town on horseback, on a journey of three leagues
to a property which his father owned in the plain, by the
sea-coast. Later in the day, he saw Signor de' Campireali, accompanied by two priests, take the road leading
to the magnificent avenue of evergreen oaks that crowns
the edge of the crater in which the lake of Albano lies.
Ten minutes later, an old woman boldly made her way
into the palazzo de' Campireali, on the pretext of offering
some fine fruit for sale; the first person that she met was
the little maid Marietta, the confidential friend of her mistress Elena, who blushed to the whites of her eyes on receiving a fine nosegay. The letter concealed in the nosegay was of a preposterous length: Giulio related all his
feelings since the night of the arquebus-shots; but, by a
very singular piece of modesty, did not venture to confess
what any other young man of his day would have been so
proud to make known, namely that he was the son of a

Captain famous for his adventures, and that he himself
had already given proof of his valour in more than one
combat. He felt that he could hear the reflexions which
these deeds would inspire in old Campireali. It must be
understood that in the sixteenth century the young women,
their outlook being more akin to republican commonsense,
esteemed a man far more highly for what he had done
himself than for the riches amassed by his fathers or for
their famous deeds. But it was principally the young
women of humble birth that entertained these ideas. Those
who belonged to the rich or noble class were afraid of the
brigands, and, as is natural, had a great regard for nobility and opulence. Giulio ended his letter with the
words: "I do not know whether the more becoming clothes
which I have brought back from Rome have made you
forget the cruel insult that a person whom you respect
addressed to me recently, with regard to my shabby appearance; I could have avenged myself, I ought to have
done so, my honour commanded it; I refrained in consideration of the tears which my revenge would have brought
to a pair of eyes that I adore. This may prove to you, if,
unfortunately for me, you should still doubt it, that one
can be extremely poor and yet have noble feelings. Apart
from this, I have to reveal to you a terrible secret; I should
certainly find no difficulty in telling it to any other woman;
but somehow I shudder when I think of making it known
to you. It is capable of destroying, in an instant, the
love that you feel for me; no protestation on your part
would satisfy me. I wish to read in your eyes the effect
that this admission will produce. One of these days, at
nightfall, I shall see you in the garden that lies behind
the palazzo. That day, Fabio and your father will be
away from home; when I have made certain that, notwithstanding their contempt for a poor and ill dressed young
man, they cannot deprive us of three quarters of an hour

or an hour of conversation, a man will appear beneath the windows of your palazzo, who will be shewing a tame fox to the village children. Later, when the Angelus rings, you will hear a shot fired from an arquebus in the distance; at that moment, go across to the wall of your garden, and, if you are not alone, sing. If all is silent, your slave will appear, trembling, at your feet, and will tell you things which will perhaps fill you with horror. Until that decisive day comes, a terrible day for me, I shall not take the risk again of offering you a nosegay at midnight; but about two o'clock in the morning I shall go by singing, and perhaps, watching from the great stone balcony, you will let fall a flower plucked by you in your garden. These may be the last signs of affection that you will give to the unhappy Giulio."

Three days after this, Elena's father and brother had gone on their horses to the property which they owned by the seashore; they were to start back shortly before sunset, so as to reach home about two o'clock in the morning. But, when the time came for them to take the road, not only their own two horses but every horse on the farm had disappeared. Greatly astonished by this audacious robbery, they hunted for their horses, which were not found until the following day in the forest of tall trees which lines the shore. The two Campireali, father and son, were obliged to return to Albano in a country cart drawn by oxen.

That evening, when Giulio was at Elena's feet, it was almost quite dark, and the poor girl was very glad of the darkness: she was appearing for the first time before this man whom she loved tenderly, who knew very well that she loved him, but to whom after all she had never yet spoken.

One thing that she noticed restored a little of her courage: Giulio was paler and trembled more than she. She saw him at her knees: "Truly, I am not in a fit state to speak," he said to her. There followed some moments, apparently of great happiness; they gazed at one another, but without the power to utter a single word, motionless as a group wrought in marble, but a group full of expression. Giulio was on his knees, holding one of Elena's hands; she, with bent head, was studying him attentively.

Giulio knew well that, following the advice of his friends, the young debauchees of Rome, he ought to have made some attempt; but the idea horrified him. He was aroused from this state of ecstasy and, perhaps, of the keenest happiness that love can give, by this thought: the time was passing rapidly, the Campireali were drawing near their palazzo. He realised that with so scrupulous a nature as his he could not find any lasting happiness so long as he had not made to his mistress that terrible admission which would have seemed to his Roman friends so dense a piece of stupidity.

"I have spoken to you of an admission which perhaps I ought not to make to you," he said at length to Elena.

Giulio turned very pale; he added with difficulty and as though his breath were failing:

"Perhaps I am going to see those feelings vanish, the hope of which constitutes my life. You think me poor; that is not all: *I am a brigand and the son of a brigand.*"

At these words Elena, a rich man's daughter filled with all the fears of her caste, felt that she was going to faint; she was afraid of falling to the ground. "What a grief that will be for poor Giulio!" she thought: "he will imagine that I despise him." He was at her knees. In order not to fall she leaned upon him, and a little later fell into his arms, apparently unconscious. As we see, in the sixteenth century they liked exactitude in love stories. This was because the mind did not criticise these stories, the imagination felt them, and the passion of the reader identified itself with that of their heroes. The two manuscripts which we follow, and especially the one which presents certain turns of speech peculiar to the Florentine dialect, give in the fullest detail the history of all the meetings that followed. Danger took away all sense of guilt from the girl. Often the danger was extreme; but it did nought but inflame these two hearts for which all the sensations that arose from their love were those of happiness. Several times Fabio and his father were on the point of surprising them. They were furious, believing themselves to be defied: common rumour informed them that Giulio was Elena's lover, and yet they could see nothing. Fabio, an impetuous young man and one proud of his birth, proposed to his father to have Giulio killed.

"So long as he remains in this world," he said to him, "my sister's life is a succession of the greatest dangers. Who knows but that at any moment our honour may oblige us to dip our hands in the blood of that obstinate girl? She has come to such a pitch of boldness that she no longer denies her love; you have seen her answer your reproaches only with a gloomy silence; very well, that silence is Giulio Branciforte's death sentence."

"Think of what his father was," replied Signor de' Campireali. "Certainly there is no difficulty in our going to spend six months in Rome, and, during that time, this Branciforte will disappear. But how do we know that his father, who, with all his crimes, was brave and generous, generous to the point of enriching many of his soldiers and remaining a poor man himself, how do we know that his father has not left friends behind him, either in the band of the Duca di Monte Mariano or in the Colonna band, which often occupies the woods of la Faggiola, half a league from us? In that case, we are all massacred without mercy, you, myself, and perhaps your unfortunate mother as well."

These conversations between the father and son, often repeated, were kept no secret from Vittoria Carafa, Elena's mother, and plunged her in despair. The upshot of Fabio's discussions with his father was that it did not become their honour to stand peacefully by and allow a continuance of the rumours that ran rife in Albano. Since it was not prudent to secure the disappearance of this young Branciforte who, every day, appeared more insolent than ever, and in addition, dressed now in magnificent clothes, carried his self-importance to the point of speaking, in the public thoroughfares, either to Fabio or to Signor de' Campireali himself, one, or possibly both of the following courses must be adopted: the whole family must return to live in Rome, or Elena must be sent back to the Convent of the Visitation at Castro, where she would remain until a suitable husband had been found for her.

Never had Elena confessed her love to her mother; daughter and mother loved one another tenderly, they spent their whole time together, and yet never had a single word been uttered on this subject which interested them both almost equally. For the first time the almost exclusive subject of their thoughts was expressed in words when the mother gave her daughter to understand that there was a question of removing the household to Rome, and perhaps of sending her back to spend some years in the Convent at Castro.

This conversation was imprudent on the part of Vittoria Carafa, and can be excused only by the unreasoning affection that she felt for her daughter. Elena, desperately in love, wished to prove to her lover that she was not ashamed of his poverty, and that her confidence in his honour knew no bounds. "Who would believe it?" cries the Florentine writer; "after all these daring assignations, attended with the risk of a horrible death, given in the garden, and once or twice even in her own

room, Elena was pure! Strong in her virtue, she proposed
to her lover that she should leave the palazzo, about midnight, by the garden, and spend the rest of the night in his
little house built amid the ruins of Alba, more than a quarter of a league away. They disguised themselves as Fran-
ciscan friars. Elena was of tall stature, and, thus at-
tired, appeared a young novice of eighteen or twenty.
What is incredible, and shews plainly enough the finger
of God, is that, in the narrow road cut through the rock,
which still passes under the wall of the Capuchin convent,
Giulio and his mistress, disguised as friars, met Signor de'
Campireali and his son Fabio, who, followed by four servants well armed, and preceded by a page carrying a lighted
torch, were returning from Castel Gandolfo, a town situated on the shore of the lake at no great distance. To
allow the lovers to pass, the Campireali and their servants
stood aside to the right and left of the road cut in the rock,
which is about eight feet wide. How much better would
it have been for Elena to be recognised at that moment!
She would have been killed by a shot from her father's
or her brother's pistol, and her punishment would have
lasted but an instant: but heaven had ordered otherwise
(*Dis aliter visum*).

"A further detail is added with regard to this strange
encounter, which Signora de' Campireali, in her extreme
old age, when almost a centenarian, used at times to relate
in Rome in the presence of persons of weight, who, themselves of a great age, repeated it to me when my insatiable
curiosity questioned them as to this matter and many
others.

"Fabio de' Campireali, who was a young man proud of
his courage and extremely arrogant, observing that the
elder of the friars gave no greeting either to his father or
to himself when passing so close to them, exclaimed:

" 'There's a conceited rascal of a friar! Heaven knows

what he is going to do outside his convent, he and his friend, at this time of night! I don't know why I don't pull off their cowls; we should see their faces.'

"At these words, Giulio gripped his dirk under his friar's habit, and placed himself between Fabio and Elena. At that moment he was not more than a foot away from Fabio; but heaven ordered otherwise, and by a miracle calmed the fury of these two young men, who were presently to see each other at such close quarters."

In the prosecution of Elena de' Campireali in after years, an attempt was made to present this nocturnal expedition as a proof of her corruption. It was the delirium of a young heart inflamed by a mad love, but that heart was pure.

## III

IT should be explained that the Orsini, the perpetual rivals of the Colonna, and all powerful at that time in the villages nearest to Rome, had recently procured the passing of a sentence of death, by the government courts, on a rich farmer named Baldassare Bandini, a native of la Petrella. It would take too long to relate here the various actions of which Bandini was accused: the majority would be crimes to-day, but could not be regarded in so severe a fashion in 1559. Bandini was imprisoned in a castle belonging to the Orsini, and situated in the mountains in the direction of Valmontone, six leagues from Albano. The *bargello* of Rome, accompanied by one hundred and fifty of his *sbirri*, spent a night on the road; he was coming to fetch Bandini to take him to Rome, to the Tordinona prison; Bandini had appealed to Rome from the sentence which condemned him to death. But, as we have said, he was a native of la Petrella, a fortress belonging to the Colonna; Bandini's wife appeared and publicly asked Fabrizio Colonna, who happened to be at la Petrella:

"Are you going to allow one of your faithful servants to die?"

Colonna replied:

"May I never, please God, be wanting in the respect I owe to the decisions of the courts of my Lord, the Pope!"

Immediately his soldiers received orders, and he sent word to all his supporters to hold themselves in readiness. The place of assembly was fixed in the neighbourhood of Valmontone, a little town built on the summit of a rock of moderate height, but with the rampart of a continuous and almost vertical precipice of from sixty to eighty feet.

[ 47 ]

It was to this town, which belonged to the Pope, that the supporters of the Orsini and the government *sbirri* had succeeded in conveying Bandini. Among the most zealous supporters of authority were numbered Signor de' Campireali and Fabio, his son, who, moreover, were distantly related to the Orsini. Giulio Branciforte and his father, on the other hand, had always been attached to the Colonna.

In circumstances in which it did not suit the Colonna to act openly, they had recourse to a very simple stratagem: the majority of the wealthy Roman peasants, then as now, belonged to some confraternity or other of penitents. These penitents, whenever they appear in public, cover their heads with a piece of cloth which hides the face and is pierced with two holes opposite the eyes. When the Colonna did not wish to avow their part in any enterprise, they used to invite their supporters to put on their penitential dress before coming to join them.

After long preparations, the removal of Bandini, which for a fortnight had been the talk of the countryside, was fixed for a Sunday. On that day, at two o'clock in the morning, the governor of Valmontone had the bells rung in all the villages of the forest of la Faggiola. The peasants were to be seen emerging in considerable numbers from each village. (The customs of the mediaeval Republics, when one fought to obtain a certain thing which one desired, had preserved a great element of courage in the peasant heart; in these days, no one would stir.)

On the day in question a curious thing might have been observed: as the little troop of armed peasants issuing from every village reached the cover of the forest, it diminished by half; the supporters of the Colonna made their way to the place of assembly given out by Fabrizio. Their leaders appeared to be convinced that there would be no fighting that day: they had received orders that morning to spread this rumour. Fabrizio ranged the forest with the picked men of his supporters, whom he had mounted on the young and half-broken horses of his stud. He held a sort of review of the various detachments of peasants; but he said nothing to any of them, as a single word might prove compromising. Fabrizio was a large, lean man, of an incredible agility and strength: although barely forty-five years old, his hair and moustache were dazzlingly white, which greatly annoyed him: by this peculiarity he could be recognised in places where he would have preferred to pass unknown. As soon as the peasants caught sight of him, they cried: *"Evviva Colonna!"* and put on their cloth hoods. The Prince himself had his hood hanging over his chest, so as to be able to draw it on as soon as he came in sight of the enemy.

Which enemy did not keep him waiting: the sun had scarcely risen when about a thousand men, belonging to the Orsini party, and coming from the direction of Valmontone, entered the forest and passed within some three hundred yards of the supporters of Fabrizio Colonna, who had made his men lie down. A few minutes after the last of the Orsini troops forming this advance guard had filed past, the Prince ordered his men to move; he had decided to attack Bandini's escort a quarter of an hour after it should have entered the wood. At this point the forest is littered with small rocks fifteen or twenty feet high; these are waves of lava, more or less ancient, on which the chestnuts flourish admirably, and almost entirely shut out the light of day. As these drifts of lava, more or less eaten away by time, make the ground very uneven, to avoid making the high road pass over a number of unnecessary little gradients, the lava has been cut into, and very often the road runs three or four feet below the level of the forest.

Near the place chosen by Fabrizio for the attack, was

a clearing covered with vegetation and crossed at one end by the high road. Beyond this the road again entered the forest, which, at this point, choked with brambles and shrubs between the trunks of the trees, was altogether impenetrable. It was at a point a hundred paces within the forest and on either side of the road that Fabrizio posted his men. At a signal from the Prince, each of the peasants arranged his hood, and took his post with his arquebus behind a chestnut; the Prince's soldiers placed themselves behind the trees nearest to the road. The peasants had a definite order to fire only after the soldiers, and these were not to open fire until the enemy should be within twenty paces. Fabrizio made them hastily fell a score of trees, which, flung down with their branches upon the road, fairly narrow at that point and three feet below the level of the forest, blocked it entirely. Captain Ranuccio, with five hundred men, followed the advance guard; he had orders not to attack it until he should hear the first arquebus shots fired from the barricade that blocked the road. When Fabrizio Colonna saw his troops and the rest of his supporters properly posted, each behind his tree, and full of determination, he set off at a gallop with all those of his men who were mounted, among whom was to be seen Giulio Branciforte. The Prince took a path to the right of the high road, which led to the farther end of the clearing.

He had been gone but a few minutes when his men saw approaching in the distance, by the road from Valmontone, a numerous troop of men on horseback; these were the *sbirri* and the *bargello,* escorting Bandini, and the whole of the Orsini horsemen. In their midst was Baldassare Bandini, surrounded by four executioners clothed in red; they had orders to carry out the sentence of the court of first instance and to put Bandini to death, if they saw the supporters of the Colonna attempting to set him free.

Colonna's cavalry had barely arrived at the end of the clearing or meadow furthest from the road, when he heard the first arquebus shots fired by the ambuscade which he had posted on the high road by the barricade. Immediately he ordered his horsemen to gallop, and made them charge upon the four executioners clothed in red who surrounded Bandini.

We shall not attempt to follow the narrative of this little affair, which was over in three quarters of an hour; the Orsini party, taken by surprise, scattered in all directions; but, in the advance guard, the gallant Captain Ranuccio was killed, an event which had a fatal influence on the destiny of Branciforte. Barely had the latter dealt a few sabre thrusts, as he made his way towards the four men clothed in red, before he found himself face to face with Fabio de' Campireali.

Mounted upon a fiery horse, and wearing a gilded *giacco* (a coat of mail), Fabio cried:

"Who are these wretched creatures in masks? Cut their masks off with your sabres; this is how I do it!"

A moment later, Giulio Branciforte received a horizontal slash from Fabio's sabre across his brow. This blow had been so skilfully aimed that the cloth which covered his face fell to the ground, while at the same time his eyes were blinded by the blood that flowed from his wound, though the latter was not at all serious. Giulio reined in his horse, to give himself time to breathe and to wipe his face. He was anxious, at all costs, not to fight with Elena's brother; and his horse was already four paces from Fabio when he received a furious sabre thrust on the chest, which did not enter his body, thanks to his *giacco,* but did take away his breath for a moment. At the same time a voice shouted in his ear:

"*Ti conosco, porco!* I know you, you swine! So this is how you make money to replace your tatters!"

[ 51 ]

Giulio, stung to anger, forgot his original intention and turned on Fabio:

"*Ed in mal punto venisti!*" [1] he cried.

After a succession of vigorous blows the garments that covered their coats of mail fell off in tatters. Fabio's coat of mail was gilded and splendid, Giulio's of the commonest kind.

"In what gutter did you pick up your *giacco?*" Fabio cried to him.

At that moment, Giulio found the opportunity which he had been seeking for the last half minute: Fabio's superb coat of mail did not fit closely enough round his throat, and Giulio aimed at his throat, which was bare in one place, a thrust that went home. Giulio's sword ran six inches into Fabio's breast, causing a huge jet of blood to spout forth.

"Take that for your insolence!" cried Giulio.

And he galloped towards the men dressed in red, two of whom were still in the saddle a hundred yards away. As he approached them, a third fell; but, just as Giulio came up to the fourth executioner, the latter, seeing himself surrounded by more than ten horsemen, fired a pistol point blank at the unfortunate Baldassare Bandini, who fell.

"Now, gentlemen, there is nothing more for us to do here!" cried Branciforte. "Let us sabre these rascals of *sbirri* who are making off everywhere."

The others all followed him.

When, half an hour later, Giulio rejoined Fabrizio Colonna, that nobleman addressed him for the first time in his life. Giulio found him mad with rage; he had expected to see him in a transport of joy, in view of the victory, which was complete and due entirely to his good

[1] "And you have come at an unlucky moment!"

[ 52 ]

arrangement; for the Orsini had nearly three thousand men, and Fabrizio, on this occasion, had not been able to muster more than fifteen hundred.

"We have lost our gallant friend Ranuccio!" the Prince exclaimed, addressing Giulio. "I have just touched his body myself; it is cold already. Poor Baldassare Bandini is mortally wounded. So, properly speaking, we have not been successful. But the ghost of the gallant Captain Ranuccio will appear before Pluto with a good escort. I have given orders to hang all these rascally prisoners from the branches of the trees. Do your duty, gentlemen," he cried, raising his voice.

And he went off again at a gallop to the place where the advance guard had been engaged. Giulio had been more or less second in command of Ranuccio's company; he followed the Prince, who, on coming up to the body of that brave soldier, which lay surrounded by more than fifty of the enemy's dead, dismounted a second time to take Ranuccio's hand. Giulio followed his example, with tears in his eyes.

"You are very young," the Prince said to him, "but I see you covered with blood, and your father was a brave man, who received more than a score of wounds in the service of the Colonna. Take command of what is left of Ranuccio's company, and carry his body to our church of la Petrella; remember that you may perhaps be attacked on the way."

Giulio was not attacked, but he killed with a stroke of his sword one of his own men, who said that he was too young to be in command. This rash act proved successful, because Giulio was still covered with Fabio's blood. All along the road, he found the trees loaded with men who were being hanged. This hideous spectacle, combined with the death of Ranuccio, and more especially with that of Fabio, drove him almost mad. His only hope was that the name of Fabio's conqueror would remain unknown.

We pass over the military details. Three days after the battle, he was able to return to spend a few hours at Albano; he told his friends there that a violent fever had detained him in Rome, where he had been obliged to keep his bed all the week.

But he was treated everywhere with a marked respect; the most important persons of the town made haste to greet him; some rash fellows even went so far as to call him *Signor Capitano*. He had passed several times in front of the palazzo Campireali, which he found entirely shut up, and, as the newly made Captain was extremely shy when it came to asking certain questions, it was not until the middle of the day that he managed to take it upon himself to say to Scotti, an old man who had always treated him kindly:

"But where are the Campireali? I see their palazzo shut up."

"My friend," replied Scotti with a sudden grimness, "that is a name which you must never utter. Your friends are quite convinced that it was he who attacked you, and they will say so everywhere; but, after all, he was the chief obstacle to your marriage; after all, his death leaves his sister immensely rich, and she is in love with you. It may even be added, and indiscretion becomes a virtue at this moment, it may even be added that she loves you to the extent of going to pay you a visit at night in your little house at Alba. So it may be said, in your interest, that you were husband and wife before the fatal combat at the Ciampi." (This was the name given in the district to the fight which we have described.)

The old man broke off, because he saw that Giulio was in tears.

"Let us go up to the inn," said Giulio.

Scotti followed him; they were given a room the door of which they locked, and Giulio asked the old man's leave to tell him everything that had happened in the last week. This long story finished:

"I can see quite well from your tears," said the old man, "that nothing in your conduct was premeditated; but Fabio's death is none the less a very terrible event for you. It is absolutely essential that Elena tells her mother that you have been her husband for some time."

Giulio made no reply; this the old man ascribed to a praiseworthy discretion. Absorbed in deep meditation, Giulio was asking himself whether Elena, enraged by the death of a brother, would do justice to his delicacy; he repented of what had happened before. Afterwards, at his request, the old man told him frankly of everything that had occurred in Albano on the day of the fight. Fabio having been killed about half past six in the morning, more than six leagues from Albano, incredible as it might sound, by nine o'clock people had begun to speak of his death. Towards midday they had seen old Campireali, in floods of tears and supported by his servants, making his way to· the Capuchin convent. Shortly afterwards, three of those good fathers, mounted on the best horses of the Campireali stable, and followed by a number of servants, had taken the road to the village of the Ciampi, in the neighbourhood of which the battle had been fought. Old Campireali was absolutely determined to accompany them; but he had been dissuaded, on the grounds that Fabrizio Colonna was furious (no one knew why) and might easily do him an ill turn should he be taken prisoner.

That evening, towards midnight, the forest of la Faggiola had seemed to be on fire: this was all the monks and all the poor of Albano who, each carrying a huge lighted candle, went out to meet the body of young Fabio.

[ 55 ]

"I shall not conceal from you," the old man went on, lowering his voice as though he had been afraid of being overheard, "that the road which leads to Valmontone and to the Ciampi. . . ."

"Well?" said Giulio.

"Well, that road passes by your house, and they say that when Fabio's body reached that point, the blood gushed out from a horrible wound which he had in his throat."

"How terrible!" cried Giulio, springing to his feet.

"Calm yourself, my friend," said the old man, "you can see for yourself that you must know all. And now I may tell you that your presence here, to-day, has seemed a trifle premature. If you should do me the honour to consult me, I should add, Captain, that it is not advisable for you to appear in Albano for another month. I have no need to warn you that it would not be prudent to shew yourself in Rome. We do not yet know what course the Holy Father is going to adopt towards the Colonna; it is thought that he will accept the statement of Fabrizio, who professes that he heard of the fight at the Ciampi only from common rumour; but the Governor of Rome, who is out and out Orsini, is furious and would be only too glad to have one of Fabrizio's gallant soldiers hanged, nor would Fabrizio himself have any reasonable grounds for complaint, since he swears that he took no part in the fight. I shall go farther, and, although you have not asked me for it, take the liberty of giving you a piece of military advice: you are popular in Albano, otherwise you would not be able to stay here in safety. Bear in mind that you have been walking about the town for some hours, that one of the Orsini's supporters might imagine that you were defying him, or at least think it an easy opportunity of winning a fine reward. Old Campireali has repeated a thousand times that he will give his richest estate to whoever kills you. You ought to have brought down to Albano some of the soldiers you have in your house."

"I have no soldiers in my house."

"In that case, Captain, you are mad. This inn has a garden, we are going to leave by the garden, and escape through the vineyards. I shall accompany you; I am an old man, and unarmed; but if we meet any ill-disposed persons, I shall talk to them, and at least be able to let you gain time."

Giulio was broken-hearted. Dare we mention the nature of his madness? As soon as he had learned that the palazzo Campireali was shut up and that its occupants had left for Rome, he had formed the plan of going to revisit that garden where so often he had conversed with Elena. He even hoped to see once again her bedroom, where he had been received when her mother was away. He felt the need of reassuring himself against her anger, by the sight of the places in which she had been so loving to him.

Branciforte and the chivalrous old man met with no misadventure as they followed the little paths that run through the vineyards and climb towards the lake.

Giulio made his companion tell him once more the details of young Fabio's burial. The body of that gallant young man, escorted by a crowd of priests, had been taken to Rome, and buried in the chapel of his family, in the Convent of Sant' Onofrio, on the summit of the Janiculum. It had been observed, as something extremely unusual, that, on the eve of the ceremony, Elena had been taken back by her father to the Convent of the Visitation, at Castro; this had confirmed the common report which insisted that she was secretly married to the soldier of fortune who had had the misfortune to kill her brother.

On nearing his own house, Giulio found the corporal of

his company and four of his men; they told him that their old captain used never to leave the forest without having some of his men at hand. The Prince had said many times that, whenever anyone wished to have himself killed by his own rashness, he must first resign his commission, so as not to cast upon him the responsibility for avenging another death.

Giulio Branciforte realised the soundness of these ideas, of which until that moment he had been completely ignorant. He had supposed, as young nations suppose, that war consisted only in fighting with personal courage. He at once complied with the Prince's wishes, only giving himself time to embrace the wise old man who had been so chivalrous as to accompany him to his house.

But, not many days later, Giulio, half mad with melancholy, returned to visit the palazzo Campireali. As night was falling, he and three of his men, disguised as Neapolitan merchants, made their way into Albano. He presented himself alone at the house of Scotti; he learned that Elena was still confined in the convent of Castro. Her father, who believed her to be married to the man whom he called his son's murderer, had sworn never to set eyes on her again. He had not seen her even when he was taking her to the convent. Her mother's affection seemed, on the contrary, to have increased, and she often left Rome to go and spend a day or two with her daughter.

## IV

"IF I do not justify myself to Elena," Giulio told himself as he made his way back, by night, to the quarters which his company were occupying in the forest, "she will come to regard me as a murderer. Heaven knows what stories they have been telling her about this fatal fight!"

He went to receive his orders from the Prince in his stronghold of la Petrella, and asked leave to go to Castro. Fabrizio Colonna frowned:

"The matter of the little disturbance is not yet settled with His Holiness. You must understand that I have told the truth, namely that I knew nothing whatever of that encounter, of which I was not even informed until the following day, here, in my castle of la Petrella. I have every reason to believe that His Holiness will finally accept this sincere statement. But the Orsini are powerful, and everybody is saying that you distinguished yourself in the skirmish. The Orsini go so far as to pretend that a number of prisoners were hanged from the branches of the trees. You know how little truth there is in that; but we may expect reprisals."

The profound astonishment revealed in the young captain's artless gaze amused the Prince: he decided, however, seeing such a display of innocence, that it would be as well to speak more plainly.

"I see in you," he went on, "that absolute bravery which has made the name of Branciforte famous throughout Italy. I hope that you will shew that loyalty towards my house which made your father so dear to me, and which I have sought to reward in you. The standing order among my troops is this: never tell the truth about anything that relates to me or to my men. If, at the moment when you are obliged to speak, you see no advantage in any particular falsehood, lie at random, and avoid as you would avoid a mortal sin ever uttering a word of the truth. You can understand that, taken in conjunction with other information, it may put people on the track of my plans. I know, as it happens, that you have a little love affair in the convent at Castro; you may go and waste a fortnight in that town, where the Orsini are certain to have friends, and even agents. Call on my steward, who will pay you two hundred sequins. The affection that I had for your father," the Prince added with a smile, "prompts me to give you a few instructions as to the best way of carrying out this amorous and military undertaking. You and three of your men will be disguised as merchants; you will not forget to lose your temper with one of your companions, who will make a show of being always drunk, and will make plenty of friends for himself by standing wine to all the vagabonds of Castro. . . . Apart from that," the Prince went on, with a change of tone, "if you are taken by the Orsini and put to death, never confess your true name, still less that you belong to me. I have no need to advise you to make a circuit of all the small towns, and always to enter by the gate farthest from the road by which you arrive."

Giulio's heart was melted by this fatherly advice, coming from a man who was ordinarily so solemn. At first the Prince smiled at the tears which he saw gathering in the young man's eyes; then his own voice altered. He slipped off one of the many rings which he wore on his fingers; as he took it, Giulio kissed that hand, famous for so many great deeds.

"My father would never have told me so much," the young man cried enthusiastically.

Two days later, shortly before dawn, he passed within the walls of the small town of Castro; five soldiers followed him, disguised like himself: two of them kept to themselves and appeared not to know either him or the other three. Even before entering the town, Giulio caught sight of the Convent of the Visitation, a vast building surrounded by dark walls, and not unlike a fortress. He hastened to the church, which was magnificent. The nuns, all of them noble and mostly belonging to wealthy families, competed among themselves in their pride for the privilege of enriching this church, the only part of the convent that was exposed to the public gaze. It had become a custom that whichever of these ladies the Pope appointed Abbess, from a list of three names presented to him by the Cardinal Protector of the Order of the Visitation, made a considerable offering, intended to perpetuate her name. Any whose offering was inferior to that of the previous Abbess was despised, and her family as well.

Giulio made his way trembling through this magnificent building, resplendent with marble and gilding. As a matter of fact, he paid little attention to the marble or the gilding; he felt that Elena's eyes were upon him. The high altar, he was told, had cost more than eight hundred thousand francs; but his gaze, scorning the treasures of the high altar, was directed at a gilded grating, nearly forty feet high, and divided into three sections by a pair of marble pillars. This grating, whose vast mass made it appear almost terrifying, rose behind the high altar, and separated the nuns' choir from the church itself, which was open to all the faithful.

Giulio told himself that behind this gilded grating were assembled, during the services, the nuns and their boarders. To this inner church might repair, at any hour of the day, a nun or a boarder who felt a desire to pray; it was upon this circumstance, known to the world at large, that the poor lover's hopes were based.

It was true that an immense black curtain screened the inner side of the grating; but "that curtain," thought Giulio, "cannot entirely block the view for the boarders when they look into the public church, since I, who am unable to approach within a certain distance of it, can see quite well, through the curtain, the windows that light the choir, and can even make out the smallest architectural details." Each bar of this magnificent grating was armed with a strong spike, pointed towards the worshippers.

Giulio chose a place where he would be clearly visible, opposite the left hand side of the grating, in the most brightly lighted part of the church; there he spent his time hearing masses. As he saw no one near him but peasants, he had hopes of being observed, even through the black curtain which draped the inside of the grating. For the first time in his life, this simple young man sought to create an effect; he dressed himself with care; he scattered alms broadcast as he entered and left the church. His men and himself paid endless attentions to all the workmen and small tradesmen who had any dealings with the convent. It was not, however, until the third day that he at last had hopes of conveying a letter to Elena. By his orders, his men closely followed the two lay sisters whose duty it was to purchase some of the provisions for the convent; one of them was on friendly terms with a small merchant. One of Giulio's soldiers, who had been in religion, made friends with this merchant, and promised him a sequin for each letter that should be conveyed to the boarder Elena de' Campireali.

"What!" said the merchant at the first overture that

was made to him in the matter, "a letter to the *brigand's wife!*"

This name was already in common use in Castro, and Elena had not been there a fortnight: so swiftly does anything that seizes hold of the imagination circulate among this people, passionately interested in all exact details! The merchant added:

"At least, she is married! But how many of our ladies have not that excuse, and yet receive a great deal more than letters from outside."

In this first letter, Giulio related with endless details everything that had occurred on the fatal day marked by the death of Fabio: "Do you hate me?" he said in conclusion.

Elena replied in a few lines that, without hating anyone, she was going to employ the rest of her life in trying to forget the man by whose hand her brother had perished.

Giulio made haste to reply; after inveighing against his fate, in a style imitated from Plato and in fashion at the time:

"So you wish," he went on, "to forget the Word of God handed down to us in the Holy Scriptures? God says: woman shall leave her family and her parents to follow her husband. Dare you pretend that you are not my wife? Remember the night of Saint Peter's day. As dawn was beginning to appear behind Monte Cavi, you flung yourself at my feet; I was good enough to grant you a respite; you were mine, had I wished to take you; you could not resist the love which you then felt for me. Suddenly it occurred to me that, as I had told you many times that I had long since offered you the sacrifice of my life and of all that I might hold most dear in the world, you were in a position to reply, although you never did, that all these sacrifices, not being marked by any outward action, might well be no more than imaginary. An idea, hard

[ 63 ]

to bear, but fundamentally just, dawned upon me. I reflected that it was not for nothing that chance was presenting me with the opportunity of sacrificing in your interest the greatest happiness that I could ever have dreamed of. You were already in my arms, and defenceless, remember; your own lips dared not refuse. At that moment the morning Angelus rang from the convent of Monte Cavi, and, by a miracle, the sound reached our ears. You said to me: 'Make this sacrifice to the Holy Madonna, the mother of all purity.' I had already, a moment earlier, had the idea of this supreme sacrifice, the only real sacrifice that I should ever have an opportunity of making for you. I felt it strange that the same idea should have occurred to you. The distant sound of that Angelus touched me, I confess; I granted your request. The sacrifice was not entirely for you; I believed that I was placing our future union under the protection of the Madonna. At that time I supposed that the objections would come not from you, faithless one, but from your rich and noble family. Had there not been some supernatural intervention, how could that Angelus have reached our ears from so great a distance, carried over the tree-tops of half the forest, stirred at that moment by the morning breeze? Then, you remember, you threw yourself at my feet; I rose, I took from my bosom the cross which I carry there, and you swore upon that cross, which is here before me, and by your own eternal damnation, that in whatever place you might at any time be, whatever might at any time happen, as soon as I should give you the order, you would place yourself entirely at my disposal, as you were at the moment when the Angelus from Monte Cavi travelled so far to strike your ear. We then repeated devoutly two *Hail Marys* and two *Our Fathers*. Very well, by the love which you then felt for me, or else, if you have forgotten it, as I fear, by your eternal damnation, I order you to receive me to-night, in your room or in the garden of the Convent of the Visitation."

The Italian author carefully reports many long letters written by Giulio Branciforte after this one; but he gives only extracts from the replies of Elena de' Campireali. After the lapse of two hundred and seventy-eight years, we are so remote from the sentiments of love and religion which fill these letters, that I have been afraid of their seeming wearisome.

It appears from these letters that Elena finally obeyed the order contained in this one, of which we have given an abridged translation. Giulio found a way of penetrating into the convent; we may conclude from a certain passage that he disguised himself as a woman. Elena received him, but only at the grating of a window on the ground floor looking out to the garden. To his unspeakable grief, Giulio found that this girl, so tender and indeed so passionate before, had become like a stranger to him; she treated him almost with *civility*. In admitting him to the garden, she had yielded almost exclusively to the obligation of her oath. Their meeting was brief: after a few moments, Giulio's pride, excited a little, perhaps, by the events that had occurred in the last fortnight, succeeded in prevailing over his intense grief.

"I see before me now," he said to himself, "only the tomb of that Elena who, at Albano, seemed to have given herself to me for life."

Immediately, the important thing for Giulio was to conceal the tears with which the polite turns of speech that Elena adopted in addressing him bathed his cheeks. When she had finished speaking and justifying a change that was so natural, she said, after the death of a brother, Giulio said to her, speaking very slowly:

"You are not abiding by your oath, you do not receive

me in a garden, you are not on your knees before me, as you were for a minute after we had heard the Angelus from Monte Cavi. Forget your oath if you can; as for me, I forget nothing; may God help you!"

So saying, he left the barred window before which he might still have remained for nearly an hour. Who would have said, a moment earlier, that he would of his own free will cut short this meeting for which he had so longed! This sacrifice rent his heart; but he felt that he might well deserve Elena's scorn if he replied to her *civilities* otherwise than by abandoning her to her own remorse.

Before dawn, he left the convent. At once he mounted his horse, giving orders to his men to wait for him at Castro for a full week, then to return to the forest. At first he rode towards Rome.

"What! I am going away from her!" he said to himself at every yard: "What! We have become strangers to one another! Oh, Fabio! How amply you are avenged!"

The sight of the men whom he passed on the road increased his anger; he urged his horse across country and made his way towards the deserted and uncultivated tract by the seashore. When he was no longer disturbed by meeting these placid peasants whose lot he envied, he drew breath; the aspect of this wild spot was in keeping with his despair and lessened his rage; then he was able to give himself up to the consideration of his sad fate.

"At my age," he said to himself, "I have one resource left: to love some other woman!"

At this melancholy thought, he felt his despair increase twofold; he saw only too clearly that there was for him but one woman in the world. He pictured to himself the torment that he would suffer should he venture to utter the word love to any woman but Elena: the idea tore his heart.

He was seized with a fit of bitter laughter.

"Here I am," he thought, "exactly like those heroes in Ariosto who travel alone through desert lands, when they have to forget that they have found their mistress in the arms of some other knight. . . . And yet she is not so much to blame," he told himself, bursting into tears after this fit of wild laughter; "her faithlessness does not reach the point of loving another. That keen, pure spirit has allowed herself to be led astray by the dreadful accounts that have been given her of me; no doubt I have been represented to her as having armed myself for that fatal expedition only in the secret hope of finding an opportunity of killing her brother. They will have gone farther still: they will have credited me with the sordid calculation that once her brother was dead she would become the sole heiress of an immense property. . . . And I have been fool enough to leave her for a whole fortnight a prey to the wiles of my enemies! It must be admitted that if I am most unfortunate, heaven has also furnished me with singularly little sense with which to conduct my life! I am a most miserable, most contemptible creature! My life has been of use to no one, and to myself least of all."

At that moment, young Branciforte had an inspiration very rare in that age: his horse was going along the water's edge, and every now and then was being splashed by the waves; he had the idea of urging the animal into the sea, and so ending the dreadful fate that overhung him. What was he to do henceforward, after the one person in the world who had ever made him feel the existence of happiness had abandoned him? Then suddenly another idea stopped him short.

"What are the pains that I am enduring," he said to himself, "compared with those which I shall suffer in a moment, once this wretched life is ended? Elena will no longer be simply indifferent to me, as she is in reality; I shall see her in the arms of a rival, and that rival will be some young Roman noble, rich and *highly esteemed;* for, to rend my heart, the devils will seek out the most cruel visions, as is their duty. So I shall never succeed in finding forgetfulness of Elena, even in death; far from it, my passion for her will be doubled, because that is the surest means which the Eternal Power can find of punishing me for the fearful sin which I shall have committed."

To banish the temptation finally, Giulio began devoutly reciting the *Hail Mary.* It was on hearing the morning Angelus, the prayer sacred to the Madonna, that he had been carried away before, and led to a generous action which he now regarded as the greatest mistake of his life. But, from a sense of reverence, he did not venture to go farther and express the whole of the idea that had seized hold of his mind.

"If, by the Madonna's inspiration, I have fallen into a fatal error, ought she not, in her infinite justice, to bring about some circumstance which will restore my happiness?"

This idea of the justice of the Madonna gradually banished his despair. He raised his head, and saw facing him, beyond Albano and the forest, that Monte Cavi, covered in its dusky greenery, and the holy convent whose morning Angelus had led him into what he now called his appalling stupidity. The unexpected sight of that holy place comforted him.

"No!" he exclaimed; "it is impossible that the Madonna should abandon me. If Elena had been my wife, as her love allowed and my dignity as a man required, the account given to her of her brother's death would have found in her heart the memory of the bond that attached her to me. She would have told herself that she belonged to me long before the fatal chance which, on a field of battle, brought me face to face with Fabio. He was two years older than I; he was more skilled in arms, bolder in every way, stronger. A thousand reasons would have occurred to my wife to prove that it was not I that had sought that combat. She would have remembered that I had never shewn the slightest feeling of hatred towards her brother, even when he fired his arquebus at me. I can recall that at our first meeting, after my return from Rome, I said to her: 'What would you have? Honour required it; I cannot blame a brother!' "

His hope restored by his devotion to the Madonna, Giulio urged on his horse and in a few hours arrived at his company's cantonment. He found his men standing to arms: they were about to take the road that runs from Naples to Rome past Monte Cassino. The young captain changed horses, and marched with his men. There was no fighting that day. Giulio never asked himself why they were on the march; it mattered little to him. The moment that he found himself at the head of his soldiers, a new vision of his destiny appeared to him.

"I am simply and solely a fool," he said to himself; "I did wrong to leave Castro; Elena is probably less to blame than I in my anger imagined. No, she cannot have ceased to belong to me, that pure and simple heart, in which I have beheld the first dawn of love! She was steeped in so sincere a passion for me! Has she not offered, ten times and more, to fly with me, poor as I am, and to have ourselves married by one of the friars of Monte Cavi? At Castro I ought, first of all, to have obtained a second assignation, and made her listen to reason. Really, passion makes me as distracted as a child! God! Why have I not a friend to whom I can turn for advice! The same course of action seems to me execrable, and, the next minute, excellent."

On the evening of that day, as they left the high road to return to the forest, Giulio rode up to the Prince and asked whether he might stay for a few days longer at the place he knew of.

[ 69 ]

"You can go to the devil!" cried Fabrizio, "do you think this is the time to bother me with your childish nonsense?"

An hour later, Giulio set off again for Castro. He found his men there, but he did not know how to write to Elena, after the summary fashion in which he had left her. His first letter contained only these words: "May I be received to-morrow evening?"

Similarly, *"You may come,"* was all the answer he received.

After Giulio's departure, Elena had imagined herself to be abandoned for ever. Then she had felt the whole force of the argument urged by that poor young man who was so unhappy: she was his wife before he had had the misfortune to encounter her brother on a field of battle.

On this occasion, Giulio was by no means received with the polite turns of speech which had struck him as so cruel at their former meeting. It was true that Elena appeared to him only behind the shelter of her barred window; but she was trembling, and as Giulio was extremely reserved and his language [1] almost that which he would have used to address a stranger, it was Elena's turn to feel all the cruelty that exists in the almost official tone when it follows the most tender intimacy. Giulio, who was especially afraid of having his soul torn asunder by some cold speech proceeding from Elena's heart, had adopted a lawyer's tone to prove that Elena was his wife long before the fatal combat at the Ciampi. Elena let him speak, because she was afraid of being overcome by tears if she answered him otherwise than with a few brief words. Finally, seeing that she was on the point of betraying herself, she bade her lover come again the next day. Giulio, who was

[1] In Italy the fashion of addressing a person as *tu, voi* or *Lei* marks the degree of intimacy. The word *tu*, a survival from the Latin, has a more restricted application than in France.

reasoning like a lover, left the garden deep in thought; he could not bring his uncertainty to the point of deciding whether he had been well or ill received; and as military ideas, inspired by conversation with his comrades, were beginning to take root in his brain:

"One day," he said to himself, "I shall perhaps have to come and carry off Elena."

And he began to consider the ways of entering the garden by force. As the convent was very rich and offered grand opportunities of pillage, it had in its pay a great number of menservants, mostly old soldiers; they were housed in a sort of barrack the barred windows of which overlooked the narrow passage which, from the outer gate of the convent, carved out of a sombre wall more than eighty feet high, led to the inner gate guarded by the portress. On the left of this narrow passage rose the barrack, on the right the wall of the garden, thirty feet high. The front of the convent, on the public square, was a massive wall black with age, and offered no openings save the outer gate and one small window through which the soldiers could see what went on outside. One may imagine the grim effect of this great black wall pierced only by a gate strengthened with broad iron bands fastened to it by enormous nails, and a single small window four feet high and eighteen inches broad.

We shall not attempt to follow the author of the original manuscript in his long account of the successive assignations which Giulio obtained from Elena. The tone mutually adopted by the lovers had once more become entirely intimate, as in the past in the garden at Albano; only Elena had never consented to come down to the garden. One night Giulio found her profoundly thoughtful: her mother had come from Rome to see her, and was staying for some days in the convent. This mother was so loving, she had always shewn such delicacy in her treatment of what she supposed to be her daughter's affections, that the latter felt a profound remorse at being obliged to deceive her; for, after all, would she ever dare to tell her that she was receiving the man who had robbed her of her son? Elena ended by admitting frankly to Giulio that if this mother who was so good to her should question her in a certain way, she would never have the strength to answer her with lies. Giulio was fully aware of the danger of his position; his fate depended on the chance which might dictate certain words to Signora de' Campireali. On the following night he said to her, with a resolute air:

"To-morrow I shall come earlier, I shall detach one of the bars of this grating, you will come down to the garden, I shall take you to a church in the town, where a priest who is devoted to me will marry us. Before daylight you will be back in this garden. Once you are my wife, I shall have nothing more to fear, and if your mother insists upon it, as an expiation of the fearful misfortune which we all equally deplore, I will consent to anything, were it even that I must spend some months without seeing you."

As Elena appeared terrified by this proposal, Giulio added:

"The Prince summons me back to his side; honour and all sorts of reasons oblige me to go. My proposal is the only one that can assure our future happiness; if you do not agree to it, let us separate for ever, here, at this moment. I shall leave you with a sense of remorse at my rashness. *I trusted in your word of honour,* you are unfaithful to the most sacred of oaths, and I hope that in the course of time the contempt which your fickleness rightly inspires in me may cure me of this love which has been for too long the bane of my life."

Elena burst into tears:

"Great God!" she exclaimed, weeping, "how terrible for my mother!"

In the end, she agreed to the proposal that had been made to her.

"But," she added, "some one may see us, going or coming; think of the scandal that would arise, consider the fearful position in which my mother would find herself placed; let us wait until she goes, which will be in a few days."

"You have succeeded in making me doubt what was to me the holiest, the most sacred thing in the world: my confidence in your word. To-morrow night we will be married, or else we see one another now for the last time, on this side of the grave."

Poor Elena could make no answer save by her tears, her heart was torn especially by the cruel and decided tone which Giulio had adopted. Had she then really merited his contempt? Could this be that same lover who was formerly so docile and so tender? At length she agreed to what had been ordered of her. Giulio withdrew. From that moment, Elena awaited the coming of the following night in an alternation of the most rending anxieties. Had she been prepared for certain death, her anguish would have been less keen; she could have found some encouragement in the thought of Giulio's love and of her mother's tender affection. The rest of that night passed in the most agonising changes of mind. There were moments when she decided to tell her mother all. Next day, she was so pale when she appeared in her mother's presence, that the latter, forgetting all her wise resolutions, flung herself upon her daughter's bosom, crying:

"What is happening? Great God! Tell me what you have done, or what you are going to do? If you were to take a dagger and thrust it into my heart, you would

[ 73 ]

hurt me less than by this cruel silence which I see you adopt with me."

Her mother's intense affection was so evident to Elena, she saw so clearly that her mother, instead of exaggerating her feelings, was seeking to moderate her expression of them, that in the end she was overcome; she fell at her feet. Her mother, who was trying to find out what the fatal secret might be, having exclaimed that Elena was shunning her society, Elena replied that, next day and every day after that, she would spend all her time with her, but she besought her not to question her further.

This indiscreet utterance was speedily followed by a full confession. Signora de' Campireali was horrified to hear that her son's murderer was so close at hand. But this grief was followed by an outburst of keen and pure joy. Who could describe her delight when she learned that her daughter had never failed in her duties?

Immediately all the plans of this prudent mother were completely changed; she felt herself entitled to employ a stratagem to outwit a man who was nothing to her. Elena's heart was torn by the most cruel impulses of passion: the sincerity of her confession could not have been greater; this tormented soul was in need of relief. Signora de' Campireali, who had begun to think that anything was permissible, devised a chain of reasoning too long to be reported here. She had no difficulty in proving to her unhappy daughter that, instead of a clandestine marriage, which always leaves a stain upon a woman's reputation, she would obtain a public and perfectly honourable marriage, if she would only agree to postpone for a week the act of obedience which she owed to so high-minded a lover.

Signora de' Campireali herself would return to Rome; she would explain to her husband that, long before the fatal combat at the Ciampi, Elena had been married to Giulio. The ceremony had been performed on that very night when, disguised in a religious habit, she had met her father and brother by the shore of the lake, on the road cut through the rock which runs by the walls of the Capuchin convent. The mother took good care not to leave her daughter all that day, and finally, towards evening, Elena wrote her lover an ingenuous and, to our ideas, extremely touching letter, in which she told him of the inward struggle that had torn her heart. She ended by begging him on her knees for a week's respite: "As I write you," she added, "this letter for which a messenger of my mother's is waiting, it seems to me that I was utterly wrong to tell her everything. I think I see you angry, your eyes look at me with hatred; my heart is torn by the most cruel remorse. You will say that I have a very weak, very cowardly, very contemptible nature; I admit it, my dear angel. But try to imagine the scene: my mother, in floods of tears, was almost at my feet. Then it became impossible for me not to tell her that a certain reason prevented me from consenting to do what she asked; and, once I had been so weak as to utter those rash words, I do not know what change occurred in me, but it became almost impossible for me not to tell her everything that had passed between us. So far as I can remember, I felt that my heart, robbed of all its strength, stood in need of advice. This I hoped to find in a mother's words. . . . I forgot, my friend, that that beloved mother had an interest opposed to yours. I forgot my first duty, which is to obey you, and apparently I am incapable of feeling true love, which is said to withstand every trial. Despise me, my Giulio; but, in God's name, do not cease to love me. Carry me off if you wish, but do me the justice to admit that, if my mother had not happened to be here in the convent, the most horrible dangers, shame itself, nothing in the world could have prevented me from obeying your orders. But that mother is so good; so clever; so generous; remember what I told you at the time; when my father burst into my room, she rescued your letters which I had no means of hiding: then, when the danger was over, she gave them back to me without wishing to read them, and without a single word of reproach! In the same way, all my life long, she has been to me, as she was at that moment, supreme. You can see whether I ought to love her, and yet, when I write to you (it is a horrible thing to say) I feel that I hate her. She has announced that on account of the heat she wishes to spend the night in a tent in the garden; I hear the tapping of the mallets, they are putting up the tent now; impossible for us to meet to-night. I am even afraid that the boarders' dormitory may be locked, as well as the two doors of the spiral staircase, a thing which is never done. These precautions would make it impossible for me to come down to the garden, even if I thought that it would have any effect in calming your anger. Oh, how I would give myself to you at this moment, if I had the means! How I should run to that church where they are going to marry us!"

This letter concludes with a couple of pages of mad sentences, in which I notice certain impassioned arguments which seem to be imitated from the philosophy of Plato. I have suppressed several elegances of this sort in the letter I have just translated.

Giulio Branciforte was amazed when he received it about an hour before the evening Angelus; he had just completed his arrangements with the priest. He was beside himself with rage.

"She has no need to advise me to carry her off, the weak, cowardly creature!"

And he set off at once for the forest of la Faggiola.

Meanwhile, Signora de' Campireali's position was as follows: her husband lay on his deathbed, the impossibility of avenging himself on Branciforte was carrying him slowly to the grave. In vain had he made his agents offer considerable sums to Roman *bravi;* none of these was prepared to attack one of the *caporali,* as they were called, of Prince Colonna; they were too certain of being exterminated, themselves and their families. It was not a year since an entire village had been burned to punish the death of one of Colonna's soldiers, and all those of the inhabitants, men and women alike, who tried to flee into the country, had their hands and feet tied together with ropes, and were then tossed into the blazing houses.

Signora de' Campireali had large estates in the Kingdom of Naples; her husband had ordered her to send there for assassins, but she had made only a show of obedience: she imagined her daughter to be irrevocably bound to Giulio Branciforte. Acting on this supposition, she thought that Giulio should go and serve for a campaign or two in the Spanish armies, which were then making war on the rebels in Flanders. If he survived, that would, she thought, be a sign that God did not disapprove of a necessary marriage; in that case she would give her daughter the estates which she owned in the Kingdom of Naples; Giulio Branciforte would take the name of one of these estates, and would go with his wife to spend a few years in Spain. After all these trials perhaps she would have the heart to see him. But the whole aspect of things had been changed by her daughter's confession: the marriage was no longer a necessity: far from it, and while Elena was writing her lover the letter which we have translated, Signora de' Campireali wrote to Pescara and Chieti, ordering her farmers to send to her at Castro a party of trustworthy men capable of a bold stroke. She did not conceal from them that it was a question of avenging the death of Fabio, their young master. The courier who conveyed these letters set off before the end of the day.

# V

B UT, two days later, Giulio was back in Castro,
bringing with him eight of his men who had vol-
unteered to follow him and expose themselves to
the anger of the Prince, who had sometimes punished with
death enterprises of the sort on which they were engag-
ing. Giulio had five men at Castro, he arrived with eight
more; and yet fourteen soldiers, however brave, seemed
to him insufficient for his task, for the convent was like a
fortress.

One had first to pass, by force or by guile, through the
outer gate of the convent; then to proceed along a passage
more than fifty yards in length. On the left, as has been
said, rose the barred windows of a sort of barrack in which
the nuns had placed thirty or forty menservants, old soldiers. From these barred windows a hot fire would be
opened as soon as the alarm should be given.

The reigning Abbess, who had a head on her shoulders,
was afraid of the exploits of the Orsini chiefs, Prince
Colonna, Marco Sciarra, and all the others that held sway
in the neighbourhood. How was one to hold out against
eight hundred determined men, suddenly occupying a little
town like Castro and imagining the convent to be full of
gold?

As a rule, the Visitation of Castro had fifteen or twenty
*bravi* in the barrack to the left of the passage which led
to the inner gate of the convent; on the right of this passage was a great wall, impossible to break through; at the

end of the passage one came upon an iron gate opening upon a pillared hall; beyond this hall was the great court-yard of the convent. This iron gate was guarded by the portress.

When Giulio, followed by his eight men, had come within three leagues of Castro, he halted in a lonely inn until the heat of the day should be past. It was only there that he announced his intention; he then traced in the dust of the courtyard the plan of the convent which he was going to attack.

"At nine o'clock this evening," he said to his men, "we sup outside the town; at midnight we enter; we shall find your five comrades who will be waiting for us near the convent. One of them, who will be mounted, will pretend to be a courier arriving from Rome to summon Signora de' Campireali to the bedside of her husband, who is dying. We shall try to get without noise past the outer gate of the convent, which is there, close to the barrack," he said, pointing to it on his plan in the dust. "If we were to begin our fight at the first gate, we should be making it easy for the nuns' *bravi* to shoot us down with their arque-buses while we were still in the little square, here, outside the convent, or while we were going along the narrow pas-sage which leads from the first gate to the second. This second gate is of iron, but I have the key.

"It is true that there are enormous iron rods, or valets, fastened to the wall at one end, and these, when they are in position, prevent the two halves of the gate from open-ing. But as these two iron rods are too heavy for the portress to be able to handle them, I have never seen them in position; and yet I have passed ten times and more through this iron gate. I expect to pass through it again to-night without difficulty. You understand that I have friends inside the convent; my object is to carry off a boarder, not a nun; we must not use our arms except in

the last extremity. If we should begin the fight before
reaching this second gate with the iron bars, the portress
would not fail to call two old gardeners, men of seventy,
who sleep inside the convent, and the old men would fix in
position the iron bars of which I have spoken. Should
this misfortune befall us, we shall be obliged, in order to
pass the gate, to destroy the wall, which will take ten
minutes; in any case, I shall advance first towards the
gate. One of the gardeners is in my pay; but I have
taken good care, as you can imagine, not to speak to him
of the abduction I have in mind. Once past this second
gate, we turn to the right, and come to the garden; as soon
as we are in the garden, the fight begins, we must go for
everyone we see. You will of course use only your swords
and dirks, a single shot from an arquebus would set the
whole town stirring, and we might be attacked on coming
out. Not that with thirteen men such as you I have any
misgivings about getting through a little place like that:
certainly no one would dare come down to the street; but
many of the townsfolk have arquebuses, and they would
fire from the windows. In that case, we should have to
keep close to the walls of the houses, so much for that.
Once you are in the convent garden, you will say in a low
voice to every man that shews his face: *Retire;* you will
kill with your dirks any that does not immediately obey.
I shall go up into the convent by the little door from the
garden, with those of you that are near me; three minutes
later I shall come down with one or two women whom we
shall carry in our arms, without allowing them to walk. We
shall then go quickly out of the convent and the town.
I shall leave two of you near the gate, they will fire twenty
rounds from their arquebuses, one every minute, to frighten
the townsfolk and keep them at a distance."

Giulio repeated this explanation a second time.

"Do you quite understand?" he asked his men. "It will

be dark in that hall; on the right the garden, on the left the courtyard; you must not lose your way."

"Count on us!" cried the soldiers.

Then they went off to drink; the corporal did not follow them but asked leave to speak to the captain.

"Nothing could be simpler," he said to him, "than your honour's plan. I have already forced two convents in my time; this will make the third; but there are not enough of us. If the enemy oblige us to pull down the wall that supports the hinges of the second gate, we must bear in mind that the *bravi* in the barrack will not be idle during that long operation; they will kill seven or eight of your men with arquebus shots, and after that they may seize the lady from us as we come out. That is what happened to us in a convent near Bologna: they killed five of our men, we killed eight of theirs, but the captain did not get the lady. I suggest to your honour two things: I know four peasants close to this inn where we are now, who have served gallantly under Sciarra, and for a sequin will fight all night like lions. They may perhaps steal some silver from the convent; that does not matter to you, the sin is upon their heads, you simply pay them to secure a lady, that is all. My second suggestion is this: Ugone is a fellow with some education, and very quick; he was a doctor when he killed his brother-in-law and took to the *macchia*. You might send him, an hour before nightfall, to the gate of the convent; he will ask to take service there, and will manage so well that he will be admitted to the guard-room; he will fill the nuns' servants with liquor; more than that, he is quite capable of wetting the matches of their arquebuses."

Unfortunately, Giulio accepted the corporal's suggestion. As the man was leaving his presence, he added:

"We are going to attack a convent, that means *major*

*excommunication,* and besides, this convent is under the immediate protection of the Madonna. . . ."

"I hear you!" cried Giulio, as though aroused by the last words. "Stay here with me."

The corporal shut the door and came back to repeat the Rosary with Giulio. Their prayers lasted for fully an hour. At dusk, they took the road again.

As midnight struck, Giulio, who had entered Castro by himself about eleven o'clock, returned to fetch his party outside the gate. He entered the town with his eight soldiers, who had been joined by three peasants, well armed; adding to these the five soldiers whom he already had in the town, he found himself at the head of a band of sixteen resolute men; two were disguised as servants, they had put on loose shirts of black cloth to hide their *giacchi* (coats of mail), and they wore no plumes in their caps.

At half past twelve, Giulio, who had cast himself for the part of courier, arrived at a gallop at the gate of the convent, making a great noise, and shouting to the inmates to open at once to a courier sent by the Cardinal. He was pleased to see that the soldiers who answered him through the little window, by the side of the outer gate, were more than half drunk already. Complying with the custom, he handed in his name on a slip of paper; a soldier went to give this to the portress, who had the key of the second gate, and on important occasions had to arouse the Abbess. For three mortal quarters of an hour he was kept waiting for an answer; during this time, Giulio had great difficulty in keeping his troop silent: some of the townsfolk were even beginning timidly to open their windows, when a favourable reply at length arrived from the Abbess. Giulio entered the guard-room by means of a ladder five or six feet in length, which was let down to him from the little window, the *bravi* of the convent not wishing to give themselves the trouble of opening the great gate: this ladder he climbed, followed by the two soldiers disguised as servants. As he jumped from the window sill into the guard-room, he caught the eye of Ugone; the whole of the guard were drunk, thanks to his efforts. Giulio told the man in charge that three servants of the Campireali household, whom he had armed like soldiers to serve as his escort on the road, had found a place where there was good brandy for sale, and asked that they might come up instead of cooling their heels on the square; this request was unanimously granted. As for himself, accompanied by his two men, he went down by the staircase which led from the guard-room into the passage.

"Try to open the big gate," he said to Ugone.

He himself arrived without the least trouble at the iron gate. There he found the good portress, who told him that as it was past midnight, if he entered the convent, the Abbess would be obliged to report it to the Bishop; accordingly she sent word asking him to hand his dispatches to a young sister whom she had sent to receive them. To which Giulio replied that in the confusion surrounding the sudden decline of Signor de' Campireali, he had been given nothing but a simple letter of credit written by the doctor, and had been ordered to communicate all the details by word of mouth to the dying man's wife and daughter, should those ladies still be in the convent, and in any event to the Lady Abbess. The portress went to convey this message. There remained by the gate only the young sister sent down by the Abbess. Giulio while he talked and joked with her, slipped his hands through the great iron bars of the gate, and, still laughing, attempted to open it. The sister, who was very timid, was alarmed and took the pleasantry amiss; then Giulio, seeing that a considerable amount of time had passed, was rash enough to offer her a handful of sequins, begging her to open the

[ 83 ]

gate for him, adding that he was too tired to wait any longer. He saw quite well that he was doing a foolish thing, says the historian: it was with steel and not with gold that he should have acted, but he had no heart for that: nothing could have been easier than to seize the sister, who was not a foot away from him on the other side of the gate. At his offer of the sequins, the girl took fright. She said afterwards that, from the way in which Giulio addressed her, she realised quite clearly that he was not a mere courier: "He will be the lover of one of our nuns," she thought, "who has come to keep an assignation," and she was devout. Seized with horror, she began to tug with all her strength the rope of a little bell which hung in the great courtyard, and at once made din enough to arouse the dead.

"The fight begins," said Giulio to his men; "look out for yourselves!"

He took his key, and, slipping his arm between the iron bars, opened the gate, to the complete despair of the young sister, who fell on her knees and began to recite the *Hail Mary*, crying out against the sacrilege. Again at this moment, Giulio ought to have silenced the girl, but had not the heart to do so: one of his men seized hold of her and clapped his hand to her mouth.

At that moment Giulio heard an arquebus fired in the passage behind him. Ugone had opened the main gate; the remainder of the soldiers were entering without a sound, when one of the *bravi*, less drunk than the rest, came up to one of the barred windows, and, in his astonishment at seeing so many people in the passage, forbade them with an oath to come any farther. The only thing was to make no answer and to continue to advance towards the iron gate; this was what the first of the soldiers did; but the man who came last of all, and who was one of the peasants recruited in the afternoon, fired a pistol shot at this servant who was speaking from the window, and killed him. This pistol shot, in the dead of night, and the shouts of the drunken men as they saw their comrade fall, awoke the soldiers of the convent, who were spending the night in bed, and had not had an opportunity of tasting Ugone's wine. Nine or ten of the *bravi* of the convent rushed into the passage half dressed, and began vigorously to attack Branciforte's men.

As we have said, this racket began at the moment when Giulio had succeeded in opening the iron gate. Followed by his two soldiers, he dashed into the garden, and ran towards the little door of the boarders' stair; but he was greeted by five or six pistol shots. His two men fell, he himself received a bullet in his right arm. These pistol shots had been fired by Signora de' Campireali's people, who, by her orders, were spending the night in the garden, authorised to do so by a special dispensation which she had obtained from the Bishop. Giulio ran by himself towards the little door, so well known to him, which led from the garden to the boarders' stair. He did all he could to force it open, but it was firmly shut. He searched for his men, who made no attempt to reply; they were dying; in the pitch darkness he ran into three of the Campireali servants against whom he defended himself with his knife.

He ran into the hall, towards the iron gate, to call his soldiers; he found this gate shut: the pair of heavy iron rods had been put in position and padlocked by the old gardeners, who had been aroused by the young sister's pealing of the bell.

"I am cut off," Giulio said to himself.

He repeated this to his men; in vain did he attempt to force one of the padlocks with his sword: had he succeeded, he would have raised one of the iron rods, and opened one side of the gate. His sword broke in the ring of the padlock; at the same moment he was wounded in the shoulder

by one of the servants who had come in from the garden;
he turned round, and resting his back against the iron
gate, found himself being attacked by a number of men.
He defended himself with his dirk; fortunately, the darkness being unbroken, almost all the sword strokes landed
on his coat of mail. He received a painful wound in the
knee; he flung himself upon one of the men who had lunged
too far to reach him with his sword, killed him by stabbing
him in the face with his knife, and was lucky enough to
gain possession of the man's sword. From that moment
he thought himself safe; he took his stand on the left-hand
side of the gate, towards the courtyard. His men, who
had hastened to his assistance, fired five or six pistol shots
between the iron bars of the gate and sent the servants
flying. Nothing was visible in the hall except in the flash
of these pistol shots.

"Do not fire in my direction!" cried Giulio to his men.

"Now you are caught like a mouse in a trap," the corporal said to him with the utmost coolness, speaking
through the bars; "we have three men killed. We are going
to break down the jamb of the gate on the opposite side
to where you are; do not come near, the bullets will be
falling on us; there seem to be some of the enemy in the
garden still."

"Those rascally servants of the Campireali," said Giulio.

He was still speaking to the corporal, when further
pistol shots, aimed at the sound of their voices and coming
from the part of the hall that led to the garden, were fired
at them. Giulio took shelter in the portress's lodge, which
was on the left as one entered; to his great joy he found
a lamp burning with an almost imperceptible glimmer before the image of the Madonna; he took it with many
precautions not to extinguish it; he noticed with regret
that he was trembling. He examined the wound in his

knee, which was giving him great pain; the blood was flowing copiously.

As he cast his eyes round him, he was greatly surprised at recognising, in a woman who had fainted in a wooden armchair, little Marietta, Elena's confidential maid; he shook her vigorously.

"Why, Signor Giulio," she exclaimed, weeping, "are you going to kill Marietta, your friend?"

"Nothing of the sort; say to Elena that I beg pardon for having disturbed her sleep, and bid her remember the Angelus on Monte Cavi. Here is a nosegay which I plucked in her garden at Albano; but it is stained a little with blood; wash it before you give it to her."

At that moment, he heard a volley of arquebus shots fired in the passage; the nuns' *bravi* were attacking his men.

"Tell me, where is the key of the little door?" he said to Marietta.

"I do not see it; but here are the keys of the padlocks of the iron bars which keep the great gate shut. You can get out."

Giulio took the keys and dashed out of the lodge.

"Stop trying to break down the wall," he said to his soldiers. "I have the key of the gate at last."

There was a moment of complete silence, while he tried to open a padlock with one of the small keys; he had mistaken the key, he tried the other; at length, he opened the padlock; but just as he was lifting the iron rod, he received a pistol shot, fired at him almost point blank, in his right arm. At once he felt that his arm refused to obey him.

"Lift up the iron valet," he cried to his men.

He had no need to tell them.

By the flash of the pistol shot, they had seen the hooked end of the iron rod almost out of the ring in the gate; when it was clear of the ring, they let it fall. Then it was possible to push open one side of the gate; the corporal entered, and said to Giulio, carefully lowering his voice:

"There is nothing more to be done, there are only three or four of us now unwounded, five are dead."

"I am losing blood," replied Giulio. "I feel that I am going to faint; tell them to carry me away."

While Giulio was speaking to the gallant corporal, the soldiers in the guard-room fired three or four more arquebus shots, and the corporal fell dead. Fortunately, Ugone had heard the order given by Giulio, he called two of the soldiers by name, and these picked up their captain. As after all he did not faint, he ordered them to carry him to the end of the garden, to the little door. This order made the men swear; they obeyed, nevertheless.

"A hundred sequins to the man who opens that door!" cried Giulio.

But it resisted the efforts of three furious men. One of the old gardeners, installed in a window on the second floor, fired a number of pistol shots at them, which served to lighten their path.

After vain efforts to break down the door, Giulio fainted completely away; Ugone told the soldiers to carry the captain out as quickly as possible. He himself went into the portress's lodge, out of which he flung little Marietta, telling her in a terrifying voice to make her escape, and never to say that she had recognised him. He pulled out the straw from the bed, broke several chairs and set fire to the room. When he saw the fire well started, he made off as fast as he could run, through a rain of arquebus shots fired by the *bravi* in the convent.

It was not until he had gone some hundred and fifty yards from the Visitation that he found the captain, who, in a dead faint, was being carried rapidly away. A few minutes later, they were out of the town; Ugone called a halt; he had now only four soldiers with him; he sent two back into the town, with orders to fire their arquebuses every five minutes.

"Try to find your wounded comrades," he told them, "and leave the town before daybreak; we are going to follow the path towards the Croce Rossa. If you can start a fire anywhere, do so without fail."

When Giulio recovered consciousness, they had gone three leagues from the town, and the sun was already high above the horizon. Ugone made his report.

"Your troop consists now of only five men, of whom three are wounded. Two of the peasants who are alive have received a reward of two sequins each, and have fled; I have sent the two men who are not wounded to the nearest village to fetch a surgeon."

The surgeon, an old man trembling with fear, arrived presently mounted upon a magnificent ass; the men had had to threaten to set fire to his house before he would make up his mind to come. They were obliged also to dose him with brandy to make him fit to work, so great was his fear. Finally he set to work; he told Giulio that his injuries were of no consequence.

"The wound in the knee is not dangerous," he went on, "but it will make you limp all your life, if you do not keep absolutely still for the next two or three weeks."

The surgeon dressed the wounds of the men. Ugone made a sign with his eye to Giulio; two sequins were bestowed on the surgeon, who was speechless with gratitude; then, on the pretext of thanking him, they made him drink such a quantity of brandy that finally he fell into a deep sleep. This was what they desired. They carried him into a neighbouring field, and wrapped four sequins in a scrap of paper which was slipped into his pocket: it was the price of his ass, on which were set Giulio and one of the soldiers who was wounded in the leg. They went to spend the period of the midday heat in an ancient ruin

by the edge of a pond; they marched all night, avoiding
the villages, which were few in number upon that road,
and at length, on the third morning, at sunrise, Giulio,
carried by his men, awoke in the heart of the forest of la
Faggiola, in the charcoal-burner's hut which was his headquarters.

## VI

O N the morning after the fight, the nuns of the
    Visitation were horrified to find nine dead bodies
    in their garden and in the passage that led from
their outer gate to the gate with the iron bars; eight of
their *bravi* were wounded.  Never had there been such a
panic in the convent: it was true that they had, now and
again, heard arquebus shots fired in the square, but never
such a quantity of shots fired in the garden, in the middle
of the nuns' buildings and beneath their windows.  The
affair had lasted fully an hour and a half, and during that
time the disorder had been complete inside the convent.
Had Giulio Branciforte had the least understanding with
any of the sisters or boarders, he must have been successful:
all that was needed was to open to him one of the many
doors that led into the garden; but, wild with indignation
and with resentment of what he called the perjury of
young Elena, Giulio had sought to carry everything before
him by main force.  He would have felt that he was failing
in his duty to himself, had he confided his plan to anyone
who could repeat it to Elena.  And yet a single word to
her little Marietta would have sufficed to assure his success: she would have opened one of the doors leading into
the garden, and one man even appearing in the dormitories
of the convent, with that terrible accompaniment of arquebus shots heard from without, would have been obeyed to
the letter.  At the sound of the first shot, Elena had trembled for the life of her lover, and her one thought had
been to fly with him.

How are we to depict her despair when little Marietta

[ 91 ]

told her of the fearful wound Giulio had received in his knee, from which she had seen the blood flowing in torrents? Elena detested her own cowardice and pusillanimity:

"I was weak enough to say a word to my mother, and Giulio's blood has been shed; he might have lost his life in that sublime assault in which it was his courage that did everything."

The *bravi,* when admitted to the parlour, had said to the nuns, who were all agog to hear them, that never in their lives had they witnessed valour comparable to that of the young man dressed as a courier who directed the efforts of the brigands. If all the rest listened to these tales with the keenest interest, one may judge of the intense passion with which Elena asked these *bravi* for a detailed account of the young chief of the brigands. After the long stories which she made them, and also the old gardeners, tell her, she felt that she no longer loved her mother at all. There was indeed a moment of extremely heated discussion between these two women who had loved each other so tenderly on the eve of the fight; Signora de' Campireali was shocked by the bloodstains which she saw on the flowers of a certain nosegay from which Elena refused to be parted for a single instant.

"You ought to throw away those flowers covered with blood."

"It was I who caused that noble blood to be spilt, and it flowed because I was weak enough to say a word to you."

"You still love your brother's murderer?"

"I love my husband, who, to my eternal misfortune, was attacked by my brother."

After this reply, not a single word passed between Signora de' Campireali and her daughter during the three more days which the Signora spent in the convent.

On the day following her departure, Elena managed to

escape, taking advantage of the confusion that prevailed
at the two gates of the convent, owing to the presence of a
large number of masons who had been let into the garden
and were engaged in erecting new fortifications there.
Little Marietta and she were disguised as workmen. But
the townsfolk were keeping a strict guard at the gates of
the town. Elena had considerable difficulty in getting out.
Finally, the same small merchant who had conveyed Branciforte's letters to her consented to let her pass as his daughter, and to escort her as far as Albano. There Elena found
a hiding-place with her nurse, whom her generosity had
enabled to open a little shop. No sooner had she arrived,
than she wrote to Branciforte, and the nurse found, not
without great trouble, a man willing to risk his life by
entering the forest of la Faggiola without having the pass-
word of Colonna's troops.

The messenger dispatched by Elena returned after three
days, in great consternation; for one thing, he had been
unable to find Branciforte, and, as the questions which he
continued to put with regard to the young captain had
ended by making him suspected, he had been obliged to
take flight.

"There can be no doubt about it, poor Giulio is dead,"
Elena said to herself, "and it is I that have killed him!
Such was bound to be the consequence of my wretched
weakness and cowardice; he should have loved a strong
woman, the daughter of one of Prince Colonna's captains."

The nurse thought that Elena was going to die. She
went up to the Capuchin convent, standing by the road cut
in the rock, where Fabio and his father had once met the
lovers in the middle of the night. The nurse spoke at
great length to her confessor, and, beneath the seal of the
sacrament, admitted to him that young Elena de' Campireali wished to go and join Giulio Branciforte, her husband, adding that she was prepared to place in the church

[ 93 ]

of the convent a silver lamp of the value of one hundred Spanish piastres.

"A hundred piastres!" replied the friar angrily. "And what will become of our convent, if we incur the anger of Signor de' Campireali? It was not a hundred piastres, but a good thousand, that he gave us for going to fetch his son's body from the battlefield at the Ciampi, not to speak of the wax."

It must be said to the honour of the convent that two elderly friars, having discovered where precisely Elena was, went down to Albano and paid her a visit, originally with the intention of inducing her by hook or crook to take up her abode in the palazzo of her family: they knew that they would be richly rewarded by Signora de' Campireali. The whole of Albano was ringing with the report of Elena's flight and of the lavish promises made by her mother to anyone who could give her news of her daughter. But the two friars were so touched by the despair of poor Elena, who believed Giulio Branciforte to be dead, that, so far from betraying her by revealing to her mother the place in which she had taken refuge, they agreed to serve as her escort as far as the fortress of la Petrella. Elena and Marietta, once more disguised as workmen, repaired on foot and by night to a certain spring in the forest of la Faggiola, a league from Albano. The friars had sent mules there to meet them, and, when day had come, the party set out for la Petrella. The friars, who were known to be under the Prince's protection, were greeted everywhere with respect by the soldiers whom they met in the forest; but it was not so with the two little men who accompanied them: the soldiers began by staring at them in the most forbidding manner and came up to them, then burst out laughing and congratulated the friars on the charms of their muleteers.

"Silence, impious wretches; know that all is being done

under Prince Colonna's orders," replied the friars as they proceeded on their way.

But poor Elena was unlucky; the Prince was not at la Petrella, and when, three days later, on his return, he at length granted her an audience, he showed himself most stern.

"Why do you come here, Signorina? What means this ill-advised action? Your woman's chatter has cost the lives of seven of the bravest men in Italy, and that is a thing which no man in his senses will ever forgive you. In this world, one must wish a thing or not wish it. It is doubtless in consequence of similar chatter that Giulio Branciforte has just been declared guilty of sacrilege, and sentenced to be tortured for two hours with red-hot pincers, and then burned as a Jew, he, one of the best Christians I know! How could anyone, without some abominable chattering on your part, have invented so horrible a lie as to say that Giulio Branciforte was at Castro on the day of the attack on the convent? All my men will tell you that they saw him that day here at la Petrella, and that in the evening I sent him to Velletri.

"But is he alive?" Elena cried for the tenth time, bursting into tears.

"He is dead to you," replied the Prince. "You shall never set eyes on him again. I advise you to return to your convent at Castro; try to commit no more indiscretions, and I order you to leave la Petrella within an hour from now. Above all, never mention to anyone that you have seen me, or I shall find a way of punishing you."

Poor Elena was broken-hearted at meeting with such a reception from that famous Prince Colonna, for whom Giulio felt so much respect, and whom she loved because Giulio loved him.

Whatever Prince Colonna might choose to say, this action on Elena's part was by no means ill-advised. If she had come to la Petrella three days earlier, she would have found there Giulio Branciforte; the wound in his knee rendered him incapable of marching, and the Prince had him carried to the market town of Avezzano, in the Kingdom of Naples. At the first news of the terrible sentence upon Giulio Branciforte which, purchased by Signor de' Campireali, denounced him as guilty of sacrilege and of violating a convent, the Prince had seen that, should he have occasion to protect Branciforte, he would have to reckon without three-fourths of his men. This was a sin against the Madonna, to whose protection each of these brigands supposed himself to have a special claim. Had there been a *bargello* in Rome sufficiently daring to come and arrest Giulio Branciforte in the heart of the forest of la Faggiola, he might have been successful.

On reaching Avezzano, Giulio took the name of Fontana, and the men who carried him there were discreet. On their return to la Petrella, they announced with sorrow that Giulio had died on the way, and from that moment each of the Prince's soldiers knew that a dagger would find its way to the heart of any who should pronounce that fatal name.

It was in vain therefore that Elena, on her return to Albano, wrote letter after letter, and spent, on their transmission to Branciforte, all the sequins that she possessed. The two aged friars, who had become her friends, for extreme beauty, says the Florentine chronicler, cannot fail to exercise some sway, even over hearts hardened by the vilest selfishness and hypocrisy; the two friars, we say, warned the poor girl that it was in vain that she might seek to convey a word to Branciforte: Colonna had declared that he was dead, and certainly Giulio would not appear in public again unless the Prince chose. Elena's nurse informed her, with tears, that her mother had at length succeeded in discovering her retreat, and that the strictest orders had been given that she should be forcibly taken to the palazzo Campireali, in Albano. Elena realised that, once inside that palazzo, her imprisonment might be one of unbounded severity, and that they would succeed in cutting her off absolutely from any communication with the outer world, whereas at the Convent of Castro she would have, for receiving and sending letters, the same facilities as all the other nuns. Besides, and this was what brought her to a decision, it was in the garden of that convent that Giulio had shed his blood for her: she could gaze once more upon that wooden armchair in the portress's lodge on which he had sat for a moment to examine the wound in his knee; it was there that he had given Marietta that nosegay stained with blood which never left her person. And so she went sadly back to the Convent of Castro, and here one might bring her history to an end: it would be well for her, and for the reader also. For we are now about to observe the gradual degradation of a noble and generous nature. Prudent measures and the falsehoods of civilisation, which for the future are going to assail her on every side, will take the place of the sincere impulses of vigorous and natural passions. The Roman chronicler here sets down a most artless reflexion: because a woman has taken the trouble to bring into the world a beautiful daughter, she assumes that she has the talent necessary to direct that daughter's life, and because, when the daughter is six years old, she said to her and was justified in saying: "Miss, put your collar straight," when the daughter is eighteen and she herself fifty, when the daughter has as much intelligence as her mother and more, the mother, carried away by the mania for ruling, thinks that she has the right to direct her daughter's life and even to employ falsehood. We shall see that it was Vittoria Carafa, Elena's mother, who, by a succession of adroit measures, most skilfully planned, brought about the death of that dearly loved daughter, after keeping her in misery for twelve years, a lamentable result of the mania for ruling.

Before his death, Signor de' Campireali had had the joy of seeing published in Rome the sentence that condemned Giulio Branciforte to be tortured for two hours with red-hot irons in the principal squares of Rome, then to be burned on a slow fire, and his ashes flung into the Tiber. The frescoes in the cloisters of Santa Maria Novella, at Florence, still survive to show us how these cruel sentences upon the sacrilegious were carried out. As a rule, a numerous guard was required to prevent the outraged populace from forestalling the headsmen in their office. Everyone regarded himself as an intimate friend of the Madonna. Signor de' Campireali had had the sentence read over to him again a few moments before his death, and had given the *avvocato* who had procured it his fine estate lying between Albano and the sea. This *avvocato* was by no means devoid of merit. Branciforte was condemned to this terrible punishment, and yet no witness had professed to have recognised him beneath the clothing of that young man disguised as a courier, who seemed to be directing with such authority the movements of the assailants. The magnificence of the reward set all the intriguers of Rome in a stir. There was then at court a certain *fratone* (monk), a deep man and one capable of anything, even of forcing the Pope to give him the Hat; he looked after the affairs of Prince Colonna, and that terrible client earned him great consideration. When Signora de' Campireali saw her daughter once more safely at Castro, she sent for this *fratone*.

"Your Reverence will be lavishly rewarded, if he will be so kind as to help to bring to a successful issue the very simple affair which I am going to explain to him. In a few days' time, the sentence condemning Giulio Branciforte to a terrible punishment is to be published and made

effective in the Kingdom of Naples also. I request Your
Reverence to read this letter from the Viceroy, a relative
of mine, by the way, who deigns to inform me of this news.
In what land can Branciforte seek an asylum? I shall
have fifty thousand piastres conveyed to the Prince, with
the request that he will give the whole sum, or a part of
it, to Giulio Branciforte, on condition that he goes to serve
the King of Spain, my Sovereign, against the rebels in
Flanders. The Viceroy will give a brevet as captain to
Branciforte, and in order that the sentence for sacrilege,
which I hope to have made operative in Spain also, may not
hamper him at all in his career, he will go by the name of
Barone Lizzara; that is a small property which I have in
the Abruzzi, and shall find a way of making over to him,
by means of fictitious sales. I do not suppose Your Reverence has ever seen a mother treat her son's murderer like
this. For five hundred piastres we could long since have
been rid of the hateful creature; but we had no wish to fall
foul of Colonna. Be so good, therefore, as to point out to
him that my respect for his rights is costing me sixty or
eighty thousand piastres. I never wish to hear that Branciforte mentioned again; that is all, and you will present my
compliments to the Prince."

The *fratone* said that in two or three days he would be
going in the direction of Ostia, and Signora de' Campireali
handed him a ring worth a thousand piastres.

A few days later, the *fratone* reappeared in Rome, and
told Signora de' Campireali that he had not informed the
Prince of her plan, but that within a month young Branciforte would have taken ship for Barcelona, where she would
be able to convey to him, through one of the bankers of
that city, the sum of fifty thousand piastres.

The Prince found considerable difficulty in handling
Giulio. Whatever the risk he must for the future run in
Italy, the young lover could not make up his mind to leave

that country. In vain did the Prince suggest to him that Signora de' Campireali might die; in vain did he promise that, in any event, after three years, Giulio might return to visit his native land; Giulio shed copious tears, but consent he would not. The Prince was obliged to request him to go, as a personal service to himself; Giulio could refuse nothing to his father's friend; but, first and foremost, he wished to take his orders from Elena. The Prince deigned to take charge of a long letter; and, what was more, gave Giulio permission to write to her from Flanders once every month. At length the despairing lover embarked for Barcelona. All his letters were burned by the Prince, who did not wish Giulio ever to return to Italy. We have forgotten to mention that, although anything like ostentation was utterly alien to his character, the Prince had felt himself obliged to say, in order to bring matters to a successful issue, that it was he himself who thought fit to assure a small fortune of fifty thousand piastres to the only son of one of the most faithful servants of the house of Colonna.

Poor Elena was treated like a Princess in the Convent of Castro. Her father's death had put her in possession of a considerable fortune, and a vast inheritance would accrue to her in time. On the occasion of her father's death she made a gift of five ells of black cloth to all such of the inhabitants of Castro or of the district who announced that they wished to wear mourning for Signor de' Campireali. She was still in the first days of her bereavement when, by the hand of a complete stranger, a letter was brought to her from Giulio. It would be hard to describe the rapture with which that letter was opened, though no less hard to describe the intense grief which followed her perusal of it. And yet it was indeed in Giulio's handwriting; she examined it with the closest scrutiny. The letter spoke of love; but what love, great heavens! Nevertheless, it was Signora de' Campireali, who was so clever, that had composed it. Her intention was to begin the correspondence with seven or eight letters of impassioned love; she wished thus to prepare the way for the next letters, in which the writer's passion would seem to die gradually away.

We may pass briefly over ten years of an unhappy life. Elena supposed herself to be completely forgotten, and yet had scornfully refused the overtures of the most distinguished young noblemen in Rome. She did, however, hesitate for a moment, when mention was made to her of young Ottavio Colonna, the eldest son of the famous Fabrizio, who had received her so coldly, long ago, at la Petrella. She felt that, being absolutely obliged to take a husband in order to provide a protector for the lands which she owned in the Roman States and in the Kingdom of Naples, it would be less repulsive to her to bear the name of a man whom Giulio had once loved. Had she agreed to this marriage, Elena would very soon have found out the truth about Giulio Branciforte. The old Prince Fabrizio spoke often and with enthusiasm of the superhuman valour shown by Colonel Lizzara (Giulio Branciforte), who, just like the heroes of the old romances, was seeking to distract his mind by gallant actions from the unfortunate love affair which made him indifferent to all pleasures. He imagined Elena to be long since married; Signora de' Campireali had surrounded him, too, with falsehood.

Elena was half reconciled to that wiliest of mothers. She, passionately anxious to see her daughter married, asked her friend, old Cardinal Santi-Quattro, Protector of the Visitation, who was going to Castro, to announce in confidence to the senior sisters in the convent that his visit to them had been delayed by an act of grace. The good Pope Gregory XIII, moved to pity for the soul of a brigand named Giulio Branciforte, who had once tried to break into their cloister, had been pleased, on learning of his death, to revoke the sentence that declared him guilty of sacrilege, being fully convinced that, beneath the load of such a condemnation, he would never be able to escape from Purgatory, assuming that Branciforte, taken by surprise in Mexico and massacred by rebellious natives, had been so fortunate as to go no farther than Purgatory. This news put the whole Convent of Castro in a stir; it reached the ears of Elena, who at once began to indulge in all the foolish acts of vanity that the possession of a great fortune can inspire in a person who is profoundly vexed. From that moment, she never left her room. It should be explained that, in order to be able to install herself in the little portress's lodge in which Giulio had taken refuge for a moment on the night of the assault, she had had half the convent rebuilt. With infinite pains and, in the sequel, a scandal which it was extremely difficult to hush up, she had succeeded in laying hands on, and in taking into her service the three *bravi* employed by Branciforte who still survived out of the five that had got away from the fight at Castro. Among these was Ugone, now old and crippled by wounds. The arrival of these three men had caused considerable murmuring; but in the end the fear that Elena's proud nature inspired in the whole convent had prevailed, and every day they were to be seen, dressed in her livery, coming to take her orders at the outer grill, and often giving long answers to her questions, which were always on the same subject.

After the six months of seclusion and detachment from all the things of this world which followed the announcement of Giulio's death, the first sensation to awaken this heart already broken by a misfortune without remedy and a long period of boredom was one of vanity.

A little time since, the Abbess had died. According to custom, Cardinal Santi-Quattro, who was still Protector of the Visitation, despite his great age of ninety-two years, had drawn up the list of the three ladies from among whom the Pope would select an Abbess. It required some very serious reason to make His Holiness read the last two names on the list; as a rule he contented himself with running his pen through those names, and the nomination was made.

One day, Elena was at the window of what had been the portress's lodge, and had now become one end of the wing of new buildings erected by her. This window stood not more than two feet above the passage once watered by the blood of Giulio and now forming part of the garden. Elena's eyes were firmly fixed on the ground. The three ladies whose names, as had been known for some days, formed the Cardinal's list of possible successors to the late Abbess, came past Elena's window. She did not see them, and in consequence could not greet them. One of the three ladies was offended, and remarked in a loud voice to the other two:

"A fine thing for a boarder to flaunt her room before everybody."

Aroused by these words, Elena raised her eyes and encountered three hostile stares.

"Very well," she said to herself as she shut the window without greeting them, "I've played the lamb in this convent quite long enough; it's time I became a wolf, if only to give a little variety to the curious gentlemen of the town."

An hour later, one of her servants, dispatched as a courier, carried the following letter to her mother, who for the last ten years had been living in Rome, and had managed to acquire great influence there.

"Most respected Mother,

"Every year you give me three hundred thousand francs upon my birthday; I make use of that money to do foolish things, perfectly honourable things I must say, but foolish nevertheless. Although it is long since you have mentioned the matter, I know that there are two ways in which I can shew my gratitude for all the thoughtful care you have taken of me. I will never marry, but I would gladly become *Abbess of this Convent;* what has given me the idea is that the three ladies whose names our Cardinal Santi-Quattro has placed on the list which he will present to His Holiness are my enemies, and, whichever of them be chosen, I may expect every sort of annoyance. Offer the usual flowers on my birthday to all the right people; let us first have the nomination postponed for six months, which will make the Prioress of the Convent, my dearest friend, who is now holding the reins, wild with joy. That alone will afford me some happiness, and it is very seldom that I can use that word in speaking of your daughter. I think my idea absurd; but if you see any chance of success, in three days I will take the white veil, eight years of residence in the convent, without a night's absence, entitling me to six months' exemption. The dispensation is never refused, and costs forty scudi.

"I am with respect, my venerable mother," etc.

On reading this letter, Signora de' Campireali's joy knew no bounds. When it reached her, she was bitterly regretting that she had sent word to her daughter of Branciforte's death; she foresaw some mad action, she was even afraid lest her daughter might decide to go to Mexico to visit the spot where Branciforte was said to have been massacred, in which case it was highly probable that she would learn in Madrid the true name of Colonel Lizzara. On the other hand, what her daughter demanded in the letter was the most difficult, one might even say the most preposterous thing in the world. That a young girl who was not even in religion, and was known only for a mad love affair with a brigand, should be set at the head of a convent in which all the Roman Princes had relatives professed! "But," thought Signora de' Campireali, "they say that every cause can be pleaded, and, if so, won." In her reply, Vittoria Carafa gave her daughter grounds for hope; that daughter, as a rule, wished only for the most absurd things, but, on the other hand, she very soon tired of them. In the evening, while seeking any information that, nearly or remotely, bore upon the Convent of Castro, she learned that for some months past her friend Cardinal Santi-Quattro had been extremely cross: he wished to marry his niece to Don Ottavio Colonna, the eldest son of that Prince Fabrizio, who has been so often mentioned in the course of this narrative. The Prince offered him his second son, Don Lorenzo, because, in order to bolster up his own fortune, fantastically compromised by the war which the King of Naples and the Pope, reconciled at last, were waging against the brigands of la Faggiola, it was essential that his eldest son's wife should bring a dowry of six hundred thousand piastres (3,210,000 francs) to the House of Colonna. Now Cardinal Santi-Quattro, even by disinheriting in the most preposterous fashion all the rest of his family, could only offer a fortune of three hundred and eighty or four hundred thousand piastres.

Vittoria Carafa spent the evening and part of the night in having these reports confirmed by all the friends of old Santi-Quattro. Next day, about seven o'clock, she sent in her name to the old Cardinal.

"Your Eminence," she said to him, "we are neither of us young; it is useless our trying to deceive one another by giving fine names to things that are not fine; I have come to propose to you something mad; all that I can say in defence of it is that it is not abominable; but I must admit that I find it supremely ridiculous. When there was some talk of a marriage between Don Ottavio Colonna and my daughter Elena, I formed an affection for the young man, and, on the day of his marriage, I will hand over to you two hundred thousand piastres in land or in money, which I shall ask you to convey to him. But, in order to enable a poor widow like myself to make so enormous a sacrifice, I require that my daughter Elena, who is at present twenty-seven years old, and since the age of nineteen has never spent a night out of the convent, be made *Abbess of Castro;* but first of all the election must be postponed for six months; it is all quite canonical."

"What are you saying, Signora?" cried the old Cardinal in horror; "His Holiness himself could not perform what you come here and ask of a poor, helpless old man."

"Did I not tell Your Eminence that the thing was absurd: fools will call it madness; but the people that are well informed of what goes on at court will say that our Excellent Prince, good Pope Gregory XIII, has chosen to reward Your Eminence's long and loyal services by facilitating a marriage which the whole of Rome knows Your Eminence to desire. Besides, it is perfectly possible, quite canonical, I will vouch for it; my daughter is going to take the white veil to-morrow."

"But the simony, Signora!" cried the old man in a terrible voice.

Signora de' Campireali prepared to go.

"What is that paper you are leaving behind you?"

"It is the list of the estates which I should present as the equivalent of two hundred thousand piastres, should that be preferred to ready money; the change of proprietor could be kept secret for a very long time: for instance, the House of Colonna might bring actions against me which I should proceed to lose. . . ."

"But the simony, Signora, the fearful simony!"

"The first thing to be done is to put off the election for

six months; to-morrow I shall call to receive Your Eminence's orders."

I feel that there is need of an explanation, for readers born north of the Alps, of the almost official tone of several passages in this dialogue: let me remind them that, in strictly Catholic countries, the majority of discussions of unpleasant subjects end in the confessional; and then it is anything but a trivial matter whether one has made use of a respectful or of an ironical expression.

In the course of the following day, Vittoria Carafa learned that, owing to a grave error in point of fact which had been discovered in the list of three ladies submitted to fill the vacant post of Abbess of Castro, that election was postponed for six months: the second lady upon the list had a renegade in her family; one of her great-uncles had turned Protestant at Udine.

Signora de' Campireali felt herself impelled to approach Prince Fabrizio Colonna, to whose House she was about to offer so notable an increase in its patrimony. After trying for two days, she succeeded in obtaining an appointment in a village near Rome, but she came away quite alarmed by her audience; she had found the Prince, ordinarily so calm, so greatly taken up with the military glory of Colonel Lizzara (Giulio Branciforte), that she had decided it to be completely useless to ask him to keep silent on that head. The Colonel was to him like a son, and, what was more, a favourite pupil. The Prince spent his time reading and re-reading certain letters that came to him from Flanders. What would become of the cherished plan to which Signora de' Campireali had sacrificed so much in the last ten years, were her daughter to learn of the existence and fame of Colonel Lizzara?

I must pass over in silence a number of circumstances which do, indeed, portray the manners of that age but seem to me wearisome to relate. The author of the Roman manu-

script has taken endless pains to arrive at the exact date
of these details which I suppress.

Two years after Signora de' Campireali's meeting with
Prince Colonna, Elena was Abbess of Castro; but the old
Cardinal Santi-Quattro had died of grief after this great
act of simony. At that time Castro had as Bishop the
handsomest man at the Papal Court, Monsignor Francesco
Cittadini, a noble of the city of Milan. This young man,
remarkable for his modest graces and his tone of dignity,
had frequent dealings with the Abbess of the Visitation,
especially with regard to the new cloister with which she
proposed to adorn her convent. This young Bishop Cittadini, then twenty-nine years old, fell madly in love with
the beautiful Abbess. In the legal proceedings which followed, a year later, a number of nuns, whose evidence was
taken, report that the Bishop made his visits to the Convent as frequent as possible, and often said to their Abbess:
"Elsewhere I command, and, I am ashamed to say, find
some pleasure in doing so; in your presence, I obey like a
slave, but with a pleasure that far surpasses that of commanding elsewhere. I find myself under the influence of
a superior being; were I to try, I could have no other will
than hers, and I would rather see myself, to all eternity,
the last of her slaves than reign as king out of her sight."

The witnesses relate that often, in the middle of these
elegant speeches, the Abbess would order him to be silent,
and in harsh language which implied scorn.

"To tell the truth," another witness goes on, "the Signora
used to treat him like a servant; when that happened the
poor Bishop would lower his eyes, and begin to weep, but
he never went away. He found a fresh excuse every day
for coming to the Convent, which greatly scandalised the
nuns' confessors and the enemies of the Abbess. But the
Lady Abbess was strongly defended by the Prioress, her

dearest friend, who carried on the internal government under her immediate orders.

"You know, my noble sisters (she used to say), that ever since that thwarted passion which our Abbess felt in her earliest girlhood for a soldier of fortune, her ideas have always been very odd; but you all know that there is this remarkable element in her character, that she never changes her mind about people for whom she has shown her contempt. Well, never, in the whole of her life, probably, has she said so many insulting words as she has uttered in our presence to poor Monsignor Cittadini. Every day, we see him submit to treatment which makes us blush for his high office."

"Yes," replied the scandalised sisters, "but he comes again the day after; so, after all, he cannot be so ill treated, and, however that may be, this suggestion of intrigue is damaging to the reputation of the Holy Order of the Visitation."

The sternest master would never address to the clumsiest servant one quarter of the abuse which, day after day, the proud Abbess heaped upon this young Bishop whose manners were so unctuous; but he was in love, and had brought from his own country the fundamental maxim that once an undertaking of this sort has been begun, one has to think only about the end and not to consider the means.

"After all," said the Bishop to his confidant, Cesare del Bene, "the true scorn is that felt for the lover who has desisted from the attack before being compelled to do so by superior forces."

Now my sad task will be confined to giving an extract, of necessity extremely dry, from the criminal proceedings which led to Elena's death. These proceedings, which I have read in a library the name of which I am obliged to keep private, occupy no fewer than eight folio volumes. The questions and arguments are in the Latin tongue, the answers in Italian. I find that during the month of November, 1572, about eleven o'clock at night, the young Bishop betook himself alone to the door of the church by which the faithful are admitted throughout the day; the Abbess herself opened this door to him, and allowed him to follow her. She received him in a room which she often occupied, one that communicated by a secret door with the galleries built over the aisles of the church. Barely an hour elapsed before the Bishop, in great bewilderment, was sent packing; the Abbess herself conducted him to the door of the church, and addressed him in these very words:

*"Return to your Palace, and leave my sight at once. Farewell, Monsignore; you fill me with horror; I feel that I have given myself to a lackey."*

Three months later, however, came Carnival. The people of Castro were famous for the festivities which they held among themselves at this season, the whole town being filled with the clamour of the masquerades. Not one of these failed to pass beneath a little window which gave a feeble light to a certain stable in the Convent. We need not be surprised to hear that three months before Carnival this stable had been converted into a parlour, which was never empty during the days of masquerade. In the midst of all the popular absurdities, the Bishop came past in his coach; the Abbess made him a signal, and, the following night, at one o'clock, he appeared without fail at the door of the church. He entered, but, within three-quarters of an hour, was angrily dismissed. Since the first assignation, in the month of November, he had continued to come to the Convent almost every week. A slight air of rather foolish triumph was to be observed on his face; this everyone noticed, but it had the special effect of greatly shocking the proud nature of the young Abbess. On Easter Monday, among other occasions, she treated him like the meanest of mankind, and addressed to him words which the humblest workman in the Convent would not have borne. Nevertheless, a few days later, she gave him a signal, on receiving which the handsome Bishop presented himself without fail at the door of the church; she had sent for him to let him know that she was with child. On hearing this, says the official account, the young man turned pale with horror and became absolutely *stupid with fear*. The Abbess took fever; she sent for the doctor, and made no mystery to him about her condition. The man knew his patient's generous nature, and promised to help her out of the difficulty. He began by putting her in touch with a woman of humble station, young and good looking, who, without bearing the title of midwife, had the necessary acquirements. Her husband was a baker. Elena was taken with the conversation of this woman, who informed her that, in order to carry out the plans by which she hoped to save her, it was necessary that she should have two other women in her confidence inside the Convent.

"A woman like yourself, well and good, but one of my equals? Never! Leave my presence."

The midwife withdrew. But, a few hours later, Elena, feeling it not to be prudent to expose herself to the risk of the woman's chattering, summoned the doctor, who sent the woman back to the Convent, where she was liberally rewarded. This woman swore that, even had she not been called back, she would never have divulged the secret that had been confided to her; but she declared once again that, if there were not, inside the Convent, two women devoted to the Abbess's interests and conversant with everything, she herself could have no hand in the matter. (No doubt, she was thinking of the possible charge of infanticide.) After prolonged reflexion, the Abbess decided to entrust this terrible secret to Donna Vittoria, Prioress of the Convent, of the ducal family of C——, and to Donna Bernarda, daughter of the Marchese P——. She made them swear

[ 111 ]

on their breviaries that they would never utter a word, even at the stool of penitence, of what she was about to confide to them. The ladies stood frozen with terror. They admit, in their examination, that, having in mind the proud nature of their Abbess, they expected to hear a confession of murder. The Abbess said to them, quite simply and coolly:

"I have failed in all my duties; I am with child."

Donna Vittoria, the Prioress, deeply moved and troubled on account of the ties of friendship which for so many years had bound her to Elena, and not urged by any idle curiosity, exclaimed with tears in her eyes:

"And who is the bold wretch that has committed this crime?"

"I have not told even my confessor; judge whether I am likely to tell you!"

The two ladies at once began to consider the best way of keeping this fatal secret from the rest of the convent. They decided first of all that the Abbess's bed should be removed from her own room, at the very centre of the building, to the Pharmacy, which had just been installed in the most remote part of the Convent, on the third floor of the great wing erected by Elena's generosity. It was in this spot that the Abbess gave birth to a male child. For three weeks the baker's wife had been concealed in the Prioress's apartment. As this woman was hurrying swiftly along the cloister carrying the child, it began to cry, and in her terror she took shelter in the cellar. An hour later, Donna Bernarda, assisted by the doctor, managed to open a little gate in the garden wall; the baker's wife hurriedly left the Convent, and, shortly afterwards, the town. On reaching the open country, still pursued by a wild terror, she took refuge in a little cave to which chance led her among some rocks. The Abbess wrote to Cesare del Bene, the Bishop's confidant and head valet, who hastened to the

cave indicated; he was on horseback; he took the infant in
his arms, and set off at a gallop for Montefiascone. The
child was baptised there in the Church of Saint Margaret,
and received the name of Alessandro. The landlady of
the local inn had procured a nurse, on whom Cesare bestowed eight scudi: a crowd of women, who had gathered
outside the church during the ceremony of baptism, called
out persistently to Signor Cesare, demanding the name of
the child's father.

"He is a great gentleman of Rome," Cesare told them,
"who has allowed himself to make free with a poor village
girl like yourselves."

So saying, he vanished.

# VII

ALL was going well so far in that immense convent, peopled with more than three hundred inquisitive women; no one had seen anything, no one had heard anything. But the Abbess had given the doctor some handfuls of sequins newly struck from the mint in Rome. The doctor gave several of these pieces to the baker's wife. The woman was pretty and her husband jealous; he searched in her box, found these pieces of gold that shone so brightly, and, supposing them to be the price of her shame, forced her, with a knife at her throat, to tell him from whence they came. After some equivocation, the woman confessed the truth, and peace was made. The couple then began to discuss the use to which they should put so large a sum. The wife wished to pay various debts; but the husband thought it better to buy a mule, which was done. This mule created a scandal among the neighbours, who knew well the poverty of the couple. All the gossips in the town, friend and foe alike, came in turn to ask the baker's wife who was the generous lover who had enabled her to buy a mule. The woman, losing her temper, sometimes replied by telling the truth. One day when Cesare del Bene had been to see the child and came to give an account of his visit to the Abbess, she, although extremely unwell, dragged herself to the grating, and reproached him for the want of discretion shewn by the agents whom he employed. The Bishop, meanwhile, fell ill with fear; he wrote to his brothers in Milan to inform them of the false accusation that was being levelled against him: he appealed to them to come to his rescue. Although seriously ill, he made up his mind to leave Castro; but, before starting, he wrote to the Abbess:

"You know already that all that happened is public property. So, if you have any interest in saving not only my reputation, but perhaps my life, and in order to avoid a greater scandal, you might lay the blame on Gianbattista Doleri, who died two days ago; so that if, in this way, you do not repair your own honour, mine at least shall be no longer imperilled."

The Bishop summoned Don Luigi, Confessor to the Monastery of Castro.

"Deliver this," he said, "into the Lady Abbess's own hands."

She, upon reading this atrocious missive, cried out in the hearing of all that happened to be in the room:

"Thus the foolish virgins deserve to be treated who set the beauty of the body above that of the soul."

The rumour of all that was occurring at Castro came rapidly to the ears of the *terrible* Cardinal Farnese (he had given himself that reputation some years back, because he hoped, at the next conclave, to have the support of the *zealous* Cardinals). He at once gave orders to the *podestà* of Castro to have Bishop Cittadini arrested. All the Bishop's servants, fearing the *question,* took flight. Cesare del Bene alone remained faithful to his master, and swore to him that he would die in torments sooner than reveal anything that might damage him. Cittadini, seeing himself under close guard in his own Palace, wrote again to his brothers, who arrived in haste from Milan. They found him detained in the Ronciglione prison.

I see from the Abbess's first examination that, while admitting her crime, she denied having had relations with the Bishop; her paramour had been Gianbattista Doleri, lawyer to the Convent.

On the 9th of September, 1575, Gregory XIII ordered that the trial should proceed with all haste and with the utmost rigour. A criminal judge, a fiscal and a commissary betook themselves to Castro and Ronciglione. Cesare del Bene, the Bishop's head valet, admitted only that he had taken an infant to a nurse. He was examined in the presence of Donna Vittoria and Donna Bernarda. He was put to the torture on consecutive days; his sufferings were acute; but, true to his word, he admitted only what it was impossible to deny, and the fiscal could extract nothing from him.

When it came to Donna Vittoria and Donna Bernarda, who had witnessed the tortures inflicted on Cesare, they admitted all that they had done. All the nuns were asked the name of the author of the crime; the majority replied that they had heard it said that it was the Bishop. One of the Sister Portresses repeated the offensive words which the Abbess had used to the Bishop when shewing him out of the church. She added: "When people talk in that tone, it means that they have long been making love to one another. And indeed Monsignore, who as a rule was remarkable for his excessive self-assurance, had quite a shamefaced air as he left the church."

One of the sisters, examined in front of the instruments of torture, replied that the author of the crime must be the cat, because the Abbess had it constantly in her arms and was always fondling it. Another sister asserted that the author of the crime must be the wind, because, on days when there was a wind, the Abbess was happy and in a good humour; she would expose herself to the force of the wind on a belvedere which she had had built on purpose; and, when anyone came to ask a favour of her in this spot, she never refused it. The baker's wife, the nurse, the gossips of Montefiascone, frightened by the tortures which they had seen inflicted on Cesare, told the truth.

The young Bishop was ill or feigning illness at Ronciglione, which gave his brothers, supported by the credit and secret influence of Signora de' Campireali, an opportunity of prostrating themselves more than once at the Pope's feet, and asking him that the proceedings might be suspended until the Bishop should have recovered his health. Whereupon the terrible Cardinal Farnese increased the number of the soldiers that were guarding him in his prison. As the Bishop could not be examined, the commissioners began all their sittings by subjecting the Abbess to a fresh examination. One day, after her mother had told her to have courage and to deny everything, she admitted all.

"Why did you first of all inculpate Gianbattista Doleri?"

"Out of pity for the Bishop's cowardice, and, besides, if he succeeds in saving his precious life, he will be able to provide for my son."

After this admission, the Abbess was confined in a room in the Convent of Castro, the walls of which, as well as its vaulting, were eight feet thick; the nuns would never speak of this dungeon without terror, and it went by the name of the monks' room; watch was kept there over the Abbess by three women.

The Bishop's health having slightly improved, three hundred *sbirri* or soldiers came for him to Ronciglione, and he was transported to Rome in a litter; he was confined in the prison called Corte Savella. A few days later, the sisters also were taken to Rome; the Abbess was placed in the Monastery of Santa Marta. Four sisters were inculpated: Donna Vittoria and Donna Bernarda, the sister through whom messages passed, and the portress who had heard the offensive words addressed to the Bishop by the Abbess.

The Bishop was examined by the Auditor of the Chamber, one of the chief personages in the judiciary. Torture was applied once again to the unfortunate Cesare del Bene,

[ 117 ]

who not only admitted nothing, but said things which *caused inconvenience to the public ministry;* these earned him a fresh dose of torture. This preliminary punishment was inflicted similarly upon Donna Vittoria and Donna Bernarda. The Bishop denied everything, with vituperation, but with a fine stubbornness; he gave an account, in the fullest detail, of all that he had done upon the three evenings which he was known to have spent with the Abbess.

Finally the Abbess and Bishop were confronted, and, albeit she continued to tell the truth, she was subjected to torture. As she repeated what she had always said from her first confession, the Bishop, sticking to his part, covered her with abuse.

After a number of other measures, reasonable enough in principle, but marred by that spirit of cruelty which, after the reigns of Charles V and Philip II, prevailed too often in the Italian courts, the Bishop was sentenced to undergo perpetual imprisonment in the Castel Sant' Angelo; the Abbess to be detained for the term of her life in the Convent of Santa Marta, where she was. But already Signora de' Campireali, in the hope of saving her daughter, had set to work to have a subterranean passage burrowed. This passage started from one of those sewers which are relics of the splendour of ancient Rome, and was to end in the deep cellar in which were deposited the mortal remains of the nuns of Santa Marta. This passage, which was barely two feet in width, was walled with planks, to keep back the earth on either side, and was roofed, as it advanced, with pairs of planks arranged like the sides of a capital A.

The tunnel was being bored about thirty feet below ground. The important thing was to carry it in the right direction; at every moment, wells and the foundations of old buildings obliged the workmen to turn aside. Another great difficulty arose as to the disposal of the earth, with which they did not know what to do; it appears that they sprinkled it during the night over all the streets of Rome. The citizens were astonished to see such a quantity of earth, fallen, as one might say, from heaven.

However large the sums Signora de' Campireali might spend in the attempt to save her daughter's life, her subterranean passage would doubtless have been discovered, but Pope Gregory XIII happened to die in 1585, and disorder reigned as soon as the See was vacant.

Elena was far from happy at Santa Marta; one may imagine whether common and distinctly poor nuns shewed zeal in annoying a very rich Abbess convicted of such a crime. She was eagerly awaiting the outcome of her mother's enterprise. But suddenly her heart was caught by strange emotions. Six months had already passed since Fabrizio Colonna, seeing the uncertain state of Gregory XIII's health, and having great plans for the interregnum, had sent one of his officers to Giulio Branciforte, now so widely known in the Spanish armies under the name of Colonel Lizzara. He recalled him to Italy; Giulio was burning to see his native land once more. He landed under a false name at Pescara, a small port on the Adriatic below Chieti, in the Abruzzi, and journeyed over the mountains to la Petrella. The Prince's joy caused general astonishment. He told Giulio that he had sent for him to make him his successor and to give him the command of his troops. To which Branciforte replied that, from the military point of view, it was no longer worth while to continue, as he was easily able to prove; if Spain ever seriously wished to do so, in six months, and at small cost to herself, she could wipe out all the soldiers of fortune in Italy.

"However," young Branciforte added, "if you wish it, Prince, I am ready to take the field. You will always find in me a successor to the gallant Ranuccio, who was killed at the Ciampi."

Before Giulio's arrival, the Prince had ordered, as he alone could order, that no one at la Petrella should dare to speak of Castro or of the Abbess's trial; the penalty of death, without hope of respite, was held out as a deterrent from any rash word. In the course of the affectionate greetings with which he welcomed Branciforte, he asked him on no account to go to Albano without himself, and his method of carrying out the expedition was to occupy the town with a thousand of his men, and to post an advance guard of twelve hundred on the road to Rome. One may imagine poor Giulio's state when the Prince, having sent for old Scotti, who was still alive, to the house in which he had established his headquarters, made him come up to the room in which he himself was sitting with Branciforte. As soon as the two old friends had flung themselves into each other's arms:

"Now, my poor Colonel," he said to Giulio, "be prepared for the worst."

Whereupon he snuffed the candle and left the room, turning the key on the friends.

Next day Giulio, who preferred not to leave his room, sent to the Prince to ask leave to return to la Petrella, and not to see him for some days. But his messenger returned to say that the Prince had disappeared, with all his troops. During the night, he had heard of the death of Gregory XIII; he had forgotten his friend Giulio and was scouring the country. There remained with Giulio only some thirty men belonging to Ranuccio's old company. The reader is aware that in those days, during a vacancy of the See, the law no longer ran, everyone thought of gratifying his own passions, and there was no force but brute force; that is why, before the end of the day, Prince Colonna had already hanged more than fifty of his enemies.

As for Giulio, albeit he had not forty men with him, he made bold to march upon Rome.

All the servants of the Abbess of Castro had remained faithful to her; they were lodged in humble houses near the Convent of Santa Marta. The death agony of Gregory XIII had lasted for more than a week; Signora de' Campireali was eagerly awaiting the troubled days that would follow his death before attacking the final fifty yards of her tunnel. As it had to pass through the cellars of several inhabited houses, she was greatly afraid lest she might be unable to keep from public knowledge the completion of her undertaking.

On the second day after Branciforte's arrival at la Petrella, the three of Giulio's old *bravi*, whom Elena had taken into her service, appeared to have gone mad. Although everyone knew only too well that she was in the strictest isolation, and guarded by nuns who hated her, Ugone, one of the *bravi*, came to the gate of the Convent and made the strangest request that he should be allowed to see his mistress, and without delay. He was refused admission and turned from the door. In his desperation, the man remained outside, and began to distribute *baiocchi* (copper coins) among all the persons employed in the service of the Convent who passed in or out, saying to them these precise words: *"Rejoice with me; Signor Giulio Branciforte has arrived, he is alive: tell this to your friends."*

Ugone's two companions spent the day in bringing him fresh supplies of *baiocchi*, which they continued to distribute day and night, always repeating the same words, until there was not one *baiocco* left. But the three *bravi*, taking turns, continued none the less to keep guard at the gate of the Convent of Santa Marta, still addressing to all that passed them the same words, followed by an obsequious salute: *"Signor Giulio has arrived,"* etc.

These worthy fellows' plan was successful: less than thirty-six hours after the giving of the first *baiocco*, poor Elena, down in her cell, in solitary confinement, knew that *Giulio was alive;* the words threw her into a sort of frenzy:

"Oh, my mother!" she cried, "what harm you have wrought me!"

A few hours later, the astonishing news was confirmed by little Marietta, who, by making a sacrifice of all her golden ornaments, obtained leave to accompany the sister who took the prisoner her meals. With tears of joy Elena flung herself into her arms.

"This is very pleasant," she said to her, "but I shall not be with you much longer."

"Indeed no!" said Marietta. "I am sure that before this Conclave is ended, your imprisonment will be changed to an ordinary banishment."

"Ah, my dear, to see Giulio again! And to see him, with this guilt on my head!"

In the middle of the third night after this conversation, part of the floor of the church fell in with a loud noise; the nuns of Santa Marta thought that their convent was going to collapse. Their commotion was extreme, everyone was calling out that there had been an earthquake. About an hour after the subsidence of the marble pavement of the church, Signora de' Campireali, preceded by the three *bravi* in Elena's service, made her way into the dungeon by the underground passage.

"Victory, victory, Signora!" cried the *bravi*.

Elena was in a mortal fear; she thought that Giulio Branciforte was with them. She was quite reassured, and her features resumed their stern expression when the men told her that they were escorting Signora de' Campireali, and that Giulio was still at Albano, which he had just invaded with several thousand troops.

She waited for some moments, and then Signora de'

Campireali appeared; she was walking with great difficulty, on the arm of her *scudiere,* who was in full costume, with sword on hip; but his gorgeous coat was all soiled with earth.

"Oh, my dear Elena, I have come to rescue you!" cried Signora de' Campireali.

"And how do you know that I wish to be rescued?"

Signora de' Campireali was left speechless; she stared helplessly at her daughter; she seemed greatly agitated.

"Well, my dear Elena," she said at length, "fate compels me to confess to you an action which was perhaps natural enough, after the misfortunes that had befallen our family, but of which I repent, and beg that you will forgive me for it: Giulio . . . Branciforte . . . is alive . . ."

"And it is because he is alive that I have no wish to live."

Signora de' Campireali did not at first grasp her daughter's meaning, then she besought her with the most tender supplications; but she could obtain no answer. Elena had turned to her crucifix and was praying without listening to her. In vain, for a whole hour, did Signora de' Campireali make every effort to win from her a word or a look. At length, her daughter, losing patience, said to her:

"It was beneath the marble of this crucifix that his letters were hidden, in my little room at Albano; it had been better to let my father stab me! Go, and leave some gold with me."

As Signora de' Campireali tried to continue speaking to her daughter, disregarding the signs of alarm shewn by her *scudiere,* Elena lost patience.

"Let me, at least, have an hour of freedom; you have poisoned my life, you wish to poison my death as well."

"We shall still have command of the passage for two or three hours; I venture to hope that you will change your mind!" exclaimed Signora de' Campireali, bursting into tears.

And she made her way out by the underground passage.

"Ugone, stay with me," said Elena to one of her *bravi,* "and see you are well armed, my lad, for you may have to defend me. Let me see your dirk, your sword, your dagger."

The old soldier shewed her these weapons, all in good condition.

"Good; now wait there, outside my cell; I am going to write Giulio a long letter which you will hand to him yourself; I do not wish it to pass through any hands but yours, having nothing with which to seal it. You may read the whole of the letter. Put in your pockets all the gold my mother has left there, I need for myself only fifty sequins; place them on my bed."

Having said these words, Elena sat down to write.

"I have not the least doubt of you, my dear Giulio; if I take my departure, it is because I should die of grief in your arms, at the sight of what would have been my happiness, had I not committed a sin. You are not to imagine that I have ever loved any creature in the world after you; far from it, my heart was filled with the bitterest contempt for the man whom I admitted to my room. My sin was solely one of distraction, and, if you like, of wantonness. Think that my spirit, greatly weakened after the futile attempt which I made at la Petrella, where the Prince whom I revered, because you loved him, received me so cruelly; think, I say, that my spirit, greatly weakened, had been assailed by twelve years of falsehood. Everything round me was lying and false, and I knew it. I received first of all some thirty letters from you; imagine the rapture with which, at first, I used to tear them open. But, as I read them, my heart froze. I examined the writing, I recognised your hand, but not your heart. Think that this first falsehood cankered the essence of my life, so that I could open a letter in your writing without any pleasure! The detestable announcement of your death finally killed in me anything that might yet survive from the happy days of our youth. My first intention, as you can well understand, was to go to see with my eyes and touch with my hands the Mexican shore upon which they said that the savages had massacred you; had I carried out that idea . . . we should be happy now, for, in Madrid, whatever the number and craftiness of the spies that a watchful hand might have managed to dispose round about me, as I myself would have appealed to every heart in which there remained a trace of pity and of goodness, it is probable that I should have arrived at the truth; for already, my Giulio, your gallant deeds had attracted the attention of the whole world towards you, and perhaps someone in Madrid knew that you were Branciforte. Would you like me to tell you what prevented our happiness? First of all, the memory of the atrocious, humiliating reception the Prince gave me at la Petrella; what a chain of obstacles to surmount between Castro and Mexico! You see, my heart had already lost its motive power. Then I had an impulse of vanity. I had erected huge buildings in the Convent, in order to be able to take as my own room the portress's lodge, in which you took shelter on the night of the assault. One day, I was looking at the ground which, for my sake, you had watered with your blood; I heard a contemptuous utterance, raised my head, saw spiteful faces; to avenge myself, I decided to become Abbess. My mother, who knew quite well that you were alive, made heroic efforts to secure that preposterous nomination. The position was nothing, for me, but a source of trouble; it completed the debasement of my nature; I took pleasure often in proving my power by the suffering of others; I committed acts of injustice. I saw myself, at the age of thirty, virtuous according to the world, rich, respected, and yet completely wretched. Then there appeared that poor man, who was goodness itself, but foolishness personified. The effect of his foolishness was that I bore with his first suggestions. My heart had been made so wretched by everything that surrounded me after your departure, that it had no longer the strength to resist the slightest temptation. Shall I confess to you something really indelicate? Yes, for I remember that everything is permitted to the dead. When you read these lines, the worms will be devouring this so-called beauty, which should have been all yours. Well, I must out with this matter which distresses me; I did not see why I should not make trial of the coarser side of love, like all our Roman ladies; I had a lascivious thought, but I was never able to give myself to that man without a feeling of horror and disgust which destroyed all the pleasure. I saw you always at my side, in the garden of our palazzo at Albano, when the Madonna inspired in you that thought, apparently so noble, but one that has, after my mother, been the bane of our lives. You were not at all threatening, but tender and good as you always were, you looked at me, then I felt moments of anger with that other man, and went so far as to beat him with all my strength. This is the whole truth, my dear Giulio: I did not wish to die without telling you it, and I thought also that perhaps this conversation with you might take away from me the idea of dying. It makes me see all the more clearly what would have been my joy on greeting you again, had I kept myself worthy of you. I order you to live and to continue that military career which caused me so much joy when I heard of your success. What would my joy have been, great God, had I received your letters, especially after the battle of Achenne! Live, and recall often to your mind the memory of Ranuccio, killed at the

Ciampi, and that of Elena, who, not to read a reproach in your eyes, lies dead at Santa Marta."

Having written this, Elena went up to the old soldier, whom she found sleeping; she took his dirk from him, without his noticing the loss, then aroused him.

"I have finished," she told him; "I am afraid of our enemies' seizing the passage. Go at once, take my letter which is on the table, and give it yourself to Giulio, *yourself,* do you understand? In addition to that, give him this handkerchief, tell him that I love him no more at this moment than I have always loved him, *always,* remember!"

Ugone was on his feet but made no move.

"Off with you!"

"Signora, have you really decided? Signor Giulio loves you so!"

"And I too, I love him, take the letter and give it to him yourself."

"Very well, may God bless you as you deserve!"

Ugone went and speedily returned; he found Elena dead; the dirk was in her heart.

# VITTORIA ACCORAMBONI

## DUCHESS OF BRACCIANO

# *VITTORIA ACCORAMBONI*

## *DUCHESS OF BRACCIANO*

U NFORTUNATELY for myself as for the reader, this is not a work of fiction, but the faithful translation of a most serious narrative written at Padua in December, 1585.

Some years ago I happened to be in Mantua; I was in search of sketches and small pictures in keeping with my small income, but I wanted only the work of painters earlier than the year 1600; about that date originality in Italian art, already greatly imperilled by the seizure of Florence in 1530, finally perished.

Instead of pictures, an aged patrician of great wealth and great avarice offered to sell me, at an extremely high price, some old manuscripts yellow with age; I asked leave to look through them; he consented, adding that he trusted to my honesty, that I would retain no memory of such spicy anecdotes as I might find, if I did not purchase his manuscripts.

On these terms, which appealed to me, I perused, to the great detriment of my eyesight, three or four hundred volumes in which had been jumbled together, two or three centuries ago, accounts of tragic adventures, letters challenging people to duels, treaties of peace between neighbouring nobles, memoranda upon every sort of subject, etc., etc. The venerable owner asked an enormous price for his manuscripts. After duly bargaining with him I acquired for a considerable sum the right to have copies made of certain stories which appealed to me and which illustrate Italian customs in the sixteenth century. I have twenty-two folio volumes of them, and it is one of these stories, faithfully translated, which the reader will find in the following pages, provided that he is endowed with patience. I know the history of the sixteenth century in Italy, and am of opinion that what follows is perfectly true. I have taken pains to arrange that the translation of that old Italian style, grave, direct, supremely obscure, and loaded with allusions to the things and ideas that occupied the world under the Pontificate of Sixtus V (in 1585) should shew no traces of the fine literature of to-day, or of the ideas of our unprejudiced age.

The unknown author of the manuscript is a circumspect person, he never judges any action, never leads up to it; his sole business is to relate things truthfully. If now and then he is unconsciously picturesque, that is because, in 1585, vanity did not enwrap a man's every action in a halo of affectation; he felt that he could exert an influence over his neighbour only by expressing himself with the utmost possible clarity. In the year 1585, with the exception of the fools kept at courts, or of poets, no one dreamed of making himself pleasant in speech. People had not yet learned to say: "I will die at Your Majesty's feet," when they had just sent out for post horses with which to fly the country; this was perhaps the one form of treachery that was not in use. People spoke little, and everyone paid the most careful attention to what was said to him.

And so, gracious reader, look not here for a quick and savoury style, sparkling with up to date allusions to the latest fashions in feelings, do not, above all, expect the captivating emotions of a novel by George Sand; that great writer would have made a masterpiece of the life and misfortunes of Vittoria Accoramboni. The sincere account which I present to you can claim only the most modest advantages of history. When it so happens that, travelling post, alone, as night is falling, your thoughts turn to the great art of knowing the human heart, you may take as a basis for your conclusions the story told in the following pages. The author says everything, explains everything, leaves nothing to the reader's imagination; he wrote twelve days after the death of the heroine.[1]

Vittoria Accoramboni was born of an extremely noble family, in a small town in the Duchy of Urbino, named Agubio. From her childhood, she was everywhere singled out, on account of her rare and extraordinary beauty; but this beauty was the least of her charms: nothing was lacking of those qualities which make one admire a girl of exalted birth; but nothing else was so remarkable in her, or as one might say nothing seemed so miraculous, amid so many extraordinary qualities, as a certain altogether charming grace which, at the first glance, won her the hearts and allegiance of all beholders. And this simplicity which gave authority to her slightest word was troubled by no suspicion of artifice; from the first one felt confidence in a lady endowed with such extraordinary beauty. One might, with a superhuman effort, have resisted this enchantment, had one merely seen her; but, if one heard her speak, if especially one was privileged to hold any conversation with her, it was quite impossible to escape so extraordinary a charm.

Many young gentlemen of the city of Rome, where her father lived, and where one still sees his palazzo in the Piazza Rusticucci, near Saint Peter's, sought to win her hand. There was much jealousy, and indeed rivalry, but

[1] The Italian manuscript is deposited at the office of the *Revue des Deux Mondes.*

in the end Vittoria's parents chose Felice Peretti, nephew of Cardinal Montalto, now Pope Sixtus V, whom God preserve.

Felice, the son of Camilla Peretti, the Cardinal's sister, was originally named Francesco Mignucci; he took the names of Felice Peretti when he was formally adopted by his uncle.

Vittoria, on entering the Peretti family, took with her, unawares, that superiority which may be called fatal, and which accompanied her everywhere; so that one might say that, in order not to adore her, one must never have set eyes on her.[1] The love that her husband felt for her was akin to madness; her mother-in-law, Camilla, and Cardinal Montalto himself, seemed to have no other occupation in the world than that of guessing Vittoria's wishes, so as to seek at once to gratify them. All Rome marvelled to see how this Cardinal, the modest limits of whose fortune were as well known as his horror of all forms of luxury, found so unfailing a source of pleasure in anticipating Vittoria's every wish. Young, brilliantly beautiful, adored by all, she could not help having, at times, some extremely costly fancies. Vittoria received from her new relatives jewels of the greatest price, pearls, in short all the rarest treasures of the goldsmiths of Rome, who at that time were very well supplied.

For love of this charming niece, Cardinal Montalto, so famous for his severity, treated Vittoria's brothers as though they had been his own nephews. Ottavio Accoramboni, as soon as he had completed his thirtieth year, was,

[1] One sees at Milan, if I remember rightly, in the Ambrosian Library, sonnets full of grace and feeling, and other pieces of poetry, the work of Vittoria Accoramboni. Sonnets of no little merit were composed at the time upon her strange fate. It appears that her intelligence was equal to her beauty and her charm.

on the representation of Cardinal Montalto, nominated by the Duke of Urbino and created, by Pope Gregory XIII, Bishop of Fossombrone; Marcello Accoramboni, a young man of fiery courage, accused of a number of crimes, and zealously pursued by the *corte*,[1] had with great difficulty escaped more than one prosecution which might have cost him his life. Honoured with the Cardinal's protection, he was able to recapture some sort of tranquillity.

A third brother of Vittoria, Giulio Accoramboni, was admitted by Cardinal Alessandro Sforza to the highest honours at his court, as soon as Cardinal Montalto had proffered the request.

In a word, if men know how to measure their happiness, not by the boundless insatiability of their desires, but by the real enjoyment of the advantages which they already possess, Vittoria's marriage to the nephew of Cardinal Montalto might have seemed to the Accoramboni the acme of human happiness. But the insensate desire for vast and uncertain advantages is capable of plunging the men most richly blessed with fortune's favours into strange and perilous channels of thought.

And very true it is that if any of Vittoria's relatives, as was widely suspected in Rome, helped, in his desire for an ampler fortune, to rid her of her husband, he very soon afterwards had occasion to realize how much wiser it would have been to content himself with the moderate benefits of a pleasant fortune, and one that was so soon to rise to the very summit of what human ambition can desire.

While Vittoria was living thus like a queen in her own house, one evening when Felice Peretti had just retired

---

[1] This was the armed body responsible for the public safety, the police and detective force of the year 1580. They were commanded by a captain styled Bargello, who was personally responsible for the execution of the orders issued by Monsignore the Governor of Rome (the Chief of Police).

to bed with his wife, a letter was handed to him by a certain Caterina, a native of Bologna and Vittoria's waiting woman. This letter had been brought by a brother of Caterina, Domenico Acquaviva, surnamed *il Mancino* (the left-handed). This man had been banished from Rome for various crimes; but, at Caterina's request, Felice had procured for him the powerful protection of his uncle the Cardinal, and the *Mancino* frequently came to the house, Felice placing great confidence in him.

The letter in question purported to be written by Marcello Accoramboni, of all Vittoria's brothers the one that her husband loved most dearly. He lived as a rule in hiding, out at Rome; at times, however, he took the risk of entering the city, and then found a place of refuge in Felice's house.

In the letter delivered at this unusual hour, Marcello appealed for help to his brother-in-law Felice Peretti; he implored him to come to his assistance, adding that, for an affair of the most urgent importance, he was waiting for him by the Montecavallo palace.

Felice informed his wife of the contents of the strange letter that had been brought to him, then put on his clothes, taking no weapon but his sword. Accompanied by a single servant who carried a lighted torch, he was about to leave the house when he found his way barred by his mother Camilla, and all the women of the house, including Vittoria herself; they all besought him, most urgently, not to leave the house at that late hour. As he did not give ear to their prayers, they fell on their knees, and, with tears in their eyes, implored him to listen.

These women, and Camilla especially, had been struck with terror by the accounts of the strange occurrences that were reported every day, and remained unpunished during the Pontificate of Gregory XIII, a time of incessant trouble and unparalleled violence. They were further struck by this consideration: Marcello Accoramboni, when he ventured to make his way into Rome, was not in the habit of sending for Felice, and such an action, at that time of night, seemed to them quite out of the question.

Filled with all the fire of his age, Felice paid no heed to these grounds for alarm; but, when he learned that the letter had been brought by the *Mancino,* a man to whom he was greatly attached and had been of service, nothing could stop him, and he stepped out of the house.

He was preceded, as has been said, by a single servant carrying a lighted torch; but the unfortunate young man had scarcely begun to ascend the Montecavallo when he fell, shot by three arquebuses. His assailants, seeing him on the ground, flung themselves upon him, and stabbed him again and again with daggers, until he appeared to be quite dead. Immediately the fatal tidings were conveyed to Felice's mother and wife, and through them reached the ears of the Cardinal his uncle.

The Cardinal, without moving a feature, without betraying the slightest emotion, promptly called for his clothes, dressed himself, and then commended himself to God, as also that poor soul (taken thus unawares). He next went to his niece, and, with admirable gravity and an air of profound peace, succeeded in restraining the womanly cries and lamentations which were beginning to ring through the house. His authority over the women was so effective that from that moment, and even when the body was being carried out of the house, nothing was to be seen or heard that in the least degree exceeded what occurs in the best regulated families on the occasion of the most natural deaths. As for Cardinal Montalto himself, no one could discover in him the signs, even in a modified form, of the most ordinary grief; nothing was altered in the order and outward show of his existence. Of this Rome was speedily convinced, after observing with her customary curiosity the slightest movements of a man whose feelings had been so profoundly outraged.

It so happened that on the day after Felice's death the Consistory, or Court of Cardinals, was summoned to meet at the Vatican. There was not a man in the city who did not suppose that on this first day, at least, Cardinal Montalto would excuse himself from this public function. For there he would have to meet the gaze of so many and such curious spectators. The slightest movements would be observed of that natural weakness which it is always so desirable to conceal when from an eminent position one aspires to another more eminent still; for everyone will agree that it is not fitting that he whose ambition it is to exalt himself above the rest of mankind should shew himself to be human like the rest.

But the persons who held these ideas were doubly mistaken, for in the first place, following his custom, Cardinal Montalto was among the first to appear in the Hall of the Consistory, and secondly it was impossible for the most discerning to discover in him any sign whatsoever of human sensibility. On the contrary, by the replies which he made to those of his fellow Cardinals who, in view of so painful an event, sought to offer him words of consolation, he succeeded in filling everyone with amazement. The constancy and apparent immobility of his nature under the shock of so fearful a tragedy at once became the talk of the town.

True it is that at this same Consistory certain persons, more conversant with the arts of the courtier, ascribed this apparent insensibility not to a want of feeling but to a wealth of dissimulation; and this point of view was shortly afterwards adopted by the mass of courtiers, for it was evidently to his advantage not to shew himself too deeply injured by an outrage the author of which was doubtless highly placed and might perhaps, later on, be able to bar the way to the supreme dignity.

Whatever might be the cause of this evident and complete insensibility, one thing certain is that it affected the whole of Rome and the court of Gregory XIII with a sort of stupor. But, to return to the Consistory, when, all the Cardinals being assembled, the Pope himself entered the hall, he at once turned his eyes towards Cardinal Montalto, and tears were seen on His Holiness's cheeks; as for the Cardinal, his features shewed no sign of departure from their normal immobility.

The astonishment waxed twofold when, during this same Consistory, Cardinal Montalto having gone up in his turn to kneel before the throne of His Holiness, and to render an account to him of the matters under his charge, the Pope, before allowing him to begin, was unable to restrain his own tears. When His Holiness was at length able to speak, he sought to console the Cardinal by promising him that prompt and stern justice would be done upon the authors of so appalling an outrage. But the Cardinal, after most humbly thanking His Holiness, begged him not to order any inquiry into what had occurred, protesting that, for his own part, he willingly forgave the author of the crime, whoever he might be. And immediately after this petition, expressed in the fewest possible words, the Cardinal passed to a detailed account of the business for which he was responsible, as though nothing out of the common had occurred.

The eyes of all the Cardinals present at the Consistory were fastened upon the Pope and upon Montalto; and although it is certainly most difficult to deceive the practised eye of a courtier, yet none of them dared say that Cardinal Montalto's face had betrayed the slightest emotion on witnessing, at such close quarters, the grief of His Holiness, who, tell the truth, was almost out of his mind. This amazing insensibility on the part of Cardinal Montalto never relaxed during the whole of the time occupied by his duty with His Holiness. Indeed, the Pope himself was impressed by this, and, the Consistory at an end, could not help remarking to the Cardinal of San Sisto, his favourite nephew:

*"Veramente, costui è un gran frate!"* (Truly, this fellow is a thorough friar![1])

Cardinal Montalto's mode of behaviour differed in no respect during the period that followed. As is the custom, he received the visits of condolence of the Cardinals, Prelates and Princes of Rome, and with none of these, whatever their existing relations, did he allow himself to give utterance to a single word of grief or lamentation. With all of them, after a brief commentary on the instability of human affairs, confirmed and fortified by sentences and texts taken from the Holy Scriptures or from the Fathers, he promptly changed the subject, and began to speak of the news of the town or of the private affairs of the person who was conversing with him, exactly as though he had wished to comfort his comforters.

Rome was particularly curious to know what would happen during the visit that would have to be paid him by Prince Paolo Giordano Orsini, Duke of Bracciano, to whom common report ascribed the death of Felice Peretti. The general opinion was that Cardinal Montalto would not be able to remain face to face with the Prince, and engaged in private conversation with him, without allowing some indication of his true feelings to appear.

[1] An allusion to the hypocrisy which their critics suppose to be frequent among friars. Sixtus V had been a mendicant friar, and persecuted in his order. See his Life, by Gregorio Leti, an amusing historian, and no more mendacious than any other. Felice Peretti was murdered in 1580; his uncle was created Pope in 1585.

At the moment when the Prince arrived at the Cardinal's, the crowd in the street and round the door was enormous; a vast number of courtiers filled every room in the house, so great was the curiosity to study the two men's faces. But on neither one nor the other could any of the observers distinguish anything out of the common. Cardinal Montalto conformed to everything that the rules of behaviour at court prescribed; he imparted to his face a most remarkable air of hilarity, and his tone in addressing the Prince was full of affability.

Immediately afterwards, as he stepped into his coach, Prince Paolo, finding himself alone with his intimate courtiers, could not help saying with a laugh: *"In fatto, è vero che costui è un gran frate!"* (Indeed, it is true, the fellow is a thorough friar!) as though he had wished to confirm the truth of the words let fall by the Pope a few days earlier.

Wise men have thought that the conduct observed in these circumstances by Cardinal Montalto paved the way for him to the throne; for many people formed the opinion of him that, whether by nature or from virtue he could not or would not do harm to anyone, even when he had every reason to be angry.

Felice Peretti had left nothing in writing with regard to his wife; consequently, she was obliged to return to her own home. Cardinal Montalto handed over to her, before her departure, the clothes, jewels, and, generally speaking, all the gifts that she had received while the wife of his nephew.

On the third day after the death of Felice Peretti, Vittoria, accompanied by her mother, went to live in the palazzo of Prince Orsini. Some said that these ladies were led to adopt this course by anxiety as to their personal safety, as they appeared to be threatened by the *corte*[1] with a charge of having *consented* to the homicide that had been committed, or of having at least had cognisance of it beforehand; others thought (and what occurred later on seemed to confirm this view) that they were led to adopt this course in order to bring about the marriage, the Prince having promised Vittoria that he would marry her as soon as she should be no longer tied to a husband.

Anyhow, neither then nor later was it ever definitely known who had been responsible for the death of Felice, although everyone had his suspicions of someone else. Most people, however, set the murder down to Prince Orsini; it was generally admitted that he had a passion for Vittoria, he had shewn signs of this which could not be mistaken; and the marriage that followed was a strong proof, for the bride was so inferior in station that only the tyranny of amorous passion could raise her to a plane of matrimonial equality.[2] The common herd were by no means discouraged in this attitude by a letter addressed to the Governor of Rome which was made public a few days after the crime. This letter purported to have been written by Cesare Palantieri, a young man of a fiery spirit who had been banished from the city.

In this letter, Palantieri said that it was unnecessary for His Most Illustrious Worship to give himself the trouble of seeking elsewhere for the author of the death of Felice Peretti, since he himself had procured his assassination in

---

[1] The *corte* dared not venture into a Prince's palazzo.

[2] Prince Orsini's first wife, by whom he had a son named Virginio, was a sister of Francesco I, Grand Duke of Tuscany, and of the Cardinal Ferdinand de' Medici. He put her to death, with the consent of her brothers, because she had had a love affair. Such were the laws of honour conveyed to Italy by the Spaniards. The unhallowed loves of a woman were as grave an offence to her brothers as to her husband.

consequence of certain differences which had arisen between them some time earlier.

Many people thought that the murder had not been committed without the consent of the Accoramboni family; they accused Vittoria's brothers, who were supposed to have been led astray by the desire for an alliance with so powerful and wealthy a prince. Marcello in particular was accused, on the strength of the letter which had made the unfortunate Felice leave his house. Harsh things were said of Vittoria herself, when people saw that she consented to go and live in the palazzo Orsini as a future bride, so soon after the death of her husband. It was highly improbable, they suggested, that two people would come like that, in the twinkling of an eye, to a hand-to-hand encounter, if they had not, for some time at least, been engaged with weapons of longer range.[1]

The inquiry into the murder was conducted by Monsignor Portici, Governor of Rome, by order of Gregory XIII. All that one gathers from it is that Domenico, surnamed Mancino, arrested by the *corte,* confesses, without being put to the question (*tormentato*), in his second examination, dated February 24th, 1582:

"That Vittoria's mother was responsible for everything, and that she was assisted by the maid from Bologna, who, immediately after the murder, took refuge in the citadel of Bracciano" (which belonged to Prince Orsini, and into which the *corte* would not dare to penetrate), "and that the instruments of the crime were Macchione of Gubbio and Paolo Barca of Bracciano, *lancie spezzate"* (soldiers) "of a gentleman whose name, for fit and proper reasons, has been omitted."

To these *fit and proper reasons* were added, I imagine,

[1] An allusion to the custom of fighting with a sword and a dagger.

the entreaties of Cardinal Montalto, who persistently begged that the inquiry should be carried no farther, and indeed there was no more talk of a prosecution. The Mancino was released from prison with the *precetto* (order) to return at once to his own home, on pain of death, and never to leave it again without express permission. The enlargement of this man occurred in the year 1583, on the feast of Saint Louis, and as that day was also Cardinal Montalto's birthday, the coincidence confirms my belief that it was at his request that the matter was thus brought to an end. Under so weak a government as that of Gregory XIII, a prosecution of that sort was liable to have the most disagreeable consequences without any compensating advantage.

The activities of the *corte* were thus suspended, but Pope Gregory XIII still declined to give his consent to the marriage of Prince Paolo Orsini, Duke of Bracciano, to the widow Accoramboni. His Holiness, having sentenced the lady to a sort of imprisonment, gave her and the Prince a *precetto* not to make any contract of marriage with one another without express permission from himself or his successors.

In due course Gregory XIII died (early in 1585), and the legal experts consulted by Prince Paolo Orsini having given the opinion that the *precetto* was annulled by the demise of the sovereign who had imposed it, the Prince decided to marry Vittoria before the new Pope should be elected. But the marriage could not be celebrated so soon as the Prince wished, partly because he was anxious to have the consent of Vittoria's brothers, and it so happened that Ottavio Accoramboni, Bishop of Fossombrone, refused absolutely to give his consent, and partly because it was not expected that the election of a successor to Gregory XIII would be so soon completed. In fact the marriage was solemnised only on the day on which the Papacy was conferred upon Cardinal Montalto, the person so deeply interested in this affair, that is to say on the 24th of April, 1585, this coincidence being either accidental on the Prince's part, or deliberate, he being glad of an opportunity to shew that he was no more afraid of the *corte* under the new Pope than he had been under Gregory XIII.

This marriage caused a profound shock to Sixtus V (for such was the name selected by Cardinal Montalto); he had already discarded the outlook upon life appropriate to a friar, and had raised his mind to the level of the exalted rank in which God had now placed him.

The Pope, however, shewed no sign of anger; only, Prince Orsini, having called upon him that same day with the rest of the Roman nobility to kiss his foot, and with the secret intention of trying to read, on the Holy Father's face, what he had to expect or to fear from a man hitherto so little known, discovered that it was no laughing matter. The new Pope having gazed at the Prince in a singular fashion, and not uttered a single word in reply to the compliments which he addressed to him, the Prince made up his mind to find out without more ado what were His Holiness's intentions with regard to himself.

Through the channel of Ferdinand, Cardinal de' Medici (the brother of his first wife), and of the Spanish Catholic Ambassador, he begged and obtained of the Pope an audience in his private chamber: there he delivered to His Holiness a studied speech, and, without making any reference to the past, congratulated him on his new dignity, and offered him as a most faithful vassal and servant all his possessions and all his forces.

The Pope [1] heard him with unusual seriousness, and

---

[1] Sixtus V, elected Pope in 1585 at the age of sixty-eight, reigned for five years and four months: there is a striking similarity between him and Napoleon.

finally replied that no one was more anxious than himself that the life and actions of Paolo Giordano Orsini should for the future be worthy of the Orsini blood and of a true Christian knight; that as for what he had been in the past in his relations with the Holy See and with the Pope's own person, no one could say more to him than his own conscience; that nevertheless he, the Prince, might be assured of one thing, namely, that just as he, the Pope, willingly forgave him anything that he might have done against Felice Peretti and against Felice Cardinal Montalto, he would never forgive him what in future he might do against Pope Sixtus; consequently he ordered him to proceed at once to expel from his household and from his domains all the *banditi* (outlaws) and evildoers to whom, until then, he had given asylum.

Sixtus V was a singularly effective speaker, whatever tone he might adopt; but when he was angry and threatening, one would have said that his eyes flashed lightning. One thing certain is that Prince Paolo Orsini, accustomed all his life to be feared by Popes, was led to think so seriously of his own position by the Pope's way of speaking, the like of which he had not heard for thirteen years, that no sooner had he left His Holiness's Palace than he hastened to Cardinal de' Medici to tell him what had occurred. After which he decided, on the Cardinal's advice, to send packing, without a moment's delay, all the fugitives from justice to whom he had given asylum in his palazzo and on his estates, and began to look about for some honourable pretext for leaving the territory subjected to the power of so resolute a Pontiff.

It should be explained that Prince Paolo Orsini had become extraordinarily stout; his legs were thicker than an ordinary man's whole body, and one of these enormous legs was afflicted with the disease known as the *lupa,* or wolf, so called because it has to be fed upon an abundance of fresh meat which is applied to the affected part; otherwise the violent distemper, finding no dead flesh to devour, would begin to attack the living flesh that surrounds it.

The Prince made this malady an excuse for going to the celebrated baths of Abano, near Padua, on territory belonging to the Venetian Republic; he set off with his new bride about the middle of June. Abano was a safe haven for him, since, for a great many years past, the House of Orsini had been tied to the Venetian Republic by a chain of mutual services.

Having reached this land of safety, the Prince's one thought was to combine the delights of several places of residence; and, with this object, he took three magnificent palazzi: one at Venice, the palazzo Dandolo, on the Rio della Zacca; the second at Padua, and this was the palazzo Foscarini, on the splendid piazza called the Arena; for his third abode he chose Salo, on the charming shore of Lake Garda: this had originally belonged to the Sforza Pallavicini.

The Signori of Venice (the Government of the Republic) learned with pleasure of the arrival within their borders of so great a Prince, and at once offered him a most noble *condotta* (that is to say a considerable sum paid annually, which the Prince would be expected to spend on raising a body of two or three thousand men, of whom he would assume the command). The Prince hastily rejected this offer: he sent word to the Senators that albeit, by a natural inclination and one hereditary in his family, he felt himself drawn to the service of the Most Serene Republic, yet, inasmuch as he was for the time being attached to His Catholic Majesty, it did not seem to him proper that he should accept any other engagement. So decided a response created some warmth of feeling among the Senators. At first they had thought of greeting him, on his arrival in Venice, and in the name of the people as a whole,

[ 147 ]

with a most honourable reception; they now decided, in view of his reply, to allow him to enter the city as a private person.

Prince Orsini, who was kept well informed, vowed that he would not go to Venice at all. He was already in the neighbourhood of Padua, he made a detour through that admirable country, and betook himself, with his whole retinue, to the house prepared for him at Salo, on the shores of Lake Garda. There he spent the whole of that summer amid splendid and varied diversions.

The time for a change (of residence) having come, the Prince made a number of little expeditions, after which he found that he could no longer endure fatigue as in the past; he began to be alarmed for his health; finally he thought of going to spend a few days at Venice, but was dissuaded by his wife, Vittoria, who begged him to remain at Salo.

There are some who have expressed the opinion that Vittoria Accoramboni was aware of the peril which threatened the life of the Prince, her husband, and that she made him stay at Salo only with the object of taking him, later on, out of Italy, to some free city, for instance, in the Swiss Cantons; in this way she would safeguard, in the event of the Prince's death, both her own person and her private fortune.

Whether or not this conjecture be well founded, the fact remains that nothing of the sort occurred, for the Prince, after a fresh attack of his malady at Salo on the 10th of November, at once had a premonition of what was in store.

He felt sorry for his unfortunate wife; he saw her, in the fine flower of her youth, left as poor in reputation as in worldly goods, hated by the reigning princes of Italy, little loved by the Orsini, and without hope of another marriage after his death. Like a great-hearted gentleman, faithful to his pledged word, he made, of his own accord, a will by which he hoped to assure the unfortunate woman's fortune.  He left her, in money or in jewels, the considerable sum of one hundred thousand piastres,[1] apart from all the horses, carriages and movable property which he had used on this expedition.  All the rest of his fortune he left to Virginio Orsini, his only son, whom he had had by his first wife, the sister of Francesco I., Grand Duke of Tuscany (the wife whom he had killed on account of her infidelity, with the consent of her brothers).

But how uncertain are all human anticipations!  The arrangements which Paolo Orsini thought must assure perfect security to that unhappy young woman, proved to be the cause of her utter and immediate ruin.

After signing his will, the Prince felt slightly better on the 12th of November.  On the morning of the 13th he was bled, and the doctors, whose only hope lay in a strict diet, left the most definite orders that he was to take no food.

But they had barely left the room before the Prince insisted that dinner should be brought to him; no one dared oppose his wishes, and he ate and drank as usual. Scarcely was the meal ended before he lost consciousness, and two hours before sunset he was dead.

After this sudden death, Vittoria Accoramboni, accompanied by Marcello, her brother, and by the whole of the deceased Prince's household, repaired to Padua to the palazzo Foscarini, situated near the Arena, the palazzo in fact that Prince Orsini had taken.

Shortly after her arrival, she was joined by her brother Flaminio, who stood high in the favour of Cardinal Farnese.  She then began to take the necessary measures to obtain payment of the legacy which her husband had bequeathed to her; this legacy amounted in cash to sixty

[1] About two million francs in 1837.

thousand piastres, which were to be paid to her within a period of two years, and this sum was independent of her dowry, jointure, and all the jewels and furniture actually in her possession. Prince Orsini had ordered, in his will, that in Rome or such other city as the Duchess might choose, a palazzo should be bought for her to the value of ten thousand piastres, and a vineyard (a country house) of six thousand; he had further laid down that provision should be made for her table and for the whole of her service as befitted a woman of her rank. The household was to consist of forty servants, with a corresponding number of horses.

Donna Vittoria had great hopes of the favour of the Princes of Ferrara, Florence and Urbino, as well as of that of Cardinals Farnese and de' Medici, appointed by the late Prince the executors of his will. It is to be observed that the will had been drafted at Padua, and submitted to the judgment of the most excellent Parrizoli and Menocchio, the leading professors of that University, and among the most famous jurists of the present day.

Prince Luigi Orsini arrived at Padua to carry out whatever might have to be done with regard to the late Duke and his widow, before proceeding to take over the government of the Isle of Corfu, to which he had been appointed by the Most Serene Republic.

There arose first of all a difficulty between Donna Vittoria and Prince Luigi with regard to the late Duke's horses, which the Prince said were not movable property in the general acceptation of the term; but the Duchess proved that they must be regarded as movable property so called, and it was decided that she should retain the use of them until the question was settled; she gave as a surety Signor Soardi of Bergamo, Condottiere to the Signori of Venice, a gentleman of great wealth and of the highest rank in his own country.

Another difficulty then arose with regard to a certain quantity of silver plate which the late Duke had handed over to Prince Luigi as a pledge for a sum of money which he had lent the Duke. Everything was decided by recourse to the law, for His Serenity (*i.e.* the Duke) of Ferrara took care that the last wishes of the late Prince Orsini should be given entire fulfilment.

This second question was settled on the 23rd of December, which was a Sunday.

That night, forty men entered the house of the aforesaid Accoramboni. They were dressed in coats of cloth, cut in a fantastic manner and so arranged that they could not be recognised, unless by the sound of their voices; and when they called to one another they made use of cant names.

They began by making a search for the Duchess herself, and, when they had found her, one of them said to her: "Now you must die."

And without giving her a moment, while she was begging to be allowed to commend her soul to God, he stabbed her with a fine dagger below the left breast; and, turning the point of it in all directions, the cruel wretch asked the unhappy woman several times to tell him if it was touching her heart; at length she breathed her last. Meanwhile the others were looking for the Duchess's brothers, one of whom, Marcello, escaped with his life, because he could not be found in the house; the other was stabbed by a hundred blows. The murderers left the dead bodies on the ground, the whole household weeping and shrieking; and, having seized the strong box containing the jewels and money, took their departure.

The news of this crime came rapidly to the ears of the magistrates of Padua; they had the bodies identified, and sent to Venice for further orders.

Throughout the Monday, an immense crowd assembled

[ 151 ]

round the aforesaid palazzo and in the church of the Eremitani, to see the bodies. The curious were moved to pity, especially when they saw the beauty of the Duchess: they wept for her misfortunes, *et dentibus fremebant* (and gnashed their teeth) at the murderers; but as yet these were not known by name.

The *corte* having arrived at the strongly founded suspicion that the crime had been committed by the order, or at least with the consent of the said Prince Luigi, summoned him before it, and as he sought to appear *in corte* (before the court) of the Most Illustrious Captain with a train of forty armed men, the door was barred, and he was told that he must enter with three or four only. But, as these were crossing the threshold, the others dashed in after them, thrusting aside the guards, and the whole body entered the court.

Prince Luigi, appearing before the Most Illustrious Captain, complained of this insult, asserting that he had never received such treatment from any Sovereign Prince. The Most Illustrious Captain having asked him if he knew anything of the death of Donna Vittoria, he replied that he did, and had ordered a report to be made to the officers of justice. It was proposed to take down his answer in writing; he protested that men of his rank were not bound by that formality, and, apparently, might not be examined at all.

Prince Luigi asked leave to dispatch a courier to Florence with a letter for Prince Virginio Orsini, to whom he was making a report of the proceedings and of the crime. He shewed a false letter, not that which he intended to send, and his request was granted.

But his messenger was arrested outside the city and carefully searched; the letter was found on him which Prince Luigi had shewn, and also a second letter concealed in one of his boots; this ran as follows:

## VITTORIA ACCORAMBONI

"To The Lord Virginio Orsini.

"Most Illustrious Lord,

"We have put into execution what was agreed upon between us, and so successfully that we have completely taken in the Most Illustrious Tondini" (this is apparently the name of the head of the *corte* which had examined the Prince), "so that I am regarded here as the most gallant gentleman alive. I did the deed in person, so do not fail to send at once you know whom."

This letter made a strong impression on the magistrates; they made haste to send it to Venice; by their orders the gates of the city were shut, and the walls manned by troops, day and night. A warning was published threatening severe penalties to any who, knowing the identity of the assassins, should fail to communicate what he knew to the authorities. Such of the assassins as gave evidence against any of their number were not to be molested, in fact a sum of money was to be paid to them. But about the seventh hour of the night, on Christmas Eve (towards midnight on the 24th of December), Aloisio Bragadin arrived from Venice, with ample authority from the Senate, and orders to secure the arrest, alive or dead, and at no matter what cost, of the afore-mentioned Prince Luigi and all his men. The said Signor Avogador Bragadin, the Signor Capitano and the Signor Podestà made their headquarters in the fortress.

Orders were issued, on pain of the gallows (*della forca*) to all the militia, horse and foot, to assemble well armed round the house of the said Prince Luigi, which stood near the fortress and adjoined the Church of Sant' Agostino on the Arena.

When the day (which was Christmas Day) came, an edict was published in the town calling upon all the sons of Saint Mark to arm themselves and hasten to the house of Don Luigi; those who had no arms were summoned to the fortress, where they would be given all that they required; this edict promised a reward of two thousand ducats to whosoever should hand over to the *corte,* dead or alive, the said Don Luigi, and five hundred ducats for the person of each of his followers. There was furthermore an order that any who were unarmed were on no account to approach the Prince's house, so that they should not be in the way of the fighting men were the Prince to think fit to make a sally.

At the same time siege guns, mortars and heavy artillery were mounted on the old walls, opposite the house occupied by the Prince; others were mounted on the new walls, which overlooked the rear of the said house. On this side the cavalry had been posted in such a way as to be able to move freely, should they be required. On the banks of the river Brenta people were busily arranging benches, cupboards, carts and other such things suitable for parapets. It was hoped in this way to put a stop to the movement of the besieged, should they attempt to march out in close order against the populace. These parapets would serve also to protect the gunners and infantry against the arquebusades of the besieged.

Last of all, a number of boats appeared on the river, opposite and on either side of the Prince's house, filled with men armed with muskets and other weapons calculated to harass the enemy should he attempt to break out: meanwhile barricades were erected in all the streets.

While these preparations were being made, a letter arrived, couched in the most dignified terms, in which the Prince complained of being found guilty, and of seeing himself treated as an enemy, and indeed a rebel, before any investigation had been made into the crime. This letter had been composed by Liveroto.

On the 27th of December, three gentlemen, among the foremost in the city, were sent by the magistrates to Don

Luigi, who had with him, in his house, forty men, old soldiers all of them and inured to danger. They were found to be engaged in fortifying the house with parapets made of planks and soaked mattresses, and in making ready their arquebuses.

These three gentlemen announced to the Prince that the magistrates were determined to seize his person; they advised him to surrender, adding that, by so doing, before the first shot was fired, he would have some hope of being treated with mercy. To which Don Luigi replied that if, first of all, the guards posted round about his house were withdrawn, he would go to the magistrates accompanied by two or three of his men, to discuss the matter, on the express understanding that he should be free to return at any time to his house.

The ambassadors took a note, written in his hand, of these proposals, and returned to the magistrates, who refused the conditions, acting especially on the advice of the most illustrious Pio Enea, and of other nobles there present. The ambassadors then returned to the Prince, and informed him that, if he did not make a surrender, pure and simple, of his person, his house would be razed to the ground by artillery; to which he replied that he preferred death to such an act of submission.

The magistrates gave the signal for the battle, and, although it would have been possible to destroy the whole house almost with a single discharge, it was decided to proceed more slowly, to see whether the besieged would not agree to surrender.

This plan proved successful, and saved Saint Mark a great deal of money which would have had to be spent on rebuilding the ruined parts of the bombarded palace; it did not, however, meet with general approval. If Don Luigi's men had acted without hesitation, and had made a dash from the house, the success of the siege would have been far from certain. They were old soldiers, they had no lack of munitions, of arms or of courage, and above all it was to their interest to win; was it not better for them, if the worse came to the worst, to die from the shot of an arquebus rather than by the hand of the executioner? Besides, with whom had they to deal? With a wretched band of besiegers with little experience of arms, and the Signori might then have had cause to repent of their clemency and their instinctive tenderness.

So they began by bombarding the colonnade that ran along the front of the house; then, aiming a little higher, destroyed the front wall of the building behind it. Meanwhile the men inside fired round after round from their arquebuses, but with no effect beyond wounding a humble citizen in the shoulder.

Don Luigi cried in the most impetuous fashion: "Battle! battle! war! war!" He was greatly taken up with casting bullets from the pewter of the plates and the lead from the windows. He threatened to make a sally, but the besiegers adopted new measures, and brought up guns of a larger calibre.

The first shot fired from these brought down a great piece of the house, and a certain Pandolfo Leupratti of Camerino was buried in the ruins. This was a man of great courage, and a bandit of considerable importance. He was banished from the States of Holy Church, and a price of four hundred piastres had been placed on his head by the most illustrious Signor Vitelli, for the death of Vincenzo Vitelli, who had been attacked in his carriage, and killed by arquebus shots and dagger thrusts, given by Prince Luigi Orsini through the instrumentality of the said Pandolfo and his associates. Stunned by his fall, Pandolfo was incapable of making any movement; a servant of the Signori Capodilista advanced upon him armed with a pistol, and very courageously cut off his head, which he made haste to take to the fortress and hand over to the magistrates.

Shortly afterwards a shot from another gun brought down a wall of the house, and with it the Conte Montemelino of Perugia, who died amid the ruins, blown to pieces by the ball.

After this a person was seen to leave the house named Colonel Lorenzo, of the nobility of Camerino, a man of great wealth who had on several occasions furnished proofs of his valour, and was highly esteemed by the Prince. He was determined not to die without striking a blow of some sort; he tried to fire his gun, but when he pressed the trigger, it so happened, doubtless by the will of God, that the arquebus missed fire, and at that moment a bullet went through his body. The shot had been fired by a poor devil, an usher in the school of San Michele. And while he, to gain the promised reward, was approaching his victim to cut off his head, he was forestalled by others nimbler, and, what was more, stronger than himself, who took the Colonel's purse, belt, gun, money and rings, and cut off his head.

The men in whom Prince Luigi had reposed most confidence being dead, he was left in great embarrassment, and it was observed that he no longer made any movement.

Signor Filenfi, his *maestro di casa* and secretary in civilian attire, made a signal from a balcony with a white handkerchief that he surrendered. He left the house and was taken to the citadel, *led by the arm,* as is said to be the custom of war, by Anselmo Suardo, Lieutenant to the Signori (the magistrates). Being immediately examined, he said that he was in no way to blame for what had occurred, because he had arrived on Christmas Eve only

from Venice, where he had been detained for some days
on the Prince's business.

He was asked how many men the Prince had with him,
and replied: "Twenty or thirty persons."

He was asked their names, and answered that there were
nine or ten of them who, being persons of quality, ate,
like himself, at the Prince's table, and that he knew their
names, but that of the others, people of a vagabond life
who had but recently joined the Prince, he had no personal knowledge.

He gave the names of thirteen persons, including the
brother of Liveroto.

Shortly afterwards the artillery placed on the city walls
opened fire. The soldiers posted themselves in the houses
adjoining that of the Prince to prevent his men from escaping. The said Prince, who had been running the same
risks as the two whose death we have related, told those
round about him to hold out until they should receive a
message written by his hand and accompanied by a certain sign; after which he surrendered to that Anselmo
Suardo, already named. And, because he could not be
taken in a coach, as was laid down, on account of the great
crowd of people and the barricades that blocked the streets,
it was decided that he should go on foot.

He marched amid a party of Marcello Accoramboni's
men; he had on either side of him the Signori Condottieri,
Lieutenant Suardo, other Captains and gentlemen of the
city, all well provided with arms. Next came a strong
company of men at arms and soldiers of the city. Prince
Luigi wore a suit of brown, his stiletto by his side, and
his cloak gathered under his arm with the most elegant
air; he remarked with a disdainful smile: "*If I had
fought!*" almost implying that he would have won.
Brought before the Signori, he at once bowed to them and
said:

"Sirs, I am the prisoner of this gentleman," pointing to Signor Anselmo, "and I am extremely annoyed at what has happened, by no fault of mine."

The Captain having ordered the stiletto which he wore at his side to be taken from him, he leaned against a balcony and began to trim his nails with a pair of small scissors which he found there.

He was asked whom he had in his house; he named among the rest Colonel Liveroto and Conte Montemelino, of whom mention has been made above, adding that he would give ten thousand piastres to redeem the life of one of them, and for the other would give his very life's blood. He asked to be taken to a place befitting a man of his rank. Matters being thus arranged, he wrote with his own hand a message to his supporters, ordering them to surrender, and sent his ring as a token. He told Signor Anselmo that he gave him his sword and his musket, requesting him, when those weapons should have been found in his house, to make use of them for his sake, as being the arms of a gentleman and not of any common soldier.

The troops entered the house, making a thorough search of it, and at once held a roll call of the Prince's men, who survived to the number of thirty-four, after which they were led out two by two to the prison of the Palace. The dead were left to be devoured by the dogs, and a report of the whole affair was sent to Venice.

It was noticed that many of Prince Luigi's soldiers, who had been implicated in the crime, were no longer to be found; the people were forbidden to harbour them, any who did so to be punished with the destruction of his house and confiscation of his property; those who denounced them were to receive fifty piastres. By this method several were apprehended.

A frigate was dispatched from Venice to Candia, bearing orders to Don Latino Orsini to return at once on a matter of great importance, and it is thought that he will lose his command.

Yesterday morning, which was the feast of Saint Stephen, everyone expected to see the death of the aforesaid Prince Luigi, or to hear it announced that he had been strangled in prison; and would have been greatly surprised had it been otherwise, since he was not a bird to be kept for long in a cage. But that evening the trial was held, and on Saint John's day, shortly before dawn, it became known that the said Lord had been strangled, and that he had made a good end. His body was carried without delay to the Cathedral, accompanied by the clergy of that church and by the Jesuit fathers. It was left exposed all day on a table in the middle of the church, to serve as a spectacle to the people and as a mirror to the inexperienced.

On the following day his body was conveyed to Venice, as he had ordered in his will, and there buried.

On Saturday two of his followers were hanged; the first and principal was Furio Savorgnano, the other a common person.

On Monday, which was the penultimate day of the aforesaid year, they hanged thirteen, several of whom were of high nobility; other two, one named Capitan Splendiano and the other Conte Paganello, were led through the town and mildly tortured; on reaching the place of execution, they were beaten, had their heads broken, and were quartered, the life being still in their bodies. These men were noble, and, before they took to evil courses, were extremely rich. Some say that it was Conte Paganello who killed Donna Vittoria Accoramboni with the cruelty that has been recorded. To this it is objected that Prince Luigi, in the letter already quoted, attests that he did the deed with his own hand; this may perhaps have been from vainglory, like that which he shewed in Rome when he had Vitelli murdered, or else to win more favour from Prince Virginio Orsini.

Conte Paganello, before receiving the fatal blow, was stabbed repeatedly with a knife below the left breast, so as to touch his heart, as he had done to the poor woman. In this way it came about that he shed a perfect torrent of blood from his breast. He remained alive for more than half an hour, to the great astonishment of all. He was a man of five and forty, who shewed signs of abundant strength.

The gibbets remain standing to dispatch the nineteen that are still alive, on the first day that is not a holiday. But, as the executioner is extremely tired, and the people in a sort of agony after witnessing so many deaths, their execution is being postponed for these two days. It is expected that none of them will be left alive. The one exception made, among the persons attached to Prince Luigi, will perhaps be Signor Filenfi, his *maestro di casa,* who is giving himself infinite pains (and indeed the matter is one of importance to him) to prove that he had no share in the crime.

No one, not even the oldest inhabitants of this city of Padua, can remember, by a more just sentence, the lives of so many persons to have been ever forfeited, on a single occasion. And the Signori (of Venice) have acquired for themselves high renown and a good reputation among the most civilised nations.

### *Added by another hand.*

Francesco Filenfi, secretary and *maestro di casa,* was sentenced to fifteen years' imprisonment, the cup-bearer (*coppiere*) Onorio Adami of Fermo, and two others, to one year's imprisonment; seven others were sent to the galleys, with fetters, while seven were released.

[ 161 ]

# THE CENCI

# *THE CENCI*

## 1599

THE Don Juan of Molière is, unquestionably, a rake, but first and foremost he is a man of the world; before giving way to the irresistible inclination that attracts him to pretty women, he feels that he must conform to a certain ideal standard, he seeks to be the type of man that would be most admired at the court of a young king of gallantry and parts.

The Don Juan of Mozart is already more true to nature, and less French, he thinks less of *what other people will say;* his first care is not for appearances, is not *parestre,* to quote d'Aubigné's *Baron de Fœneste.* We have but two portraits of the Italian Don Juan, as he must have appeared, in that fair land, in the sixteenth century, in the dawn of the new civilisation.

Of these two portraits, there is one which I simply cannot display, our generation is too straitlaced; one has to remind oneself of that great expression which I used often to hear Lord Byron repeat: "This age of cant." This tiresome form of hypocrisy, which takes in no one, has the great advantage of giving fools something to say: they express their horror that people have ventured to mention this, or to laugh at that, etc. Its disadvantage is that it vastly restricts the field of history.

If the reader has the good taste to allow me, I intend to offer him, in all humility, an historical notice of the second of these Don Juans, of whom it is possible to speak in 1837; his name was Francesco Cenci.

To render a Don Juan possible, there must be hypocrisy

in society. A Don Juan would have been an effect without
a cause in the ancient world; religion was a matter for rejoicing, it urged men to take their pleasure; how could
it have punished people who make a certain pleasure their
whole business in life? The government alone spoke of
*abstinence,* it forbade things that might harm the state,
that is to say the common interest of all, and not what
might harm the individual actor.

And so any man with a taste for women and plenty of
money could be a Don Juan in Athens; no one would have
made any objection; no one professed that this life is a vale
of tears and that there is merit in inflicting suffering on
oneself.

I do not think that the Athenian Don Juan could arrive
at the criminal stage as rapidly as the Don Juan of a
modern monarchy; a great part of the latter's pleasure
consists in challenging public opinion, and he has made a
start, in his youth, by imagining that he was only challenging hypocrisy.

*To break the laws* under a monarchy like that of Louis
XV, to fire a shot at a slater and bring him crashing down
from his roof, does not that prove that one moves in royal
circles, has the best possible tone, and laughs at one's
judge, who is a *bourgeois? To laugh at the judge,* is not
that the first exploit of every little incipient Don Juan?

With us, women are no longer in fashion, that is why
the Don Juan type is rare; but when it existed, such men
invariably began by seeking quite natural pleasures, boast-
ing the while of their courage in challenging ideas which
seemed to them not to be founded on reason in the religion
of their contemporaries. It is only later on, and when he
is beginning to become perverted that your Don Juan
finds an exquisite pleasure in challenging opinions which
he himself feels to be just and rational.

This transition must have been difficult and rare in an-

cient times, and it is only when we come to the Roman
Emperors, after Tiberius and Capri, that we find libertines
who love corruption for its own sake, that is to say for
the pleasure of challenging the rational opinions of their
contemporaries.

Thus it is to the Christian religion that I ascribe the
possibility of the Satanic part played by Don Juan. It
was this religion, doubtless, which taught the world that
a poor slave, a gladiator had a soul absolutely equal in
capacity to that of Cæsar himself; we have, therefore, to
thank it for having produced a delicacy of feeling. Not
that I have any doubt that sooner or later such feelings
would have grown up spontaneously in the human breast.
The *Æneid* is considerably more *tender* than the *Iliad*.

The theory held by Jesus was that of the Arab philosophers of His day; the only new thing introduced into the
world as a result of the principles preached by Saint Paul
is a body of priests absolutely set apart from their fellow
citizens and having, indeed, diametrically opposite interests to theirs.[1]

This body made it its sole business to cultivate and
strengthen the *religious sense;* it invented privileges and
habits to stir the hearts of all classes, from the uncultured
shepherd to the jaded courtier; it contrived to stamp the
memory of itself on the charming impressions of early
childhood; it never allowed the slightest pestilence or general calamity to pass without profiting by it to intensify
the dread and *sense of religion,* or at any rate to build a
fine church, like the Salute at Venice.

The existence of this body produced that admirable spectacle: Pope Saint Leo resisting without *physical force* the
savage Attila and his hordes of barbarians who had just
overrun China, Persia and the Gauls.

[1] See Montesquieu, *Politique des Romains dans la religion.*

And so, religion, like that absolute power tempered by popular songs, which we call the French Monarchy, has produced certain singular things which the world might never, perhaps, have seen had it been deprived of those two institutions.

Among these several things, good or bad but all alike singular and curious, which would indeed have astonished Aristotle, Polybius, Augustus, and the other wise heads of antiquity, I have no hesitation in including the wholly modern character of Don Juan. He is, to my mind, a product of the *ascetic institutions* of the Popes that came after Luther; for Leo X and his court (1506) followed more or less closely the religious principles of the Athenians.

Molière's Don Juan was performed early in the reign of Louis XIV, on the 15th of February, 1665; that monarch was not as yet devout, nevertheless the ecclesiastical censure ordered the scene of the *beggar in the forest* to be omitted. These censors, to strengthen their positon, tried to persuade the young king, so prodigiously ignorant, that the word Jansenist was synonymous with Republican.[1]

The original is by a Spaniard, Tirso de Molina;[2] an Italian company played an imitation of it in Paris about the year 1664, and created a furore. It has probably been acted more often than any other comedy in the world. This is because it contains the devil and love, the fear of hell and an exalted passion for a woman, that is to say the most terrible and the most attractive things that exist

---

[1] Saint-Simon, *Mémoires de l'abbé Blache.*

[2] This was the name adopted by a monk, a man of parts, Fray Gabriel Tellez. He belonged to the Order of Mercy, and we have several plays by him in which there are inspired passages, among others *El Timido á la Corte.* Tellez was the author of three hundred comedies, some seventy or eighty of which still survive. He died about 1610.

in the eyes of all men who have to any degree risen above the level of savagery.

It is not surprising that the portrait of Don Juan was introduced into literature by a Spanish poet. Love fills a large place in the life of that nation; it is a serious passion there, and one that compels the sacrifice of every other passion to itself, including that, incredible as it may seem, of *vanity!* It is the same in Germany and in Italy. Properly speaking, France is the only country completely free from this passion, which makes these foreigners commit so many acts of folly: such as marrying a penniless girl, making the excuse that she is pretty and you are in love with her. Girls who lack beauty do not lack admirers in France; we are a cautious people. Otherwise they are reduced to entering religion, and that is why convents are indispensable in Spain. Girls have no dowry in that country, and this rule has maintained the triumph of love. In France has not love fled to the attics, taken refuge, that is, among the girls who do not marry by the intervention of the family lawyer?

Nothing need be said of the Don Juan of Lord Byron, he is merely a Faublas, a good looking but insignificant young man, upon whom all sorts of improbable good fortune are heaped.

So it is in Italy alone, and there only in the sixteenth century that this singular character could make his first appearance. It was in Italy and in the seventeenth century that a Princess said, as she sipped an ice with keen enjoyment on the evening of a hot day: *"What a pity, this is not a sin!"*

This sentiment forms, in my opinion, the foundation of the character of a Don Juan, and, as we see, the Christian religion is necessary to it.

As to which a Neapolitan writer exclaims: "Is it nothing to defy heaven, and to believe that at that very instant heaven may consume one to ashes? Hence, it is said, the intense pleasure of having a nun for one's mistress, and a nun full of piety, who knows quite well that she is doing wrong, and asks pardon of God with passion, as she sins with passion." [1]

Let us take the case of a Christian extremely perverse, born in Rome at the moment when the stern Pius V had just restored to favour or invented a mass of trifling practices absolutely alien to that simple morality which gives the name of virtue only to *what is of use to mankind*. An inexorable Inquisition, so inexorable indeed that it lasted but a short time in Italy, and was obliged to take refuge in Spain, had been given fresh powers,[2] and was inspiring terror in all. For some years, the severest penalties were attached to the non-observance or public disparagement of these minute little practices, raised to the rank of the most sacred duties of religion; the perverse Roman of whom we have spoken would have shrugged his shoulders when he saw the whole of his fellow citizens trembling before the terrible laws of the Inquisition.

"Very good!" we can imagine him saying to himself, "I am the richest man in Rome, this capital of the world; I am going to be the most courageous man also; I shall publicly deride everything that these people respect, and

[1] Don Domenico Paglietta.

[2] Saint Pius V (Ghislieri), a Piedmontese, whose thin, stern face is to be seen on the tomb of Sixtus V in Santa Maria Maggiore, was *Grand Inquisitor* when he was called to the throne of Saint Peter, in 1586. He governed the Church for six years and twenty-four days. The reader should refer to his letters, edited by M. de Potter, the only man of our time with any knowledge of this detail of history. The work of M. de Potter, an inexhaustible mine of facts, is the fruit of fourteen years of conscientious research in the libraries of Florence, Venice and Rome.

that bears so little resemblance to what people ought to respect."

For a Don Juan, to be true to his type, must be a man of feeling, and be endowed with that quick and keen mind which gives one a clear insight into the motives of human actions.

Francesco Cenci must have said to himself: "By what speaking actions can I, a Roman, born in Rome in the year 1527, during those six months in which the Lutheran troops of the Connétable de Bourbon were committing the most appalling profanations in the holy places; by what actions can I call attention to my own courage and give myself, as fully as possible, the pleasure of defying public opinion? How am I to astonish my foolish contemporaries? How can I give myself that keenest of pleasures, of feeling myself to be different from all that vulgar rabble?"

It could never have entered the head of a Roman, and of a Roman of those days to stop short at words. There is no country in which brave words are more despised than Italy.

The man who might have conversed thus with himself was called Francesco Cenci: he was killed before the eyes of his wife and daughter on the 15th of September, 1598. No pleasant memories remain to us of this Don Juan, his character was in no way softened and *modified*, like that of Molière's Don Juan, by the idea of being, first and foremost, a man of the world. He paid no heed to the rest of mankind except by shewing his superiority to them, making use of them in carrying out his plans, or hating them. For your Don Juan finds no pleasure in sympathy, in sweet musings or in the illusions of a tender heart. He requires, above all, pleasures which shall be triumphs, which can be seen by others, and *cannot be denied;* he requires the list flaunted by the insolent Leporello before the sorrowful eyes of Elvira.

The Roman Don Juan took good care to avoid the signal folly of giving the key to his character and confiding his secrets to a lackey, like the Don Juan of Molière; he lived without a confidant, and uttered no words save those that would be useful in the *advancement of his projects.* No one ever surprised him in one of those moments of true tenderness and charming gaiety which make us forgive the Don Juan of Mozart; in short, the portrait which I am about to reproduce is appalling.

Had I been free to choose, I should not have written of this character, I should have confined myself to studying it, for it is more horrible than strange; but I must explain that it was demanded of me by travelling companions to whom I could refuse nothing. In 1823 I had the pleasure of visiting Italy with certain charming people, whom I shall never forget; like them, I was captivated by the portrait of Beatrice Cenci which is to be seen in Rome, at the palazzo Barberini.

The gallery of that palazzo is now reduced to seven or eight pictures; but of these four are masterpieces: there is first of all the portrait of the famous *Fornarina,* Raphael's mistress, by Raphael himself. This portrait, of the authenticity of which no doubt can be entertained, for we find copies of it made at the time, differs entirely from the figure which, in the gallery at Florence, is described as that of Raphael's mistress, and has been engraved, with that title, by Morghen. The Florence portrait is not even by Raphael. In deference to that great name, will the reader kindly pardon this little digression?

The second priceless portrait in the Barberini gallery is by Guido; it is the portrait of Beatrice Cenci, of which one sees so many bad engravings. That great painter has placed a meaningless piece of drapery over Beatrice's throat: he has crowned her with a turban; he would have been afraid of carrying accuracy to the pitch of horror had he reproduced exactly the toilet that she made before appearing at the place of execution, and the dishevelled hair of a poor girl of sixteen, abandoned to the wildest despair. The face has sweetness and beauty, the expression is most appealing and the eyes very large: they have the startled air of a person who has just been caught in the act of shedding large tears. The hair is golden and of great beauty. This head has nothing of the Roman pride and consciousness of its own strength which one often detects in the assured glance of a daughter of the Tiber, *una figlia del Tevere,* as they say of themselves with pride. Unfortunately the flesh tints of this portrait have turned to *brick red* during the long interval of two hundred and thirty-eight years which separates us from the catastrophe of which you are about to read.

The third portrait in the Barberini gallery is that of Lucrezia Petroni, Beatrice's stepmother, who was executed with her. She is the type of the Roman matron in her natural beauty and pride.[1] The features are large and the flesh of a dazzling whiteness, the eyebrows are black and strongly marked, the gaze commanding and at the same time sensuous. She makes a fine contrast with so sweet, so simple a face, almost a German face, as that of her stepdaughter.

The fourth portrait, rendered striking by the accuracy and brightness of its colouring, is one of the masterpieces of Titian; it is that of a Greek slave who was the mistress of the famous Doge Barbarigo.

Almost invariably, foreigners coming to Rome ask to be taken, at the outset of their tour of inspection, to the Barberini gallery; they are attracted, the women especially, by the portraits of Beatrice Cenci and her stepmother. I had my share of the general curiosity; then,

---

[1] This pride is not in the least dependent on social *rank,* as in portraits by Vandyck.

like everyone else, I sought to obtain access to the reports
of the famous trial. If you are similarly privileged, you
will be quite surprised, I expect, as you peruse these documents, which are all in Latin except the replies made by
the accused persons, to find almost no indication of the
facts of the case. The reason is that in Rome, in 1599,
there was no one who was not acquainted with the facts.
I purchased the right to transcribe a contemporary account; I felt that it would be possible to give a translation
of it without shocking any sensibility; anyhow this translation could be read aloud before ladies in 1823. It must
be understood that the translator ceases to be faithful to
his original when he can no longer be so: otherwise the
sense of horror would soon outweigh that of curiosity.

The tragic part played by a Don Juan (one who seeks
to conform to no ideal standard, and considers public opinion only with a view to outraging it) is here set forth in
all its horror. The enormity of his crimes forces two
unhappy women to have him killed before their eyes; of
these two women one was his wife and the other his daughter, and the reader will not dare to make up his mind as
to whether they were guilty. Their contemporaries were
of the opinion that they ought not to have been put to
death.

I am convinced that the tragedy of *Galeotto Manfredi*
(who was killed by his wife: the subject is treated by the
great poet Monti) and ever so many other domestic tragedies of the *cinquecento*, which are less well known, and
barely mentioned in the local histories of Italian cities,
ended in a scene similar to that in the castle of Petrella.
What follows is my translation of the contemporary account; it is in the *Italian of Rome*, and was written on
the 14th of September, 1599.

# THE CENCI

## A TRUE NARRATIVE

Of the deaths of Giacomo and Beatrice Cenci,
and of Lucrezia Petroni Cenci, their stepmother, executed for the crime of parricide,
on Saturday last, the 11th of September,
1599, in the reign of our Holy Father the
Pope, Clement VIII, Aldobrandini.

THE execrable life consistently led by Francesco Cenci,
a native of Rome and one of the wealthiest of our fellow
citizens, has ended by leading him to disaster. He has
brought to a precocious death his sons, stout hearted young
fellows, and his daughter Beatrice, who, although she
mounted the scaffold when barely sixteen years old (four
days since), was reckoned nevertheless one of the chief
beauties of the States of the Church, if not the whole of
Italy. The rumour has gone abroad that Signor Guido
Reni, one of the pupils of that admirable school of
Bologna, was pleased to paint the portrait of poor Beatrice,
last Friday, that is to say on the day preceding her execution. If this great painter has performed this task as he
has done in the case of the other paintings which he has
executed in this capital, posterity will be able to form
some idea of the beauty of this lovely girl. In order
that it may also preserve some record of her unprecedented
misfortunes, and of the astounding force with which this
truly Roman nature was able to fight against them, I have
decided to write down what I have learned as to the action
which brought her to her death, and what I saw on the day
of her glorious tragedy.

The people who have supplied me with my information
were in a position which made them acquainted with the
most secret details, such as are unknown in Rome even

to-day, although for the last six weeks people have been speaking of nothing but the Cenci trial. I shall write with a certain freedom, knowing as I do that I shall be able to deposit my *commentary* in respectable archives from which it will certainly not be released until after my day. My one regret is that I must pronounce, but truth will have it so, against the innocence of this poor Beatrice Cenci, as greatly adored and respected by all that knew her as her horrible father was hated and execrated.

This man who, indisputably, had received from heaven the most astounding sagacity and eccentricity, was the son of Monsignor Cenci, who, under Pius V, had risen to the post of *Tesoriere,* or Minister of Finance. That saintly Pope, entirely taken up, as we know, with his righteous hatred of heresy and the re-establishment of his admirable Inquisition, felt only contempt for the temporal administration of his State, so that this Monsignor Cenci, who was Treasurer for some years before 1572, found himself able to leave to this terrible man who was his son and the father of Beatrice Cenci a clear income of one hundred and sixty thousand piastres (about two and a half millions of our francs in 1837).

Francesco Cenci, apart from this great fortune, had a reputation for courage and prudence to which, in his youth, no other Roman could lay claim; and this reputation established him all the more firmly at the Papal court and among the people as a whole, inasmuch as the criminal actions which were beginning to be imputed to him were all of the kind which the world is most ready to forgive. Many citizens of Rome still recalled, with a bitter regret, the freedom of thought and action which they had enjoyed in the days of Leo X, who was taken from us in 1513, and under Paul III, who died in 1549. Already, in the reign of the latter of these Popes, people were beginning to speak of young Francesco Cenci on account of certain singular love affairs, carried to a successful issue by means more singular still.

Under Paul III, at a time when one could still speak with a certain degree of freedom, many people said that Francesco delighted most of all in strange incidents such as might give him *peripezie di nuova idea,* novel and disturbing sensations; those who take this view find support in the discovery, among his account books, of such entries as the following:

"For the adventures and *peripezie* of Toscanella, three thousand five hundred piastres" (about sixty thousand francs in 1837) *"e non fu caro"* (and not dear at that).

It is not known, perhaps, in the other cities of Italy, that our destinies and our mode of conduct in Rome vary with the character of the reigning Pope. Thus, for thirteen years, under the good Pope Gregory XIII (Buoncompagni), everything was permitted in Rome; if you wished, you had your enemy stabbed, and were never punished, provided that you behaved in a modest fashion. This excessive indulgence was followed by an excessive severity during the five years of the reign of the great Sixtus V, of whom it has been said, as of the Emperor Augustus, that he should either never have occurred or have remained for ever. Then one saw wretched creatures executed for murders or poisonings which had been forgotten for ten years, but which they had been so unfortunate as to confess to Cardinal Montalto, afterwards Sixtus V.

It was chiefly under Gregory XIII that people began to speak regularly of Francesco Cenci; he had married a wife of great wealth and such as befitted a gentleman of his high standing; she died after bearing him seven children. Shortly after her death, he took as his second wife Lucrezia Petroni, a woman of rare beauty, and distinguished especially for the dazzling whiteness of her skin, but a little too plump, a common fault among our Roman women. By Lucrezia he had no children.

The least fault to be found with Francesco Cenci was his propensity towards an infamous form of love; the greatest was that of unbelief in God. Never in his life was he seen to enter a church.

Three times imprisoned for his infamous love affairs, he secured his freedom by giving two hundred thousand piastres to the persons most in favour with the twelve successive Popes under whom he lived. (Two hundred thousand piastres amount to about five millions in 1837.)

When I first set eyes on Francesco Cenci his hair was already grey, during the reign of Pope Buoncompagni, when every licence was allowed to such as dared take it. He was a man of about five feet four inches, and very well built, though a trifle thin; he was reputed to be extremely strong, possibly he spread this rumour himself; he had large and expressive eyes, but the upper lids were too much inclined to droop; his nose was too large and prominent, his lips thin, and parted in a charming smile. This smile became terrible when he fastened his gaze on one of his enemies; if anything moved or annoyed him, he would begin to tremble in an alarming fashion. I have known him when I was young, in the days of Pope Buoncompagni, go on horseback from Rome to Naples, doubtless upon some amorous errand; he would pass through the forests of San Germano and la Faggiola, regardless of brigands, and would complete the journey, it was said, in less than twenty hours. He travelled always by himself, and without informing anyone; when his first horse was worn out, he would buy or steal another. Should any objection be offered by the owner, he had no objection, himself, to using his dagger. But it is true to say that in the days of my youth, that is to say when he was about forty-eight or fifty, there was no one bold enough to withstand him. His great pleasure was to defy his enemies.

He was very well known on all the roads in the States of His Holiness; he paid generously, but he was capable also, two or three months after an injury had been done him, of sending one of his *sicarj* to dispatch the person who had offended him.

The one virtuous action which he performed in the whole of his long life was to build, in the courtyard of his vast palazzo by the Tiber, a church dedicated to Saint Thomas; and even to this good deed he was prompted by the curious desire to be able to look down [1] upon the graves of all his children, whom he hated with an extravagant and unnatural loathing, even in their earliest infancy, when they were incapable of offending him in any way.

*"That is where I wish to put them all,"* he would often say with a bitter laugh to the masons whom he employed to build his church. He sent the three eldest, Giacomo, Cristoforo and Rocco, to study at the University of Salamanca in Spain. Once they were in that distant land he took an evil delight in never sending them any money, so that these unfortunate youths, after addressing a number of letters to their father, who made no reply, were reduced to the miserable necessity, for their return journey, of borrowing small sums of money or begging their way along the roads.

In Rome, they found a father more severe and rigid, more harsh than ever, who, for all his immense wealth, would neither clothe them nor give them the money necessary to purchase the cheapest forms of food. They were obliged to have recourse to the Pope, who forced Francesco Cenci to make them a small allowance. With this very modest provision they parted from their father.

[1] In Rome people are buried beneath the floors of churches.

Shortly afterwards, on account of some scandalous love affair, Francesco was put in prison for the third and last time; whereupon the three brothers begged an audience of our Holy Father the Pope now reigning, and jointly besought him to put to death Francesco Cenci their father, who, they said, was dishonouring their house. Clement VIII had a great mind to do so, but decided not to follow his first impulse, so as not to give satisfaction to these unnatural children, and expelled them ignominiously from his presence.

The father, as we have already said, came out of prison after paying a large sum of money to a powerful protector. It may be imagined that the strange action of his three elder sons was bound to increase still further the hatred that he felt for his children. He continually rained curses on them all, old and young, and every day would take a stick to his two poor daughters, who lived with him in his palazzo.

The eldest daughter, although closely watched, by dint of endless efforts managed to present a petition to the Pope; she implored His Holiness to give her in marriage or to place her in a convent. Clement VIII took pity on her distress, and married her to Carlo Gabrielli, of the noblest family of Gubbio; His Holiness obliged her father to give her an ample dowry.

Struck by this unexpected blow, Francesco Cenci shewed an intense rage, and to prevent Beatrice, when she grew older, from taking it into her head to follow her sister's example, confined her in one of the apartments of his huge palazzo. There, no one was allowed to set eyes on Beatrice, at that time barely fourteen years old, and already in the full splendour of her enchanting beauty. She had, above all, a gaiety, a candour and a comic spirit which I have never seen in anyone but her. Francesco Cenci carried her food to her himself. We may suppose that it was then that the monster fell in love with her, or pretended to fall in love, in order to torment his wretched daughter. He often spoke to her of the perfidious trick which her elder sister had played on him, and flying into a rage at the sound of his own voice, would end by showering blows on Beatrice.

While this was happening, Rocco Cenci, his son, was killed by a pork-butcher, and, in the following year, Cristoforo Cenci was killed by Paolo Corso of Massa. On this occasion, he displayed his black impiety, for at the funerals of his two sons he refused to spend so much as a single baiocco on candles. On learning of the death of his son Cristoforo, he exclaimed that he could never be truly happy until all his children were buried, and that, when the last of them died, he would, as a sign of joy, set fire to his palazzo. Rome was astounded at this utterance, but considered that everything was possible with such a man, who gloried in defying the whole world, including the Pope himself.

(Here it becomes quite impossible to follow the Roman narrator in his extremely obscure account of the strange actions by which Francesco Cenci sought to astonish his contemporaries. His wife and his unfortunate daughter were, to all appearance, made the victims of his abominable ideas.)

All this was not enough for him; he attempted with threats, and with the use of force, to outrage his own daughter Beatrice, who was already fully grown and beautiful; he was not ashamed to go and lie down in her bed, being himself completely naked. He walked about with her in the rooms of his palazzo, still stark naked; then he took her into his wife's bed, in order that, by the light of the lamps, poor Lucrezia might see what he was doing to Beatrice.

He taught the poor girl a frightful heresy, which I scarcely dare repeat, to wit that, when a father has carnal

[ 181 ]

knowledge of his own daughter, the children born of the union are of necessity saints, and that all the greatest saints whom the Church venerates were born in this manner, that is to say, that their maternal grandfather was also their father.

When Beatrice resisted his execrable intentions, he belaboured her with the cruellest blows, until the wretched girl, unable to endure so miserable an existence, decided to follow the example that her sister had given her. She addressed to our Holy Father the Pope a petition set forth in great detail; but there is reason to believe that Francesco Cenci had taken due precautions, for it does not appear that this petition ever came into the hands of His Holiness; at least, it could not be found in the secretariat of the *Memoriali,* when, after Beatrice's imprisonment, her counsel was in urgent need of the document; it would to some extent have furnished proof of the appalling excesses committed in the castle of la Petrella. Would it not have been evident to all that Beatrice Cenci had found herself legally entitled to protection? This memorial was written also in the name of Lucrezia, Beatrice's stepmother.

Francesco Cenci learned of this attempt, and one may guess with what fury he intensified his maltreatment of these two wretched women.

Life became absolutely intolerable to them, and it was at this point that, seeing that they had nothing to expect from the justice of the Sovereign, whose courtiers were seduced by Francesco's lavish gifts, they conceived the idea of adopting those extreme measures which ended in their ruin, but had nevertheless the advantage of ending their sufferings in this world.

It should be explained that the famous Monsignor Guerra was a frequent visitor to the palazzo Cenci; he was a man of tall stature and extremely handsome to boot, and had received this special gift from fortune that, to whatever task he might apply himself, he performed it with a grace that was quite peculiarly his own. It has been supposed that he was in love with Beatrice and had thoughts of discarding the *mantellata* and marrying her; [1] but, albeit he took the utmost care to conceal his feelings, he was execrated by Francesco Cenci, who accused him of having been the intimate friend of all his children. When Monsignor Guerra knew that Signor Cenci was not in his palazzo, he went up to the ladies' rooms, and spent several hours in conversing with them and listening to their complaints of the incredible treatment to which they were both subjected. It appears that Beatrice was the first to speak openly to Monsignor Guerra of the plan upon which they had decided. After a time, he promised them his support; and finally, after strong and repeated pressure from Beatrice, consented to convey their strange design to Giacomo Cenci, without whose consent nothing could be done, since he was the eldest brother, and head of the family after Francesco.

Nothing was easier than to draw him into the conspiracy; he was treated extremely ill by his father, who gave him no assistance, a deprivation which Giacomo felt all the more keenly, inasmuch as he was married and had six children. The conspirators chose as a meeting place, in which to discuss the means of putting Francesco Cenci to death, Monsignor Guerra's apartment. They conducted their business with due formality, and the votes of the stepmother and the girl were taken on all points. When at length a decision had been reached, they chose two of Francesco Cenci's vassals, each of whom had conceived an undying hatred for him. One of these was named Marzio; he was a stout fellow, deeply attached to Francesco's unfortunate children, and, in order to do something that would

[1] The majority of the *monsignori* are not in holy orders, and are free to marry.

give them pleasure, he consented to take part in the parricide. Olimpio, the second, had been chosen as warden of the fortress of la Petrella, in the Kingdom of Naples, by Prince Colonna; but, by using his all-powerful influence with the Prince, Francesco Cenci had procured his dismissal.

Everything was arranged with these two men; Francesco Cenci having announced that, in order to escape from the unhealthy air of Rome, he was going to spend the summer in this fortress of la Petrella, it occurred to them that they might collect there a dozen Neapolitan *banditi*. Olimpio undertook to provide these. It was decided to conceal the men in the forests adjoining la Petrella, to warn them of the hour at which Francesco Cenci was to start on his journey; they would intercept him on the road, and send word to his family that they would release him on payment of a large ransom. Then his children would be obliged to return to Rome to collect the sum demanded by the brigands; they would pretend to be unable to find this sum immediately, and the brigands, carrying out their threat, and seeing no sign of the money, would put Francesco Cenci to death. In this way, no one would be led to suspect the true authors of the crime.

But, when summer came and Francesco Cenci left Rome for la Petrella, the spy who was to give notice that he had started was too late in warning the *banditi* posted in the woods, and they had not time to come down to the high road. Cenci arrived without interference at la Petrella; the brigands, tired of waiting for an uncertain booty, went off to rob elsewhere on their own account.

For his part, Cenci, grown prudent and cautious with advancing years, never ventured to emerge from his fortress. And, his ill humour increasing with the infirmities of age, which he found insupportable, he intensified the atrocious treatment which he made the two poor women

[ 184 ]

undergo. He pretended that they were rejoicing in his weakness.

Beatrice, driven to desperation by the horrible things which she had to endure, summoned Marzio and Olimpio beneath the walls of the fortress. During the night, while her father slept, she conversed with them from one of the lower windows and threw down to them letters addressed to Monsignor Guerra. By means of these letters, it was arranged that Monsignor Guerra should promise Marzio and Olimpio a thousand piastres if they would take upon themselves the responsibility for putting Francesco Cenci to death. A third of the sum was to be paid in Rome, before the deed, by Monsignor Guerra, and the other two-thirds by Lucrezia and Beatrice, when, the deed done, they should be in command of Cenci's strong-box.

It was further agreed that the deed should be done on the Nativity of the Virgin, and for this purpose the two men were secretly admitted to the fortress. But Lucrezia was overcome by the respect due to a festival of the Madonna, and she made Beatrice postpone the action until the following day, so as not to be guilty of a twofold crime.

It was therefore on the evening of the 9th of September, 1598, that, mother and daughter having with great dexterity administered opium to Francesco Cenci, that man so hard to deceive, he fell into a deep sleep.

Towards midnight Beatrice herself let into the fortress Marzio and Olimpio; next, Lucrezia and Beatrice led them to the old man's room, where he lay fast asleep. There, they were left by themselves that they might do what had been determined upon, and the women withdrew to wait in an adjoining room. Suddenly they saw the two men appear with pallid faces, and apparently out of their wits.

"What has happened?" cried the ladies.

"It is a shame and a disgrace," the men answered, "to kill a poor old man in his sleep! Pity stayed our hands."

On hearing this excuse, Beatrice grew indignant, and began to abuse them, saying:

"And so you two men, thoroughly prepared to act, have not the courage to kill a man in his sleep![1] You would be a great deal less willing to look him in the face if he were awake! And so it is for nothing more than this that you dare to ask for money? Very well! Since your cowardice forces me, I will kill my father myself; and as for you, you have not long to live either!"

Animated by these few scathing words, and fearing a reduction of the fee that had been promised them, the assassins boldly returned to the bedroom, followed by the women. One of them had a great nail which he placed vertically over the sleeping man's eye; the other, who had a hammer, drove the nail into his head. Another large nail was driven similarly into his breast, so that the wretched soul, burdened with all its recent sins, was carried off by devils; the body struggled, but in vain.

The deed accomplished, the girl gave Olimpio a great purse filled with money: she gave Marzio a cloak of broadcloth with a gold stripe, which had belonged to her father, and dismissed them.

The women, left to themselves, began by withdrawing the large nail driven into the head of the corpse, and the other in his throat; then, after wrapping the body in a sheet from the bed, they dragged it through a long series of rooms to a gallery which overlooked a small, deserted garden. From this gallery, they threw down the body upon a great elder tree which grew in that lonely spot. As there was a privy at the end of this little gallery, they hoped that when, in the morning, the old man's body was found caught in the branches of the elder, it would be supposed

[1] All these details were proved at the trial.

that his foot had slipped and that he had fallen while on his way to the privy.

Things fell out exactly as they had foreseen. In the morning, when the body was found, a great clamour arose in the fortress; they did not forget to utter piercing cries, and to bewail the lamentable death of their husband and father. But the young Beatrice had the courage of outraged modesty, not the prudence necessary in this life; early in the morning, she had given to a woman who washed the linen in the fortress a sheet stained with blood, telling her not to be surprised at such a quantity of blood, because she herself, all night long, had been suffering from a copious issue; and in this way, for the moment, all went well.

Francesco Cenci was given a pompous funeral, and the women returned to Rome to enjoy that tranquillity which they had for so long desired in vain. They imagined themselves to be happy now for ever, for they did not know what was happening at Naples.

The justice of heaven, which would not allow so atrocious a parricide to remain unpunished, brought it about that, as soon as the news reached that city of what had occurred in the fortress of la Petrella, the principal judge there felt misgivings, and sent a royal commissioner to examine the body and arrest any suspected persons.

The royal commissioner ordered the arrest of everyone living in the fortress. They were all taken to Naples in chains; and nothing in their depositions appeared suspicious, except that the laundress professed to have received from Beatrice a sheet or sheets stained with blood. She was asked whether Beatrice had attempted to explain these great stains of blood; she replied that Beatrice had spoken of a natural infirmity. She was asked whether stains of such a size could be due to such an infirmity;

she replied that they could not, and that the stains on the sheet were of too bright a red.

This information was immediately sent to the judicial authorities in Rome, and yet many months elapsed before it occurred to anyone here to order the arrest of Francesco Cenci's children. Lucrezia, Beatrice and Giacomo could have escaped a thousand times over, either by going to Florence on the pretext of making some pilgrimage, or by taking ship at Civita-Vecchia; but God withheld from them this life-giving inspiration.

Monsignor Guerra, having had word of what was happening in Naples, at once sent out a number of men with orders to kill Marzio and Olimpio; but Olimpio alone did they succeed in killing at Terni. The Neapolitan authorities had arrested Marzio, who was taken to Naples, where he immediately confessed all.

This terrible deposition was at once sent to the authorities in Rome, who at last decided to arrest and confine in the Corte Savella prison Giacomo and Bernardo Cenci, the only surviving sons of Francesco, as also Lucrezia, his widow. Beatrice was guarded in her father's palazzo by a numerous troop of *sbirri*. Marzio was brought from Naples, and likewise confined in the Savella prison; there he was confronted with the two women, who denied everything consistently, Beatrice in particular refusing steadfastly to recognise the striped cloak which she had given to Marzio. The brigand, overcome by enthusiasm for the marvellous beauty and astonishing eloquence of the girl as she answered the judge, denied everything that he had confessed in Naples. He was put to the question, he admitted nothing, preferring to die in agony; fit homage to the beauty of Beatrice!

After the death of this man, there being no proof of the crime, the judges found that there was not sufficient reason for putting to the torture either Cenci's two sons or the

two women.  All four were taken to the Castel Sant'
Angelo, where they remained for some months in peace and
quietness.

The matter seemed to be at an end, and no one in Rome
had any doubt that this girl, of such beauty and courage,
who had aroused so keen an interest, would shortly be set
at liberty, when, unfortunately, the officers of justice succeeded in arresting the brigand who, at Terni, had killed
Olimpio; he was brought to Rome, where he confessed
everything.

Monsignor Guerra, whom the brigand's confession so
dangerously compromised, was summoned to appear before
the court without delay; imprisonment was certain, death
probable.  But this remarkable man, whom fate had endowed with the art of doing everything well, succeeded in
escaping in a manner which seems miraculous.  He was
reckoned the handsomest man at the Papal court, and was
too well known in Rome to have any chance of escape;
besides, a close watch was being kept at the gates, and
probably, from the moment of his summons, his house had
been under supervision.  It should be added that he was
very tall, with an extremely fair skin, and a fine beard
and hair, fair also.

With inconceivable rapidity, he procured a charcoal
seller, took his clothes, had his own head and beard shaved,
stained his face, bought a pair of asses, and began to
perambulate the streets of Rome selling charcoal, limping
as he went.  He assumed with admirable skill an air of
plebeian stupidity, and went about crying his charcoal with
his mouth full of bread and onions, while hundreds of
*sbirri* were searching for him not only in Rome, but on all
the roads as well.  At length, when his appearance was
familiar to most of the *sbirri,* he ventured to leave Rome,
still driving before him his pair of asses laden with charcoal.  He met several troops of *sbirri,* who had no thought

of stopping him. Since then, only one letter has been received from him; his mother has sent money to him at Marseilles, and it is supposed that he is serving in the French war, as a private soldier.

The confession of the Terni assassin and this flight of Monsignor Guerra, which created an enormous sensation in Rome, so revived suspicion, and indeed seemed so to point to the guilt of the Cenci, that they were taken from the Castel Sant' Angelo and brought back to the Savella prison.

The two brothers, put to the torture, were far from imitating the magnanimity of the brigand Marzio; they were so pusillanimous as to confess everything. Signora Lucrezia Petroni was so habituated to the ease and comfort of a life of the greatest luxury, and besides was so stout in figure that she could not endure the question by the *cord;* she told everything that she knew.

But it was not so with Beatrice Cenci, a girl full of vivacity and courage. Neither the kind words nor the threats of the judge Moscati had any effect on her. She endured the torture of the *cord* without a moment's faltering and with perfect courage. Never once could the judge induce her to give an answer that compromised her in the slightest degree; indeed, by her quick-witted vivacity, she utterly confounded the famous Ulisse Moscati, the judge responsible for examining her. He was so much surprised by the conduct of the girl that he felt it his duty to make a full report to His Holiness Pope Clement VIII, whom God preserve.

His Holiness wished to see the documents and to study the case. He was afraid lest the judge Ulisse Moscati, so celebrated for his deep learning and the superior sagacity of his mind, might have been overpowered by Beatrice's beauty, and be helping her out in his examinations of her. The consequence was that His Holiness took the case out of his hands, and entrusted it to another and a more severe judge. Indeed, this barbarian had the heart to subject without pity so lovely a body *ad torturam capillorum* (that is to say, questions were put to Beatrice Cenci while she was hanging by her hair[1]).

While she was fastened to the cord, this new judge confronted Beatrice with her stepmother and her brothers. As soon as Giacomo and Donna Lucrezia saw her:

"The sin has been committed," they cried; "you should perform the penance also, and not let your body be torn to pieces through a futile obstinacy."

"So you wish to cover our house with shame," replied the girl, "and to die an ignominious death. You are greatly mistaken; but, since you wish it, so be it."

And, turning to the *sbirri:*

"Release me," she said to them, "and let someone read over to me my mother's examination. I will admit what must be admitted, and deny what must be denied."

This was duly done; she admitted everything that was true.[2] Immediately the chains were removed from them all, and because for five months she had not seen her brothers, she expressed a wish to dine with them, and all four spent a very happy day together.

But next day they were separated once more; the two brothers were taken to the prison of Tordinona, while the women remained in the Savella. Our Holy Father the Pope, having seen the authentic document containing all their confessions, ordered that without further delay they

[1] See the treatise *de Suppliciis*, by the celebrated Farinacci, a jurist of the time. It contains horrible details which our nineteenth century sensibility cannot endure even to read about, but which were very creditably endured by a Roman girl of sixteen abandoned by her lover.

[2] Farinacci quotes several passages from Beatrice's confession; they seem to me touching in their simplicity.

should be tied to the tails of wild horses, and so put to death.

The whole of Rome shuddered on learning of this rigorous decree. A great number of cardinals and princes went to throw themselves on their knees before the Pope, imploring him to allow the poor wretches to present their defence.

"And they, did they give their aged father time to present his?" the Pope replied angrily.

Finally, by a special grace, he was pleased to allow a respite of five and twenty days. At once the leading *avvocati* in Rome began to write their pleadings in this case which had filled the town with pity and dismay. On the twenty-fifth day, they appeared in a body before His Holiness. Niccolò de' Angelis was the first to speak, but he had barely read the first line of his defence when Clement VIII interrupted him:

"And so, here in Rome," he exclaimed, "we find people who kill their father, and counsel afterwards to defend such people!"

All stood speechless, until Farinacci ventured to raise his voice.

"Most Holy Father," he said, "we are here not to defend the crime, but to prove, if we can, that one or more of these unfortunate people are innocent of the crime."

The Pope made a sign to him to speak, and he spoke for fully three hours, after which the Pope took their briefs from them all and dismissed them. As they were leaving the presence, Altieri was the last to go; he was afraid that he might have compromised himself, and turned to kneel before the Pope, saying:

"I could not help appearing in this case, since I am counsel for the poor."

To which the Pope replied:

"We are not surprised at you, but at the others."

The Pope refused to go to bed, but spent the whole night reading the pleadings of counsel, calling upon the Cardinal of San Marcello to help him in this task; His Holiness appeared so deeply touched that many people felt a spark of hope for the lives of the unhappy prisoners. In the hope of saving the sons, the counsel threw the whole onus of the crime upon Beatrice. As it had been proved in the trial that her father had on several occasions employed force with a criminal intention, the lawyers hoped that the murder would be pardoned in her case, as being justified in self-defence; and if so, when the principal author of the crime was granted her life, how could her brothers, who had acted at her persuasion, be put to death?

After this night devoted to his judicial duties, Clement VIII ordered that the accused persons should be taken back to prison and placed in *secret confinement*. This circumstance gave rise to great hopes in Rome, which throughout the whole of this case considered no one but Beatrice. It was alleged that she had been in love with Monsignor Guerra, but that she had never infringed the rules of the strictest virtue; it was impossible, therefore, in justice, to impute to her the crimes of a monster, and she was to be punished because she had made use of her right of self-defence; what would have been her punishment had she consented? Was it necessary that human justice should step in to increase the misery of a creature so lovable, so deserving of pity, and already in such a plight? After so sad a life, which had heaped upon her every form of misery before her sixteenth birthday, had she not acquired the right to a few days of greater happiness? The whole of Rome seemed to be briefed in her defence. Would she not have been pardoned if, when for the first time Francesco Cenci made a criminal assault upon her, she had stabbed him?

Pope Clement VIII was mild and merciful. We were

beginning to hope that, a little ashamed of the burst of ill temper which had made him interrupt the counsels' pleadings, he would pardon one who had repelled force with force, not, to be accurate, at the moment of the original crime, but when the assailant tried to commit it anew. The whole of Rome was on tenterhooks, when the Pope received the news of the violent death of the Marchesa Costanza Santa Croce. Her son, Paolo Santa Croce, had killed the lady in question, who was sixty years old, by stabbing her with his dagger, because she would not bind herself to make him the heir to her whole fortune. The report added that Santa Croce had taken flight, and that there was little or no hope of arresting him. The Pope remembered the fratricide by the Massini, which had occurred quite recently. Appalled by the frequency of these murders of near relatives, His Holiness felt that he would not be entitled to grant a pardon. When he received this fatal report of the Santa Croce murder, the Pope was at the palace of Monte Cavallo, where he was spending the 6th of September, in order to be nearer, next morning, to the Church of Santa Maria degli Angeli, where he was to consecrate as Bishop a German Cardinal.

On the Friday at the twenty-second hour (4 P.M.) he sent for Ferrante Taverna, the Governor of Rome (afterwards made Cardinal, for so singular a reason), and addressed him in the following words:

*"We entrust the case of the Cenci to your hands, in order that justice may be done without delay."*

The Governor returned to his Palace deeply moved by the order he had received; he at once signed the sentence of death, and convened a congregation to decide upon the method of execution.

On Saturday morning, the 11th of September, 1599, the first gentlemen of Rome, members of the Confraternity of the Confortatori, repaired to the two prisons, that of Corte

Savella, where were Beatrice and her stepmother, and Tordinona, in which Giacomo and Bernardo Cenci were confined. Throughout the whole of the night between the Friday and the Saturday, the Roman nobles who were aware of what was happening did nothing but hasten from the palace of Monte Cavallo to those of the principal Cardinals, hoping to obtain at least the concession that the women might be put to death inside the prison, and not upon an ignominious scaffold; and that mercy be shewn to the young Bernardo Cenci, who, being only fifteen years old, could not have been admitted to the secret. The noble Cardinal Sforza was conspicuous for his zeal during that fatal night, but albeit so powerful a prince he could obtain nothing. The Santa Croce crime was a vile crime, committed for the sake of money, and the crime of Beatrice Cenci was committed in defence of her honour.

While the most powerful Cardinals were taking such fruitless pains, Farinacci, our great jurist, actually dared to make his way into the Pope's presence; face to face with His Holiness, this remarkable man contrived to stir his listener's conscience, and at length, by sheer importunity, wrested from him the life of Bernardo Cenci.

When the Pope made this important utterance, it was about four o'clock in the morning (of Saturday, the 11th of September). All night long men had been at work on the piazza of the Ponte Sant' Angelo preparing the scene of this cruel tragedy. All the necessary copies of the death sentence could not, however, be completed before five o'clock in the morning, so that it was not until six o'clock that the fatal tidings could be conveyed to the wretched prisoners, who were peacefully asleep.

The girl, for the first few moments, could not even summon up strength to put on her clothes. She uttered piercing and continuous shrieks and gave way uncontrollably to the most terrible desperation.

"How is it possible, oh, God," she cried, "that I must die suddenly, like this?"

Lucrezia Petroni, on the other hand, said nothing that was not entirely proper; first of all, she fell on her knees and prayed, then calmly exhorted her daughter to accompany her to the chapel, where they would make preparation together for the great journey from life to death.

These words restored to Beatrice all her calm; just as she had shewn extravagance and want of control at first, so now she was reasonable and wise as soon as her stepmother had summoned up the resources of that noble soul. From that moment she was a mirror of constancy which all Rome admired.

She asked for a notary to draw up her will, which was permitted. She ordered that her body should be taken to San Pietro in Montorio; she left three hundred thousand francs to the Stimate (nuns of the Stigmata of Saint Francis); this sum was to provide dowries for fifty poor girls. This example moved the heart of Donna Lucrezia, who also made her will and ordered her body to be taken to San Giorgio; she left five hundred thousand francs to that church and made other pious bequests.

At eight o'clock they made their confession, heard mass and received the Holy Communion. But, before going to mass, Donna Beatrice reflected that it was not proper to appear on the scaffold, in the sight of the whole populace, in the rich garments which she was wearing. She ordered two gowns, one for herself, one for her mother. These gowns were made like nuns' habits, without ornaments on bosom or shoulders, and gathered only at the wide sleeves. The stepmother's gown was of black cotton; the girl's of blue taffeta, with a large cord fastening it at the waist.

When the gowns were brought, Donna Beatrice, who was on her knees, rose and said to Donna Lucrezia:

"My lady mother, the hour of our passion approaches;

it would be well for us to make ready, to put on these other clothes, and for the last time to perform the mutual service of dressing each other."

There had been erected on the Piazza del Ponte Sant' Angelo a huge scaffold with a block and a *mannaja* (a sort of guillotine). About the thirteenth hour (eight o'clock in the morning), the Company of the Misericordia came with their great crucifix to the gate of the prison. Giacomo Cenci was the first to emerge; he fell devoutly upon his knees at the threshold, made his prayer, and kissed the Sacred Wounds on the crucifix. He was followed by Bernardo Cenci, his young brother, who also had his hands bound and a little board before his eyes. The crowd was enormous, and a disturbance arose owing to a basin which fell from a window almost upon the head of one of the penitents who was holding a lighted torch by the side of the banner.

Everyone was gazing at the brothers, when suddenly the Fiscal of Rome came forward, and said:

"Don Bernardo, Our Sovereign Lord grants you your life; prepare to accompany your family, and pray to God for them."

Thereupon his two *confortatori* removed the little board that covered his eyes. The executioner installed Giacomo Cenci on the cart and had removed his coat, as he was to be tortured with the *pincers*. When the executioner came to Bernardo, he verified the signature on the pardon, unbound him, removed his handcuffs, and, as he had no coat, for he was awaiting the pincers, the executioner set him on the cart and wrapped him in a rich cloak of broadcloth striped with gold. (It was said that this was the same cloak that was given by Beatrice to Marzio after the deed in the fortress of la Petrella.) The vast crowd that filled the street, the windows and the roofs, was suddenly stirred;

one heard a deep and sullen murmur, people were beginning to tell one another that the boy had been pardoned.

The intoning of the Psalms began, and the procession moved slowly across the Piazza Navona towards the Savella prison. On reaching the prison gate the banner halted, the two women came out, made an act of adoration at the foot of the holy crucifix and then proceeded on foot, one following the other. They were dressed in the manner already described, the head of each being draped in a great taffeta veil which reached almost to her waist.

Donna Lucrezia, as a widow, wore a black veil and slippers of black velvet without heels, according to custom.

The girl's veil was of blue taffeta, like her dress; she had in addition a great veil of cloth of silver over her shoulders, a petticoat of violet cloth, and slippers of white velvet, elegantly laced and fastened with crimson cords. She appeared singularly charming as she walked, in this costume, and a tear came to every eye as the spectators caught sight of her slowly advancing in the rear of the procession.

Both women had their hands free, but their arms tied to their sides, so that each of them was able to carry a crucifix; they held these close to their eyes. The sleeves of their gowns were very wide, so that one saw their arms, which were covered by sleeved shifts fastened at the wrists, as is the custom in this country.

Donna Lucrezia, whose heart was less stout, wept almost continuously; the young Beatrice, on the other hand, shewed great courage; and, turning to gaze at each of the churches by which the procession passed, would fall on her knees for a moment and say in a firm voice: *"Adoramus Te, Christe!"*

Meanwhile, poor Giacomo Cenci was being tortured upon the cart, and shewed great constancy.

The procession had difficulty in crossing the lower end

[ 198 ]

of the Piazza del Ponte Sant' Angelo, so great was the number of carriages and the crowd of people. The women were taken straight to the chapel which had been made ready, and there Giacomo Cenci was afterwards brought.

Young Bernardo, wrapped in his striped cloak, was taken straight to the scaffold; whereupon everyone thought that he was going to be put to death, and had not been pardoned. The poor boy was so frightened that he fell in a faint as soon as he had stepped on to the scaffold. He was revived with cold water and made to sit opposite the *mannaja*.

The executioner went to fetch Donna Lucrezia Petroni; her hands were tied behind her back, the veil no longer covered her shoulders. She appeared on the piazza accompanied by the banner, her head wrapped in the veil of black taffeta; there she made an act of reconciliation to God and kissed the Sacred Wounds. She was told to leave her slippers on the pavement; as she was very stout, she had some difficulty in climbing the scaffold. When she was on the scaffold and the black taffeta veil was taken from her, she was greatly ashamed to be seen with bare shoulders and bosom; she examined herself, then the *mannaja,* and, as a sign of resignation, raised her shoulders slightly; tears came to her eyes, she said: "O my God! . . . And you, my brethren, pray for my soul."

Not knowing what was expected of her, she asked Alessandro, the chief headsman, what she ought to do. He told her to place herself astride the plank of the block. But this position seemed to her offensive to modesty, and she took a long time to assume it. (The details which follow are endurable by the Italian public, which likes to know everything with the utmost exactitude; let it suffice the French reader to know that this poor woman's modesty led to her injuring her bosom; the executioner shewed her head to the people and then wrapped it in the black taffeta veil.)

While the *mannaja* was being put in order for the girl, a scaffold loaded with spectators fell, and many people were killed. They thus appeared in God's presence before Beatrice.

When Beatrice saw the banner returning to the chapel to fetch her, she asked boldly:

"Is my lady mother really dead?"

They replied that it was so; she fell on her knees before the crucifix and prayed fervently for her stepmother's soul. Then she spoke aloud and at great length to the crucifix.

"Lord, Thou hast come back for me, and I will follow Thee with a willing heart, despairing not of Thy mercy for my great sin," etc.

She then repeated several Psalms and prayers, all in praise of God. When at length the executioner appeared before her with a cord, she said:

"Bind this body which is to be punished, and unbind this soul which is to win immortality and an eternal glory."

Then she rose, said her prayer, left her slippers at the foot of the steps and, having mounted the scaffold, stepped nimbly across the plank, placed her neck beneath the *mannaja,* and made all the arrangements perfectly herself, so as to avoid being touched by the executioner. By the swiftness of her movements she prevented the crowd, at the moment when the taffeta veil was taken from her, from seeing her shoulders and bosom. The blow was a long time in falling, as an interruption occurred. During this time she called in a loud voice upon Jesus Christ and the Most Holy Virgin.[1] Her body sprang with an impulsive

[1] A contemporary writer states that Clement VIII was extremely uneasy as to the salvation of Beatrice's soul; as he knew that she had been unjustly sentenced, he feared an impatient revulsion. The moment she had placed her head upon the *mannaja,* the fortress of Sant' Angelo, from which the *mannaja* was plainly visible, fired a gun. The Pope, who

movement at the fatal instant. Poor Bernardo Cenci, who had remained seated on the scaffold, fell once again in a faint, and it took his *confortatori* a good half hour and more to revive him. Then there appeared upon the scaffold Giacomo Cenci; but here again we must pass over details that are too harrowing. Giacomo Cenci was "broken" (*mazzolato*).

Immediately, Bernardo was taken back to prison; he was in a high fever and was bled.

As for the poor women, each of them was placed in her coffin and laid down a few feet away from the scaffold, near the statue of Saint Paul, which is the first on the right-hand side on the Ponte Sant' Angelo. Round each coffin burned four candles of white wax.

Later, with all that remained of Giacomo Cenci, they were conveyed to the palace of the Florentine Consul. At a quarter past nine in the evening,[1] the body of the girl, dressed in her own clothes and covered with a profusion of flowers, was carried to San Pietro in Montorio. She was exquisitely beautiful; looking at her, one would have said that she was asleep. She was buried in front of the high altar, and of Raphael's *Transfiguration*. She was escorted by fifty great candles, lighted, and by all the Franciscans in Rome.

Lucrezia Petroni was carried, at ten o'clock at night, to the Church of San Giorgio. During the course of this tragedy, the crowd was beyond number; as far as the eye

was engaged in prayer at Monte Cavallo, awaiting this signal, at once gave the girl the Papal major absolution *in articulo mortis*. This accounts for the delay in carrying out the sentence, of which the chronicler speaks.

[1]This is the hour set apart, in Rome, for the obsequies of Princes. The funeral of a citizen starts at sunset; the lesser nobility are carried to church at the first hour of night, Cardinals and Princes at half-past two of the night, which, on the 11th of September, corresponds to a quarter to ten.

could reach, one saw the streets packed with carriages and people, scaffoldings, windows and roofs covered with curious spectators. The sun's heat was so intense that day that many people lost consciousness. Any number of them took fever; and when the whole affair was at an end, at the nineteenth hour (a quarter to two), and the crowd dispersed, many people were suffocated, others trampled down by the horses. The number of deaths was considerable.

Donna Lucrezia Petroni was of middle height, or a little shorter, and, although fifty years old, was still a handsome woman. She had very fine features, a small nose, dark eyes, the skin of her face quite white with a fine complexion; her hair, which was not abundant, was chestnut.

Beatrice Cenci, who must inspire undying regret, was just sixteen; she was of short stature; her figure was charmingly rounded, and there were dimples in the centre of her cheeks, so that, lying dead and garlanded with flowers, she appeared to be asleep and even smiling, as she had so often lain when she was alive. Her mouth was small, her hair golden, and naturally curling. As she went to the scaffold these fair ringlets fell over her eyes, which gave her a certain charm and inspired pity.

Giacomo Cenci was of short stature, stout, with a pale face and black beard; he was about twenty-six years old when he died.

Bernardo Cenci closely resembled his sister, and as he wore his hair long like hers, many people, when he appeared on the scaffold, mistook him for her.

The heat of the sun had been so intense that a number of the spectators of this tragedy died during the night, and among them Ubaldino Ubaldini, a young man of rare beauty who had until then been in perfect health. He was brother to Signor Renzi, so well known in Rome.

Thus the shades of the Cenci left this world numerously escorted.

Yesterday, which was Tuesday the 14th of September, 1599, the penitents of San Marcello, on the occasion of the Feast of the Holy Cross, made use of their privilege to deliver from prison Don Bernardo Cenci, who has bound himself to pay within a year four hundred thousand francs to the Santissima Trinità del Ponte Sisto.

*Added by another hand.*

It is from him that the Francesco and Bernardo Cenci, now alive, descend.

The famous Farinacci, who, by his persistence, saved young Cenci's life, afterwards published his pleadings. He gives only an extract from pleading no. 66, which he declaimed before Clement VIII on behalf of the Cenci. This pleading, in the Latin tongue, would occupy fully six pages, and I cannot insert it here; this I regret, as it portrays the mental attitude of 1599; it seems to me eminently reasonable. Many years after 1599, Farinacci, when sending his pleadings to the press, added a note to this speech in defence of the Cenci: *Omnes fuerunt ultimo supplicio effecti, excepto Bernardo qui ad triremes cum bonorum confiscatione condemnatus fuit, ac etiam ad interessendum aliorum morti prout interfuit.* The end of this Latin note is touching, but I expect the reader is tired of so long a story.

# THE DUCHESS OF PALLIANO

# THE DUCHESS OF PALLIANO

Palermo, July 22nd, 1838.

I AM nothing of a naturalist, I have only a very moderate acquaintance with the Greek language; my chief object in coming to visit Sicily has not been to observe the phenomena of Etna, nor to throw light, for my own or for other people's benefit, on all that the old Greek writers have said about Sicily. I sought first of all the pleasure of the eyes, which is considerable in this strange land. It resembles Africa, or so people say; but what to my mind is quite certain is that it resembles Italy only in its devouring passions. The Sicilians are a race of whom one might well say that the word *impossible* does not exist for them once they are inflamed by love or by hatred, and hatred, in this fair land, never arises from any pecuniary interest.

I observe that in England, and above all in France, one often hears people speak of *Italian passion,* of the frenzied passion which was to be found in Italy in the sixteenth and seventeenth centuries. In our time, that noble passion is dead, quite dead, among the classes that have become infected with the desire to imitate French ways, and the modes of behaviour in fashion in Paris or in London.

I am well aware that I may be reminded that, from the time of Charles V (1530), Naples, Florence and Rome even were inclined to imitate Spanish ways; but were not these noble social customs based upon the boundless respect which every man worthy of the name ought to have for the motions of his own heart? Far from excluding emphasis, they exaggerated it, whereas the first maxim of the *fats* who imitated the Duc de Richelieu, round about 1760, was to appear *moved by nothing*. The maxim of the English dandies, whom they now copy at Naples in preference to the French *fats,* is it not to appear bored by everything, superior to everything?

Thus *Italian passion* has ceased to exist, for a century past, among the good society of that country.

In order to form some idea of this *Italian passion,* of which our novelists speak with such assurance, I have been obliged to turn to history; and even then the major histories, written by men of talent, and often too pompous, give us practically no details. They do not condescend to take note of the foolish actions except when these are committed by kings or princes. I have had recourse to the local history of each city; but I am appalled by the abundance of material. Every little town proudly offers you its history in three or four quarto volumes of print, and seven or eight volumes in manuscript; the latter almost undecipherable, teeming with abbreviations, giving unusual shapes to the letters, and, at the most interesting moments, crammed with forms of speech in use in the district but unintelligible twenty leagues away. For, in the whole of this fair land of Italy, whose surface love has sown with so many tragedies, three cities only, Florence, Siena and Rome, speak more or less as they write; everywhere else the written language is a hundred leagues apart from the spoken.

What is known as Italian passion, that is to say the passion that seeks its own satisfaction, and not to give one's neighbour an enhanced idea of oneself, begins with the revival of society, in the twelfth century, and dies out, among people of refinement at least, about the year 1734. At this date the Bourbons ascend the throne of Naples in the person of Don Carlos, son of a Farnese heiress married

as his second wife to Philip V, that melancholy grandson
of Louis XIV, so intrepid amid shot and shell, so listless,
and so passionately fond of music. We know that for
twenty-four years the sublime eunuch Farinelli sang to
him every day three favourite airs, which never varied.

A philosophic mind may find something curious in the
details of a passion as felt in Rome or Naples, but I must
say that nothing seems to me more absurd than those novels
that give Italian names to their characters. Are we not all
agreed that passions alter whenever we move a hundred
leagues farther north? Is love the same thing at Marseilles as in Paris? At most, we may say that countries
which have long been subjected to the same form of government shew a sort of outward similarity in their social
customs.

Scenery, like passions and music, changes also whenever
we move three or four degrees farther north. A Neapolitan
landscape would seem absurd in Venetia, were there not a
convention, even in Italy, to admire the fine works of
nature round Naples. In Paris, we go one better, we
imagine that the appearance of the forests and tilled plains
is absolutely the same round Naples as round Venice, and
would like Canaletto, for instance, to use absolutely the
same colours as Salvator Rosa.

But the crowning absurdity, surely, is an English lady
endowed with all the perfections of her Island, but considered not to be in a position to portray *hatred* and *love,*
even in that Island: Mrs. Anne Radcliffe giving Italian
names and grand passions to the characters of her celebrated novel: *The Italian, or the Confessional of the Black
Penitents.*

I shall make no attempt to adorn the simplicity, the
occasionally startling bluntness of the all too true narrative which I submit to the reader's indulgence; for instance,
I translate literally the reply of the Duchess of Palliano

to the declaration of love made by her cousin Marcello Capecce. This family monograph occurs, for some reason, at the end of the second volume of a manuscript history of Palermo, of which I can furnish no details.

This narrative, which I have shortened considerably, much to my regret (I omit a mass of characteristic features), consists of the ultimate adventures of the ill-fated house of Carafa, rather than of the interesting history of a single passion. Literary vanity suggests to me that perhaps it might not have been impossible for me to enhance the interest of several situations by developing them farther, that is to say, by guessing and relating to the reader, with details, what the characters felt. But can I, a young Frenchman, born north of Paris, be quite sure of my power to guess what was felt by these Italian hearts in the year 1559? At the very most, I can hope to be able to guess what may appear elegant and thrilling to French readers in 1838.

This passionate manner of feeling which prevailed in Italy about the year 1559 required deeds, not words. And so the reader will find very little conversation in the following narrative. This is a handicap to my translation, accustomed as we are to the long conversations of the characters in our fiction; for them a conversation is a duel. The story for which I claim all the reader's indulgence shews a singular element introduced by the Spaniards into Italian manners. I have nowhere departed from the office of a translator. The faithful reproduction of the mental attitudes of the sixteenth century, and even of the narrative style of the chronicler who, apparently, was a gentleman attached to the household of the unfortunate Duchess of Palliano, constitutes, to my mind, the chief merit of this tragic tale, if there be any merit in it.

The strictest Spanish etiquette prevailed at the *court* of the Duke of Palliano. Bear in mind that each Cardinal, each Roman Prince had a similar court, and you will be able to form some idea of the spectacle furnished, in 1559, by the civilisation of the city of Rome. Do not forget that this was the period in which Philip II, requiring for one of his intrigues the support of two Cardinals, bestowed upon each of them a revenue of two hundred thousand lire in ecclesiastical benefices. Rome, although lacking an effective army, was the capital of the world. Paris, in 1559, was a city of barbarians not without charm.

LITERAL TRANSLATION OF AN OLD NARRATIVE WRITTEN
ABOUT THE YEAR 1566

Gian Pietro Carafa, although sprung from one of the noblest families of the Kingdom of Naples, behaved in a harsh, rude, violent manner more befitting a keeper of flocks or herds. He assumed the *long coat* (the cassock) and left at an early age for Rome, where he benefited by the favour of his cousin, Olivero Carafa, Cardinal and Archbishop of Naples. Alexander VI, that mighty man, who knew everything and could do anything, made him his *cameriere* (roughly what we should call nowadays groom of the chambers). Julius II nominated him Archbishop of Chieti; Pope Paul created him Cardinal, and finally, after endless intriguing and disputes among the Cardinals enclosed in Conclave, he was elected Pope, taking the name of Paul IV; he was then seventy-eight years old. The very Cardinals who had just called him to the Throne of Saint Peter soon shuddered when they thought of the firmness and fierce, inexorable piety of the master whom they had set over themselves.

The news of this unexpected election caused a revolution at Naples and Palermo. Before many days had passed, Rome saw arrive within her gates innumerable members of the illustrious house of Carafa. All of them found places; but, as was only natural, the Pope shewed particular favour to his three nephews, sons of the Conte di Montorio, his brother.

Don Giovanni, the eldest, who was already married, was made Duke of Palliano. This duchy, taken from Marcantonio Colonna, to whom it belonged, included a large number of villages and small towns. Don Carlo, the second of His Holiness's nephews, was a Knight of Malta and had seen active service; he was created Cardinal, Legate of Bologna and First Minister. He was a man of great determination; loyal to the traditions of his family, he made bold to hate the most powerful monarch in the world (Philip II, King of Spain and of the Indies), and furnished him with proofs of his hatred. As for the new Pope's third nephew, Don Antonio Carafa, since he was married, the Pope made him Marchese di Montebello. Finally he proposed to give in marriage to Francis, Dauphin of France and son of King Henry II, a daughter whom his brother had got by a second marriage; Paul IV was to settle upon her as her dowry the Kingdom of Naples, which would first be taken from Philip II, King of Spain. The Carafa family hated this mighty king, who, with the help of the said family's own weaknesses, succeeded in wiping it out, as you shall see.

After he had ascended the throne of Saint Peter, the mightiest in the world, and one which, at that time, eclipsed even that of the illustrious Spanish monarch, Paul IV, as we have seen occur with most of his successors, set an example of all the virtues. He was a great Pope and a great Saint; he set to work to reform abuses within the Church, and by so doing to avoid the General Council for which all parties at the Roman Court were clamouring, but which a wise policy refused to grant.

In accordance with the custom of that age, which our

age has let fall into oblivion, the custom which forbade a
Sovereign to repose his confidence in men who might have
interests other than his own, the States of his Holiness
were governed despotically by his three nephews. The
Cardinal was First Minister and carried out his uncle's
wishes; the Duke of Palliano had been created General of
the forces of Holy Church; and the Marchese di Montebello, Captain of the Palace Guard, allowed only such
persons as it suited him to admit to cross its threshold.
Soon these young men were committing the wildest excesses; they began by appropriating for their own use the
possessions of the families opposed to their rule. The
people did not know where to turn to obtain justice. Not
only had they cause to be afraid for their possessions, but,
horrible to relate in the land of the chaste Lucrece, the
honour of their wives and daughters was not safe. The
Duke of Palliano and his brothers carried off the most
beautiful women; it was enough to have been so unfortunate as to take their fancy. People were amazed to see
them shew no respect for exalted birth; worse still, they
were in no way restrained by the sanctity of the cloister.
The people, in despair, knew of no one to whom they might
complain, so great was the terror which the three brothers
had inspired in everyone who approached the Pope's
presence; they were insolent to the Ambassadors even.

The Duke had married, before his uncle's rise to great-
ness, Violante di Cardone, of a family of Spanish origin
which, at Naples, belonged to the highest aristocracy.

It was numbered in the *Seggio di nido*.

Violante, famed for her rare beauty and for the charm
which she knew how to assume when she sought to attract,
was famed even more for her overweening pride. But, to
do her justice, it would have been difficult to have a more
exalted mind, as she shewed to all the world by admitting
nothing, in the hour of her death, to the Capuchin friar

who came to shrive her. She knew by heart and used to repeat with infinite charm the admirable *Orlando* of Messer Ariosto, most of the *Sonnets* of the divine Petrarch, the *Tales* of Pecorone, etc. But she was even more entrancing when she deigned to entertain her company with the odd ideas that suggested themselves to her mind.

She had a son who was styled Duca di Cavi. Her brother, Don Ferrante, Conte d'Aliffe, came to Rome, attracted by the prosperous state of his brothers-in-law.

The Duke of Palliano maintained a splendid court; the scions of the first families of Naples fought for the honour of belonging to it. Among those whom he most cherished, Rome marked out, by its admiration, Marcello Capecce (of the *Seggio di Nido*), a young gentleman celebrated at Naples for his intelligence, no less than for the godlike beauty which heaven had bestowed upon him.

The Duchess had as favourite Diana Brancaccio, then thirty years of age, closely related to the Marchesa di Montebello, her sister-in-law. It was rumoured in Rome that, with this favourite, she threw off her pride; that she confided to her all her secrets. But these secrets related only to politics; the Duchess aroused passions in others, but reciprocated none.

On the advice of Cardinal Carafa, the Pope declared war against the King of Spain, and the King of France sent to the Pope's assistance an army commanded by the Duc de Guise.

But we must confine ourselves to events at home, inside the court of the Duke of Palliano.

Capecce had long appeared more or less mad; he was seen to perform the strangest actions; the fact was that the poor young man had fallen passionately in love with the Duchess, his *mistress,* but dared not reveal his condition to her. At the same time, he did not absolutely despair of attaining his end, for he saw the Duchess intensely annoyed by a husband who neglected her. The Duke of Palliano was all powerful in Rome, and the Duchess knew, without any shadow of doubt, that almost every day the most famous beauties among the ladies of Rome came to visit her husband in her own palazzo, and this was an insult to which she could not grow reconciled.

Among the chaplains to His Holiness Pope Paul IV was a respectable cleric with whom he used to repeat his breviary. This gentleman, at the risk of his own downfall, and perhaps at the instigation of the Spanish Ambassador, made bold one day to reveal to the Pope all his nephews' misdeeds. The holy pontiff was ill with grief; he tried not to believe the report; but overwhelming evidence came in from every side. It was on the first day of the year 1559 that the event occurred which confirmed all the Pope's suspicions, and perhaps brought him to a decision. It was therefore, on the actual Feast of the Circumcision of Our Lord, a coincidence which greatly aggravated the offence in the eyes of so pious a Sovereign, that Andrea Lanfranchi, secretary to the Duke of Palliano, gave a magnificent supper to Cardinal Carafa, and wishing to add to the excitement of the palate that of the flesh, invited to this supper Martuccia, one of the most beautiful, most notorious and wealthiest courtesans of the noble city of Rome. Fate so willed it that Capecce, the Duke's favourite, the same who was secretly in love with the Duchess, and was reckoned the handsomest man in the capital of the world, had for some time past been attached to Martuccia. On the evening in question he searched for her in all the places where he had any hope of finding her. Not seeing her anywhere, and having heard that there was a supper party at Lanfranchi's house, he had a suspicion of what was happening, and towards midnight appeared at Lanfranchi's door, accompanied by a numerous body of armed men.

The door was opened to him; he was invited to sit down and partake of the feast; but, after a few words had been exchanged with a certain constraint, he made a signal to Martuccia to rise and leave the house with him. While she was hesitating, greatly confused and with an inkling of what was going to happen, Capecce rose from the chair on which he was sitting, and, going up to the girl, took her by the hand, and attempted to carry her off with him. The Cardinal, in whose honour she had come to the party, strongly opposed her departure; Capecce persisted, endeavouring to drag her from the room.

The Cardinal First Minister, who, that evening, had assumed a garb very different from that which indicated his high rank, took his sword in hand, and endeavoured, with the vigour and courage which all Rome knew him to possess, to prevent the girl from leaving. Marcello, blind with rage, summoned his men; but they were mostly Neapolitans, and, when they recognised first of all the Duke's secretary and then the Cardinal, whom the unusual clothes which he was wearing had at first disguised from them, they sheathed their swords again, declined to fight, and intervened to settle the dispute.

During this uproar, Martuccia, who was surrounded by the rest, while Marcello Capecce kept hold of her left hand, was clever enough to escape. As soon as Marcello noticed her absence he hastened after her, and his men all followed him.

But the darkness of the night gave rise to the strangest reports, and on the morning of January 2nd the capital was filled with accounts of the perilous encounter which had occurred, it was said, between the Cardinal's nephew and Marcello Capecce. The Duke of Palliano, Commander in Chief of the forces of the Church, understood the affair to be more serious than it actually was, and, as he was not on the best of terms with his brother the Min-

ister, had Lanfranchi arrested that same night, while early
on the following morning Marcello himself was put in
prison.   Then it was discovered that no life had been lost,
and that these imprisonments served only to increase the
scandal, the whole of which fell upon the Cardinal's shoulders.   The prisoners were quickly set at liberty, and the
three brothers combined their enormous influence to hush
up the affair.   They expected at first to be successful;
but, on the third day, the whole story came to the ears of
the Pope.   He sent for his two nephews and spoke to them
as a Prince might speak who was so pious and so profoundly shocked.

On the fifth day of January, which saw a great number
of Cardinals assembled in the congregation of the Holy
Office, the Pope was the first to speak of this horrible affair;
he asked the Cardinals present how they had dared refrain
from bringing it to his knowledge:

"You keep silence!   And yet the scandal affects the
sublime dignity with which you are invested!   Cardinal
Carafa has had the audacity to appear in the public streets
in lay attire and with a drawn sword in his hand.   And
with what object?   To take forcible possession of a shame-
less harlot!"

One may imagine the deathly silence that prevailed
among all his courtiers during this outburst against the
First Minister.   Here was an old man of eighty inveighing
against a beloved nephew, the master until then of his will.
In his indignation, the Pope spoke of taking the hat from
his nephew.

The Pope's anger was fanned by the Ambassador of the
Grand Duke of Tuscany, who came to complain to him of
a recent insult on the part of the Cardinal First Minister.
This Cardinal, so powerful until then, presented himself
before His Holiness in the course of his duty.   The Pope
kept him for four whole hours in the ante-room, waiting

where everyone could see him, then sent him away without admitting him to an audience. One may imagine the blow to the Minister's unbounded pride. The Cardinal was annoyed, but not disposed to yield; he felt that an old man bowed down with years, dominated all his life long by the love he bore his family, and moreover little accustomed to the handling of temporal matters, would be obliged to have recourse to his activity. The saintly Pope's virtue won the day; he summoned the Cardinals together, and after gazing at them for a long time without speaking, finally burst into tears and had no hesitation in making what apology he could.

"The feebleness of age," he said to them, "and the attention that I pay to matters of religion, in which, as you know, I am trying to destroy all the abuses, have led me to entrust my temporal authority to my three nephews; they have abused that authority, and I banish them now for ever."

A brief was then read by which the nephews were deprived of all their dignities and confined to miserable villages. The Cardinal Prime Minister was banished to Città Lavinia, the Duke of Palliano to Soriano, and the Marchese to Montebello; by this brief, the Duke was deprived of his fixed revenue, which amounted to seventy-two thousand piastres (more than a million in 1838).

There could be no question of disobeying these stern orders: the Carafa had as enemies and watchers the entire population of Rome, who detested them.

The Duke of Palliano, escorted by the Conte d'Aliffe, his brother-in-law, and by Leonardo del Cardine, established his quarters in the little village of Soriano, while the Duchess and her mother-in-law came to live at Gallese, a wretched hamlet within two leagues of Soriano.

The neighbourhood is charming, but they were in exile;

and they were banished from Rome, where but a little while since they had held an insolent sway.

Marcello Capecce had followed his mistress, with the rest of the courtiers, to the wretched village to which she had been banished. Instead of the devotion of all Rome this woman, so powerful a few days earlier, who had exulted in her position with all the arrogance of her pride, now found herself surrounded only by simple peasants, whose very amazement kept her in mind of her downfall. She had no consolation; her uncle was so old that probably death would overtake him before he had recalled his nephews, and, to complete their misfortune, the three brothers hated one another. It was even said that the Duke and the Marchese, who were not liable to the fiery passions of the Cardinal, alarmed by his excesses, had gone the length of denouncing them to the Pope their uncle.

Amidst the horror and shame of this abject disgrace, something occurred which, unfortunately for the Duchess and for Capecce himself, shewed plainly that, in Rome, it had not been a genuine passion that had drawn him in the wake of Martuccia.

One day when the Duchess had sent for him to give him an order, he found himself alone with her, a thing which did not happen more than once, perhaps, in a whole year. When he saw that there was no one else in the room in which the Duchess received him, Capecce stopped short and remained silent. He went to the door to see whether there was anyone that could hear them in the next room, then found courage to speak as follows:

"Signora, do not vex yourself, do not take offence at the strange words which I am about to have the temerity to utter. For a long time past I have loved you more than life itself. If, in a rash moment, I have ventured to gaze as a lover upon your heavenly beauty, you must impute the fault not to me, but to the supernatural force which urges and distracts me. I am in torment, I burn; I ask for nothing to quench the flame that is consuming me, but simply that your generosity may take pity upon a servant filled with misgivings and humility."

The Duchess appeared surprised, and, what was more, annoyed.

"Why, Marcello, what have you ever seen in me," she said to him, "to encourage you to speak to me of love? Does my life, does my conversation so far depart from the rules of decent behaviour as to afford you any justification for such insolence? How could you have the audacity to suppose that I could give myself to you or to any other man, except my lord and master? I forgive you for what you have said to me, because I consider that you are in a frenzied state; but take care not to make the same mistake again, or I swear I will have you punished for both pieces of impertinence at once."

The Duchess left him in a towering passion, and indeed Capecce had failed to observe the laws of prudence: he should have let his love be guessed and not have spoken. He stood there speechless, greatly alarmed lest the Duchess should tell her husband of what had happened.

But the sequel proved to be very different from his apprehensions. In the solitude of this village, the proud Duchess of Palliano could not help taking into her confidence and revealing what had been said to her to her favourite lady in waiting, Diana Brancaccio. This was a woman of thirty, devoured by burning passions. She had red hair (the chronicler harps again and again upon this peculiarity, which to him seems to account for all Diana Brancaccio's mad actions). She was hotly in love with Domiziano Fornari, a gentleman attached to the household of the Marchese di Montebello. She wished to take him as her husband; but would the Marchese and his wife, with whom she had the honour to be connected by ties of blood, ever consent to her marriage to a man actually in their service? This obstacle was insurmountable, or seemed so at least.

There was but one chance of success: she would have to obtain some practical support from the Duke of Palliano, the Marchese's elder brother, and Diana was not without some hope in this direction. The Duke treated her as one of his family rather than as a servant. He was a man with an element of simplicity and goodness in his nature, and attached infinitely less importance than his brothers to questions of pure etiquette. Although, as a young man would, the Duke made full use of all the advantages of his exalted position, and was anything but faithful to his wife, he loved her dearly, and, so far as one might judge, could not refuse her any favour were she to ask it with a certain amount of persistence.

The confession which Capecce had ventured to make to the Duchess seemed to the dark mind of Diana an unlooked-for piece of good fortune. Her mistress had been until then maddeningly prudent; should she prove capable of feeling passion, were she to commit a sin, at every moment she would need Diana, who in turn might look for anything in the world from a woman whose secrets she would know.

So far from giving any hint to the Duchess first of all of what she owed to herself, and then of the terrible danger to which she would be exposing herself amid so sharp-sighted a court, Diana, carried away by the heat of her passion, spoke of Marcello Capecce to her mistress as she was in the habit of speaking to herself of Domiziano Fornari. In the long conversations with which they beguiled their solitude, she found some pretext daily for recalling to the Duchess's memory the charm and beauty of that poor Marcello who seemed so unhappy; he belonged, like the Duchess, to one of the first families in Naples, his manners were as noble as his blood, and he lacked only those worldly possessions which a caprice of fortune might at any time bestow upon him, in order to become in every respect the equal of the woman whom he ventured to love.

Diana was delighted to observe that the first effect of these speeches was to increase the confidence which the Duchess placed in her.

She did not forget to give a report of what was happening to Marcello Capecce. During the burning heat of that summer the Duchess often strolled in the woods which surround Gallese. At the close of day she would await the turn of the sea breeze on the charming hills which rise in the midst of those woods, hills from the summit of which the sea is visible at a distance of less than two leagues.

Without infringing the strict laws of etiquette, Marcello also might stroll in these woods: he would conceal himself there, it was said, and took care only to catch the Duchess's eye when she had been led to think kindly of him by the speeches of Diana Brancaccio. The latter would then give Marcello a signal.

Diana, seeing her mistress on the point of yielding to the fatal passion the seeds of which she herself had sown in the other's heart, herself gave way to the violent love which Domiziano Fornari had inspired in her. Now at last she was certain of being able to marry him. But Domiziano was a sober-minded young man, cold and reserved by nature; the extravagances of his fiery mistress, so far from attaching him to her, soon became distasteful to him. Diana Brancaccio was closely related to the Carafa; he might be certain of being stabbed, should the faintest rumour of his amours come to the ears of the terrible Cardinal Carafa who, albeit younger than the Duke of Palliano, was, as a matter of fact, the real head of the family.

The Duchess had yielded, some time since, to Capecce's passion, when one fine day Domiziano Fornari was not to be found in the village to which the court of the Marchese di Montebello had been banished. He had disappeared: it was learned later on that he had taken ship in the little port of Nettuno; doubtless he had changed his name, and nothing more was ever heard of him.

How is one to describe Diana's feelings? After listening good-humouredly for some time to her inveighings against fate, one day the Duchess of Palliano let her see that this topic of conversation seemed to her to be exhausted. Diana saw herself scorned by her lover; her heart was a prey to the most cruel forces; she drew the strangest conclusion from the momentary irritation which the Duchess had felt on hearing a repetition of her complaints. Diana persuaded herself that it was the Duchess who had compelled Domiziano Fornari to leave her for ever, and who, moreover, had furnished him with the means of travelling. This fantastic idea had no basis apart from certain remonstrances which the Duchess had once addressed to her. Her suspicion was swiftly followed by revenge. She sought an audience of the Duke and told him all that had occurred between his wife and Marcello. The Duke refused to believe her.

"Bear in mind," he told her, "that during the last fifteen years I have not had the least fault to find with the Duchess; she has withstood the temptations of the court and the pitfalls of the brilliant position we enjoyed in Rome; the most attractive Princes, the Duc de Guise himself even, the General of the French Army, found it a waste of time, and you would have her yield to a mere Esquire!"

As ill luck would have it, the Duke finding time hang on his hands at Soriano, the village to which he had been banished, and which was but a couple of leagues from that in which his wife was living, Diana managed to secure frequent audiences from him, without their coming to the Duchess's knowledge. Diana had an amazing faculty of invention; her passion made her eloquent. She furnished the Duke with a mass of details; revenge had become her sole pleasure. She repeated that, almost every night, Capecce made his way into the Duchess's room about eleven o'clock, and did not leave until two or three in the morning. These reports made so little impression, at first, on the Duke's mind, that he refused to take the trouble to ride a couple of leagues at midnight in order to go to Gallese and pay a surprise visit to his wife's room.

But one evening when he happened to be at Gallese, the sun had set, and yet it was still light; Diana, quite dishevelled, made her way into the room in which the Duke was. Everyone else withdrew. She informed him that Marcello Capecce had just entered the Duchess's bedroom. The Duke, who doubtless was in an ill humour at the moment, took up his dagger and ran to his wife's room, which he entered by a secret door. There he found Marcello Capecce. The lovers did, indeed, change colour when they saw him come in; but, as a matter of fact, there was nothing reprehensible in their attitude. The Duchess was in bed, engaged in making a note of a small sum which she had just paid; a maid was in the room; Marcello was on his feet, at a distance of three yards from the bed.

The Duke in his fury seized Marcello by the throat, and dragged him into an adjoining closet, where he ordered him to fling away the dirk and dagger with which he was armed. After which the Duke summoned the men of his guard, by whom Marcello was at once led away to the prisons of Soriano.

The Duchess was left in her own house, but under close guard.

The Duke was by no means a cruel man; it appears that

he did think of concealing the scandal of the affair, so as not to be obliged to have recourse to the extreme measures which honour required of him. He wished it to be thought that Marcello was being kept in prison for a wholly different reason, and taking as a pretext a number of huge toads which Marcello had bought at a high price two or three months previously, he gave out that the young man had attempted to poison him. But the true nature of the crime was too well known, and the Cardinal, his brother, sent to ask him when he was going to think of washing out in the blood of the guilty the insult that had been offered to their family.

The Duke called to his assistance the Conte d'Aliffe, his wife's brother, and Antonio Torando, a friend of the family. The three of them, forming a sort of tribunal, passed judgment upon Marcello Capecce, accused of adultery with the Duchess.

The instability of human affairs brought it to pass that Pope Pius IV, who succeeded Paul IV, belonged to the Spanish faction. He could refuse nothing to King Philip II, who demanded of him the lives of the Cardinal and of the Duke of Palliano. The brothers were brought before the local tribunal, and from the minutes of the trial which they had to undergo we learn all the circumstances of the death of Marcello Capecce.

One of the many witnesses who were called gave evidence as follows:

"We were at Soriano; the Duke, my master, held a long conversation with the Conte d'Aliffe. . . . Late at night we went down into one of the cellars, where the Duke had made ready the cords required for putting the accused to the question. There were present the Duke, the Conte d'Aliffe, Don Antonio Torando and myself.

"The first witness to be called was Captain Camillo

Griffone, the intimate friend and confidant of Capecce. The Duke addressed him thus:

" 'Tell the truth, my friend. What do you know of Marcello's doings in the Duchess's room?'

" 'I know nothing: for the last three weeks and more I have not spoken to Marcello.'

"As he refused obstinately to say anything further, the Lord Duke called in some of his guards from outside. Griffone was tied to the cord by the Podestà of Soriano. The guards pulled the cords, and in this way raised the witness four fingers'-breadth from the ground. After the Captain had been suspended thus for fully a quarter of an hour, he said:

" 'Let me down and I will tell you all I know.'

"When they had set him down on the ground, the guards withdrew, and we remained alone in the cellar with him.

" 'It is true that on several occasions I have gone with Marcello to the Duchess's room,' said the Captain, 'but I know nothing more than that, because I used to wait for him in a courtyard near at hand until one o'clock in the morning.'

"The guards were at once recalled, and, on an order from the Duke, drew him up again, so that his feet were clear of the ground. Presently the Captain cried out:

" 'Let me down, I will speak the truth. It is true,' he went on, 'that, for many months past, I have observed that Marcello was making love to the Duchess, and I meant to inform Your Excellency or Don Leonardo. The Duchess used to send every morning to inquire for Marcello; she kept making him little presents, among other things, preserves of fruit prepared with great care and very costly; I have seen Marcello wearing little golden chains of marvellous workmanship which he had obviously had from the Duchess.'

"After making this statement, the Captain was taken

back to prison. The Duchess's porter was brought in, but said that he knew nothing; he was bound to the cord and raised in the air. After half an hour he said:

" 'Let me down and I will tell you all I know.'

"Once on the ground again, he pretended to know nothing; he was raised once more. After half an hour he was let down; he explained that he had been only a short time in the Duchess's personal service. As it was possible that the man did really know nothing, he was sent back to prison. All this had taken a long time on account of the guards, who were made to leave the room each time. They were intended to suppose that the trial was one of an attempt at poisoning, with the venom extracted from the toads.

"The night was already far advanced when the Duke ordered in Marcello Capecce. The guards having left the room, and the door being duly locked:

" 'What business have you,' he asked him, 'in the Duchess's room, that you stay there until one, two, and sometimes four o'clock in the morning?'

"Marcello denied everything; the guards were called, and he was strung up; the cord dislocated his arms; unable to endure the pain, he asked to be let down; he was set upon a chair; but after that became confused in his speech and did not seem himself to know what he was saying. The guards were called and strung him up once more; after a long spell, he asked to be let down.

" 'It is true,' he said, 'that I have entered the Duchess's apartment at these improper hours; but I was making love to Signora Diana Brancaccio, one of her Excellency's ladies, to whom I had given a promise of marriage, and who has granted me all, save such things as honour forbids.'

"Marcello was led back to prison, where he was confronted with the Captain; also with Diana, who denied everything.

"After this Marcello was brought back to the cellar; when we were near the door:

"'My Lord Duke,' he said, 'Your Excellency will recall that he has promised me my life if I tell the whole truth. It is not necessary to give me the cord again; I am going to tell you everything.'

"He then went up to the Duke, and, in a tremulous and barely articulate voice, told him that it was true that he had won the favour of the Duchess. At these words, the Duke flung himself upon Marcello and bit him in the cheek; he then drew his dagger, and I saw that he was on the point of stabbing the culprit. At this point I suggested that it would be as well for Marcello to write down in his own hand what he had just confessed, and that such a document would serve as a justification of His Excellency's action. We went into the cellar where there were writing materials; but the cord had so injured Marcello's arm and hand, that he was able to write only these few words: 'Yes, I have betrayed my lord; yes, I have stolen his honour.'

"The Duke read the words as Marcello wrote them. At this point, he flung himself upon Marcello and struck him three blows with his dagger, from which he expired. Diana Brancaccio was present, within an arm's-length, more dead than alive, and, no doubt, repenting a thousand times over what she had done.

"'Woman unworthy to be of noble birth,' cried the Duke, 'and sole cause of my dishonour, for which you have laboured to serve your own infamous pleasures, I must now give you the reward of all your treacheries.'

"So saying he seized her by the hair and sawed through her throat with a knife. The wretched woman shed a torrent of blood, and at length fell down dead.

"The Duke had the two bodies flung into a sewer that ran by the prison."

The young Cardinal Alfonso Carafa, son of the Marchese di Montebello, the one member of the family that Paul IV had kept in his court, felt it his duty to tell him of these events. The Pope's only answer was:

"And the Duchess, what have they done with her?"

It was generally thought, in Rome, that these words were tantamount to the unfortunate woman's death warrant. But the Duke could not steel himself to that great sacrifice, either because she was pregnant or because of the intense affection he had felt for her in the past.

Three months after the great act of virtue which the saintly Pope Paul IV had performed in parting from the whole of his family, he fell ill, and, after three months of illness, expired on the 18th of August, 1559.

The Cardinal wrote letter after letter to the Duke of Palliano, incessantly reiterating that their honour demanded the death of the Duchess. Seeing their uncle dead and not knowing what the next Pope's attitude might be, he was anxious to have the whole affair finished as quickly as possible.

The Duke, a simple man, good natured and far less scrupulous than the Cardinal over mere points of honour, could not bring himself to the terrible extremes demanded of him. He reminded himself that he had frequently been unfaithful to the Duchess, without taking the slightest pains to conceal his infidelities from her, and that they might have led so proud a woman to take her revenge. At the very moment of entering the Conclave, after hearing mass and receiving the Holy Communion, the Cardinal wrote to him again that he was being tormented by these continual delays, and vowed that, if the Duke did not finally make up his mind to do what the honour of their house required of him, he would take no further interest in his affairs, and would make no attempt to be of use to him either in the Conclave or with the new Pope. A reason quite unconnected with the point of honour helped to determine the Duke's action. Although the Duchess was closely guarded, she contrived (it is said) to send word to Marcantonio Colonna, the Duke's mortal enemy, on account of his Duchy of Palliano which Carafa had secured for himself, that if Marcantonio were to succeed in saving her life and delivering her from captivity, she, for her part, would put him in possession of the fortress of Palliano, the commandant of which was her devoted servant.

On the 28th of August, 1559, the Duke sent to Gallese two companies of soldiers. On the 30th, Don Leonardo del Cardine, the Duke's kinsman, and Don Ferrante, Conte d'Aliffe, the Duchess's brother, arrived at Gallese, and entered the Duchess's apartments to take her life. They told her that she was to die; she received the news without the slightest change of countenance. She wished first to make her confession and to hear the Holy Mass. Then, on these two gentlemen's approaching her, she observed that they were not acting in concert. She asked whether there were an order from the Duke, her husband, authorising her death.

"Yes, Signora," replied Don Leonardo.

The Duchess asked to see it; Don Ferrante shewed it to her.

(I find in the report of the Duke's trial the deposition of the friars who were present on this terrible occasion. These depositions are greatly superior to those of the other witnesses, this being due, I should say, to the fact that these monks had no fear when speaking before a court of justice, whereas all the other witnesses had been more or less the accomplices of their master.)

Fra Antonio di Pavia, a Capuchin, gave evidence as follows:

"After mass, at which she devoutly received the Holy Communion, and while we were giving her comfort, the Conte d'Aliffe, brother of the Lady Duchess, entered the room with a cord and a hazel rod of the thickness of my thumb, and about half an ell in length. He bandaged the Duchess's eyes with a handkerchief, which she, with great coolness, pulled lower down over her eyes, so that she should not see. The Conte put the cord round her throat; but, as it did not run well, removed it and drew back a few feet; the Duchess hearing his step pulled the handkerchief from her eyes, and said:

" 'Well, what is happening now?'

"The Conte answered:

" 'The cord was not running well, I am going to fetch another, so that you shall not suffer.'

"So saying, he left the room; shortly afterwards he returned with another cord, arranged the handkerchief once more over her eyes, placed the cord round her throat, and, passing the rod through the loop, twisted it and so strangled her. The whole affair, on the Duchess's part, was conducted in the tone of an ordinary conversation."

Fra Antonio di Salazar, another Capuchin, concludes his evidence with these words:

"I wished to retire from the pavilion, from a scruple of conscience, so as not to see her die, but the Duchess said to me:

" 'Do not go away from here, for the love of God.' "

(Here the friar relates the incidents of her death, exactly as we have reported them.) He adds:

"She died like a good Christian, frequently repeating: *'Credo, credo.'* "

The two friars, who apparently had obtained the necessary authority from their superiors, repeat in their depositions that the Duchess always insisted upon her complete innocence, in all her conversations with them, in all her

[ 231 ]

confessions, and particularly in that preceding the mass at which she received the Holy Communion. If she was guilty, by this act of vanity she cast herself into hell.

When Fra Antonio di Pavia, the Capuchin, was brought face to face with Don Leonardo del Cardine, the friar said:

"My companion said to the Count that it would be as well to wait until the Duchess had been confined; 'she is in the sixth month,' he went on, 'we must not destroy the soul of the poor little creature she is carrying in her womb, he must have an opportunity of baptism.'

"To which the Conte d'Aliffe replied:

"'You know that I have to go to Rome, and I do not wish to appear there with this mask on my face,'" (meaning, "with this insult unavenged.")

Immediately the Duchess was dead, the two Capuchins insisted that her body be opened without delay, so that the rite of baptism might be administered to the child; but the Conte and Don Leonardo would not listen to their entreaties.

Next day, the Duchess was buried in the local church, with ceremony of a kind (I have read the account of it). This event, the news of which at once spread abroad, made but little impression, it had long been expected; her death had several times already been reported at Gallese and in Rome, and in any event an assassination outside the city and during a vacancy of the Holy See was nothing out of the common. The Conclave that followed the death of Paul IV was very stormy, and lasted for no less than four months.

On the 26th of December, 1559, the unfortunate Cardinal Carafa was obliged to concur in the election of a Cardinal supported by Spain, and unable, consequently, to decline to take any of the harsh measures which Philip

II would invoke against Cardinal Carafa. The new Pope took the name of Pius IV.

Had the Cardinal not been in banishment at the moment of his uncle's death, he would have had control of the election, or at least would have been in a position to prevent the nomination of an enemy.

Soon after this, both the Cardinal and the Duke were arrested. King Philip's order was evidently that they should be put to death. They had to reply to fourteen separate charges. Everyone who could throw any light upon these charges was examined. The report, which is extremely well drafted, consists of two folio volumes, which I have read with great interest, because one finds on every page of them details of custom which the historians have not thought worthy of the solemn garb of history. I observed among others certain extremely picturesque details of an attempt at assassination aimed by the Spanish party against Cardinal Carafa, then the all-powerful Minister.

Anyhow, he and his brother were condemned for crimes which would not have been crimes in anyone else, that for instance of having put to death the lover of an unfaithful wife and the wife herself. A few years later, Prince Orsini married the sister of the Grand Duke of Tuscany; he suspected her of infidelity and had her poisoned in Tuscany itself, with the consent of the Grand Duke her brother, and yet this was never imputed to him as a crime. Several Princesses of the House of Medici died in this way.

When the trial of the two Carafa was ended, a long summary of it was prepared, and this, on several occasions, was examined by congregations of Cardinals. It is obvious that once it had been decided to punish with death a murder committed to avenge an act of adultery, a sort of crime to which justice never paid any attention, the Cardinal was guilty of having persecuted the Duke until the crime was committed, as the Duke was guilty of having ordered its execution.

On the 3rd of March, 1564, Pope Pius IV held a Consistory which lasted for eight hours, and at the end of which he pronounced sentence on the Carafa in the following words: *"Prout in schedula."*

On the night of the 4th, the Fiscal sent the Bargello to the Castel Sant' Angelo, to carry out the sentence of death passed upon the two brothers, Carlo, Cardinal Carafa, and Giovanni, Duke of Palliano, which he did. They dealt first with the Duke. He was transferred from the Castel Sant' Angelo to the prisons of Tordinone, where everything was in readiness; it was there that the Duke, the Conte d'Aliffe and Don Leonardo del Cardine had their heads cut off.

The Duke bore that dread moment not merely like a gentleman of exalted birth, but like a Christian ready to endure all for the love of God. He addressed a few noble words to his two companions, encouraging them in the hour of death; then wrote to his son.[1]

The Bargello returned to the Castel Sant' Angelo, with an announcement of death to Cardinal Carafa, giving him no more than an hour to prepare himself. The Cardinal shewed a greater strength of character than his brother, all the more as he said less; speech is always a strength which one seeks outside oneself. He was heard only to mutter these words in a low tone, on receiving the grim tidings:

"I to die! O Pope Pius! O King Philip!"

[1] The learned Signor Sismondi confuses the whole of this story. See the article *Carafa* in the *Biographie Michaud;* he maintains that it was the Conte di Montorio who had his head cut off on the day of the Cardinal's death. The Conte was father of the Cardinal and of the Duke of Palliano. The learned historian confuses the father with the son.

He made his confession; repeated the seven Penitential Psalms, then sat down on a chair and said to the executioner:

"Proceed."

The executioner strangled him with a silken cord, which broke; he was obliged to make a second and a third attempt. The Cardinal looked at him without deigning to utter a word.

(*Note added.*)

Not many years later, the sainted Pope Pius V ordered a revision of the proceedings, which were annulled; the Cardinal and his brother had all their honours restored to them, and the Procurator General, who had done most to cause their death, was hanged. Pius V ordered the suppression of the report; all the copies existing in the libraries were burned; people were forbidden to preserve one on pain of excommunication: but the Pope forgot that he had a copy of the report in his own library, and it was from this copy that all those were made which we see to-day.

# VANINA VANINI

## or

## SOME PARTICULARS OF THE LATEST ASSEMBLY OF CARBONARI DISCOVERED IN THE STATES OF THE CHURCH

IT was a spring evening in 182—. All Rome was astir: the Duca di B——, the famous banker, was giving a ball in his new palazzo on the Piazza di Venezia. All the most sumptuous treasures that the arts of Italy, the luxury of Paris and London can furnish had been collected for the adornment of this palace. The gathering was immense. The fair, retiring beauties of noble England had intrigued for the honour of being present at this ball; they arrived in crowds. The most beautiful women of Rome vied with them for the prize of beauty. A girl whom her sparkling eyes and ebon tresses proclaimed of Roman birth entered, escorted by her father; every eye followed her. A singular pride was displayed in her every gesture.

One could see the foreigners who entered the room struck by the magnificence of this ball. "None of the courts of Europe," they were saying, "can compare with this."

Kings have not a palace of Roman architecture: they are obliged to invite the great ladies of their courts; the Duca di B—— invites only lovely women. This evening he had been fortunate in his invitations; the men seemed dazzled. Amid so many remarkable women it was hard to decide which was the most beautiful: the award was for some time undetermined; but at length Principessa Vanina Vanini, the girl with the raven hair and fiery eye, was proclaimed queen of the ball. Immediately the foreigners and the young Romans, deserting all the other rooms, crowded into the room in which she was.

Her father, Principe Don Asdrubale Vanini, had wished her to dance first of all with two or three Sovereign Princes from Germany. She then accepted the invitations of certain extremely handsome and extremely noble Englishmen; their starched manner irritated her. She appeared to find more pleasure in teasing young Livio Savelli, who seemed deeply in love. He was the most brilliant young man in Rome, and a Prince to boot; but, if you had given him a novel to read, he would have flung the book away after twenty pages, saying that it made his head ache. This was a disadvantage in Vanina's eyes.

Towards midnight a report ran through the ball-room, which caused quite a stir. A young carbonaro, in detention in the Castel Sant' Angelo, had escaped that evening, with the help of a disguise, and, with an excess of romantic daring, on coming to the outermost guardroom of the prison, had attacked the soldiers there with a dagger; but he had been wounded himself, the *sbirri* were pursuing him through the streets, following the track of his blood, and hoped to recapture him.

While this story was going round, Don Livio Savelli, dazzled by the charms and the success of Vanina, with whom he had just been dancing, said to her as he led her back to her seat, being almost mad with love:

"Why, in heaven's name, what sort of person could please you?"

"This young carbonaro who has just made his escape,"

was Vanina's reply; "he at least has done something more than take the trouble to be born."

Principe Don Asdrubale approached his daughter. He is a wealthy man who for the last twenty years has kept no accounts with his steward, who lends him his own income at a high rate of interest. If you should pass him in the street, you would take him for an elderly actor; you would not notice that his fingers were loaded with five or six enormous rings set with huge diamonds. His two sons became Jesuits, and afterwards died insane. He has forgotten them, but it vexes him that his only daughter, Vanina, declines to marry. She is already nineteen, and has refused the most brilliant suitors. What is her reason? The same that led Sulla to abdicate, her *contempt for the Romans.*

On the day after the ball, Vanina remarked that her father, the most casual of men, who never in his life had taken the trouble to carry a key, was very careful in shutting the door of a little stair which led to an apartment on the third floor of the palazzo. The windows of this apartment looked on to a terrace planted with orange trees. Vanina went out to pay some calls in Rome; on her return, the main door of the palazzo was blocked with the preparations for an illumination, the carriage drove in through the courtyards at the back. Vanina raised her eyes, and saw with astonishment that one of the windows of the apartment which her father had so carefully closed was now open. She got rid of her companion, climbed up to the attics of the palazzo and after a long search succeeded in finding a small barred window which overlooked the orange tree terrace. The open window which she had observed from below was within a few feet of her. Evidently the room was occupied; but by whom? Next day, Vanina managed to secure the key of a small door which opened on to the terrace planted with orange trees.

She stole on tiptoe to the window, which was still open. It was screened by a sunblind. Inside the room was a bed, and somebody in the bed. Her first impulse was to retire; but she caught sight of a woman's gown flung over a chair. On looking more closely at the person in the bed, she saw that this person was fair, and evidently quite young. She had no longer any doubt that it was a woman. The gown flung over the chair was stained with blood; there was blood also on the woman's shoes placed beneath a table. The stranger moved in the bed; Vanina saw that she had been wounded. A great bandage stained with blood covered her bosom; this bandage was fastened with ribbons only; it was not a surgeon's hand that had so arranged it. Vanina noticed that every day, about four o'clock, her father shut himself up in his own rooms, and then went to visit the stranger; presently he came downstairs and took his carriage to call upon the Contessa Vitelleschi. As soon as he had left the house, Vanina went up to the little terrace, from which she could see the stranger. Her compassion was strongly aroused towards this young woman who was in such a plight; she tried to imagine what could have befallen her. The bloodstained gown that lay on the chair appeared to have been stabbed with a dagger. Vanina could count the rents in it. One day she saw the stranger more distinctly: her blue eyes were fastened on the ceiling; she seemed to be praying. Presently tears welled in those lovely eyes; the young Princess could hardly refrain from addressing her. Next day, Vanina ventured to hide on the little terrace before her father came upstairs. She saw Don Asdrubale enter the stranger's room; he was carrying a small basket in which were provisions. The Prince appeared ill at ease, and said but little. He spoke so low that, although the window stood open, Vanina could not overhear his words. He soon left.

"That poor woman must have very terrible enemies," Vanina said to herself, "for my father, who is so careless by nature, not to dare to confide in anyone and to take the trouble to climb a hundred and twenty steps every day."

One evening, as Vanina was cautiously extending her head towards the stranger's window, their eyes met, and she was discovered. Vanina fell on her knees, crying:

"I love you, I am your devoted servant."

The stranger beckoned to her to come in.

"How can I apologise to you?" cried Vanina; "how offensive my foolish curiosity must appear to you! I swear to keep your secret, and, if you insist on it, I will never come again."

"Who would not be delighted to see you?" said the stranger. "Do you live in this palazzo?"

"Certainly," replied Vanina. "But I see that you do not know me: I am Vanina, Don Asdrubale's daughter."

The stranger looked at her with an air of surprise, then went on:

"Please let me hope that you will come to see me every day; but I should prefer the Prince not to know of your visits."

Vanina's heart beat violently; the stranger's manner seemed to her most distinguished. This poor young woman had doubtless given offence to some powerful man; possibly in a moment of jealousy she had killed her lover. Vanina could not conceive any common reason for her trouble. The stranger told her that she had received a wound in the shoulder, which had penetrated her breast and gave her great pain. Often she found her mouth filled with blood.

"And you have no surgeon!" cried Vanina.

"You know that in Rome," said the stranger, "the surgeons have to furnish the police with an exact report of all the injuries that they treat. The Prince is kind enough to dress my wounds himself with the bandage you see here."

The stranger refrained with the most perfect taste from any commiseration of her accident; Vanina loved her madly. One incident, however, greatly surprised the young Princess, which was that in the middle of a conversation which was certainly most serious the stranger had great difficulty in suppressing a sudden impulse to laughter.

"I should be happy," Vanina said to her, "to know your name."

"I am called Clementina."

"Very well, dear Clementina, to-morrow at five I shall come to see you."

Next day Vanina found her new friend in great pain.

"I am going to bring you a surgeon," said Vanina as she embraced her.

"I would rather die," said the stranger. "Would you have me compromise my benefactors?"

"The surgeon of Monsignor Savelli-Catanzara, the Governor of Rome, is the son of one of our servants," Vanina answered firmly; "he is devoted to us, and in his position has no fear of anyone. My father does not do justice to his loyalty; I am going to send for him."

"I do not want any surgeon!" cried the stranger with a vivacity which surprised Vanina. "Come and see me, and if God is to call me to Himself, I shall die happy in your arms."

On the following day the stranger was worse.

"If you love me," said Vanina as she left her, "you will see a surgeon."

"If he comes, my happiness is at an end."

"I am going to send to fetch him," replied Vanina.

Without saying a word, the stranger seized hold of her, and took her hand, which she covered with kisses. A long silence followed; tears filled the stranger's eyes. At length she let go Vanina's hand, and with the air of one going to her death, said to her:

"I have a confession to make to you. The day before yesterday, I lied when I said that my name was Clementina; I am an unhappy carbonaro . . ."

Vanina in her astonishment thrust back her chair, and presently rose.

"I feel," went on the carbonaro, "that this confession is going to make me forfeit the one blessing which keeps me alive; but I should be unworthy of myself were I to deceive you. My name is Pietro Missirilli; I am nineteen; my father is a poor surgeon at Sant' Angelo in Vado, I myself am a carbonaro. Our *venuta* was surprised; I was brought, in chains, from the Romagna to Rome. Cast into a dungeon lighted day and night by a lamp, I lay there for thirteen months. A charitable soul conceived the idea of helping me to escape. I was dressed as a woman. As I was leaving the prison and passing by the guard at the outer gate, one of them cursed the carbonari; I dealt him a blow. I swear to you that it was not a piece of vain bravado, but simply that I was not thinking. Pursued by night through the streets of Rome after that act of folly, stabbed with bayonet wounds, I had begun to lose my strength, I entered a house the door of which stood open, I heard the soldiers coming in after me, I sprang into a garden; I fell to the ground within a few feet of a woman who was walking there."

"Contessa Vitelleschi! My father's mistress," said Vanina.

"What! Has she told you?" cried Missirilli. "However that may be, this lady, whose name must never be uttered, saved my life. As the soldiers were coming into her house to seize me, your father took me away in his carriage. I feel very ill: for some days this bayonet wound in my shoulder has prevented me from breathing. I am going to die, and in despair, since I shall not see you again."

Vanina had listened with impatience; she swiftly withdrew from the room. Missirilli read no pity in those lovely eyes, but only the signs of a proud nature which had been deeply offended.

When it was dark, a surgeon appeared; he was alone. Missirilli was in despair; he was afraid that he would never see Vanina again. He questioned the surgeon, who bled him and made no reply. A similar silence on each of the days that followed. Pietro's eyes never left the window on the terrace by which Vanina used to enter; he was very miserable. Once, about midnight, he thought he could see someone in the dark on the terrace: was it Vanina?

Vanina came each night to press her face against the panes of the young carbonaro's window.

"If I speak to him," she said to herself, "I am lost! No, I must never see him again!"

Having come to this resolution, she recalled, in spite of herself, the affection that she had formed for this young man when she had so stupidly taken him for a woman. After so pleasant an intimacy, must she then forget him? In her most reasonable moments, Vanina was alarmed by the change that was occurring in her ideas. Ever since Missirilli had told her his name, all the things of which she was in the habit of thinking were, so to speak, wrapped in a veil of mist, and appeared to her now only at a distance.

A week had not gone by before Vanina, pale and trembling, entered the young carbonaro's room with the surgeon. She had come to tell him that he must make the Prince promise to let his place be taken by a servant. She was not in the room for ten seconds; but some days later she came back again with the surgeon, from a sense of humanity. One evening, although Missirilli was much better, and Vanina had no longer the excuse of being alarmed for his life, she ventured to come unaccompanied. On seeing her, Missirilli was raised to a pinnacle of joy, but he was careful to conceal his love; whatever happened, he was determined not to forget the dignity befitting a man. Vanina, who had come into the room blushing a deep crimson, and dreading amorous speeches, was disconcerted by the noble and devoted, but by no means tender friendliness with which he greeted her. She left without his making any attempt to detain her.

A few days later, when she returned, the same conduct, the same assurances of respectful devotion and eternal gratitude. So far from being occupied in putting a check on the transports of the young carbonaro, Vanina asked herself whether she alone were in love. This girl, hitherto so proud, was bitterly aware of the full extent of her folly. She made a pretence of gaiety, and even of coldness, came less frequently, but could not bring herself to abandon her visits to the young invalid.

Missirilli, burning with love, but mindful of his humble birth and of what he owed to himself, had made a vow that he would not stoop to talk of love unless Vanina were to spend a week without seeing him. The pride of the young Princess contested every inch of ground.

"After all," she said to herself at length, "if I see him, it is for my own sake, to please myself, and I will never confess to him the interest that he arouses in me."

She paid long visits to Missirilli, who talked to her as he might have done had there been a score of persons present. One evening, after she had spent the day hating him, and promising herself that she would be even colder and more severe with him than usual, she told him that she loved him. Soon there was nothing left that she could withhold from him.

Great as her folly may have been, it must be admitted that Vanina was sublimely happy. Missirilli no longer thought of what he believed to be due to his dignity as a man; he loved as people love for the first time at nineteen and in Italy. He felt all the scruples of "impassioned love," going so far as to confess to this haughty young Princess the stratagem which he had employed to make her love him. He was astounded by the fulness of his happiness. Four months passed rapidly enough. One day the surgeon set his patient at liberty. "What am I to do now?" thought Missirilli; "lie concealed in the house of one of the most beautiful people in Rome? And the vile tyrants who kept me for thirteen months in prison without ever allowing me to see the light of day will think they have disheartened me! Italy, thou art indeed unfortunate, if thy sons forsake thee for so slight a cause!"

Vanina never doubted that Pietro's greatest happiness lay in remaining permanently attached to herself; he seemed only too happy; but a saying of General Bonaparte echoed harshly in the young man's heart and influenced the whole of his conduct with regard to women. In 1796, as General Bonaparte was leaving Brescia, the municipal councillors who were escorting him to the gate of the city told him that the Brescians loved freedom more than any of the Italians.

"Yes," he replied, "they love to talk about it to their mistresses."

Missirilli said to Vanina with a visible air of constraint: "As soon as it is dark, I must go out."

"Be careful to come in again before daybreak; I shall be waiting for you."

"By daybreak I shall be many miles from Rome."

"Very well," said Vanina coldly, "and where are you going?"

"To the Romagna, to have my revenge."

"As I am rich," Vanina went on with perfect calmness, "I hope that you will let me supply you with arms and money."

Missirilli looked at her for some moments without moving a muscle; then, flinging himself into her arms:

"Soul of my life," he said to her, "you make me forget everything, even my duty. But the nobler your heart is, the better you must understand me."

Vanina wept freely, and it was agreed that he should not leave Rome until the following night.

"Pietro," she said to him on the morrow, "you have often told me that a well-known man, a Roman Prince, for instance, with plenty of money at his disposal, would be in a position to render the utmost services to the cause of freedom, should Austria ever be engaged abroad, in some great war."

"Undoubtedly," said Pietro in surprise.

"Very well, you have a stout heart; all you lack is an exalted position: I have come to offer you my hand and an income of two hundred thousand lire. I undertake to obtain my father's consent."

Pietro fell at her feet; Vanina was radiant with joy.

"I love you passionately," he told her; "but I am a humble servant of the Fatherland; the more unhappy Italy is, the more loyal I should be to her. To obtain Don Asdrubale's consent, I shall have to play a sorry part for many years. Vanina, I decline your offer."

Missirilli made haste to bind himself by this utterance. His courage was failing him.

"My misfortune," he cried, "is that I love you more than life itself, that to leave Rome is for me the most agonising torture. Oh, that Italy were set free from the barbarians! With what joy would I set sail with you to go and live in America."

Vanina's heart was frozen. The refusal of her hand

had dealt a blow to her pride; but presently she threw herself into Missirilli's arms.

"Never have you seemed so adorable," she cried; "yes, my little country surgeon, I am yours for ever. You are a great man, like our ancient Romans."

All thoughts of the future, every depressing suggestion of common sense vanished; it was a moment of perfect love. When they were able to talk reasonably:

"I shall be in the Romagna almost as soon as you," said Vanina. "I am going to have myself sent to the baths of la Porretta. I shall stop at the villa we have at San Niccolò, close to Forlì. . . ."

"There I shall spend my life with you!" cried Missirilli.

"My lot henceforward is to dare all," Vanina continued with a sigh. "I shall ruin myself for you, but no matter. . . . Will you be able to love a girl who has lost her honour?"

"Are you not my wife," said Missirilli, "and the object of my lifelong adoration? I shall know how to love and protect you."

Vanina was obliged to go out, on social errands. She had barely left Missirilli before he began to feel that his conduct was barbarous.

"What is the *Fatherland?*" he asked himself. "It is not a person to whom we owe gratitude for benefits received, or who may suffer and call down curses on us if we fail him. The *Fatherland* and *Freedom* are like my cloak, a thing which is useful to me, which I must purchase, it is true, when I have not acquired it by inheritance from my father; but after all I love the Fatherland and Freedom because they are both useful to me. If I have no use for them, if they are to me like a cloak in the month of August, what is the good of purchasing them, and at an enormous price? Vanina is so beautiful! She has so singular a nature! Others will seek to attract her; she will forget me. What

woman is there who has never had more than one lover?
Those Roman Princes, whom I despise as citizens, have
so many advantages over me! They must indeed be attractive! Ah, if I go, she will forget me, and I shall lose
her for ever."

In the middle of the night, Vanina came to see him; he
told her of the uncertainty in which he had been plunged,
and the criticism to which, because he loved her, he had
subjected that great word "Fatherland." Vanina was very
happy.

"If he were absolutely forced to choose between his
country and me," she told herself, "I should have the
preference."

The clock of the neighbouring church struck three, the
time had come for a final leave-taking. Pietro tore himself from the arms of his mistress. He had begun to descend the little stair, when Vanina, restraining her tears,
said to him with a smile:

"If you had been nursed by some poor woman in the
country, would you do nothing to shew your gratitude?
Would you not seek to repay her? The future is uncertain,
you are going on a journey through the midst of your
enemies: give me three days out of gratitude, as if I were
a poor woman, and to pay me for the care I have taken
of you."

Missirilli stayed. At length he left Rome. Thanks to
a passport bought from a foreign embassy, he returned in
safety to his family. This was a great joy to them; they
had given him up for dead. His friends wished to cele-
brate his home-coming by killing a carabiniere or two
(such is the title borne by the police in the Papal States).

"We must not, when it is not necessary, kill an Italian
who knows how to handle arms," said Missirilli; "our
country is not an island, like happy England: it is soldiers

that we need to resist the intervention of the Sovereigns of Europe."

Some time later Missirilli, hard pressed by the carabinieri, killed a couple of them with the pistols which Vanina had given him. A price was set on his head.

Vanina did not appear in the Romagna: Missirilli imagined himself forgotten. His vanity was hurt; his thoughts began to dwell upon the difference in rank which divided him from his mistress. In a moment of weakness and regret for his past happiness it occurred to him that he might return to Rome to see what Vanina was doing. This mad idea was beginning to prevail over what he believed to be his duty when one evening the bell of a church in the mountains sounded the Angelus in a singular fashion, and as though the ringer were thinking of something else. It was the signal for the assembling of the *venuta* of carbonari which Missirilli had joined on his arrival in Romagna. That night, they all met at a certain hermitage in the woods. The two hermits, drugged with opium, knew nothing of the use to which their little dwelling was being put. Missirilli, who arrived in great depression, learned there that the leader of the *venuta* had been arrested, and that he, a young man not twenty years old, was about to be elected leader of a *venuta* which included men of fifty and more, who had taken part in all the conspiracies since Murat's expedition in 1815. On receiving this unexpected honour, Pietro felt his heart beat violently. As soon as he was alone, he determined to give no more thought to the young Roman who had forgotten him, and to devote his whole mind to the duty of *freeing Italy from the barbarians*.[1]

Two days later, Missirilli saw in the reports of arrivals

[1] *Liberar l'Italia de' barbari*: the words used by **Petrarch** in 1350, and since then repeated by **Julius II, Machiavelli** and **Conte Alfieri.**

and departures which were supplied to him, as leader of the *venuta,* that the Principessa Vanina had just arrived at her villa of San Niccolò. The sight of that name caused him more uneasiness than pleasure. It was in vain that he imagined himself to be proving his loyalty to his country by undertaking not to fly that very evening to the villa of San Niccolò; the thought of Vanina, whom he was neglecting, prevented him from carrying out his duty in a reasonable manner. He saw her next day; she loved him still as in Rome. Her father, who wished her to marry, had delayed her departure. She brought him two thousand sequins. This unexpected assistance served admirably to accredit Missirilli in his new office. They had daggers made for them in Corfu; they won over the Legate's private secretary, whose duty it was to pursue the carbonari. Thus they obtained a list of the clergy who were acting as spies for the government.

It was at this time that the organisation was completed of one of the least senseless conspiracies that have been planned in unhappy Italy. I shall not enter here into irrelevant details. I shall merely say that if success had crowned the attempt, Missirilli would have been able to claim a good share of the glory. At a signal from him, several thousands of insurgents would have risen, and awaited, armed, the coming of their superior leaders. The decisive moment was approaching when, as invariably happens, the conspiracy was paralyzed by the arrest of the leaders.

Immediately on her arrival in Romagna, Vanina felt that his love of his country would make her young lover forget all other love. The young Roman's pride was stung. She tried in vain to reason with herself; a black melancholy seized her: she found herself cursing freedom. One day when she had come to Forlì to see Missirilli, she was powerless to check her grief, which until then her pride had managed to control.

"Truly," she said to him, "you love me like a husband; that is not what I have a right to expect."

Soon her tears flowed; but they were tears of shame at having so far lowered herself as to reproach him. Missirilli responded to these tears like a man preoccupied with other things. Suddenly it occurred to Vanina to leave him and return to Rome. She found a cruel joy in punishing herself for the weakness that had made her speak. After a brief interval of silence, her mind was made up; she would feel herself unworthy of Missirilli if she did not leave him. She rejoiced in the thought of his pained surprise when he should look around for her in vain. Presently the reflexion that she had not succeeded in obtaining the love of the man for whom she had done so many foolish things moved her profoundly. Then she broke the silence, and did everything in the world to wring from him a word of love. He said, with a distracted air, certain quite tender things to her; but it was in a very different tone that, in speaking of his political enterprises, he sorrowfully exclaimed:

"Ah, if this attempt does not succeed, if the government discovers it again, I give up the struggle."

Vanina remained motionless. For the last hour, she had felt that she would never look upon her lover again. The words he had now uttered struck a fatal spark in her mind. She said to herself:

"The carbonari have had several thousands from me. No one can doubt my devotion to the conspiracy."

Vanina emerged from her musings only to say to Pietro:

"Will you come and spend the night with me at San Niccolò? Your meeting this evening can do without you. To-morrow morning, at San Niccolò, we can take the air

[ 254 ]

together; that will calm your agitation and restore the cool judgment you require on great occasions."

Pietro agreed.

Vanina left him to make ready for the journey, locking the door, as usual, of the little room in which she had hidden him.

She hastened to the house of one of her former maids who had left her service to marry and keep a small shop in Forlì.  On reaching the house, she wrote in haste on the margin of a Book of Hours which she found in the woman's room, an exact indication of the spot at which the *venuta* of carbonari was to assemble that evening.  She concluded her denunciation with the words: "This *venuta* is composed of nineteen members; their names and addresses are as follows."  Having written this list, which was quite accurate except that the name of Missirilli was omitted, she said to the woman, on whom she could rely:

"Take this book to the Cardinal Legate; make him read what is written in it, and give you back the book.  Here are ten sequins; if the Legate ever utters your name, your death is certain; but you will save my life if you make the Legate read the page I have just written."

All went well.  The Legate's fear prevented him from standing upon his dignity.  He allowed the humble woman who asked to speak with him to appear before him with only a mask, but on condition that her hands were tied. In this state the shop-keeper was brought into the presence of the great personage, whom she found entrenched behind an immense table, covered with a green cloth.

The Legate read the page in the Book of Hours, holding it at a distance, for fear of some subtle poison.  He gave it back to the woman, and did not have her followed.  In less than forty minutes after she had left her lover, Vanina, who had seen her former maid return, appeared once more before Missirilli, imagining that for the future he was entirely hers. She told him that there was an extraordinary commotion in the town; patrols of carabinieri were to be seen in streets along which they never went as a rule.

"If you will take my advice," she went on, "we will start this very instant for San Niccolò."

Missirilli agreed. They proceeded on foot to the young Princess's carriage, which, with her companion, a discreet and well-rewarded confidant, was waiting for her half a league from the town.

Having reached the San Niccolò villa, Vanina, disturbed by the thought of what she had done, multiplied her attentions to her lover. But when speaking to him of love she felt that she was playing a part. The day before, when she betrayed him, she had forgotten remorse. As she clasped her lover in her arms, she said to herself:

"There is a certain word which someone may say to him, and once that word is uttered, then and for all time, he will regard me with horror."

In the middle of the night, one of Vanina's servants came boldly into her room. This man was a carbonaro, and she had never known it. So Missirilli had secrets from her, even in these matters of detail. She shuddered. The man had come to inform Missirilli that during the night, at Forlì, the houses of nineteen carbonari had been surrounded and they themselves arrested as they were returning from the *venuta*. Although taken unawares, nine of them had escaped. The carabinieri had managed to convey ten to the prison of the citadel. On their way in, one of these had flung himself down the well, which was deep, and had killed himself.

Vanina lost countenance; happily Pietro did not observe her; he could have read her crime in her eyes. . . . "At the present moment," the servant went on, "the Forlì garrison is lining all the streets. Each soldier is close enough to the next to be able to speak to him. The inhabitants cannot cross from one side of the street to the other except at the places where there is an officer posted."

After the man had left them, Pietro remained pensive for a moment only.

"There is nothing to be done for the present," he said finally.

Vanina was half dead; she trembled under her lover's gaze.

"Why, what is the matter with you?" he asked her.

Then his thoughts turned to other things, and he ceased to look at her. Towards midday she ventured to say to him:

"And so another *venuta* has been surprised; I hope that you are going to be undisturbed now for some time."

"Quite undisturbed," replied Missirilli with a smile which made her shudder.

She went to pay a necessary call upon the parish priest of San Niccolò, who might perhaps be a spy of the Jesuits. On returning to dine at seven o'clock, she found the little room in which her lover had been concealed empty. Beside herself with alarm, she ran over the whole house in search of him. In despair, she returned to the little room, and it was only then that she saw a note; she read:

"I am going to give myself up to the Legate; I despair of our cause; heaven is against us. Who has betrayed us? Evidently the wretch who flung himself down the well. Since my life is of no use to poor Italy, I do not wish that my comrades, seeing that I alone have not been arrested, should imagine that I have sold them. Farewell; if you love me, try to avenge me. Destroy, crush the scoundrel who has betrayed us, even if he should be my own father."

Vanina sank down on a chair, half unconscious, and plunged in the most agonizing grief. She could not utter a word; her eyes were parched and burning.

At length she flung herself upon her knees:

"Great God!" she cried, "hear my vow; yes, I will punish the scoundrel who has betrayed them; but first I must set Pietro free."

An hour later, she was on her way to Rome. Her father had long been pressing her to return. During her absence, he had arranged her marriage with Principe Livio Savelli. Immediately on Vanina's arrival, he spoke to her of this marriage, in fear and trembling. Greatly to his surprise, she consented from the first. That evening, at Contessa Vitelleschi's, her father presented to her, semi-officially, Don Livio; she conversed with him freely. He was the most exquisite young man, and had the finest horses of any; but although he was admitted to have plenty of intelligence, he was regarded as so frivolous that he was held in no suspicion by the government. Vanina reflected that, by first of all turning his head, she might make a useful agent of him. As he was the nephew of Monsignor Savelli-Catanzara, Governor of Rome and Minister of Police, she supposed that the government spies would not dare to follow him.

After shewing herself most kind, for some days, to the charming Don Livio, Vanina broke to him that he could never be her husband; he had, according to her, too light a mind.

"If you were not a mere boy," she told him, "your uncle's clerks would have no secrets for you. For instance, what action is being taken with regard to the carbonari who were surprised the other day at Forlì?"

Don Livio came to inform her, a few days later, that all the carbonari taken at Forlì had escaped. She let her large black eyes rest on him with a bitter smile of the most profound contempt, and did not condescend to speak to him throughout the evening. Two days later, Don Livio came to confess to her, blushing as he did so, that he had been misinformed at first.

"But," he told her, "I have secured a key to my uncle's room; I see from the papers I found there that a *congregation* (or commission) composed of the Cardinals and prelates who are most highly considered is meeting in the strictest secrecy, and discussing whether it would be better to try these carbonari at Ravenna or in Rome. The nine carbonari taken at Forlì and their leader, a certain Missirilli, who was fool enough to give himself up, are at this moment confined in the castle of San Leo.[1]

At the word "fool," Vanina gripped the Prince with all her strength.

"I wish," she said, "to see the official papers myself, and to go with you into your uncle's room; you must have misread what you saw."

At these words, Don Livio shuddered; Vanina asked a thing that was almost impossible; but the girl's eccentric nature intensified his love for her. A few days later, Vanina, disguised as a man and wearing a neat little jacket in the livery of the casa Savelli, was able to spend half an hour among the most secret documents of the Minister of Police. She started with joyful excitement when she came upon the daily report on *Pietro Missirilli, on remand*. Her hands shook as she seized the paper. On reading the name again, she felt as though she must faint. As they left the palace of the Governor of Rome, Vanina permitted Don Livio to embrace her.

"You are coming very well," she told him, "through the tests to which I mean to subject you."

After such a compliment, the young Prince would have set fire to the Vatican to please Vanina. That evening, there was a ball at the French Ambassador's; she danced

---

[1] Near Rimini in Romagna. It was in this castle that the famous Cagliostro died; the local report is that he was smothered there.

frequently, and almost always with him. Don Livio was wild with joy; he must be kept from thinking.

"My father sometimes acts oddly," Vanina said to him one day; "this morning he dismissed two of his servants, who came to me in tears. One asked me to find him a place with your uncle the Governor of Rome; the other, who served as a gunner under the French, wishes to be employed in the Castel Sant' Angelo."

"I will take them both into my service," said the young Prince impulsively.

"Is that what I am asking you to do?" Vanina answered haughtily. "I repeat to you word for word the request made by these poor men; they must obtain what they have asked for, and nothing else."

It was the hardest thing imaginable. Monsignor Catanzara was the most serious of men, and admitted into his household only people well known to himself. In the midst of a life filled, apparently, with every pleasure, Vanina, crushed by remorse, was most unhappy. The slow course of events was killing her. Her father's man of business had supplied her with money. Ought she to fly from the paternal roof and make her way to the Romagna to try to compass her lover's escape? Absurd as this idea was, she was on the point of putting it into execution, when chance took pity on her.

Don Livio said to her:

"The ten carbonari of the Missirilli *venuta* are going to be transferred to Rome, except that they will be executed in the Romagna after they have been sentenced. My uncle obtained the Pope's authority for that this evening. You and I are the only two people in Rome who know this secret. Are you satisfied?"

"You are growing into a man," replied Vanina; "you may make me a present of your portrait."

On the day before that on which Missirilli was to reach

Rome, Vanina found an excuse for going to Città Castellana. It is in the prison of this town that carbonari are lodged on their way from the Romagna to Rome. She saw Missirilli in the morning, as he was leaving the prison: he was chained by himself upon a cart; he struck her as very pale but not at all despondent. An old woman tossed him a bunch of violets; Missirilli thanked her with a smile.

Vanina had seen her lover, her mind seemed to revive; she felt fresh courage. Long before this she had procured a fine advancement for the Abate Cari, Chaplain of the Castel Sant' Angelo, in which her lover was to be confined; she had chosen this worthy priest as her confessor. It is no small matter in Rome to be the confessor of a Princess, who is the Governor's niece.

The trial of the carbonari from Forlì did not take long. To be revenged for their transfer to Rome, which it had been unable to prevent, the "ultra" party had the commission which was to try them packed with the most ambitious prelates. Over this commission presided the Minister of Police.

The law against the carbonari is clear: the men from Forlì could entertain no hope; they fought for their lives nevertheless by every possible subterfuge. Not only did their judges condemn them to death, but several were in favour of cruel tortures, amputation of the right hand, and so forth. The Minister of Police, whose fortune was made (for one leaves that office only to assume the Hat), was in no need of amputated hands: on submitting the sentence to the Pope, he had the penalty commuted to some years of imprisonment for all the prisoners. The sole exception was Pietro Missirilli. The Minister regarded the young man as a dangerous fanatic, in addition to which he had already been sentenced to death as guilty of the murder of the two carabinieri whom we have mentioned. Vanina knew of the sentence and its commutation within a few minutes of the Minister's return from seeing the Pope.

On the following evening, when Monsignor Catanzara returned to his palace about midnight, his valet was not to be found; the Minister, somewhat surprised, rang several times; finally an aged and half-witted servant appeared; the Minister, losing patience, decided to undress himself. He turned the key in his door; it was a hot night: he took off his coat, and flung it in a heap upon a chair. This coat, thrown with excessive force, went beyond the chair, and fell against the muslin curtain of the window, behind which it outlined the figure of a man. The Minister sprang swiftly to his bedside and seized a pistol. As he was returning to the window, a man quite young, wearing his livery, came towards him, pistol in hand. Seeing him advance, the Minister raised his own pistol to his eye; and was about to fire. The young man said to him with a laugh:

"Why, Monsignor, do not you recognise Vanina Vanini?"

"What is the meaning of this ill-timed foolery?" replied the Minister angrily.

"Let us discuss the matter calmly," said the girl. "In the first place, your pistol is not loaded."

The Minister, taken aback, found that this was so; whereupon he took out a dagger from the pocket of his waistcoat.[1]

[1] A Roman prelate would doubtless be incapable of commanding an Army Corps with gallantry, as happened more than once in the case of a divisional general who was Minister of Police in Paris, at the time of the Malet conspiracy; but he would never allow himself to be held up so simply as this in his own house. He would be too much afraid of the satirical comment of his colleagues. A Roman who knows himself to be hated always goes about well armed. It has not been thought necessary to give authority for various other slight differences between Parisian and Roman habits of speech and behaviour. So

Vanina said to him with a charming little air of authority: "Let us be seated, Monsignore."

And she took her seat calmly upon a sofa.

"Are you alone, tell me that?" said the Minister.

"Absolutely alone, I swear to you!" cried Vanina.

The Minister took care to verify this assurance: he made a tour of the room and searched everywhere; after which he sat down upon a chair three paces away from Vanina.

"What object could I have," said Vanina with a calm and winning air, "in attempting the life of a man of moderate views, who would probably be succeeded by some weak hothead, capable of destroying himself and other people?"

"What is your purpose then, Signorina?" said the Minister crossly. "This scene is highly improper and must not continue."

"What I am going to add," Vanina went on haughtily, suddenly forgetting her gracious manner, "concerns you rather than myself. The life of the carbonaro Missirilli must be saved: if he is executed, you shall not outlive him by a week. I have no interest in the matter; the foolish action of which you complain was planned, first of all, for my own amusement, and also to oblige one of my friends. I wished," went on Vanina, resuming her air of good breeding, "to do a service to a man of talent, who will shortly become my uncle, and ought, one would say, to enhance considerably the fame and fortune of his house."

The Minister ceased to appear angry: Vanina's beauty no doubt contributed to this rapid alteration. Monsignor Catanzara's fondness for pretty women was well known in Rome, and in her disguise as a footman of the casa Savelli, with close-fitting silk stockings, a red waistcoat, her little

far from minimising these differences, we have felt it our duty to indicate them boldly. The Romans whom we are describing have not the honour to be French.

[ 263 ]

sky-blue jacket with its silver braid, and the pistol in her hand, Vanina was irresistible.

"My future niece," said the Minister, almost laughing, "you are doing a very foolish thing, and it will not be the last."

"I trust that so wise a person as yourself," replied Vanina, "will keep my secret, especially from Don Livio; and to bind you, my dear uncle, if you grant me the life of my friend's favourite, I will give you a kiss."

It was by continuing the conversation in this half jocular tone, with which Roman ladies know how to discuss the most serious matters, that Vanina succeeded in giving to this interview, begun pistol in hand, the semblance of a visit paid by the young Principessa Savelli to her uncle the Governor of Rome.

Soon Monsignor Catanzara, while rejecting with lofty scorn the idea that he could let himself be influenced by fear, found himself explaining to his niece all the difficulties that he would meet in trying to save Missirilli's life. As he talked, the Minister strolled up and down the room with Vanina; he took a decanter of lemonade that stood on the mantelpiece and poured some of the liquid into a crystal glass. Just as he was about to raise it to his lips, Vanina took it from him, and, after holding it in her hand for some time, let it fall into the garden, as though by accident. A moment later the Minister took a chocolate drop from a comfit box. Vanina seized it from him, saying with a smile:

"Take care, now; everything in the room is poisoned; for your death was intended. It was I who obtained a reprieve for my future uncle, that I might not enter the house of Cavelli absolutely empty handed."

Monsignor Catanzara, greatly astonished, thanked his niece, and gave her good reason to hope for the life of Missirilli.

"Our bargain is made!" cried Vanina, "and in proof of it, here is your reward," she said, kissing him.

The Minister accepted his reward.

"You must understand, my dear Vanina," he went on, "that I myself do not like bloodshed. Besides, I am still young, though to you perhaps I may appear very old, and I may survive to a time in which blood spilt to-day will leave a stain."

Two o'clock was striking when Monsignor Catanzara accompanied Vanina to the little gate of his garden.

A couple of days later, when the Minister appeared before the Pope, considerably embarrassed by the action which he had to take, His Holiness began:

"First of all, I have a favour to ask of you. There is one of those carbonari from Forlì who is under sentence of death; the thought of him keeps me awake at night: the man's life must be spared."

The Minister, seeing that the Pope had made up his mind, raised a number of objections, and ended by writing out a decree or *motu proprio*, which the Pope signed, regardless of precedent.

Vanina had thought that she might perhaps obtain her lover's reprieve, but that an attempt would be made to poison him. The day before, Missirilli had received from the Abate Cari, his confessor, several little packets of ship's biscuit, with a warning not to touch the food supplied by the State.

Having afterwards learned that the carbonari from Forlì were to be transferred to the Castle of San Leo, she decided to attempt to see Missirilli as he passed through Città Castellana; she arrived in that town twenty-four hours ahead of the prisoners; there she found the Abate Cari, who had preceded her by several days. He had obtained the concession from the gaoler that Missirilli might hear mass, at midnight, in the prison chapel. This was not all: if Missirilli would consent to have his arms and legs chained together, the gaoler would withdraw to the door of the chapel, in such a way as not to lose sight of the prisoner, for whom he was responsible, but to be out of hearing of anything he might say.

The day which was to decide Vanina's fate dawned at last. As soon as morning came, she shut herself up in the prison chapel. Who could describe the thoughts that disturbed her mind during that long day? Did Missirilli love her sufficiently to forgive her? She had denounced his *venuta*, but she had saved his life. When reason prevailed in her tormented brain, Vanina hoped that he would consent to leave Italy with her: if she had sinned, it was from excess of love. As four was striking, she heard in the distance, on the cobbled street, the hooves of the carabinieri's horses. The sound of each hoof-beat seemed to strike an echo from her heart. Presently she could make out the rumbling of the carts in which the prisoners were being conveyed. They stopped in the little piazza outside the prison; she saw two carabinieri lift up Missirilli, who was alone on one cart, and so loaded with irons that he could not move. "At least he is alive," she said to herself, the tears welling into her eyes, "they have not poisoned him yet." The evening was agonising; the altar lamp, hanging at a great height, and sparingly supplied with oil by the gaoler, was the only light in the dark chapel. Vanina's eyes strayed over the tombs of various great nobles of the middle ages who had died in the adjoining prison. Their statues wore an air of ferocity.

All sounds had long ceased; Vanina was absorbed in her sombre thoughts. Shortly after midnight had struck, she thought she heard a faint sound, like the fluttering of a bat. She tried to walk, and fell half fainting against the altar rail. At that moment, two spectres appeared close beside her, whom she had not heard come in. They were the gaoler and Missirilli, so loaded with chains as to be almost smothered in them. The gaoler opened a dark lantern which he placed on the altar rail, by Vanina's side, in such a way as to give him a clear view of his prisoner. He then withdrew to the other end of the chapel, by the door. No sooner had the gaoler moved away than Vanina flung herself on Missirilli's bosom. As she clasped him in her arms, she felt only the cold edges of his chains. "To whom does he owe these chains?" was her thought. She felt no pleasure in embracing her lover. This grief was followed by another even more poignant; she fancied for a moment that Missirilli was aware of her crime, so frigid was his greeting.

"Dear friend," he said to her at length, "I regret the affection that you have formed for me; I seek in vain to discover what merit in me has been capable of inspiring it. Let us return, believe me, to more Christian sentiments, let us forget the illusions which hitherto have been leading us astray; I cannot belong to you. The constant misfortune that has dogged my undertakings is due perhaps to the state of mortal sin into which I have so often fallen. To listen only to the counsels of human prudence, why was not I arrested with my friends, on that fatal night at Forlì? Why, in the moment of danger, was I not found at my post? Why has my absence then furnished grounds for the most cruel suspicions? I had another passion besides that for the liberation of Italy."

Vanina could not get over her surprise at the change in Missirilli. Without being perceptibly thinner, he had the air of a man of thirty. Vanina attributed this change to the ill treatment which he had undergone in prison, and burst into tears.

"Ah!" she said, "the gaolers promised so faithfully that they would treat you well."

The fact was that at the approach of death all the religious principles consistent with his passion for the liberation of Italy had revived in the heart of the young carbonaro. Gradually Vanina realised that the astonishing change which she had remarked in her lover was entirely moral, and in no way the effect of bodily ill treatment. Her grief, which she had supposed to have reached its extreme limit, was intensified still further.

Missirilli was silent; Vanina seemed to be on the point of being suffocated by her sobs. He spoke, and himself also appeared slightly moved:

"If I loved any single thing in the world, it would be you, Vanina; but, thanks be to God, I have now but one object in life; I shall die either in prison or in seeking to give Italy freedom."

Another silence followed; evidently Vanina was incapable of speech: she attempted to speak, but in vain. Missirilli went on:

"Duty is cruel, my friend; but if it were not a little difficult to perform, where would be the heroism? Give me your word that you will not attempt to see me again."

So far as the chain that was wound tightly about him would allow, he made a slight movement with his wrist and held out his fingers to Vanina.

"If you will accept the advice of one who was once dear to you, be sensible and marry the deserving man whom your father has chosen for you. Do not confide in him anything that may lead to trouble; but, on the other hand, never seek to see me again; let us henceforward be strangers to one another. You have advanced a considerable sum for the service of the Fatherland; if ever it is delivered from its tyrants, that sum will be faithfully repaid to you in national bonds."

Vanina was crushed. While he was speaking, Pietro's eye had gleamed only at the moment when he mentioned the Fatherland.

# VANINA VANINI

At length pride came to the rescue of the young Princess; she had brought with her a supply of diamonds and small files. Without answering Missirilli, she offered him these.

"I accept from a sense of duty," he told her, "for I must seek to escape; but I will never see you, I swear it by this latest token of your bounty. Farewell, Vanina; promise me never to write, never to attempt to see me; leave me wholly to the Fatherland, I am dead to you: farewell."

"No," replied Vanina, grown furious, "I wish you to know what I have done, led on by the love that I bear you."

She then related to him all her activities from the moment when Missirilli had left the villa of San Niccolò to give himself up to the Legate. When her tale was finished:

"All this is nothing," said Vanina: "I have done more, in my love for you."

She then told him of her betrayal.

"Ah, monster," cried Pietro, mad with rage, hurling himself upon her; and sought to crush her to the ground with his chains.

He would have succeeded but for the gaoler, who came running at the sound of her cries. He seized Missirilli.

"There, monster, I will not owe anything to you," said Missirilli to Vanina, flinging at her, as violently as his chains would allow him, the files and diamonds, and he moved rapidly away.

Vanina was left speechless. She returned to Rome: and the newspapers announce that she has just been married to Principe Don Livio Savelli.

THE END